P9-CER-234

CLOSE CALL

LAURA DISILVERIO

MIDNIGHT INK
WOODBURY, MINNESOTA

FIRST EDITION
First Printing, 2016

Book format by Bob Gaul
Cover design by Lisa Novak
Cover image by iStockphoto.com/80017671/©NemanjaMiscevic

Midnight Ink, an imprint of Llewellyn Worldwide Ltd.

This is a work of fiction. Names, characters, places, and incidents are either the product of the author's imagination or are used fictitiously, and any resemblance to actual persons living or dead, business establishments, events, or locales is entirely coincidental.

Library of Congress Cataloging-in-Publication Data
Names: DiSilverio, Laura A. H., author.
Title: Close call / Laura DiSilverio.
Description: First Edition. | Woodbury, Minnesota : Midnight Ink, [2016]
Identifiers: LCCN 2016016806 (print) | LCCN 2016021719 (ebook) | ISBN 9780738749204 | ISBN 9780738749624 ()
Subjects: | GSAFD: Mystery fiction.
Classification: LCC PS3604.I85 C58 2016 (print) | LCC PS3604.I85 (ebook) | DDC 813/.6—dc23
LC record available at https://lccn.loc.gov/2016016806

Midnight Ink
Llewellyn Worldwide Ltd.
2143 Wooddale Drive
Woodbury, MN 55125-2989
www.midnightinkbooks.com

Printed in the United States of America

For Hank
Mentor, sage, partner in crime, voice of sanity
and, most of all, dear friend.

SUNBURN AND A HANGOVER. Those were the dangers Emily most associated with tubing trips down the Guadalupe River, even after spring storms pushed the water level higher than usual, churning the river's gentle undulations into wannabe rapids in one or two places. Having kayaked Class Four rapids in her native Maryland, Emily disdained the slight drops that had her University of Texas roommate squealing.

"Puh-leeze, Rach," she said, tummy-down on the tube, stroking with her arms. "There are kiddie rides at Six Flags more thrilling than this."

The green water cooled her skin and dragged at the T-shirt she wore to prevent her upper arms from chafing when she paddled. The river bottom flowed past below her, not more than three feet down, smooth pebbles and sand. By the bank, brush submerged by the rains frothed the water. The water's clean scent mingled with the petroleum stink of sun-warmed rubber and a whiff of coconut oil. Bliss.

Rachel shrieked again as she floated backward over a two-foot drop and swirled to face Emily, her legs hanging over the inner tube's side, her hand clutching a pink straw hat to her head. "Mark!" She pushed at their buddy as he playfully bumped her tube with his, making it lurch.

Emily could see freckles popping out on her redheaded friend's fair skin, despite the hat. And Mark's shoulders virtually glowed. Sunburn and hangover, she thought again, and maybe a stray moccasin or two. She glanced into a quiet pool notched into the bank and scanned the cottonwood branches overhanging the river, their shadows offering brief sanctuary from the glaring sun. No snakes. Satisfied, she flipped over on the tube so her cutoff-clad butt hung into the water. She'd tubed this river when it was so low her ass scraped the bottom. Thank God for rain. With one hand, she hoisted the gallon milk jug tied to her tube. Her blond braid trailed in the water as she swallowed two gulps of rum and Gatorade and carefully replaced the cap.

"Catch," she called to Mark, unclipping the bottle from the carabiner that secured it to a loop of rope. She flung the jug and it plopped into the water within an arm's length of her target, sinking for a moment before bobbing to the surface.

"This is the life, huh? Done with finals, graduation next week, Spit in the Wind concert tonight…" Mark drank deeply and wiped his mouth with the back of his hand. "We'll be bona fide MBAs in a week. That would mean more if I had a job to go with it like you two." He took another swig and ducked his chin to peer at Emily from over the top of his sunglasses. "You sure you want to get shackled so soon? Gainful employment plus a hub sounds way too adult. Call it off, live a little. You can always get married later."

"Just because you're still into hook-ups and beer pong doesn't mean we all are," Emily said, splashing him. "I'm ready. Ready to settle down with the man I've loved since I was twelve. I can't wait."

Mark lobbed the jug back her way and it sideswiped her temple, toppling her into the river with a splash.

Mark doubled over and almost laughed himself into the water.

"Mark!" Rachel reprimanded him, half laughing too.

The milk jug popped to the surface, several yards down river. "Get the booze," Mark called.

"What about Emily?"

"She's fine. Just get the—"

Rachel screamed and pointed. Mark jerked his head back to where Emily had gone under as a blood-dark cloud stained the river's surface. Tendrils of red diluted to pink as the flow tugged them away.

"Emily!"

Sydney
Tuesday, August 1

WHEN SOMEONE STARTS A conversation with "Are you okay?" and you have no idea what they're talking about, it's a sure sign that fate has trampled you with cleats and you just don't know it yet.

That thought zipped through Sydney Ellison's head as she slowed in the middle of a rush hour DC sidewalk to answer a call from her mother.

"Are you okay?" Connie Linn asked, anxiety tightening her voice.

"Why wouldn't I be?" A man jostled Sydney and she walked faster. The sidewalk was almost as jammed as the street, and the pedestrians had fewer hesitations about ramming into each other.

Connie inhaled sharply. "You haven't heard. Oh my God. Sydney, it's George."

"George?" There had only ever been one George in her life, one George who had *been* her life, but she asked anyway. "Manley?" The name brought with it memories she tried to keep corralled in an *Off*

Limits part of her brain. Nausea roiled her stomach and she swallowed hard. "What about him?"

"He's dead."

"How? Wha—" Sydney was abreast of an Electronics Emporium, its display window crowded with high-def TVs. Images of her and George from long ago played on the screens. She sucked in her breath and stopped dead. "Connie, I can't—not now." She hung up on her mother without apology and edged closer. She was fifteen years younger and twenty pounds heavier on the screen; it was like looking at a badly distorted image, a fun-house mirror. Her face flamed and she looked over her shoulder. No one was pointing or staring. People trotted down the Metro stairs. Jaywalkers snarled traffic. Thank God for small favors. She turned back to the window as her younger self shrouded her head with a coat to escape the reporters jabbing microphones at her.

George's image filled the screens. *Oh my God.* In his sixties, his silver hair matched the gray of his suit and his hooded eyes challenged the viewer. A name and a brace of years underscored the photo: *George Manley (D/Ohio), former Speaker of the House, 1948–2016.*

He was really dead. *Oh my God.* Her knees buckled. She splayed a hand on the cool glass to keep from falling.

"Hey, lady, this yours?" A beefy stranger held out her briefcase. She hadn't even felt it fall.

"What? Oh, thank you." She strangled the handle, torn between wanting to know what had happened to George and an unwillingness to hear newscasters rehash their past. The anchor, face solemn, narrated silently, and she tried to read his lips. Had he said "affair"? Anger prickled in her scalp and in her hands and feet. She swung away from the window. God knew she had plenty of reason to hate George, but he was dead. Why did the networks always—*always*—have to zoom in on the sordid? How sad—tragic, even—that their affair was haunting

George even in death. He'd have wanted to be remembered for his education bill, for three decades of public service, not for screwing a coed younger than his daughter. Even if that girl had loved him more than … more than was safe.

Anger, humiliation, and something that wasn't quite sadness—more like regret—mixed it up in Sydney's stomach as she pushed open the deli door four storefronts away. A bell tinkled, drowned by customers shouting their orders to harried clerks, cell phones spraying Bach or the Beatles, and cash registers pinging. She inhaled a peppery hint of salami and the vinegar tang of pickles and pepperoncini. Better. Her jangled nerves quieted. Leaning against a glass-fronted case, she let the cool seep through her sweat-damp dress. DC summers could double as a Dantean circle of hell—one reserved for politicians, George used to say.

She tore her thoughts away from George Manley. Even though she'd never live down her past, she didn't have to relive it just because he was dead. She didn't need the painful memories spoiling her evening with Jason.

Half a pound of sharp cheddar, she forced herself to think instead. Two roasted chicken dinners and a few of those garlic olives Jason liked. Did they need more coffee? Supplies like coffee and toilet paper seemed to evaporate with Jason in the house. One more week and he'd be back in his newly renovated condo. A pang of guilt zipped through her at the thought and she bit the inside of her lip. It'd been a little claustrophobic at first, having Jason around more, but she liked bumping against him now as they cooked dinner in the small kitchen, liked hearing the details of his day and snuggling with him every night, not just on weekends. She could live with the whiskers in the sink, but his racing bicycle couldn't stay in the living room, even for just another week. They'd have to find somewhere else to keep it if—

"Ma'am? It's your turn." A man nudged Sydney from behind. He bounced from one foot to the other, horn-rimmed glasses balanced on his sharp nose. "Can you hurry it up? I've gotta get my kids from day-care. They charge ten bucks for every minute you're late. Per kid."

"Sorry."

She stepped to the deli counter with its four cash registers and ordered, on impulse getting a piece of chocolate cheesecake for Mrs. Colwell, her neighbor with the chocolate jones and fixed income. She had to lean forward to be heard over the men on either side, both jabbering into their cell phones. The aproned clerk dumped two white bags with handles onto the counter, and Sydney's phone rang.

"Sorry." She checked the number. Connie. Calling back to check on her okayness. She didn't answer. Putting the phone beside her deli bags, she pulled out a fifty, maneuvering around the man on her left and his six pizza boxes and the man on her right scrambling after dropped coins.

"Sorry. I don't have anything smaller," Sydney told the clerk, a youth with pimples and straw-colored hair. Good grief, she sounded like the battered women she'd set up Winning Ways to help: *sorry, sorry, sorry*.

"It's cool," the clerk said, counting out her change. He peered at her in a way she'd come to dread. "You look familiar—"

She didn't need this. "Thanks." She gave him a small smile and looked away, desperate to be gone before he said more.

"Hey—I just saw you on TV!" He jerked his head toward the tiny television suspended above the counter's far end. "Cool! You're that—"

Impatient, the man behind Sydney elbowed her aside and knocked against a pickle jar, streaming briny water over the counter. The clerk sprang back. Warty green pickles rolled across the Formica and plunked to the floor. She swept her phone and damp change into her purse and almost ran out the door, praying that no one had heard the clerk.

"Jesus H. Christ!" and "Oh, shit, I'm sorry!" followed her out of the deli.

Two blocks away, she paused to take a deep breath, not minding the exhaust fumes held at street level by the oppressive humidity that slicked her skin. In another half hour, this part of DC would quiet as the commuters fled to suburbia. She and Jason could enjoy dinner on the balcony, have a glass of wine, talk. She picked up her pace. Ten minutes brought her to the one-way quiet of G Street Southeast. Townhomes lined both sides, cooled by mighty oaks old enough to remember flames erupting from the White House just three miles away, the eerie quiet of the streets during the flu pandemic, and windows darkened by blackout curtains.

A block from home, she heard a cell phone's faint *brrr*—a plain ring, not her "Rhapsody in Blue" ringtone. She looked around. No one in earshot. *Funny*. It trilled again, from inside her purse. *Oh, shoot.* She knew what must have happened even as she set the deli bags down and found the phone. It was a simple pay-as-you-go model, just like hers—she hadn't had a cell phone contract since her account got hacked by unscrupulous journalists when the relationship with George made the headlines.

A man's voice started speaking before she could even say hello. "Time for round two. Remember to make the Montoya job look like an accident. There's a bonus if you take care of it before the election." The voice was terse, accentless. "Payment as previously arranged. Make it happen."

Click.

2

Paul

PAUL JONES HAILED A taxi outside Sol's Deli. He reeked of pickle juice, and a splash of tomato soup marred his white shirt. Moira had called to tell him his father had started a small fire in the kitchen but not to worry. Not to worry! He clambered into the cab. How was he supposed to not worry when Pop's behavior grew more erratic every day? When he eluded Moira and wandered off, sometimes dressed, sometimes in bathrobe and socks ... when he started to fill the tub and got caught up watching *Judge Judy* so the water overflowed and soaked the linoleum so Paul had to replace it ... when—

"Address?" the taxi driver asked, looking at him in the rearview mirror. His fingers tapped the steering wheel to the beat of a rap song.

Paul closed his eyes and took a deep breath through flared nostrils. *Calm.* He had a job to do this week. He couldn't afford to be distracted. Moira was an RN; she could handle Pop. *Concentrate.* After a moment he opened his eyes and gave the driver the motel's address.

With a grunt, the driver started the meter and pulled into traffic, making the hula girl suction-cupped to the dash shimmy.

Paul eased his head back against the vinyl seat. He wasn't sure what smelled worse—the cab's mildewy plastic or his clothes. His ability to blend in with a crowd, to rate no more detailed a description than "sixty-something white guy," was key to his success. Smelling like a pickle factory jeopardized his anonymity. As the taxi sludged along in the stop-and-go traffic, he concentrated on clearing his mind, emptying it of all thought and emotion. It was a trick he'd developed working with a Buddhist monk in Laos when he was in country for the third time in the late '70s, after the war was officially over. It kept him focused.

The opening glissando of Gershwin's "Rhapsody in Blue" trilled from his pocket, almost drowned out by the cabbie's rap crap. What the—? He pulled out the cell phone, conscious of the driver's gaze, and answered cautiously, "Yes?"

A recorded voice said, "This call is for Sydney Ellison from Dr. Field's office to remind you of your dental appointment on Tuesday, August eighth, at eight o'clock. If you need to reschedule, please call—"

"Go back," he told the startled cabbie.

"Huh?"

"To the deli. And turn off that fucking noise."

Paul's fingers worried at the curling end of duct tape that patched a foot-long tear in the seat beside him. Every red light and delay twanged his taut nerves. There was no relief at the deli—his phone wasn't there. No one remembered seeing it. He should never have set it on the counter, not for an instant. At least he'd emptied the call log, as always, when he'd hung up. He didn't give a damn about the phone—it was pay-as-you-go and replaceable—but he needed to make sure his client didn't call and say something to this Sid Ellison guy that could incriminate both of them. He'd have to alert his client via email—that was safer and quicker than a face-to-face with Ellison to trade phones.

He climbed back into the cab and pulled his laptop out of its case. "Starbucks. The closest one."

3

Sydney

SYDNEY STARED AT THE phone in her hand. Damn. How could she have picked up the wrong phone? It was identical to hers, but still. A black man wrapped in an Army surplus jacket, fingerless mittens, and several scarves despite the heat wandered closer, eyeing the deli bags at her feet. A Heinz 57 dog with hound ears pasted himself to the man's shin. She could count his ribs.

"D'ya have any change?" the man asked, bloodshot eyes flitting to her face, then to the neon bar sign behind her, the squirrel chittering from a nearby tree, the crack in the sidewalk. She'd seen the man around since early spring and thought his name was Eli. The dog sat and scratched one floppy ear vigorously with his hind paw.

She found one of the fast-food gift cards she kept on hand and made a mental note to stick some dog biscuits in her briefcase for the next time she saw the pair. And maybe a flea collar, she thought as the dog kept scratching. "Here, sir."

He glanced at the card, sucked air through his teeth, and shuffled off, turning to say thank you after a few yards. The dog ambled after him.

She waved, picked up the bags, and started walking again. She couldn't go back to the deli now; she'd lose half an hour. Jason was waiting with "big news," he'd said, and she'd promised to be home by six, which was five minutes ago. Plus, she didn't feel up to dealing with the deli clerk's speculation or questions. She could use the new phone to dial her cell number and arrange an exchange with whoever had her phone.

But something about the call she'd answered kept her from dialing. *The job? Accident?* The only part of the call that had made sense was the reference to Montoya and the election. Clearly the caller was talking about Fidel Montoya and his Senate bid. He'd been a congressman from Maryland for ten years and was looking to move up, in next week's special election, to a Senate seat. Already pundits were talking about him as a presidential candidate somewhere down the road. A bead of sweat trickled down Sydney's spine and she shivered. Come to think of it, the call had sounded almost like ... but no, that was ridiculous. The stuff of movies. People didn't really put out hits, take out contracts—whatever the terminology was—on politicians, did they?

Once the thought had invaded her mind, it refused to budge. She tried to think of an innocent explanation for the "job" looking like an "accident." Maybe someone was arranging some sort of political trick or campaign disaster? The Montoya campaign had certainly attracted a lot of attention and more than its fair share of detractors. Fidel Montoya was a well-educated liberal who supported open immigration, gay rights, and abortion; right-wing loonies stuck to his campaign like gum to a shoe. They hefted posters, shouted slogans, hacked into his web page, tried to "persuade" people not to attend his rallies. She'd heard some of the more militant groups, given air time by the media, mention lynching, deportation (to the Mexico of his parents), and boiling in oil.

While Sydney thought, her feet had carried her home. She bumped open the waist-high gate with her hip and let it swing shut with a clang. A demanding mew drew her gaze down. Indigo, the neighbor's gray cat, rubbed against her leg.

"Hi, Indy." She stooped to pat the friendly guy. Surprised to find the cell phone still gripped in her hand, she turned it off and slid it into a pocket. She'd call the deli instead, see if maybe they had her phone. She stroked the cat's back. He arched and let out a series of burp-like purrs, slitting his eyes with bliss.

"You're home." Jason stood in the open doorway, his dark, gray-streaked hair looking even curlier than usual in the humidity. One hand dug into the pocket of the chinos that slipped off his narrow waist, revealing sharp hipbones and toned abs. The other hand held a champagne bottle. He smiled. A curl of heat warmed the pit of Sydney's stomach. She loved the way his smile split his face, revealing deep dimples and white teeth.

"I'm home." She went to him and leaned into his kiss. His lips lingered on her. Maybe they could skip dinner... "Mmm. What are we celebrating?"

He held the bottle aloft like a trophy. "Yours truly, Dr. Jason Nygaard, economics professor extraordinaire, was notified today of his selection for a Fulbright grant—"

Oh, no. Sydney hugged him, dropping the deli bags and briefcase.

"—to teach in Indonesia for a year."

Indonesia! She'd known it was a possibility, since he applied four months ago, but—"Congratulations, sweetheart. I'm so happy for you." Stifling her dismay, she planted kisses along his jaw and neck. "Pour some bubbly and let's toast your achievement properly." She retrieved the bags, nudging Indigo to get his nose out of the chicken bag.

When they were settled on the small balcony off the back bedroom, champagne fizzing in crystal flutes, she said, "Tell me everything. When did you hear? What did they say?" She kicked off her shoes—*aah, bliss*—and propped her heels on the tiny tabletop no larger than a manhole cover. Sipping the Perrier-Jouet, she fought the urge to sneeze as bubbles tickled the roof of her mouth.

"They said I'm going to Indonesia," Jason said, plunking the bottle onto the table. He went to the rail and leaned against it, gazing down into the garden—geraniums, marigolds, and petunias in planters, and shrubs around a brick patio. A patchwork of neighbors' gardens and yards spread out beyond, some with flowering fruit trees, some with manicured grass, some with ivy-covered walls and bird feeders, all small. Honeysuckle sweetness drifted from a hidden corner; Sydney found it comforting.

"I know. I heard you. I mean, did they say anything like, 'It was the brilliance of Dr. Nygaard's recent journal article and the enthusiastic endorsements of his colleagues that convinced us to award him this grant'?" Excitement for him sped up her words and she finished with a bounce.

He turned to face her, a half smile on his lips. "Something like that. But did you hear me, Syd? I'm going to Indonesia." He rolled the champagne flute between his palms.

She knit her brows. "I heard, honey. I'm thrilled for you." She reached out a hand, but he stayed where he was.

"A little too thrilled, I'd say."

The words hung between them. Her hand dropped.

She swung her feet down and padded barefoot to where he leaned back against the railing. "What is it, Jason?" She searched his face.

"I guess I was hoping for something more along the lines of 'Don't go, Jason. I'll miss you, Jason.'"

"I didn't want to be selfish. Don't go, Jason. Stay." Her stomach lurched in a way that had nothing to do with hunger. "I'd miss you dreadfully."

"Enough to go with me?" He put his hands on her shoulders, met her gaze squarely.

His offer stole her breath. She opened her mouth but no words came out. She swallowed. "To Indonesia?"

"Yes, to Indonesia," he said, his green eyes blazing with excitement. "There're bound to be women there who need your kind of help. You could start up an Indonesian branch of Winning Ways, put them on the path to training, jobs, careers..."

"How would I get funding? Wait." She held up a hand, pulling back. Jason's hands fell to his sides. Going to Indonesia would mean leaving Winning Ways, the nonprofit she'd worked so hard to build; leaving the women who depended on her. It would mean leaving Connie, leaving her house. She loved Jason, but Indonesia! Sydney's breaths came fast and dizziness made her clutch at the railing. "I can't go."

"You mean you won't."

"I can't. I have responsibilities here."

"Now that your dad's passed, you don't need to stay in the area for him anymore. Your mom's doing fine. You can—"

"It's only for a year," she said desperately. "We can write, call, every day. I'll be here when you get back. Military families do it all the time."

"But we're not a family, are we, Syd?" His tone was bleak. "I can tell it's all you can do to put up with me staying here for a couple of weeks."

"No! Maybe at first. Jason—" Memories of her momentary irritation in the deli overwhelmed her with guilt. She almost missed his next words.

"If you won't come with me, it's over."

The ultimatum darkened the space between them as the sun set and shadows overtook the garden, swarming the balcony. Pinpricks of light flashed at grass-level. Sydney barely noticed the fireflies as confusion and hurt swamped her.

"That's not fair."

"It can't always be about 'fair.'" Jason reached out a hand and tucked an auburn strand of hair behind her ear. "You caught some raw breaks, Syd. Manley was a sexual predator—"

"I was eighteen the first time we—"

"Don't defend him!"

"He's—" She'd meant to tell him George had died, but Jason stopped her with a sharp headshake.

"And Dirk was an asshole. But I'm not, damn it. Don't tar me with the same brush as them."

"I'm not! I don't want to break up with you."

"But you don't want to commit to me—to us—either. Because you don't trust yourself."

"Don't psychoanalyze me!"

"You're playing it safe. You made a couple of bonehead choices when you were young—hell, hardly more than a kid—and now you're afraid, hiding behind family commitments and your work. Grow up, Syd. Life—living—isn't about being safe."

"Those women need me."

"Hell, I need you. Doesn't that count for anything?"

His weariness cut through her rising anger. "You know it does."

"Do I? Look, I want a family—"

"So do I. Someday." She couldn't think clearly. Her mind jammed with competing images: an infant's head, fuzzed with dark down, resting against her breast; Dirk's cruel smile as he handed her an autographed copy of the tell-all book he'd published after the divorce; her father's hand, drawn down to bone threaded with ropey blue veins, resting in hers. Tears threatened.

"I'll be forty-two in October, Syd. I don't want to be changing diapers when I'm sixty. 'Someday' has to be now."

Jason's voice was calm. She knew he'd anticipated her every possible response to his news, and to his ultimatum. Knew he'd prepared himself to walk away.

He drained the champagne from his glass in one swallow. "I leave in ten days. They want me to come over early for some sort of training session. I presume I'm still welcome to stay here, since my condo's not ready and I'll need to rent it out anyway?"

"Of course. Please, Jason, let's talk—"

"Here kitty, kitty."

The reedy voice startled Sydney. She looked down to see Mrs. Colwell, Indigo's mother, staring up from her side of the low brick wall, not ten feet away. She could tell from the old woman's avid expression that she'd heard every word of their conversation. She battled a surge of irritation. Incurable busybody.

"Have you seen Indigo?" Mrs. Colwell called as Sydney made eye contact. She was only in her sixties but looked older. Hair like spider filaments wisped in patches thinned by radiation treatments. She clutched a robe closed at her neck. Scarlet cashmere. It didn't fit her style or her income—a gift from her daughter, maybe. Over-large glasses magnified her eyes.

"Not for half an hour or so," Sydney said tightly. Jason brushed past her into the house. "I'm sure he'll turn up. 'Night." She flipped a hand in an abbreviated wave and went after Jason, knowing it was too late.

4

Paul

"IT'S TOO LATE," THE voice on the other end of the phone told Paul. "I already called the number you gave me. I thought I was talking to you, Mr. Jones."

Paul had no defense against the hard accusation in the voice. He'd set up the call by sending an email to his client's anonymous account with the phone number of his new burner phone. Not that anything online was really anonymous in this day and age. He might not be a tech whiz, but he knew that much.

"Look, no harm, no foul," Paul said now. "You didn't give your name, so the guy can't identify you or me. We'll just go from here." He sat on a concrete bench set in a square of tired grass too small to be called a park. Suited men and women strode by, most of them on their phones or checking texts, avoiding eye contact. You'd think they were late for a plane, the way they hurried. Did no one fucking stroll anymore? Pigeons pecked at bread crumbs on the sidewalk. Rats with wings. A woman in spandex capris, Rollerblades on her feet, was tossing crumbs from a baggie she'd pulled from a fanny pack. Some cities had made it illegal to feed pigeons. If DC hadn't, it should.

"That's not acceptable." The voice brooked no argument. "It's a risk I can't afford to take. God knows what exactly I said. What if he can ID my voice? You have to eliminate the risk."

"That wasn't part of the contract." His client was being overly cautious. That was why he'd used a burner phone, for God's sake. So it was anonymous, untraceable.

"It is now." He broke the connection.

Fuck. Paul took pride in avoiding collateral damage. He didn't want to kill anyone unless he was paid for it or it was absolutely necessary for his own safety and freedom. He thrust the phone into his pocket and stood, his knee hitching. He gave it a moment, wondering if he should take his doc's advice. Nah. A replacement would necessitate too much downtime. The knee was a minor nuisance on occasion, no big deal. Deliberately marching through the flock of pigeons, he took pleasure in the way they heaved themselves into the air, wings laboring. The Rollerblader glared at him but didn't say anything. He didn't look back, knowing the birds would have resettled on the sidewalk within moments of his passing.

Back in his motel room, he called Moira to give her the new phone number.

"Want to talk with your father?" she asked, catching him off-guard. "He's right here."

"Paul? Moira says you're working? I hope you've got a live one on the hook."

The voice was surprisingly lucid and Paul closed his eyes in relief. "Yeah, Pop, I'm in New York." The lie came automatically. "I think I can sign a couple of new accounts." For his fictitious hotel linens sales job. Nobody ever asked a follow-up question if you told them you sold sheets and tablecloths to hotels. "I should be home by Sunday." With any luck.

As he half listened to his dad recount the day's events, apparently mixing them with the plot of some *Knots Landing* rerun he'd been watching, Paul pulled out the cell phone he'd taken by mistake and thumbed his way through the menu to *Contacts*. As he had hoped, there was a listing for "Home." Plug the number into a reverse directory and Sid Ellison was halfway to dead.

Bingo.

5

Sydney
Wednesday, August 2

SYDNEY COULDN'T CONCENTRATE AT work the next morning. She'd picked up a new pay-as-you-go phone on the way to work, and arrived late to find messages from seven reporters on her desk, all wanting to get her reaction to George's death, squeeze more mileage out of the fifteen-year-old scandal. When hell froze over. She'd crumpled the pink slips into a ball and banged them into the trash can. And the argument with Jason was a steady ache that Motrin wasn't going to help. Now, five women filled the tiny Winning Ways classroom, their hopeful gazes fixed on her as she gave them pointers on professional dress and appearance, using her own navy suit, mid-heeled pumps, hose—yes, even in summer, she told Belinda—and understated jewelry as visual aids for interview attire.

"No bling," Sydney emphasized, pointing at Bo-Bae's chandelier earrings and Malayna's armful of jangly bangles.

Victims of abuse or their own bad choices, these women were looking to turn their lives around, to find jobs that might become careers, to learn to value themselves and the contributions they could make. Winning Ways helped by offering free classes on job hunting, interviewing, and workplace etiquette; supplying interview attire; running mock interviews; and doing job placement. *These women need me*, Sydney reminded herself, her gaze lighting on the cast covering Belinda's forearm, courtesy of the abusive husband she'd finally left. So many of them had suffered at the hands of men who had more power—physical, emotional, or financial—than they did. As Sydney had suffered. But where she'd had all the advantages of wealth and education to help her make it after the scandal, and again after Dirk, these women had only their pride and determination and whatever Winning Ways could give them in the way of a leg up. It wasn't right of Jason to expect her to desert them.

"And keep your hair neat and conservative," she finished, not letting her thoughts show. At least her time in the political spotlight had taught her that much. She turned to show how her auburn hair was skewered at the nape of her neck with a tortoiseshell slide.

"But that's boring," Malayna complained, smoothing the sculpture of shellacked swirls and curls that made up her 'do.

"Employers crave boring," Sydney said with a sympathetic smile, but the word caught her unaware. Was her look boring? Conservative, yes—but boring? She let the thought go as another woman launched into a question.

Even as she fielded the women's questions with half her brain, the other half dwelled on the scene with Jason the night before and the chill that had permeated their evening. They'd lain in bed together, each turned away from the middle, and the gap between them, though mere inches, had felt like an icy crevasse on Mt. Everest. Jason slipped out of bed at five for a bike ride and Sydney snuggled into the warm depression left by his body, breathed in his lingering scent, and dozed. She was vaguely aware of the shower raining against the tile when he returned. Next thing she knew, he was leaning over her, all clean-shaven skin and toothpaste breath, to brush her cheek with his lips. She hadn't known what to say, so she'd feigned sleep. After a moment's hesitation, he'd left. A sense of loss tugged at her as she dismissed the class and headed to her office.

"Sydney, a moment."

The mellifluous bass voice, perfect for its owner's weekly radio show "Come to Jesus," came from behind her. She groaned. Pasting a small smile on her face, she turned to greet the Chairman of Winning Ways' Board of Directors. "Marlon, good to see you." A lie.

Wearing a sober gray suit and white shirt banded with a clerical collar, Marlon Hotchkiss slowed as he approached. More than half a foot taller than Sydney's five-eight, he had a gangly build, outsized hands, and hunched his shoulders forward in a way that made him look like he was protecting something. His immortal soul, Sydney thought acidly, or the secrets of the confessional. Except he wasn't Catholic. A crag of a nose dominated his face and he used it to sniff out sin, lecturing the single mothers who came to Winning Ways for help, sermonizing on the evils of not only alcohol and drugs but also desecration of the flesh (piercings and tattoos); vanity (painted nails, jewelry, and fashionable clothes); and anything else he found self-indulgent or wasteful.

"My spirit was greatly troubled by yesterday's news," he proclaimed.

"Oh?" Sydney stood her ground in the hall, determined not to invite him into her office and extend the session one moment longer than necessary. Since securing the chairmanship a year ago—by one vote—he'd concerned himself far too much with Winning Ways' daily workings.

"I prayed for the repose of Manley's soul," he continued, "and have every confidence that he is at peace in the Lord's bosom. But we—"

His mention of Manley stung. "I don't want to talk about George Manley."

"So angry, Sydney." He shook his head, not disturbing the abundant white hair combed back from his brow. "The Lord is grieved by an angry soul. But I'm afraid we must talk about Manley since the press is displaying so much interest. I've drafted some comments for you to—"

"I'm not talking to reporters or issuing a statement of any kind," she said. "My relationship with George ended fifteen years ago, and my feelings about his death are private."

His small smile was a slice of condescension. "Nothing is private when it reflects upon our work, which is God's work," he said. "And, unfortunately, the wrongful choices you made as a young woman are now casting Winning Ways in a bad light. We don't want the efforts of so many hard-working people to be undermined by scandal."

Sydney stared at him in disbelief. Taking a long breath through her nostrils, she reminded him, "I founded Winning Ways. It was my concept, my money, and my hard work that got Winning Ways started. I—"

He held up one liver-spotted hand. "That's as may be, my dear, but the responsibility for charting Winning Ways' course, for protecting its reputation, now rests with me. And the rest of the board," he added. "We're in agreement that a brief statement to the press is in the organization's best interests. It will stifle the media's curiosity and ensure the story dies a quick death."

He held out a single sheet of paper and Sydney accepted it, her hand trembling, unable to read the short paragraph through the red mist clouding her vision. Turning her back on Hotchkiss, she strode to her office, wanting to slam the door but closing it with a controlled click instead. "And I'm not your 'dear,'" she whispered furiously to the door. Not trusting her reaction if she read his press release, she folded the page in half and tore it into strips. Each rip purged a bit of anger until she dropped the confetti into the trash can.

Her office was small but cozy, with two velvet overstuffed chairs arranged before the desk and an art deco lamp she'd bought in college on a small table between them. A colorful Indian rug spanned the space between the chairs and the desk. A glass-fronted bookcase brimming over with books took up most of the back wall, which she'd painted a warm terra-cotta. The local news played on a small television atop the bookcase. A reporter on a street corner was saying, "This is where another member of the city's homeless population was set on fire last night, the second such incident in only three weeks. The woman, known only as Donna, is in critical condition and police—"

Sydney winced and blanked the screen with the remote. At least they weren't still talking about George. She slumped into her chair and scowled. The cell phone from the deli sat on her desk. She'd just as soon have confronted a pile of dog poop. As if she didn't have enough on her plate. She picked it up. Last night, while undressing for bed, she'd found it in her pocket and her suspicions had come flooding back. She'd wanted to ask Jason's advice, tell him about the strange phone call, but he was hunched over his computer in her spare bedroom/office, earphones on, clearly not wanting to talk. She'd drifted downstairs and eaten the cheesecake, half in revenge against Mrs. Colwell for interrupting her talk with Jason and half in hopes that the heavy chocolate would drug her to sleep.

Sydney called the deli. No one knew anything about her phone. Of course not. After a moment's hesitation, she punched keys to see the call log. There was only one number. She knew from the date/time stamp that it was the call she'd answered. The outgoing calls list was empty. Curious. Either it was a brand-new phone or the owner habitually erased numbers from the memory. Maybe a cheating spouse? She centered it on the desk, trying to find a reason why she shouldn't go to the police and warn them that a prominent politician might be an assassin's target. She could hear the jeers and speculation now, echoes from the past coming back to haunt her. She couldn't do it.

The office phone rang and she swiveled to answer it, eager to put off making a decision.

Topaz Johnson, Winning Ways' young receptionist, said hesitantly, "Sydney, there's a reporter from Channel 9 on the line for you. She wants to interview—"

"No way in hell." She bit down on her lip as soon as the words escaped.

Topaz giggled.

Sydney fought to regain her calm. "I'm sorry. Just tell her I'm not available."

"You got it," Topaz said, sounding like she'd have preferred to relay the first response.

Hanging up, Sydney smacked the cell phone off the desk with the flat of her hand.

6

Sydney

"WHOA, BOSS, SERIOUS FACE. Who died? Oops." D'won Duvalier, Sydney's right-hand man, stood in the doorway holding a steel mug.

He slapped a hand over his mouth. "Me and my big mouth. It's Manley, right?" He wore a short-sleeved, apricot seersucker shirt tucked into khaki slacks, with a coordinating paisley tie. His hair this week fell in short dreadlocks to mid-ear and was its natural black. Born to Haitian immigrants, D'won had been with Winning Ways from the beginning, first as a consultant on dress and presentation, then as Sydney's deputy and friend. She often thought she couldn't run the place without him.

"Not so much. It was a shock to hear he'd died, but it's been more than a decade since I've even spoken to him." Sydney tried a smile. She was tempted to tell D'won about Hotchkiss's interference, but talking about it would only fan the flames of her anger. "I've just got something to work out."

"Tell Uncle D'won all about it," he said, seating himself in the comfier of the moss-green chairs facing her desk. At thirty, he was actually five years younger than she was. He fixed a mock serious look on his cocoa-colored face. "Is it that Jason? Is he cheating on you? I always knew he wasn't good enough for you. Do you want me to beat him up, teach him a lesson?" D'won balled his hands into fists and leaned forward, his slight frame tensing.

Sydney choked on something between a laugh and a sob. "No, it's not Jason. Well, it's partly Jason. He's leaving for Indonesia in just over a week. He'll be gone for a year."

"In-do-ne-sia." D'won opened his eyes wide. "Wow, boss, I've heard of couples wanting some time apart, but that's ridiculous."

She didn't want to discuss Jason, not even with D'won. "Actually," she said to distract him, "I'm really trying to decide what to do about this." She nodded at the cell phone she'd retrieved from the floor and stuck in her inbox.

"It's a cell phone. You don't do something about it, you make calls on it," D'won said in the voice of one talking to a slow child. "If you're rude and thoughtless—which, of course, you're not, boss—you carry on loud conversations in the subway, at restaurants, on planes, at the theater, in the john."

She laughed and D'won looked pleased with himself. His mobile lips stretched into a grin. "Tell Uncle D'won why you need a remedial course on cell phone use."

She told him about the chaos at the deli, walking out with the wrong phone, and the call. He set his mug down with a snap on the end table. "Say what? Give me that again."

As she repeated the caller's words, D'won wrote them down. "Those are his exact words?"

"Near as I can remember. 'Time for round two. The Montoya job has to look like an accident. You'll get a bonus if you do it before the election. Payment as previously arranged. Get it done.' Do you think I should tell the police?"

"Of course, Syd." Coming from D'won, with his well-earned antipathy toward the police, that was no small endorsement.

Panic fluttered her muscles and she wove her fingers together to keep her hands from shaking. "I can't. There'll be reporters, cameras, headlines saying there's something between Montoya and me—"

"You're right." D'won nodded sagely and stood. "And if some assassin offs Montoya, he'll have only himself to blame for running for office in the first place. The world'll be better off with one less politician."

"I didn't say that! I don't want him to get killed." She bit her lower lip, her stomach knotted with indecision.

"Didn't think so. I'll do the mock interviews with Belinda and Bo-Bae. You head to the cop shop." D'won grabbed his mug and headed for the door. "I cannot exist for another instant without more caffeine. Ciao, boss."

She sat for a moment twiddling two paperclips. Her gaze rested on the photo of her mother and father as newlyweds that sat beside her computer. Her indecision bugged her. She'd been sliding into a pit of indecisiveness for a couple of months, struggling to make choices that would've come easily three months ago, before her father died. At work, she was fine. Her personal life was the kicker—she couldn't seem to make a decision more complicated than sesame bagel or onion.

D'won could run Winning Ways while she was in Indonesia.

The thought popped fully formed into her head. Her mouth fell open slightly at the suddenness of it. She *could* go to Indonesia. Jason was right; there was nothing except Winning Ways keeping her here now that her dad was dead and her mom, more freed than grieved by his passing, was playing tennis and poker with friends, taking line dancing lessons, and chairing fundraising balls for at least two charities. And they'd only be gone a year. She knew nothing about Indonesia beyond the fact it had one of the largest Muslim populations in the world, but she could read up on it. She'd rent out her townhouse— Connie could take care of that if necessary—put her winter clothes in storage at the family home near Mt. Vernon, prep D'won…

Sydney stood and paced the small office. Could she really desert Winning Ways for a year? Starting the organization, helping other women, had saved her sanity after her marriage imploded. Would she be leaving them in the lurch? The truth hit her: the organization would get along fine. She was the one who needed Winning Ways. Maybe Jason was right…maybe she could start something like Winning Ways in Indonesia. Her mind whirled with the list of things to do in ten short days.

First things first. Sydney picked up the phone to call Jason. He answered on the first ring. "Jason Nygaard."

"Is that travel offer still open?"

"Sydney? Are you serious?" Cautious joy sounded in his voice.

"Yes. I love you."

"Oh, darling. I love you, too. Will you marry me? I'll ask you properly tonight, on my knees if you want, but I've got to know."

Peaceful certainty settled on her. "Yes. Should we do it next week? Before we go?"

Jason's delighted laughter set her heart on fire. "Tomorrow if you want. Let's get home early, do that celebrating we missed out on last night. My last class is at noon. I could make it home by two—no, call it two thirty. There's a department meeting."

"It's a date."

She hung up, happiness bubbling through her, a carbonation lifting her mood. She pressed her palms to her cheeks. Indonesia! What was she thinking? She twirled, already thinking about what to pack. The cell phone caught her eye.

Damn. Some of her euphoria evaporated. She picked it up and tossed it in the air like it was a quarter. Heads, she'd go to the police. Tails, she wouldn't. It slapped into her palm face up and another option occurred to her. She could mail the phone to the police with an anonymous note about the call and send a copy of her note to Montoya. Stifling the niggling thought that the police might dismiss it all as a prank, she searched the desk for a padded mailer. A note would give Montoya a heads-up. Why should she risk her peace of mind and privacy for what was probably no more than someone setting up a campaign trick of some kind?

7

Paul

PAUL GOT OFF THE Metro at the Eastern Market stop at the corner of 7th and Pennsylvania Avenue SE at noon. He avoided taxis whenever possible if on a job; just because a cabbie could barely speak English didn't mean he wouldn't remember your face. Ditto for rental cars. There were records and you always ran the risk of accidents, attracting police attention. No, in cities with public transportation, buses and subways were a killer's best friend.

He cursed the heat rising up from the asphalt as he crossed 8th Street SE. A night's thinking had convinced him to dispose of Ellison, per the client's instructions, before proceeding with the main target. No telling what Ellison might tell the police about the strange call he'd answered once word of Montoya's death hit the streets. No, the client was right: it was best to eliminate the risk—no matter how slight—up front. After matching Sid Ellison's home number with its street address, he'd memorized the address and the route to the house;

he'd learned early in his career never to commit anything to paper. In the Army they called it "sanitizing." You never carried anything on a mission—not a photo, letter, ID card, laundry list—that could give the enemy a wedge in interrogation. Of course, operating conditions were different here and he had to carry a wallet, money, credit card, and driver's license. But they weren't in his real name. He carried nothing that would connect him to his real life in Pennsylvania.

A purple car set ridiculously low on wide wheels honked at him as it made an illegal U-turn. Four youths laughed and gave him the finger, speeding past in an exhaust cloud. One of them yelled something in Spanish. Paul let it roll off his back. He was three blocks from the target's house, passing a military facility, it looked like. Two Marines in uniform stood at attention outside the front door and other Marines—identifiable by their high-and-tights—policed the block, picking up trash, wielding a leaf blower, pulling weeds. Paul almost greeted them with "Semper Fi," catching himself in time. He'd worked with a few Marines in 'Nam, understood their closeness. The brassy notes of a Sousa march drifted from behind the mansion-like facility. Paul wondered what it was but didn't dare question the Marines. He'd look it up later, when he was clear of the scene.

The music diminished as he kept walking, not fast but not slow, a forgettable man following his doctor's instructions to be more active, lose ten pounds. The target's house was ahead on the right. A trash truck trundled down the road and disappeared around the corner. Good. Halfway down the block on the other side of the street a woman spread mulch under some azalea bushes, reminding Paul of the yard tasks he had to complete at home. Although Moira provided care for his father and even undertook light household chores when Paul was traveling, he couldn't ask her to aerate the lawn or fertilize the shrubs.

The crack of a bat from further down the block jerked his head around. All of a sudden he was a senior in high school again, dropping the bat, knowing he'd connected for a double, maybe a triple. His powerful thigh muscles bunched and he pounded down the baseline to first, tagging the base and rounding the corner, headed for second. The center fielder was scrambling for the ball, coming up with it. His chest expanded and deflated, the tightness feeling good. He vaguely heard his teammates' screams, the crowd's cheers as his feet thudded into the dirt. He could make third. His peripheral vision caught the ball headed straight for the third baseman's mitt. Instinctively his body set up to slide, his hip joints loosening, his left leg easing out from under him.

He never knew how it happened, but suddenly he and the third baseman were lying in a twisted heap, coated with dust, the base knocked askew. His shoulder hurt like a son-of-a-bitch. "Safe!" yelled the ump. The runner they put in for him made it home on the next hit, and the Panthers won the state championship. But a torn rotator cuff ended his career as a shortstop, lost him his baseball scholarship to Penn State. Where would he be now, he wondered for perhaps the thousandth time, if he'd stopped at second base? If he'd gone to Penn State as planned—he didn't have the money for it without the scholarship—maybe he never would've ended up in the Army, never found his niche in Special Forces, never been trained to do what he did.

The thought brought him back to the present and he saw that the noise he'd thought was a bat was really a homeowner with a broom, whacking at a rug draped over the porch rail. *Focus*, he told himself, sniffing the air to make sure it didn't really carry a whiff of hot dogs. He was abreast of the address he'd memorized. He squatted, his knees making a sound like crinkling wax paper, and pretended to tie his shoe directly in front of Ellison's townhouse. Painted dark green, it was mated with a red brick-faced house on the left and a gray one with black trim on the right. The scrap of lawn was neatly maintained. No sign of kids' toys or animals. Good. Maybe, if he were really lucky, Sid Ellison lived alone. Paul moved on, glancing between the houses as he walked. No fence.

Playing it safe, he strolled two blocks past the target's house before turning. Sweat beaded his forehead and trickled down his sides. The nylon pullover he wore was good for concealing his weapon but damned uncomfortable in the heat. He swiped his sleeve across his forehead. A mail carrier stopping her square vehicle two blocks up gave him an idea. When he reached the Ellison house again he pulled open the mailbox, careful to use the fleshy ball under his thumb so as not to leave prints, and pantomimed slipping an envelope inside, as if he were delivering a note. Bills, flyers, a Sharper Image catalog, and *The Economist* half filled the small space. The items he could see without touching anything were all addressed to *S. L. Ellison*. Bingo.

Nudging the box closed with his elbow, he looked around. Across the street, a realtor's sign and a tube of brochures were staked in the front yard. Not that you could really call it a yard, he thought, crossing the road. More like a patch or a tuft. In fact, why bother putting grass in a space that small? Just pave it or tile it, put out a table and chairs or a grill and call it done. The house next door had a dark green ivy groundcover instead of grass. That looked better. Maybe he should try ivy in that shady patch on the side of his pop's house where the grass kept dying. Paul pulled open the tube and took a brochure. Looking like a prospective buyer would give him an excuse for lingering.

His new burner phone rang, making him drop the flyer. Only two people had the number, his client and Moira. "Yes?"

"Paul, I hate to bother you … I know you've got meetings, but I think you need to come home. Your father—" Anxiety and exasperation in equal measures tinged Moira's voice.

"What's happened?"

"He's been arrested."

"What! He's a cop. He was a cop." Paul forced himself to lower his voice.

"They picked him up for indecent exposure. He slipped out and walked down to the 7-Eleven to buy some cigarettes, wearing nothing but his slippers. He went past a bus stop where middle school girls were waiting for the school bus. They—"

Paul closed his eyes and sighed heavily. "I get the picture."

"The police released him to me, but someone must have talked about institutionalizing him because he's traumatized, keeps asking for you. Actually, he's asking for Eldon—"

"His older brother, dead twenty years."

"—but I assume he means you. I'm so sorry."

"It's not your fault, Moira. I'll be home tonight."

He hung up, bending to retrieve the brochure without really seeing it. Shit. This could screw up his timetable massively. Three hours to Barrytown, a stop at his old stomping grounds to ask what the fuck they meant by hauling in his father, a visit with his pop, three hours back ... He needed to take care of Ellison and hit the road.

His eyes swiveled back to the target's house, just in time to see a tall man with dark hair approach the gate. He held a briefcase in one hand, and a laptop case was slung over his shoulder. Could it be ... ? He looked somewhat familiar. He could've been in that deli.

Paul crumpled the flyer, his eyes scanning the neighborhood, looking for movement in the windows or on the street, anything to indicate witnesses. No shadows flickering behind curtains, no blinds dented down by curious fingers, no kids riding trikes. Nothing. Maybe this was his lucky day. Slipping his hand into the pullover pocket, he started across the street.

8

Sydney

SYDNEY SAT AT HER desk and studied her online calendar, fighting off the anxiety that nibbled at her as she noted all the appointments she'd be missing just in the next couple of weeks: the mock interview with Malayna, who was making such good progress; the lunch with Dan Soto to persuade him he needed to recruit Winning Ways' clients for his corporation; the introductory class with seven new women; her end-of-fiscal-year report to the Board of Directors. Well, she didn't mind handing that off to D'won. But the others, the ones involving the women... she gnawed on a pencil eraser, hand hovering over the delete key. She couldn't leave. Closing down the calendar, she reminded herself that Indonesia had Internet access. She could keep in touch with Winning Ways, and she'd only be gone a year. She needed to focus on the immediate future: she was getting married! Executing a little spin, she banged her hip against the desk's corner and grabbed the phone.

She wanted to share her news with someone. Phone in hand, she hesitated. Her best friend Helena was backpacking in Tibet with her partner. Not reachable. Sydney knew she should want to call her mother, or Reese, her older sister. That's what brides did, right? But Connie would be crushed to know they were going to marry simply, within the week, denying her the angst, frustration, and headaches of planning a major society wedding. She'd railed at Sydney for six months after she'd eloped with Dirk. Reese—well, the gap between them was as wide as ever.

Cradling the phone, Sydney walked next door to D'won's office. Little bigger than a storage closet, everything in it was sleek and pale gray with white accents: baseboards, shelves, the melamine desk, the laptop. D'won's apricot shirt popped against the neutral background. He was on the phone, dreadlocks swishing as he shook his head in response to what the person on the other end of the line was saying. "No, no, no—" he started.

"I'm getting married," Sydney announced.

D'won jerked his head up, said "Let me call you back" into the phone, and stood. "Say what?"

"I'm getting married. To Jason."

"Finally." A grin split his face and he came around the desk to hug her so tightly her back cracked and she could feel his ribs. He smelled of coconut-lime aftershave. "I wish you every happiness, Syd. You'll be happy—Jason's a good dude. He loves you."

She hugged him back and then pulled away. "There's more. I'm moving to Indonesia, so you'll be in charge here. But don't get any delusions of permanent emperorhood. I'll be back in a year."

His smile faltered. "I don't know if I'm ready—"

"You're ready." She smiled at him through a strange mist. She blinked it away. "You'll do a fabulous job. Hotchkiss and the board will probably tell me to stay in Indonesia."

"Not likely, boss," D'won said drily. "Hotchkiss would kick my Catholic black ass to the curb tomorrow if he could. I swear that man thinks I practice voodoo in my basement." He flapped a hand as if to clear away a bad smell. "I'm not spoiling your big news by thinking about him. Have you talked about a date?"

"Next week. Maybe Tuesday."

"Damn, that's fast. This calls for a celebration. I'm taking you to lunch."

"You don't have to—"

"Downstairs. Ten minutes."

"It's only ten o'clock."

"So?" He cocked a challenging brow.

She smiled, feeling giddy. "Meet you down there."

———

Sydney was waiting on the sidewalk in front of Winning Ways when D'won pulled to the curb in his yellow Miata. She hopped in and he wedged his way back into traffic, sticking his arm out the window to give the finger to a honking station wagon behind them. "Moron."

"Where are we lunching?" she asked, used to D'won's continuing commentary on road hogs, tailgaters, speeders, and generic incompetents who should never have received a driver's license. He was endlessly tolerant and patient in the classroom but a total flamer on the road.

His glance darted to her hand. "Where's your ring? The engagement's not official until there's a great big sparkly on your finger." He lifted his left hand from the wheel to waggle his fourth finger.

"He's a college professor," Sydney objected, massaging her ring-less finger. "I'm pretty sure he'll have a ring for me tonight," she added, wanting to fast-forward to the moment when she could be with Jason again.

"He's probably had it for a year and a half, waiting for the right moment, waiting for you to get over your commitment phobia enough that you wouldn't run screaming for the hills like someone avoiding a chain-saw-wielding serial killer at the mention of the M word," D'won said, swooping into a small parking lot outside a two-story brick building with *Delia's* in elegant script across the front. Only one other car, a late-model Mercedes, sat in the lot.

"It doesn't seem very popular," Sydney said, choosing to ignore D'won's exaggerated description of her natural caution about a second marriage. They walked around the side of the building and approached the entrance. "What kind of food—?" She didn't finish the question as she stared at the display windows, then turned a disbelieving face to D'won, who was grinning like a fool.

"D'won! What—?"

"This is where my brother's wife, Angelique—you've met her—got her dress." He shrugged as if taking Sydney shopping for a wedding dress was no big deal. "I called for an appointment and we got lucky. You don't have any time to waste if you want to get married before flying off to Indonesia."

She flung her arms around him and hugged convulsively, unable to say anything because of the lump blocking her throat.

"Just don't get anything white," D'won said, pulling away, "because the whole world knows for damned sure you ain't no virgin."

She laughed and they ascended the two shallow stairs leading into the bridal shop. Pushing through the glass doors took them out of the DC heat into the hushed cool of another world. Regency England, maybe, Sydney thought, noting the satin-upholstered chairs with their spindly legs, and the bronze and crystal chandeliers that cast a very modern light on the extravagant dresses that lined the showroom's walls; there were more shades of white, ecru, oyster, vanilla, and even pink than she knew existed.

A petite woman of a certain age, wearing an exquisitely fitted lavender suit, glided across the Aubusson-style carpet, hands out in welcome. She could have been anywhere between fifty and sixty-five, with expensively maintained ash-blond hair. Sydney suspected she accessorized her weekend wear with a Pekinese or two peeking out of a Kate Spade handbag. Her shrewd eyes flitted between D'won and Sydney, assessing their relationship. Her gaze lingered on D'won's apricot shirt and paisley silk tie, and Sydney could see it on her face when she decided he was not the groom but a gay buddy along to advise on a dress. D'won wasn't gay but didn't mind when people assumed he was, misled by his fashion taste.

"Congratulations on your engagement and welcome to my shop. I am Delia." Her eyes noted Sydney's bare left hand but she was too polite, or too much the saleswoman, to comment. Sydney slid the hand surreptitiously behind her back. "Have you set a date?"

"Next week," Sydney said.

Delia took the news without blinking. "Then we'd better get started. Did you have a style in mind?"

"I was thinking maybe a suit..." She hadn't actually given the matter any thought, but a suit seemed appropriate for a second marriage. It was dignified.

Delia nodded. Before she could say anything, D'won broke in. "What's this suit shit, Syd? You need yards of train and sparkles"—his hands waved in front of his chest—"and a veil."

"I don't think—"

"What did you wear to the registrar—or whatever they call 'em in Austria? Jeans, I'll bet."

"A perfectly nice skirt and—"

"You've finally found the right guy, Syd. A suit does not say 'I'm giddy with love and excited about starting a life on the other side of the planet with you,'" D'won said in the same voice he used when telling Winning Ways clients what constituted acceptable interview attire. "Indulge. She'll try that one." He pointed to the confection of eggshell-colored satin and lace in the display window.

A delicious feeling of irresponsibility drifted over her. Not the bad kind. The kind that said she could go with the flow, cede control, try on a few dresses if it made D'won happy. *And me*, she admitted.

"A wonderful choice with your height and your coloring," Delia said approvingly, moving to the racks to locate the gown. She surged toward the dressing room, swathes of material draped over her arms. "Do you need foundation garments?"

"Does she think I need a girdle?" Sydney whispered to D'won.

He lifted both hands in an "I'm not going there" gesture and she giggled. She was not a giggler and the sound surprised her.

All urge to laugh left when she stood on the round dais in front of floor-to-ceiling mirrors and surveyed the gown's effect. The shimmering satin cast a glow on her skin and made her auburn hair look redder. The crystal-encrusted bodice, fitted to high hip, minimized her full bust and made her look slim as a lily. She hadn't worn anything so form-fitting in a long, long time. Lifting her hair off her neck, she piled it atop her head. An up-do would be elegant. She spun around, the gown's weight making her movements languid and graceful, and asked, "Well?"

D'won gave a thumbs-up and said, "Now that's what I'm talking about. And you wanted a suit." He snorted.

Delia nodded crisply and said, "Charming."

Sydney's heel caught as she turned back to the mirror and she lurched slightly. "Do you think Jason will like it?"

"Good Lord, Syd," D'won said with an eye roll. "Of course he will. The man's not dead."

9

Paul

PAUL STUMBLED ON THE curb by Ellison's townhome but caught himself. Habit made him scan the area again—still no one in sight. The target was just unlocking his door. He had broad shoulders and gray-flecked hair curling over his collar. A cat wound around his ankles, making *prrp-prrp* sounds.

Paul came within ten feet of the man and called out as the door opened inward. "Sir, can I have a word?"

His right hand around the Ruger .22, he pulled the bi-fold wallet out with his left hand and flipped it open to display the badge. His badge from his days on the Barrytown force—the same department his dad had retired from—which he joined when he'd mustered out after 'Nam. He'd told the chief he'd lost it when they ordered him to turn it in after the Jorgenson incident. The chief hadn't believed him, but what could he do? The badge came in very handy in his current line of work; it disarmed all sorts of people who might otherwise be more cautious.

"Yes?" The target turned, his brows arching up.

Two more steps. Drawing the silenced .22 from his pocket, Paul surged toward the man, who took an involuntary step back, tripping over the cat. As he lurched into the foyer, Paul shot him.

The first bullet caught the man in the chest. He thudded to the floor, one hand groping at his chest, fear and confusion in his eyes. Paul bumped the door closed with his hip. Swinging around, he took one smooth step forward and fired the gun, arms extended, at point-blank range into the target's forehead. The man's hand flopped to his side and he laid still, his brown eyes glazing over. A last breath gargled out.

His every sense tuned to its sharpest, Paul stood for a moment looking down at Ellison. The familiar stink of blood and shit mixed with lemony wax. Relatively little blood pooled on the floor, although some had soaked into the man's sport coat and shirt from the chest wound. His face showed very white against the dark wood, his dulled irises staring at the ceiling. Much less gory and far quieter than combat. War's loudness—the whine of incoming rounds, the ack-ack of machine guns, the explosions and screams—had pummeled young Private Jones in Vietnam, and Paul still sub-consciously expected death to be noisy. It rarely was anymore. The *chunk* of an air conditioner kicking on startled him until he identified the quiet hum. He breathed in … out, centering himself, easing the adrenaline and 'Nam out of his system.

Okay, task completed—target terminated. He turned away from the body. Now he only had to worry about egress. Normally he'd have had a plan roughed out, based on surveillance, but Moira's call had prompted him to take advantage of the unexpected opportunity. Careful not to step in the blood, he crossed to the door and peered out the vertical window that paralleled it. The yuppie neighborhood looked empty and somnolent in the early-afternoon sun.

A whisper whipped him around. The cat, inspecting the body with curiosity, had bloodied its front paws. It sat in the middle of the foyer, shaking one paw, its ears laid flat, hissing.

"Hey, puss, puss." The cat glared at him through slitted eyes and Paul opted to leave it alone.

He stole another glance through the window. The front door was his best bet; if he were seen, no one would think much of it, whereas an unknown man walking out the back might excite more scrutiny. He took one last, assessing look at the scene. Ellison was dead. No one could tie him to the victim: he'd touched nothing, left no evidence other than the hair and skin flakes everybody shed. They'd be no good to anyone unless he was arrested someday and the cops thought to check his DNA against the samples collected at this scene. He had a better chance of being hit by lightning. This was a textbook operation. He thought about looking for his cell phone—it might have his prints on it—but decided he couldn't risk the time. Slipping the gun back into his pocket, he waited until an electrician's van moved past, then opened the door with his hand wrapped in his windbreaker.

"Thanks, Sid. See you Tuesday, then," he said in a normal voice for anyone who might be listening. He raised a hand in a farewell wave and walked down the front sidewalk, confident in his anonymity, the mediumness of his build, hair, and features. His forgettableness was one of his chief assets. Two blocks away, sweat dripping from his forehead, he took a deep breath. The Metro entrance was around the next corner. He was clear.

10

Sydney

SYDNEY WAS PRACTICALLY SKIPPING as she rode the escalator up from the Metro depths at two o'clock. With a delicious feeling of irresponsibility, she'd opted to play hooky instead of returning to the office after trying on the wedding dress. Instead, after D'won returned to the office, she'd done wedding stuff, hiring a photographer and a florist, both of whom were happy to accept commissions for the Thursday night Jason and Sydney had decided on after consulting via cell phone. Her hair swung gently against her shoulders and she smiled at strangers as she passed, surprising smiles out of some, suspicious looks from others. In one hand she clutched a bouquet of Gerbera daisies whose bright colors and open faces she'd been unable to resist. In the other, she had a bottle of Dom Perignon to replace the champagne they'd wasted last night. Humming, she passed the Marine Commandant's house on the corner. Almost home.

Crossing 9th Street, she spotted an ambulance parked in the middle of the block. Oh, no. Poor Mrs. Colwell! Had she fallen? Had a heart attack? Sydney sped up. A knot of police cars blocked the street and one's light bar sent red and blue stripes flashing across the neighborhood. A clump of neighbors stood outside a perimeter of yellow tape, watching as two EMTs wheeled a gurney to the waiting ambulance. They moved without urgency, their load unmoving under a white sheet. *Damn.* Had anyone contacted Mrs. Colwell's daughter? As Sydney moved closer, she saw Mrs. Colwell standing just off her stoop talking to a policewoman. *What was—?*

The woman petted Indigo as she talked, breaking off to point. "There she is," the old woman said. Indigo struggled to get free but Mrs. Colwell snuggled him tighter against her meager bosom.

"Miss Ellison?" Someone stood at Sydney's elbow.

She turned to see a man in his late thirties, flanked by a short African-American woman. He had a commanding presence, although he was only medium height with brown hair cut military-short, brows that peaked rather than arched, and deep-set brown eyes. The woman was petite, dowdily dressed in a shapeless mud-colored suit, and had the air of a cat about to pounce on an unsuspecting mouse.

"Miss Ellison, I'm Detective Benjamin West. This is my partner, Detective Graves. We need—"

Just then, two men in utility overalls stenciled with *Metropolitan Police Department* emerged from Sydney's open front door.

"Oh, God, no," she gasped. The truth began to sink in, shocking her cold like the first plunge into Wood Lake in May. "Jason! Where's Jason?" She tried to push past West but he grabbed her arm. The roughness of his palm against her skin surprised her; maybe he was a do-it-yourselfer who wielded a hammer on weekends. She struggled against his grasp, but he held on.

"You can't go in there."

"What's happened to Jason?" Sydney looked wildly from West to Graves.

"I'm sorry to have to tell you, Miss Ellison," the woman said, not sounding sorry. "Mr. Jason Nygaard is dead. Was he a friend of yours?" Sloe eyes set above sharp cheekbones watched for her reaction.

"My ... my fiancé. We were going to Indonesia." A wave of dizziness washed over her and she would have fallen if West hadn't tightened his hold on her arm. He saved the bottle of champagne as it slipped from her grasp. The daisies fell, splattering the sidewalk with red, orange, yellow, and purple. "What happened?"

Could the shape on the gurney really be Jason? Sydney's eyes followed it as the EMTs hoisted it into the rear of the ambulance. She needed to see him. Wrenching free, she ran toward the men with the gurney, losing one of her pumps and almost falling before kicking the other shoe off and limping the last couple of steps to Jason's side.

"Hey—!" one of the EMTs said as she reached the gurney, taking in jerky breaths.

His partner shushed him with a gesture and, after a glance at Detective West, peeled the sheet down to expose Jason's face and shoulders.

His eyes were closed. His beautiful green eyes. Trying hard to block out the dark hole in his forehead, Sydney stretched one hand to caress the hair at his temple. It sprang away from her touch as if still alive. She didn't realize she was crying until she tasted the saltiness of tears. She dashed them away with the back of her hand, then put her fingertips to Jason's lips. The unfamiliar feel of cooling flesh jolted her back a step. The sympathetic EMT took advantage of her retreat to flick the sheet back into place and collapse the legs of the gurney so they could slide it between the open doors. Sydney stood in a vacuum of silence, not hearing the voices around her or the traffic noises or the rising wind in the leaves until the metallic clang of the ambulance door tore into her consciousness.

"Jason—" She took a step, wanting to follow the ambulance, but a hand on her elbow stopped her. Confused, she looked into West's not unsympathetic face. It was a strong face with cop's eyes, firm lips, and a nose that had been broken more than once.

"Sit down." West guided her to the open door of an unmarked police car and she sank onto the edge of the seat.

"Someone shot Jason," she whispered. The import of that dark hole in his forehead sank in. "Why?"

"Don't you know?" Detective Graves asked, arching thin brows. "Where were you today?" Her pen hovered over the notepad she held in one hand. Her hands were square, short-fingered, with nails bitten past the quick.

"No! How would I—? I was at work, at Winning Ways, then I was shopping with my deputy in the afternoon."

"Winning Ways? Is that a sports bar, a betting parlor?"

"No, it's—" Sydney turned away from the snide woman and concentrated on West, trying to read the neutral planes of his face, the trace of concern in his eyes. "What happened?" she asked. "Where are they taking him?" Her voice broke and tears welled. Jason was gone. Not to Indonesia. Gone. Forever.

"Mr. Nygaard was shot twice, execution style, in your home, Miss Ellison."

"Oh my God." The word "execution" bit into her. The cell phone. The hit man had used her phone to track her down. He'd shot Jason. She looked around. "My briefcase … where's my briefcase?"

West made a calming motion. "Over there." He pointed.

"I need it now!" She tried to get out of the car but he restrained her, directing his partner to get the case with a nod of his head.

Grudgingly, Graves retrieved it from the sidewalk, crushing a red daisy underfoot. She opened the case and scanned the contents before handing it to Sydney.

She pulled out the manila envelope with the cell phone inside. She tried to pry open the metal clasp but her trembling fingers couldn't do it. She thrust it at West. "Here. I was going to mail this to you." She pointed at the police department address inscribed on the front.

"What is it?" West ripped open the envelope and the phone fell into his hand in a shower of gray fuzz. "A cell phone?" He looked at her from under his brows, turning the phone over in his hands.

"It belongs to a hit man." Semi-coherently, Sydney told them about the phone mix-up and the call she'd answered. "I wasn't really sure it was about a … a contract," she finished, "and I was afraid of the publicity, so I decided to mail it to you. And now Jason … "

"You're saying this hit man you supposedly talked to came here and killed your boyfriend?" Detective Graves asked, her voice dripping with disbelief. "Give the lady this week's prize for creativity, Ben," she said with a harsh laugh. Her eyes never smiled. "What time did you say you left work?"

Her tone drilled through Sydney's grief. Willing away tears, she met Graves's eyes, staying silent for a full thirty seconds. "You think I had something to do with this?" Not for nothing was she the daughter of one of the country's most powerful lawyers. "I want a lawyer."

West shot his partner a look that said, "Way to go." The female detective shrugged, but Sydney caught a glimpse of satisfaction in her eyes.

"Do you have someone you can go to? Someone you want us to call?" West asked. "You can't stay here." She turned back to him, not fooled for an instant by the concern she knew must be fake. He was only playing good cop to his partner's bad cop.

"Don't worry about me," Sydney said, standing. The heat clubbed her, made her sway. West caught her arm again, his fingers tight around her biceps, until she steadied. She arched her brows and his hand dropped away.

"We'll need a number where we can reach you," West said, his voice cooler. He rubbed a curled forefinger over his eyebrow. "You'll need to make a statement."

"I'll be with my mother, Constance Linn." Sydney reeled off the number. "Hilary Trent will be in touch. I presume you're familiar with her."

From the look on West's face, she knew he recognized the name of the city's most prominent, successful, and acerbic criminal defense attorney. She also happened to be one of Connie's tennis partners.

"I'm sorry about your fiancé," he said, giving her ringless finger a pointed look.

"Thank you," she said, cursing inwardly as her cheeks warmed. "Did he … was he in pain?"

"He died instantly," West said in a gentler voice. He started to say something more, but then stopped.

Sydney kept her eyes fixed on him, hoping for—what?—but realized he had no more to offer. She thought about asking if she could get some clothes from the bedroom but couldn't face the idea of entering the house, maybe seeing Jason's blood. Instead, she turned away from West and groped for her cell phone, not caring that the briefcase dropped and spilled files, pens, and business cards onto the sidewalk. With a trembling finger, she punched in the familiar number. While she waited for her mother to answer, her gaze landed unseeingly on the daisies, their vibrance already wilted and browned by the griddle-hot sidewalk.

11

Sydney

SYDNEY SAT AT HER mother's kitchen table, clutching a mug of tea liberally laced with honey and bourbon; Connie's panacea for everything from sore throats to career disasters to murder, apparently. The lowering sun streamed through the windows, warming the cream-colored walls and the brick tile floors of their Mount Vernon–area home. It highlighted the gouges and indentions on the oak plank table that had been in her mother's family for generations. In a rare burst of sentimentality, Connie had refused to replace the table when she'd had the kitchen redone five years ago. Sydney scraped at a purple mark with a thumbnail; probably a stain that had been there for years.

Without looking up, she knew her mother was studying her. She sniffed, grateful the tears had finally stopped. For now. She knew there'd be more when she was alone. Her eyes felt swollen, puffed up like ping-pong balls, and her nose was raw from where she'd kleen-exed it repeatedly. She took a long swallow from the mug, both hands cupped around it. Despite the sunshine flooding the kitchen, she was cold.

The last time she'd felt so cold was a year ago March when she and Jason had gone hiking in the Poconos and been caught in a freak snowstorm. Jason, raised in upstate New York, had known what to do, fashioning a shallow snow cave to shelter them from the wind. He was good at practical stuff like that; could fix his bike or replace a broken window, too. They'd huddled together, legs intertwined, testing each other for hypothermia, until the wind died down and they could see where they were going. That was the first time Jason had told her he loved her, whispering it in her ear as the wind howled. Sydney pushed away the memories, took another swallow of tea, and topped up the half-empty mug from the Wild Turkey bottle sitting within arm's reach. Connie had abandoned tea for straight bourbon half an hour earlier.

Silence lingered between mother and daughter, more noticeable now that Sydney had stopped crying. Connie and her younger daughter had never been on the same wavelength, as the saying goes, and Jason's death hadn't changed that. Something about the situation—Sydney's grief, the fact that Jason was murdered?—was making her antsy. Her foot tapped against the table leg and she sprang up to put more hot water on to boil. Sydney watched her fill the copper teapot, her knuckles gleaming white from her grip on the handle, and then switch on the gas burner.

She stared into the flames for a moment, clearly not wanting to return to the table in the breakfast nook where Sydney sat. Then, grabbing a sponge, she sopped up a water dribble from the granite counter. She looked incongruous, Sydney thought, holding a sponge while dressed in tennis whites with a platinum Patek Philippe watch on one bony wrist and a courtesan's nest egg in diamonds encircling the other.

"I think Jason was killed instead of me," Sydney said into the silence. The raspiness of her voice surprised her. From the crying, she guessed.

"That doesn't sound very likely." Connie's gaze fastened on her daughter momentarily before she carried the sponge to the sink and rinsed it.

"I've been thinking about it," Sydney said, the words coming slowly. "No one would want to kill Jason. It was me." She told her mother about taking the wrong cell phone, listening to the caller who wanted to make the Montoya job look like an accident. "The killer must think I can identify him or something. He killed Jason by mistake because he was at the house. I told the detectives, but they didn't believe me."

Connie came to the table and sank into a chair with the perfect posture Sydney had always envied. Pulling a cigarette from a pack on the table, she fiddled with it, turning it over and over between her fingers. She'd quit smoking a decade ago but still carried a cigarette with her wherever she went. When one wore out, crumbled to tobacco flakes, she'd appropriate another. One pack could last weeks.

Her brows rose in skeptical arches. "Don't you think the simplest explanation is that Jason surprised a burglar? Maybe he tried to stop him."

"Look at the timing. I get a strange phone call that sounds like someone setting up a hit, and the next day Jason is killed? Shot? Isn't that a bit too coincidental?" Sydney's voice gained strength as she talked. She needed her mother to believe her.

"The whole thing is strange," Connie hedged. "But the most important thing is to keep the story away from the media and convince the police that you had nothing to do with his death."

Sydney suspected most normal people would have reordered those priorities, but she didn't quibble with them. "You believe me, don't you, Mom? About the phone call?"

Connie buried her face in her mug, swallowing the last of the bourbon. Then she pushed back from the table. "We shouldn't speculate too much before talking to Hilary tomorrow morning. She wants to go over your statement with you before you talk to the police. She's set up an interview for you tomorrow at nine. Her office."

Sydney kept her eyes fixed on her mother for a long moment, hoping for more. "I'll need some clothes," she said finally, when it was clear Connie had nothing more to offer. She set down the mug of bourbon tea and considered her crumpled blouse and skirt. Her soiled suit jacket was draped over a chair. A smear of blood on the sleeve made her swallow hard. "This is all I have. I couldn't get any clothes from … I didn't … " Tears threatened again.

"Reese is bringing some clothes over," Connie said hastily. Her petite-size clothes would never fit Sydney; her wrists and ankles would poke out.

Sydney stiffened. "You called Reese? Isn't she in Oklahoma?"

"She got back two weeks ago," Connie said testily, responding to the hostility in Sydney's tone. "She can help."

"I don't want her help."

"Oh, for God's sake, Sydney, it's time you got over it." Connie snapped the cigarette she was fiddling with in half and flung it onto the table. "It was fifteen years ago. Reese admitted she made a mistake and said she's sorry. You're sisters." The way she said it made it clear that she thought the genetic bond should trump any betrayal or difference of personality.

"That's what made it worse."

Reese's "mistake" was breaking the story of Sydney's relationship with George Manley in order to jump-start her lackluster reporting career. At twenty-three, she was three years older than Sydney and working for a weekly rag in central Virginia when she capitalized on Sydney's sisterly lack of discretion, writing a five-part exposé about the Speaker of the House's affair with a girl young enough to be his daughter. She had plenty of photos, since all she'd had to do was follow Sydney to their rendezvous. She'd ended George's career, wrecked his relationship with his kids (although his marriage survived after a fashion), ruined Sydney's life, and landed a job with the *Washington Post*.

Everyone had expected more political exposés from her, but she'd ditched DC after a year to be a war correspondent. She'd spent most of the next ten years out of the country, reporting from Iraq and Afghanistan, Israel, Syria, Darfur, Georgia, Congo, Nigeria, and India, earning acclaim and a Pulitzer—all before thirty—prior to abruptly leaving the news business to write true crime books. Those books took her to wherever the crimes and their stories had happened, and she'd spent months in small towns in California, Louisiana, Maine, and Bermuda, and almost a year in Chicago, making it easy for Sydney to avoid her.

In the years after their initial confrontation—a confrontation replete with tears, name-calling, and Reese's lame apologies cancelled out by rhetoric about the public's right to know—Sydney had only seen her sister a handful of times. There'd been Nana Linn's funeral five years after the scandal broke, where they'd stood on opposite sides of the grave and didn't exchange a word. Then they'd collided at a cousin's wedding where some well-meaning fool, probably Aunt Rose, had seated them at the same table. Reese had spent the evening in the bar, seducing the bartender, and Sydney, recently divorced, had pleaded a headache and left before the cake-cutting. Finally, they'd met at their father's funeral three months ago, where they'd managed a few chilly civilities. Reese hadn't shed a tear at the service, but then neither had Sydney. Her sister was the last person Sydney wanted to see now.

Which was unfortunate, because Reese sailed through the kitchen door before she could run off and hide in her old bedroom. Sydney couldn't help staring at her, searching for—what? Signs of aging? That felt petty. A hint of repentance? How likely was it that a scarlet *A* for *apology* was going to pop out on her chest, or that she was going to drop to her knees and beg Sydney's forgiveness? If it hadn't happened in fifteen years, it was unlikely to happen now.

As Sydney studied her sister, she had to admit that she looked good. Better than good. Sydney was tall at five foot eight, but Reese was taller, with a slim, no breasts/no hips elegance that Sydney had always envied, even in the khaki cargo pants and white camp shirt she currently wore. Where Sydney had the Linn family auburn hair, Reese had their father's blond hair, cut in a short pixie with bangs that almost hid the strong black brows they both got from Connie. Her face had more angles than Sydney remembered, the softness of youth planed away to reveal the square jaw, prominent cheekbones, and aquiline nose. She exuded good health and her skin was tan, probably from six months in Oklahoma researching her latest book. A trace of crow's feet fanned from the corners of her eyes, and a chunk was missing from her right earlobe, torn away by a guerrilla bullet in Chechnya, but those were the only blemishes. She brought with her a Nordstrom's bag, a Starbucks cup, and a vitality that seemed to jangle the very air. It wasn't really harder to breathe, Sydney told herself.

Kicking the door shut with one foot, Reese said, "Hi, Con," but her gaze slipped to Sydney. She set the Nordstrom's bag and her coffee on the table and stopped two feet away.

"I'm very sorry for your loss, Syd," she said formally. "From what I've heard—"

From their mother, no doubt.

"—Jason was a good man."

Her sister's proximity made Sydney's scalp prickle and she had a fleeting vision of herself as a cat, fur standing on end, facing a junkyard dog. She stopped short of hissing. "He was. We were getting married."

Reese's brows rose at that news, but she merely nodded without saying anything. "I brought you some clothes." She gestured to the bag. "Wasn't sure what you needed, or how much, but that should last you. You're welcome to borrow anything you need. Anything but bras." She offered a half smile, making fun of her flat chest.

Sydney crossed her arms over her full breasts. "Thanks."

After an awkward beat, Reese asked, "Do the police know—"

"Nothing." Sydney didn't amplify.

"They clearly consider Sydney a suspect," Connie broke in. "Hilary Trent is dealing with them."

"She's the best," Reese said. "Dad thought so, anyway. I'm sure she's got a good investigator, but if there's anything I can do—"

"There's not."

Reese reached for her Starbucks cup and must have squeezed it too hard, because the top popped partway off and coffee ran down the sides. "Damn." She shook droplets off her fingers. Connie handed her a paper towel. As she blotted the cup and dried her fingers, she said, "The police are overwhelmed. There've been 214 homicides in DC already this year. A quarter of them are still unsolved. I've got time on my hands since I turned in my manuscript on the Bingle murders."

The mass murder of a five-person family by the fourteen-year-old daughter; the story that had taken Reese to Oklahoma.

"I could poke around—"

60

"Last time you poked around, it didn't turn out so well for me," Sydney said, "so I think I'll pass."

Reese took the blow without batting an eye.

"Oh, for heaven's sake," Connie huffed. "Your sister's only trying to—"

Reese stopped her with an upraised hand and continued to study Sydney with eyes that held more sympathy than Sydney was comfortable with.

Before either her sister or her mother could say more, Sydney slipped her arms through the carry hoops on the bag. "I need to change." She was running away from Reese; she didn't have the energy to overturn the habit of fifteen years. Not today. She left the kitchen, headed for the sanctuary of her old bedroom.

12

Paul

HOME IN BARRYTOWN, PENNSYLVANIA, Paul gazed down at his sleeping father, listening to the breaths whistling between his loose lips. William Jones lay on his back under a light sheet, his prominent nose pointing straight up, bold as a ship's prow. His arms lay outside the sheet, straight along his sides. Spikes of hair poked out of his nostrils and ears, stiff as the fibers on a boar bristle hair brush. Paul had taken to trimming the hairs from his own nose and ears, finding that sign of aging much more abhorrent than wrinkles, age spots, or creaky knees. His thumb and forefinger absently tugged at one earlobe. He breathed shallowly through his mouth, trying to avoid inhaling the sting of camphor from the vaporizer, the singed smell of sheets dried at too high a temperature, and the scent of old man's body.

His father coughed, opening eyes with pale blue irises awash in corneas like half-cooked egg whites. Sleep stickies caked the corners.

Confusion clouded his face as he stared up at Paul. Finally, he smiled, creasing his sunken cheeks. "Eldon!"

"No, Pop, it's me, Paul." He took his father's hand in his. It felt too light, as if the bones were hollow. "How're you doing?"

"Paul?"

"Your son." He bit down on the urge to ask "Remember?" while knowing his father didn't. "Moira tells me you had a little adventure."

Paul had stopped by the Barrytown, Pennsylvania, precinct on his way into town, shot the shit with the few cops he still knew from his time on the job, and dropped a hint that he'd appreciate it if the fellows didn't roust his father, just took him home.

"Sure, Paulie, sure," his former partner, a polar bear of a Swede named Johanssen, told him. "Landon picked him up. New guy, a rookie. We told him what's what." Johanssen shook his ursine head at the thought of the rookie's many failings.

"I appreciate it, Lars. He needs his dignity, you know?"

"Absolutely, Paulie. But ya gotta keep him from walking around stark in front of teenage girls." Johanssen pulled a cruller from the box of donuts Paul had brought and took a large bite. "It's sad to see him like this, y'know? When he was with the force, he had such presence. Like, you always knew he was in the room, even if he wasn't saying anything. Now ..." He stuffed the rest of the donut in his mouth and chewed. Swallowing, he said, "Anyways, we'll look out for him."

"Thanks, Lars. That's all I ask."

"How's the lingerie business?" A smirk disfigured the large face. "Think you could introduce me to one of those Victoria's Secrets models?"

"Linens. I sell hotel linens. Business is great."

"Sure it is. It was a shame, you getting kicked off the force for beating up that punk," Johanssen said, easing into a familiar complaint. "He deserved it, and more."

Paul knew what was coming: *The guy who invented...*

"I tell you what, buddy, the guy who invented the video camera oughta be shot. That's all there is to it. Shot. Why does video always work against the cops, huh? Tell me that. How come you never see a dirtball get convicted with video evidence but cops get suspended or fired or brought up on charges when some commie-pinko-liberal catches 'em doing their job? You got screwed, buddy. You ever want to get out of sales, I know a guy could hook you up with a security gig, bodyguard work, the like, not patrolling some construction site at midnight. Good money, too."

"Thanks. I'll let you know."

Johanssen grabbed a second donut as Paul headed for the door. "Don't be a stranger."

———

A stranger was what his dad was, Paul thought, carrying on a one-sided conversation with the man who'd taught him to hit a baseball, walloped his behind when he caught him shoplifting a paperback from the mom-and-pop store on the corner, helped him pick out perfume for his mom's birthday. Tabu. The spicy scent still lingered in some corners of the house, or maybe just in his memories.

"I bought a snow blower today, Eldon," William Jones announced.

"Great, Pop," Paul said, glancing out the window at the sunny day.

They chatted for another half hour, Paul answering variously to Eldon, Mark (his father's partner on the force for eighteen years), and his own name. When his father drifted back to sleep, he tucked the sheet around him and went into the kitchen where Moira was making a pot of tea. She was maybe ten years younger than he, with wiry strands of gray threaded through her light brown hair, and she moved with an economy of motion he appreciated. He thought maybe she found him attractive, but he hadn't pursued it, unwilling to risk upsetting his father's situation if a few dates led to awkwardness. He'd never wanted a wife: watching his mom and dad go at it had soured him on marriage, and he'd trained himself to do without women, satisfying the occasional urge with a hooker. Now, though, he felt a stirring as he watched Moira cross the linoleum floor, her rounded hips stretching the fabric of her simple skirt.

"You startled me," she said, catching sight of him in the doorway. One hand went to her chest. Then she smiled, the curve of lip and flash of teeth brightening the room with its porcelain sink turned the color of old sheets washed with black socks, its wallpaper grimed with grease from meals cooked in his childhood, its linoleum worn as thin as a bee's wing in spots. His father had refused to change anything after Paul's mother died of ovarian cancer in 1990.

"Would you like some tea? I've been reading that green tea is full of antioxidants, so that's what I'm having. But there's Earl Grey or chamomile if you prefer."

"Coffee. I'll make it."

"No, no." She beat him to the cupboard, pulling out the two-cup coffee maker and crossing to the freezer for the Seattle's Best he stored there. He hovered in the doorway, feeling almost like an intruder in his own home, the house he'd grown up in. He knew suddenly he'd sell it when his father died. The idea intrigued him and he lost himself in imagining what kind of a house he'd buy in its place. Not a condo or townhome … too many neighbors to watch his comings and goings. And he wanted a yard, someplace to have a garden.

"Let's sit outside. We don't want Bill to overhear us," Moira said, bumping the screen door open with her shoulder. "He seems better today," she observed as they lowered themselves awkwardly to the cement stoop and sat, hips almost, but not quite, touching. "Yesterday, when the police officer brought him back in borrowed clothes, he was shivering like an abandoned kitten. I've never seen him look like that."

"I've talked with the cops. It won't happen again." Paul blew on his coffee and sipped. Sheets flapped on the neighbor's clothesline and a bee buzzed nearby. He could sleep for a week in the sun's warmth.

"But something will. I can't—you can't—watch him twenty-four hours a day."

Paul tilted his head, met Moira's gaze. "Are you saying... what? That he needs to be institutionalized?"

She paused before answering, holding the cup close to her plump bosom. "It's something to consider."

The thought of his pop cooped up in a Lysol-scented facility, surrounded by octogenarians who couldn't control their bodily functions, made Paul feel like his intestines were coiled around his stomach, squeezing. "He'd hate it."

She put a soft hand on his arm. "He doesn't know where he is or who you are most of the time, Paul. He knows me, but—"

The tinny ring of his cell phone from inside the house brought Paul to his feet. His client. Letting the screen door bang shut behind him, he jogged to his father's bedroom where the phone rang from the pocket of the jacket he'd left draped over a chair. "Yeah?" he said on the fifth ring.

"You killed the wrong person," the familiar voice said.

"What?"

"You didn't kill Sydney Ellison. You killed her fucking boyfriend. It's all over the news."

"Her?" How was he supposed to know "Sidney" was a girl? Shit.

"Her. Sydney Linn Ellison. The bimbo who got caught with the Speaker of the House fifteen years ago? Her. And now she'll be on her guard."

"She can't know anything that ties us—"

"Do you still have the .22 you used on Nygaard?"

"Who?" Paul felt like he was three steps behind in this conversation and losing ground.

"Jason Nygaard, the guy you shot at Ellison's house. Do you still have the gun?"

"Of course." Paul liked the Ruger .22. He'd seen no need to dispose of the gun after yesterday's killing.

"You need to plant it in the house or her car, make it look like Ellison killed him. I hear the cops are already looking at her for it. It'll confuse the issue, cast doubt on anything she says, at the very least—anything she might happen to mention about a phone call on a burner phone, for instance. I have the address where she's staying now."

Paul memorized the address and Ellison's license plate number as the man read them out. "The gun won't have her prints," he pointed out. "There won't be a record of her buying it."

"Don't worry about that. Just fucking make it happen." As if he sensed Paul's impending rebellion, the client added, "I'll double the bonus if they're both taken care of by the election Tuesday."

Paul thought of Moira's insistence that his father needed full-time care. With the money from this job, he'd be able to stay home for three or four months, not take another contract for a while. He could maybe even retire. "Done."

The line went dead. Paul pocketed the phone. He would leave immediately, drive back to DC, and take out Montoya on Friday, as he'd planned before this whole Ellison thing came up. He'd spent three weeks doing recce, planning the hit. He could plant the gun on Ellison beforehand. Flexibility was the key to airpower, the flyboys always said.

Maybe he could catch something on the news about the investigation. He crossed to the dresser to turn on the small television that sat there. A picture blossomed on the screen, resolving itself into a reporter standing in front of the townhouse on G Street. Great. Turning to find the remote to dial up the volume, Paul came face to face with his .22, held in his father's trembling hand.

13

Sydney

SYDNEY GOT OUT OF the shower, dressed in Reese's clothes, and French-braided her wet hair. Her nerves twanged with the conviction that she had to see Montoya immediately. This evening. The urge had come to her while she was shampooing her hair, stabbing through her grief. She needed to talk to Fidel Montoya, to warn him.

The way the detectives had pooh-poohed her story about the hit man, she couldn't trust them to get in touch with Montoya. With Jason dead, her fears about publicity looked petty—unbelievably trivial—and she couldn't believe she'd let them stop her from doing the right thing. Well, she was going to do it now. She descended to the kitchen, where she found Connie at the table, unlit cigarette in one hand, the *Wall Street Journal* spread out before her. It took Sydney ten minutes to convince her to call and set up an appointment with the Congressman. Not for the first time, she thought how useful it was to have politically connected parents who donated generously to a variety of campaigns and causes.

"It's after five," Connie protested. "He'll be gone."

"Then get him at home."

"You think I have the phone number of every congressman in my Rolodex?" Without waiting for an answer, she disappeared into her bedroom and made the call. Five minutes later she was back. "He's still at the office. He'll see you." Her voice was neutral, but the stiffness of her shoulders and back shouted disapproval. Sydney was used to it.

"I'll drive you."

They turned to see Reese standing in the archway between the kitchen and the formal dining room, clearly having overheard enough of their conversation to get the gist. Sydney thought her sister had left.

"I don't need—"

"That's a great idea," Connie said briskly. "I'll feel better about you if you're with your sister. You don't look like you're in any shape to drive. I've always thought that people in the grip of strong emotion can be just as dangerous behind the wheel as drunks. On the way home from the hospital after your father died, I jumped a curb and ran into a fire hydrant. If there was a blow-test for measuring stress or grief, I'd have been way over the limit."

Sydney was too weary to argue about it, and her mother had a point. She didn't feel up to driving, and the thought of being packed into a Metro car in her current condition was so unappealing that she said "Fine."

Silence hung like a casting net over their ride into DC, full of holes that looked like escape routes but with rasping ropes that bit into them and bore them down. Their father, Howard Linn, used to cast such a net on their annual vacation to the Outer Banks. Sydney remembered standing well back and watching him when she was twelve or thirteen, marveling at the way his large hands spun the net wide, the way the rising sun made a sparkling web of it as it landed on the water's surface, and the way the fish gasped and flopped when her father pulled the net in with a crow of triumph. She'd run inside then, the sea breeze tangling her long auburn hair.

This was the first time she and Reese had been alone together in a decade and a half. It was almost like hitching a ride with a stranger, but not quite. A stranger you had history with. Dismissing that thought as a useless paradox, Sydney kept her hands in her lap, her gaze fixed straight ahead, half hoping Reese would say something and praying she wouldn't. If she'd had room for any more sad, the entangling silence might have distressed her.

Reese pulled the SUV over to the sidewalk a block away from the Rayburn House Office Building and broke the silence. "I'll drive around, maybe take a walk if I find an easy parking place. Text me when you're done."

Sydney nodded, relieved that Reese wasn't expecting to be part of the meeting with Montoya. She got out and Reese drove off. Even coming up on six o'clock, it was still steamy and sweat immediately beaded Sydney's forehead and trickled between her breasts. She faced the building, took a deep breath, and went in search of Congressman Fidel Montoya.

———

His office, when she found it, had a small reception area with three doors opening off it and two L-shaped walnut-veneer desks, staffed by young-twenties professionals who had that "political aspirant" look, an amalgam of earnestness and ambition that all but made their eyes glow red. Apparently, the work day didn't end at five for Montoya's team. A nubby green carpet squished underfoot as she approached the closest desk, occupied by a young man wearing yellow suspenders and a matching bow tie. Wheat-colored hair flopped over his brow and was cut short around the ears. Sydney's ability to assess attire, which she'd gained coaching the women at Winning Ways, made her instinctively note that he'd have to ditch the suspenders and bow ties if he wanted to be taken for a power player rather than a quirky academic or research librarian.

Conscious of the borrowed suit which was too snug across her chest and rear, she said, "Sydney Ellison. I have an appointment with the Congressman."

The receptionist clicked a few keys and smiled. "The Congressman will be with you in just one moment, Ms. Ellison. Please have a seat."

Before she could settle into the leather club chair he indicated, the inner office door swung open and Montoya stepped out, talking to a reserved-looking man in a sharp gray suit. Shorter, older, more compact than the congressman—Sydney pegged him as Montoya's chief of staff or campaign manager. Some high-up political player.

"The poll numbers look good, John. That last television ad you put together did the trick."

Or maybe he was the communications guru.

"Let's hope." The man's smile was mostly a faint crinkling of the skin around his eyes. His gaze slid to Sydney and she got the feeling he knew her history. He coughed. "Want me to sit in?" he asked Montoya.

The Congressman gave his easy smile. "Not necessary. You take off. Tell my future daughter-in-law I said hi."

"Will do." John gave a quick nod and crossed the reception area to talk with a striking woman who had emerged from one of the other offices.

Turning to Sydney, Montoya held out his hand, his famous smile breaking the angular planes of his handsome face. "Sydney Linn Ellison," he said, retaining her hand when she would have pulled it back. "You've changed."

She didn't have to ask from when. The whole country—at least people of a certain age—remembered her as the bleached-blond college coed with the cleavage who'd appeared in steamy television footage with the Speaker of the House. "The Manley Trap," they'd called her. Late-night hosts told almost as many jokes about her as they had about Monica Lewinsky. It was the primary reason she'd kept Dirk's name—Ellison—after they divorced.

"Most people change as they age," she said, withdrawing her hand from his warm, firm grasp. "I daresay your hairline has slipped back a bit from where it was in college."

"Touché!" His grin moved to his brown eyes. He gestured for her to precede him into his office. "Hold my calls."

He did have charisma, she had to give him that. More in person, even, than on television. In his early fifties, six foot two with black hair only slightly receding from a broad forehead, he exuded sex appeal. He had a lanky body and dressed well, in athletic-cut suits that showed off the results of his fitness program. A sense of humor and quick mind only added to his appeal … both to voters and to women, if the rumors were true.

Sydney took in the office with a glance. A conversation area made up of a leather loveseat and two wing chairs sat kitty-corner to a desk big enough to double as an aircraft carrier. Framed pictures of the congressman, with everyone from Bill and Hillary to Barbra Streisand, filled an entire wall, from six inches below the ceiling to a foot above the floor. Photos and paintings of Maryland—Chesapeake Bay, the pony round-up at Assateague, Baltimore's Inner Harbor; all of them places she'd been—hung on the opposite wall.

When Montoya gestured for her to sit, she sank onto the squishy leather loveseat and tugged at her skirt hem. Reese wore her skirts shorter than Sydney was comfortable with, and she caught Montoya sliding a glance at the expanse of thigh exposed by the skirt. For a moment she worried that by choosing the loveseat, she'd put the wrong idea in his head, but he sat across from her on a blue velvet-upholstered wing chair.

"I was sorry to hear of your father's passing," Montoya said. "Water?" He gestured toward a bottle of Perrier on a tray. "Or I can have Carter find a soda, if you prefer."

"Water, thank you." Sydney suddenly realized she was thirsty; she'd cried out all her moisture. She pushed away thoughts of Jason and accepted the glass Montoya poured.

"How's Connie doing?"

"You know my mom." Sydney dredged up a smile. Everyone knew Connie Linn. "She's coping. She's playing tennis at the club and took up line dancing with a friend. After fifteen years of caring for my father, she's ready to start a new life, and who can blame her?" She set the glass down on a coaster after taking a long swallow. She wasn't here to talk about her parents.

"Look, Congressman Montoya, I appreciate your—"

"Call me Fidel." He flashed that killer smile.

Sydney fought the urge to tell him not to bother. She wasn't interested, and even if she'd felt a spark, she'd more than learned her lesson. "I think someone might be trying to kill you."

That erased the smile. "Explain."

Sydney told him about the phone switch at the deli, the phone call, and Jason's death, all the while struggling to see only words in her mind and not Jason on the gurney. Trying to gauge Montoya's expression as she talked, she could read nothing in his watchful eyes, the suddenly stern mouth.

Silence fell when she finished. He poured more water from the sweating Perrier bottle into his glass, took a sip. "Just what are you after, Miss Ellison?" he asked finally.

"After? Nothing," Sydney said, confused.

"You don't ask me to believe this fairy tale, do you?"

"I don't give a damn what you believe," she said, anger flashing through her. The hell with him. She stood.

"The election's in less than a week. You expect me to believe this isn't some attempt to drag my name through the mud, ridicule me, lose me voters? I suppose I can expect to find Channel 5's reporter waiting in the lobby." His eyes had hardened and seemed almost black in the dim light of the office.

"Congressman Montoya, I only came to you because I thought you deserve a warning, and I'm not sure the police are taking me seriously despite my fiancé's death. Apparently, you aren't either. You don't mind if I say 'I told you so' at your funeral, do you? And, for the record, I wouldn't voluntarily talk to a journalist if she offered me a winning Powerball ticket."

Fury warmed her cheeks and made her neck prickle. This had been a total waste of time. She should've known. She was madder at herself than at him, because she'd known how it would play out and had come anyway. She turned and made for the door.

Her anger seemed almost to ameliorate his. His voice was placating when he said, "Calm down, Sydney. I appreciate your coming in, really I do."

"You're welcome," she bit out, reaching for the door.

"And I'm sorry about your fiancé. Really. His death has clearly hit you hard." He joined her at the door, close enough that his cologne enveloped her with hints of teak and ocean spray. Like he had spent the afternoon sailing on Chesapeake Bay, Sydney thought sourly.

His practiced charm wasn't going to work this time. "I'll tell my mom you said hello." Ignoring his outstretched hand, she yanked open the door and stalked into the reception area, blowing past a startled Carter and causing two constituents to look up from the magazines they were reading. She felt Montoya's eyes on her as she strode toward the door but refused to give him the satisfaction of turning around.

In the hall, she worked to slow her breaths. Angry tears blurred her vision and she swiped at them with an impatient hand, ducking into a restroom. The mirror showed a flushed face and angry eyes with mascara smeared beneath them, making her look like a pissed-off raccoon. Jerking a paper towel from the dispenser, she doused it with cold water and held it to her heated face for a moment, then gently scrubbed at the makeup smears.

These tears were for Jason, not Montoya. Fidel Montoya was not worth a single tear. Not one. She'd cried an ocean over George, whom she'd loved, and cried again when her marriage to Dirk ended in a blaze of publicity, lawsuits, and acrimony. Montoya was nothing. It was just that his ridicule brought the humiliation back. She sniffled, blew her nose, and glared at her reflection. She hoped the contract killer got him. Right away, she retracted that thought. She didn't really hope it; she couldn't wish anyone dead.

Stepping out of the bathroom, Sydney nodded at a young woman in a power suit race-walking down the hall and picked up her own pace. She needed to get out, away from this building brimming with the toxic cocktail of politician sweat and dandruff, ruthlessness, corruption, and self-interest. If she stayed any longer, she'd need another shower.

14

Paul

PAUL'S EYES DARTED FROM the muzzle of the silenced .22 in his pop's hand to the jacket draped over the chair back. How could he have been so criminally careless as to forget about the gun?

"Pop—" He raised his arms placatingly.

"Harmon Nowicki, I know why you're here, you bastard," the old man said, his voice surprisingly strong.

Paul groaned inwardly. "Pop, I'm not Nowicki. He moved to Minneapolis years ago."

It was as if he hadn't spoken. "My Elspeth doesn't want you, Nowicki, so stop sniffing around." The old man took a stuttering step forward.

Paul held out a hand and said in an authoritative voice, "Give me the gun."

"If I ever catch you so much as looking at Elspeth again, I'll kill you, Nowicki, so help me God I will!" His voice trailed off to a whisper as his foot caught the edge of a rag rug. He tripped and the gun went off. The report crashed around the walls in the confined space.

Paul staggered back as the bullet smacked into his shoulder. Damn, it hurt. Visions of doctors removing the bullet and telling the cops, questions about the unregistered gun, his father being carted off to a home, the bullet being matched with the one in DC ... all flashed through Paul's mind as he thudded against the bedroom wall and slid to his haunches, his left hand going automatically to the wound in his right shoulder. Blood leaked through his fingers.

"Oh my God." Moira stood on the threshold, her hand at her chest, taking in the scene. Her nurse's training kicked in and she started for Paul.

"It's not as bad as it looks," he said, pushing to his feet with effort. He winced at the pain. Taking two steps, he plucked the gun from the floor where his father had dropped it. "Look after Pop."

His father was standing in the middle of the room, uncomprehending, looking from one of them to the other. "Paul?" He blinked his eyes slowly.

"Yeah, Pop, everything's okay."

As Moira helped the old man back into bed, distracting him with a list of the things they'd do the next day—visit the grocery store, stop off to chat with Mrs. Kimmett from church—Paul ducked into the bathroom and grabbed a hand towel to staunch the bleeding. Drops of blood spattered on the one-inch square aqua tiles, staining grout that had once been white but was now the color of dirt. Shit. He didn't fucking need this right now. What shitty luck. Never took a round or even a scrap of shrapnel in 'Nam, never got more than some bruises and a couple of knife cuts in his current profession, and now this: shot by his pop in his own goddamn house. He lifted the edge of the cloth and saw the bleeding had slowed to a sluggish trickle. Good. But the slug was still in there and he couldn't risk going to the ER in town. He knew a guy, but he was three hours away, close to Baltimore.

Moira's face appeared in the mirror. "Let me see. Keep the pressure on."

Without waiting for an answer, she urged him toward the toilet and began snipping away his shirt as he seated himself. When she'd cut away his sleeve with the sewing scissors, she gently lifted the pad to inspect the wound. "You need a doctor," she pronounced.

Her face was not five inches away from his, her breath warm on the bare skin of his chest. The citrus scent of her shampoo was bright and he sniffed deeply. Suddenly, he was embarrassed by his pasty skin, the wiry gray and white hairs on his chest. He was damned near sixty-five years old, for God's sake. When was the last time a woman saw him naked? Hookers didn't count.

"I'll get the keys."

He caught her arm as she turned to go. As her biceps flexed under his hand, he realized it was the first time he'd ever touched her. "I can't. My pop."

"We'll take him with us."

He was shaking his head as he finished. "No. I mean, what will they do to him if ... "

Understanding flickered in her eyes. "But you need medical care. There's a bullet in your shoulder!"

"I know a guy who can help. Just pack it tight so it doesn't start bleeding again."

"What set him off?" she asked, pulling pads and bandages from the medicine cabinet.

"He thought I was a jerk my mom had an affair with years ago. I'd forgotten all about it until he pointed the gun at me and called me Harmon." He recalled the shouting, the tears, the slap of an open hand meeting skin. His parents hadn't spoken to each other for weeks after his pop found out. Paul had been thirteen or fourteen, old enough to understand what his mom had done. She'd done *it* with Mr. Nowicki, the beefy guy who ran the hardware store in town, who always wore overalls and smelled like licorice. He'd tried to block the images from his mind and spent a lot of time at his friend Tim's house.

Moira's forehead wrinkled but she didn't say anything as she washed the wound out, swabbed it with alcohol—"This will sting"—and packed it with sterilized gauze before wrapping a bandage over it, across his shoulder and back several times, and securing it.

"That should hold for a while," she said, taking a step back.

"Thank you. Do we have any painkillers?"

She handed him a bottle of 800mg ibuprofen without comment. He shook two into his hand and swallowed them dry.

"Where'd he get the gun?"

The question came softly. For a moment, he couldn't make out what she'd said. Her face was averted as she scrubbed at a splotch of blood on the tub. He bought himself time by pretending to choke on the pill, using his cupped hands to drink from the faucet. "It's mine," he said finally. "Traveling as much as I do, I got it for protection."

She stood, and her hazel eyes searched his face. He wondered what she saw there. Did she suspect? If he had to kill her, what would happen to his pop? He could snap her neck in an instant, but then there was the body to dispose of ... He liked Moira. He'd only once killed someone he knew. His first contract. His muscles tensed.

"Well, don't leave it where your dad can get it again," she said, stooping to pick up the blood-stained towels. "Keep it in the car, maybe."

He hadn't realized he was holding his breath. It came whooshing out as she left the bathroom. Sinking to the toilet seat again, he rubbed his hands up and down his face. The slosh of the washing machine filling came to his ears as he organized his thoughts. The hole in his shoulder was inconvenient but not a show-stopper. Already the Motrin was taking the edge off the pain. He needed to hit the road, visit the doc outside Baltimore, check into a different motel in DC, and take care of the Montoya assignment first thing in the morning. Then he could tie up the loose ends, namely one Sydney Ellison.

15

Paul
Thursday, August 3

THE TRIP TO THE southeast corner of Baltimore Wednesday night into Thursday morning had been tedious and pain-filled. The hours-long delay caused by an overturned tractor-trailer rig hauling a flammable chemical had pushed Paul to his limit. Police had siphoned traffic onto a detour, and by the time Paul finally arrived at the doctor's house it was past eleven. His shoulder throbbed as he dragged himself from the car. In the dim light cast by a gibbous moon, he saw blood had leaked from beneath the bandages. Good thing the cops had been too busy directing traffic to pay attention to the cars' occupants. He rang the bell by the narrow house's front door, not worried about waking the doctor. Late-night visitors were commonplace here, and even though the doctor had long been banned from practicing medicine, he made a good living tending to people who wanted care without questions or official reports.

Pulling Paul into the house, the slight man extracted the bullet and re-bandaged the wound in his kitchen, apologizing for not being able to supply him with antibiotics. He spoke with a slight Eastern European accent. "Barbiturates, opiates, and the like I can purchase on the street. Antibiotics? Well, there's not much market for them and you know I can't prescribe. You could maybe visit your physician, tell him you've got strep throat or bronchitis or something... get him to give you a scrip for antibiotics."

Paul looked around the brightly lit kitchen with the blackout curtains shrouding the windows, the red enamel teapot on the range, the week's worth of crusty dishes piled in the sink, the overflowing trash can. A vaguely fishy smell made him wonder about the doctor's dinner. A cockroach as long as a credit card stuck its antennae out from under the sink, then skulked along the baseboards. Paul decided he would make finding antibiotics a priority.

"Thanks, Doc," he said, handing over enough cash to pay for his care and the doc's silence. "Can I crash on your couch for a few hours?"

He slept for three hours, then drove his car to one of the long-term lots at BWI early Thursday morning. Taking the shuttle to a satellite lot, he stole a car. It was an absolute crime how many people left keys magneted to their fenders when they went on long trips. Afraid they'd drop their key rings in a Venetian canal or leave them in a Japanese sake bar or something, Paul supposed. The drive from Baltimore to DC took only forty-five minutes in the stolen Taurus at three in the morning.

He glided to a halt down the block from Ellison's townhouse. One light shone from an upstairs window six houses away, but other than that, everything was still and dark.

It took him less than fifteen minutes to jimmy the back door and silently plant the .22 as his client had directed. It was probably a waste of time, but the client wanted him to do it, and he was in the customer service business. Just as if he sold recliners or owned a bar, he thought morosely. And the client was always right. Except when he was a lying, cheating son-of-a-bitch, which was most of the time, because how many good honest folks hired contract killers? Paul had long ago learned to take precautions to avoid getting stiffed—or worse—by his clients.

He headed back to the motel room rented in the name of Lionel Ross just as the first wave of government workers, lobbyists, and military people were washing into the city, clogging every major road. He'd sleep all morning and then make a quick trip out to visit a safety deposit box he kept in a suburban Maryland bank. He had several such caches around the country, stocked with guns, cash, and fake IDs. He would get his sniper pistol, do one last recce, and be ready to kill Montoya Friday morning as he'd planned. The cops, Ellison, getting shot by his pop—none of that was going to get in the way of this payday.

16

Sydney

SYDNEY WOKE SLOWLY THURSDAY morning, clinging to sleep to cushion herself from the grief pulsing just beyond wakefulness. She blinked in confusion at the sight of her old Breyer horses on a bookshelf. Memory returned with crushing force. Jason was dead. She'd spent the night at Connie's. The evening was a blur of take-out Chinese and far too much bourbon. Her pillow was damp, and she got out of the single bed now with a grief or bourbon hangover pounding inside her skull. Brushing her teeth, she swallowed painkillers she found in the medicine cabinet and dressed reluctantly in Reese's clothes. Whatever else she did today, she needed to return home and get some of her own clothes. First, though, she had to meet with her lawyer and confront the police.

———

"Ms. Ellison, what did you and Mr. Nygaard fight about Tuesday night?"

The female detective, Graves, was in Sydney's face, and Sidney had had about enough of the woman's attitude and the faint chemical scent of dry cleaning fluid wafting off her. She flicked a glance at Hilary Trent, seated beside her. In her mid-fifties, with strong features and a short Afro threaded with gray, wearing a cranberry-colored Armani suit and stiletto heels, the attorney exuded power. Her relaxed posture signaled her disdain for the interview taking place in front of her. Sydney wished she could project that same aura of "We've got to go through the motions, even though this is ridiculous."

Hilary held up a forefinger and sighed. "Detective Graves, sit down and stop harassing Miss Ellison or we're done here."

"We didn't fight," Sydney said as Graves reluctantly dropped into a chair beside Detective West on the other side of the conference table. At Hilary Trent's insistence, they were in her law offices, luxuriously ensconced in rolling leather chairs, drinking designer water from cut-crystal glasses. "He told me he was going to Indonesia for a year. He'd won an award. I was surprised, that's all."

Graves's expression brought to mind a cat sneaking up on a canary. She leaned forward, her too-short suit sleeves revealing bony wrists. Even Sydney's borrowed suit fit better. Tugging one sleeve down, Graves caught Sydney watching and scowled. "But one of your neighbors told us that"—she referred to a notebook—"'there was a lot of yelling, and then he told her that it was over.' Sounds like a fight to me." Her self-satisfied smile made Sydney want to put a fist through her face.

Mrs. Colwell, she thought, exasperated. "He asked me to come to Indonesia with him. I needed some time to think about it. I called him the next morning from work to tell him I'd go and he asked me to marry him. I guess Mrs. Colwell didn't manage to eavesdrop on that conversation."

86

Hilary nudged Sydney's leg under the table, a cue to cut the sarcasm.

"Did anyone else?" It was West's even voice. He sat at ease with his chair pushed back from the table so one ankle could rest on his knee. Argyle socks made a playful contrast with his navy suit. They were unexpected. Sydney eyed him, trying to read him. He met her gaze with no sign of his partner's hostility, but no sympathy, either. "No," she said finally. "It was a private conversation."

"So no one else knew you were engaged?"

"I told my deputy. Why does it matter?"

"And you and your deputy, D'won Duvalier, were shopping yesterday afternoon, right?" Graves's tone condemned her for shirking work in addition to murdering her fiancé. The detective referred to her notebook again. "But you and Duvalier went your separate ways 'a bit after twelve thirty,' he says, and no one can vouch for your whereabouts until you showed up at the crime scene at two. Even supposing it took you forty-five minutes to get home, that still leaves the better part of an hour unaccounted for."

"I sat for a while in the park, people-watching, then went to a couple of stores for the flowers and champagne," Sydney said, holding onto her temper with an effort. "I told you that. Then I took the Metro and walked home from there. Jason wasn't supposed to be home until two. I guess his department meeting got cancelled."

"But no one remembers you at the florist or the liquor store you said you went to, and you didn't use a credit card."

"So now it's against the law to pay cash?" Sydney glared at Graves.

West leaned forward, claiming her attention. "Can you think of anyone who might have wanted to kill Mr. Nygaard?"

She found herself watching his eyelashes as he blinked. If he were a woman, he could make a fortune as a mascara model. "No one."

"Everyone's got enemies," Graves put in.

"Speak for yourself," Sydney said, unable to keep the dislike out of her voice. "Jason didn't. His students loved him, his coworkers respected him. He wasn't the kind of guy who made enemies."

West ran a finger back and forth along his eyebrow. "Were there any students who loved him too much?"

She didn't follow, and it must have shown, because he asked, "Did any of them call him at home, pester him, leave him love notes?"

"Good heavens, no," Sydney said. "Nothing like that. I told you, Jason was killed by mistake. Whoever did it was trying to kill me."

"Because of that phone call," West said.

She heard his doubt. "Yes." She fixed him with a steady gaze. "Why is that so hard to believe?" She felt him trying to read her, his narrowed gaze weighing the dark hollows under her eyes, her clenched jaw and interwoven fingers. She could almost hear him thinking, "Grief ... or guilt?" Her mouth tightened. To hell with him.

"Oh, let's see," Graves jumped in. "Maybe it's because no one else can verify the nature of the conversation you had with this alleged contract killer. In fact, no one can even verify you didn't buy the phone yourself and make up the call to throw us off the track when you killed the boyfriend—your alleged fiancé—who was dumping you. Maybe it's—"

"Okay, party's over," Hilary Trent said, standing. "Thank you for coming in today, detectives," she said, for all the world as if she'd invited them to a soiree. "Give me a call if you need any further information."

The detectives stood as well. "Thank you for your time, Miss Ellison," West said neutrally.

Sydney had rarely come up against someone so hard to read. He must be a whiz at poker. His partner remained silent. She offered her hand and West shook it, his hand hard and warm against her palm.

"I want to help you catch Jason's killer," she said, meeting his eyes squarely.

He studied her face for a moment. "We'll get him." His unspoken "or her" sounded loud in the air around them.

He lingered a moment, looking like he might say something more, then crossed to the glass doors and pushed through them with unnecessary force, his partner trailing behind.

Hilary's voice recalled Sydney's attention. "That Detective Graves has a real chip on her shoulder, but overall, that went off well." She kicked off her Jimmy Choo heels and padded stocking-foot to the door leading into her office.

They entered a suite bigger than Sydney's whole downstairs. "Will they want to interview me again?" she asked.

Hilary nodded. "Undoubtedly. But they've got nothing on you. So your neighbor overheard a tiff ... foo!" She waved a hand in airy dismissal. "You have an alibi—half a dozen people can vouch for your presence at the office in the morning and from there on out you were with your deputy almost until you arrived home. My investigator will turn up someone who saw you at one of the shops. You don't have access to a gun and you have no discernible motive. Jason didn't carry life insurance and his will leaves everything to his parents. Not that you'd care about his paltry estate when you have those millions in trust from your grandmama." She smiled, probably counting up the portion of those millions she'd get as her fee.

Sydney didn't begrudge her a penny. "Thanks, Hilary," she said, massaging her tense neck muscles.

The older woman gave her a serious look. "It'll go away, Sydney. Everything but the pain of missing Jason." As if regretting the moment of compassion, she added, "Tell Con she's not going to win a single game tomorrow. Not one. I've got a new racket." She shooed Sydney out of the office.

Sydney got on the elevator and pulled out her cell phone. She started to text Reese, who had insisted on being her ride again, but the jolt of the elevator as it started down kicked her back to an elevator ride with Jason, shortly after they'd met. They'd climbed the stairs to the top of the Washington Monument on a cold, rainy day that scared off the tourists and found themselves alone in the elevator on the ride down, thigh muscles aching from the climb, cheeks dusted with pink from the strong wind and the exhilarating view. As Sydney laughed at something he said, Jason leaned over and kissed her, the feel of his firm lips on hers warming her to the core. Their first kiss. She put her fingers to her lips at the memory, then deliberately steered her thoughts away from Jason. She'd have time to cry later. Right now, she was going to figure out who killed him. That resolve carried her off the elevator and out to the sidewalk, where camera flashes burned into her retinas.

Reflexively, she closed her eyes. Oh, God, it was starting again. Questions pelted her.

"Ms. Ellison! We understand the police have questioned you about your boyfriend's murder. Do you have a comment?"

"Sydney, over here. How has Manley's death affected you?"

"Do you feel like you're in danger, Ms. Ellison?"

Microphones waved in Sydney's face. The flashes reduced her pupils to pinpricks. It was as if she were twenty again, a pestilence of journalists and paparazzi lying in wait outside her parents' Mount Vernon home, pouncing on her whenever she stepped out the door. She remembered the humiliating questions—Does he get you off, Sydney? Do you prefer an older man's experience?—and the insulting offers to write a tell-all book, be interviewed on Oprah, sleep with some reporter who told her he could make her forget George Manley. She'd broken down one morning after a draining bout of throwing up her breakfast in the toilet—nerves, she'd told Connie—and screamed at the media stalking her, run at the nearest photographer and tried to pull the camera from around his neck. The others clicked their shutters non-stop as she crumpled to the ground, sobbing hysterically. Her mom and dad had carried her into the house and called a doctor, who sedated her.

Well, she wasn't a twenty-year-old who needed sedation now. Walk. Just keep walking. Walk away. Putting a hand up to shield her face from the photographer's flashes, she tried to push through the knot of journalists to cross the street. She'd learned the hard way that saying so much as "hello" to a reporter was an invitation to be misquoted.

"Get back," a stern voice said. "Miss Ellison has nothing to say." A hard hand gripped her arm above the elbow and pulled her free, dragging her half a block before the reporters dropped back. "Are you okay, Sydney?"

She lowered her hand and looked into Detective West's brown eyes. The concern and warmth she saw there took her off-guard. His solid frame sheltered her from the rabid reporters. She looked around. "Where's your partner?"

West released her arm and said, "Taking some personal time. I saw the jackals waiting and thought you might need help."

"That'd seem really thoughtful if you hadn't told them about me in the first place," she snapped, stalking away. Her heart beat fast and she was shaking. But her brain was working just fine: the police must have tipped off the reporters. No way had anyone in Hilary Trent's office leaked.

He caught up with her in a few strides. "Not me."

She quickened her pace.

He stopped her with a hand on her shoulder, then caught the other shoulder as she slowed, turning her to face him. "Not me," he repeated, gazing down into her face. "Turning you over to the media doesn't help us solve the case."

"Now that I buy," Sydney said, not fighting against his hold. He seemed sincere. "Who does it help? Your partner? She thinks I'm responsible for Jason's death, global warming, and the rise of ISIS."

He let his hands slide down her arms and then drop to his sides. "Let's just say that if the department is known to be questioning an affluent white woman about a crime, we dodge accusations of only persecuting the poor misunderstood black youth in DC."

"Equal opportunity persecution, then?"

"Absolutely," West deadpanned. "Look, can I buy you a cup of coffee?"

She hesitated. "Do I need my lawyer?"

"This is social, not official." His smile lit his eyes, crinkling his face in all the right places. This is what he looks like at home, Sydney thought, with a beer in one hand and barbecue tongs in the other.

"I didn't know you were allowed to do 'social' with murder suspects." She bit her lip, considering. The opportunity to learn what the police knew about Jason's murder overcame her suspicion. "Make mine a bottled water. And let's walk. I've been edgy since … I can't sit still."

They dodged tourists with cameras and kids surging toward the Mall with its monuments and museums until they reached a street vendor's cart with a short line. West queued for drinks while Sydney lingered in a tree's shade. It was going to be another muggy day, she thought, watching a young couple argue over a map. She lifted her hair off her neck. A slight breeze cooled her. Would West tell her anything useful? She eyed him thoughtfully as he returned and handed her a Poland Spring bottle dewed with condensation.

Well-tailored navy Nordstrom's suit, she noted automatically, plus ironed shirt, polished shoes, and handsome tie. He looked more like a lawyer or a senior-level government official than a cop. Except for those argyle socks.

"Do I pass inspection?" he asked. He stirred sugar into his coffee and took a sip.

Sydney laughed, half embarrassed, and resumed walking. "I'm sorry. It's a bad habit. I've been assessing interview attire for so many years that I go into auto-pilot mode without thinking about it."

"Do you teach people how to dress for interviews?"

"Women. And teach them interviewing skills, professional etiquette, a whole host of things."

"How'd you get into that?"

Alight with interest, his eyes focused on her face, and she found herself telling him about looking for a purpose after getting her MBA and divorcing Dirk. "I came into a trust fund when I turned twenty-five and I always knew I wanted to use it to help people. After the scandal"—she glossed over it, assuming he'd read up on her background—"I looked for a way to help disadvantaged women make something of themselves. It's too easy to be pulled off course, even when you have all the advantages of money and education and family. Sorry, I'm on my soapbox." She smiled sheepishly and took a swallow of water.

"No, I'm interested. Really." West moved closer to let a skateboarder rocket by. "Do you fund it all yourself?"

She shook her head. "No. I provided seed money, but we established a board of directors a year after I got the organization going. They do fundraising, among other things. My mom's on it. She's good at separating the wealthy from their hard-earned cash."

"Useful."

They strolled another half block in silence. West's undemanding companionship made her uneasy. What was his agenda? Suspicious of the silence, she asked, "Did you check on that phone number from the cell phone, the one that called me?"

He nodded. "It was another burner phone, which is consistent with your story. If I were calling a contract killer, I certainly wouldn't do it from my home phone. And I followed up with Congressman Montoya. It was brave of you to go warn him."

The unlooked-for understanding of her revulsion for politicians and all things political caught her unaware. "He thought I made it up, too," she said, hiding her feelings by pretending to read graffiti spray-painted onto a construction sign.

They looked up as Marine One *whop-whopped* overhead, descending toward the White House, then walked on. "What do you do now?" Sydney asked. "How do you find Jason's killer?"

"We process the evidence from the scene, interview neighbors and anyone who might have been in the area. We look at his bank accounts, talk to his coworkers, look for a motive."

"You won't find one," she said positively. "Because the killer wasn't after him." She stopped. "My sister's waiting for me to text. She's probably worried that the carrion stripped my carcass bare. She used to be one of them, so she should know."

"Your sister's a reporter?"

"Was. She writes true crime now. Reese Linn."

"I've heard of her. She wrote that book about the Secret Service killer." He looked down at her, eyes intent. They had flecks of sherry-gold and caramel in them. "We're keeping an open mind, Sydney, looking at all the possibilities."

"I'm glad to hear it." She offered a hand in pointed farewell, and he shook it. "I'm going to find the man who lost that cell phone. Even if I have to offer myself up as bait to do it. When can I move back into my house?" The thought of being in the space where Jason had died made her shiver, but she couldn't think of any other way of finding the killer.

"We're done with it," he said, a crease appearing between his brows. He pulled out a card, scribbled something on it, and passed it to her. "That's my cell phone number so you can reach me directly."

She nodded and tucked the card into her pocket. "Thanks for the escort, Detective."

"Ben."

She acknowledged him with an uplifted hand as he threaded his way through stopped cars to the far sidewalk and the Metro stop. He might just be good-copping her, but he seemed like a decent guy. Reasonable.

She texted Reese, half-regretting that she'd let her sister bring her to the meeting. Part of her was grateful, but part of her was suspicious of her sister's seeming concern. Regardless, she needed to go home.

17

Sydney

REESE PULLED TO THE curb ten minutes later, and Sydney got into the Highlander. Reese's blond hair was tousled and she wore a variation of the khakis-and-T-shirt ensemble she'd had on yesterday. It was the one thing Sydney could remember perfect Reese and their mom fighting about—her clothes. She rarely dressed up enough to suit Connie Linn's sense of what was appropriate. "You can't wear jeans to church" and "Don't tell me you're wearing that hoodie to Kelsey's birthday party? Go change this instant, young lady" were phrases that had echoed through their home when Reese was younger.

"You've got a real future with Uber if you decide to give up true crime writing," Sydney said in greeting, trying to forestall any questions about the police interview.

"Not in this lifetime," Reese said. "Inviting strangers into my car? No thanks. I've written too many stories about women who did that. Where to now? Connie's?"

"Home. The townhouse."

Reese's blond head turned, and even though she was wearing sunglasses, Sydney knew she was eyeing her doubtfully. "Are you sure you're ready for that?"

"I'm a big girl, Reese. Just drop me, okay?"

Reese's jaw tightened. She didn't say anything, either about Sydney wanting to return home or her tone, but she sped up with a force that rocked them back in their seats. They finished the drive to the townhouse in silence, the safest option. Nothing had changed overnight in the neighborhood, which seemed impossible when everything had changed for Sydney. A little girl rode a scooter at the end of the block, a sprinkler scented the air with water, and someone out of sight fired up a lawn mower. The oaks still lined the sidewalk, sturdy and resolute, capped with leaves so green they made Sydney want to cry.

"Are you going to stay here now?" Reese asked in a carefully neutral tone when she found a parking spot only two houses away.

"I'm not sure," Sydney said, hand on the door handle, suddenly not so sure about a lot of things, including the wisdom of returning home so soon. Nothing would have made her admit that to Reese.

"I've got time to come in," Reese offered.

"I don't need a babysitter," Sydney said, but her reply lacked fire, and she wasn't surprised when Reese got out of the car, shut the door, and said, "I'm coming. I'd like to see the place."

"Why? You're not thinking about writing about Jason's murder, are you?" Sydney's suspicion was instantaneous and flared to anger. "Forget about it. You do not get to capitalize on Jason's death, his parents' grief, my—"

Reese threw up her hands. "Jesus, Syd! Do you hear yourself? Stop being paranoid for one moment. You live here. I'd like to see your place. Idle curiosity about my little sister's life. That's it. Forget it. I'll wait here." She stopped and crossed her arms over her chest. A man with a briefcase glanced at them from across the street and then hurried on, careful not to make eye contact.

A wisp of shame made Sydney say, "No, it's okay. Come on in."

She unlocked the door and pushed it inward. Air sifted out, sharp with the odor of ammonia. The cleaning team Connie had called had already been here. Thank God. She couldn't have faced … she didn't even want to imagine it. She hesitated on the threshold, unable to take the next step.

Reese eyed her. "It's always hard, walking into a place where there's been a murder," she observed."I'm the last person to go all *Amityville Horror* on you, but it gets me every time."

Sydney knit her brows, and Reese explained. "For every book, I have to see the scene. Where the murder or murders happened. It's not like I'm a cop or even a reporter anymore. I don't get there when the scene is fresh, when there's a body or blood. It's months after, sometimes years. Still, it always takes an extra bit of effort to get myself over the threshold. For the most part, the houses are just houses. They don't give me the willies. I don't believe in ghosts or in disembodied evil. All of the evil I've come up against has been firmly lodged in living bodies."

"'For the most part'?"

"There was one place," Reese said. An unusual hesitance dragged at her words. "In California. It was part of the Secret Service case, Hibling's last victim before he got caught. It was a bungalow, 1940s vintage, two bedrooms, the most beautiful hibiscus bushes I ever saw blooming on either side of the front door, with huge, frilly, pink and coral blossoms."

The way Reese dwelled on the flowers, it was like she was reluctant to enter the house, even in memory.

"Inside ... I smelled blood," Reese said. "The murder happened fourteen months before I got there, and the house had been completely redone—new paint, carpet ripped out and laminate floors put in, everything—but I still smelled blood. The family that lived there, a mom and dad and two little girls who'd gotten the house cheap because of its history, clearly didn't notice the smell. I snapped a couple of photos and got out." She cleared her throat, as if embarrassed about her reaction, and shoved the door wide so the sunbeams could reach in, dance along the wide planks of the oak floor. "If we're going to do this, let's do it." She cocked her head so blond bangs flopped into her eyes.

Sydney's gaze followed the path the sun had taken, and she felt weak with relief to see that the cleaning crew had completely obliterated any sign of the murder. She entered the house and stood still for a moment. Nothing, thank God. No cold, creeping feeling of horror, no vibes from the killer, no sense of Jason. He wasn't the type who'd hang around, even if there were such things as ghosts, which there weren't. She shook her head and snorted at the strange direction her thoughts had taken.

Shoving her sunglasses atop her head, Reese looked around. "Nice place. Feels like you."

"Thanks." Sydney didn't say more, but she felt a strange wince of sadness that Reese had never been to her home. She tamped it down.

She drifted into the kitchen and opened the fridge. She'd need to pick up some skim milk and eggs. The sight of the kiwi-flavored yogurt Jason liked brought tears. What would she do with it? She couldn't eat the vile stuff and it seemed impossible to just throw it in the trash. Worse, though, to let it molder away for months, incubating strange life forms. She was losing it. She slammed the door shut, earning a curious look from Reese. "I suppose I should give his stuff to his parents," she said, her mind moving from yogurt to Jason's clothes and personal items in the bedroom and bathroom.

"Want me to help sort through it?" Reese asked.

"No." The response came too quickly. Sydney tempered it. "Not today. I can't do it yet." Her sister's incessant helpfulness after years of no connection was grating on her. Part of her couldn't help thinking Reese had an ulterior motive. She crossed to the back door and looked out at the small garden patio. The geraniums needed water. A squirrel was busily burying acorns in the pot with the maidenhair ferns. No wonder they looked so weedy. She reached for the knob, planning to unlock the door and step outside for a breath of air on the patio, but it was already unlocked. Strange. Could the police have left her house unsecured when they finished with … with whatever they needed to do? Or the cleaning team. The cleaning team must not have locked up when they left. She made a mental note to tell Connie, locked the door, and turned back to the kitchen.

Reese rummaged in the pantry, emerged with a bag of Oreos, and popped one into her mouth. It was totally unfair the way she could eat anything without gaining an ounce. "So, how are you planning to summon this hit man?" she asked around a mouthful of cookie.

Sydney blinked. "How did—"

"Oh, come on, Syd. I've known you for thirty-five years." She flipped up a hand when Sydney started to speak. "Strike that."

Sydney had opened her mouth to say Reese didn't know her at all, that she didn't know the first thing about her, that the media version of her Reese had helped create bore little resemblance to the person she was fifteen years ago and none at all to who she was now, but since Reese had correctly guessed her intention, she held back, hating that her sister had read her so easily.

"At any rate, I make my living sussing things out, reading people. Connie told me what you'd said about switching phones with a killer. Clearly, you blame yourself in part for Jason's death."

"It's my fault. I should have gone to the police immediately."

Reese ignored her interjection. "Of course you're going to try to track this guy down, the same way you followed Alana Boetcher around in sixth grade and got a video of her bullying that girl with Tourette's, Cindy—"

"Candy."

"—and took it to the principal so she got expelled, because Candy wouldn't report her. The same way you stole the neighbors' collie because they left him outside all the time without food or water and he kept getting his head stuck under the fence trying to dig his way out."

"Dad made me give him back." Sydney had been upset and furious, pleading with her dad for the dog's sake, but he had gone with the letter of the law rather than with mercy. Like he always did. She'd done her best to help Wooster the collie by organizing her friends to report the neighbors to the humane society and animal control so frequently that they ended up giving the dog away to avoid the headache.

"Point is, you're not one to let wrongs go unrighted. And murder is the biggest wrong of all." Reese paused as if to consider that. "Well, one of them."

Sydney wondered what her sister was thinking about, to make her qualify her statement.

"So, what'd you have in mind... Ouija board, billboard on Fourteenth Street saying 'Nyah, nyah, you missed'?" Reese chomped another cookie, holding the bag out in mute invitation.

Sydney took one, twisting it apart. It was like taking the lid off a memory. She and Reese used to eat Oreos this way under a sheet tent draped over the dining room table, when they were maybe five and eight. They sat on cushions commandeered from the couch, played endless games of Go Fish, and sang along to a tape of children's songs.

She dropped her uneaten cookie in the trash. "I don't know. Surely he's figured out by now that he got the wrong person? He must know I'm still alive and kicking. He might try again."

"And what are you going to do if he shows up here? Ask him to turn himself in? Say 'pretty please'? Call the cops? You'll be dead before the call goes through. You don't even have a gun, for God's sake."

Something about the way Reese said it made Sydney think that Reese did. Her sister was making her feel stupid, and she realized she hadn't thought this through. "I can get one."

"If you get a gun, the one most likely to get shot with it is you," Reese said matter-of-factly. "What you need is a bodyguard. I'm moving in with you until this is over."

"The hell you are." It was an instantaneous response, but Sydney didn't feel like revoking it on second thought. Her feelings were a mishmash of resentment at Reese taking over, embarrassment that she was so ill-prepared to lure the killer out of hiding, and fear of the possible consequences if she succeeded. She lashed out. "What—you think all this will make a good story? Wasn't once enough for you?"

"You're in trouble and I want to help," Reese said flatly. "I screwed you over once, but I'm trying to make up for it. You need someone to watch your back and I can be that someone." She stood in the middle of the small kitchen, backlit by the window so her hair was a pale nimbus and her face was shadowed. She was tall and lean and fit, but something about the tilt of her head or the set of her shoulders felt vulnerable.

It threw Sydney off-balance. "You picked up your bodyguard certification when I wasn't looking?" Even she wasn't sure if she was being snide or stalling for time. The fridge compressor thumped on and she jumped.

"I learned a lot hanging out with special forces guys and freedom fighters. I've got a few tricks up my sleeve, not to mention a nine mil in my purse," Reese said. She leveled a look at Sydney. "Don't be dumb, Syd. You can't do this alone. You getting killed doesn't make any of this better." She paused, and the corner of her mouth crooked up the tiniest bit. "If you don't let me stay, I'll tell Connie on you."

"You always were a tattletale," Sydney said without heat.

"Oh, I like that. Who was it told Mom when she saw Corky Tyler sneaking in the basement window? I was grounded for six weeks and missed prom."

"Corky Tyler was an asshole."

"Yeah, he was," Reese said. "But he could kiss like nobody's business."

They were out of practice with banter and it felt slightly off, like one instrument in an orchestra a half beat behind the rest; still, Sydney was suddenly absurdly grateful that they were trying. Despite that, she didn't want her sister moving in. Reese really might be looking to make up for what she did, but there was no making up for it. Even though they were connecting a bit more easily than usual, and even though Sydney believed her sister was genuinely sorry about Jason, she couldn't stomach the thought of her staying in the house. There was enough tension in her life at the moment.

"I've got this. Don't worry about me." After a beat, she added, "But thanks for the offer."

Reese sucked her lips in and then release them with a faint smack. Her voice was level as she said. "Fine. It's your funeral. Offer's open if you change your mind."

"I won't."

Reese gave a brusque nod, tossed her keys in the air, caught them, and said, "Lock the doors after me."

Sydney drifted into the front room after Reese left. Jason's bicycle, three thousand dollars' worth of sleek red and silver, glinted at her from behind the sofa. How could she ever have objected to its presence in the living room? It wasn't like they entertained heads of state or Martha Stewart, for heaven's sake. She squeezed the brake handle gently. He'd tried to talk her into riding with him numerous times, but she'd told him she didn't have a bicycle, didn't have the time, was afraid she'd ruin his workout by being too slow, when really she was embarrassed to tell him she'd never learned how to ride a bicycle. Five-year-olds could ride bikes, for heaven's sake. He'd have been happy to teach her. She could have done that for him, should have learned to ride a damned bike. Tearing up, she let her hand glide over the bike's seat before crossing to the stairs. She hesitated, looking up. She put a tentative foot on the first tread, unwilling to face the bedroom but needing to change into her own clothes. As she reluctantly climbed two more steps, a noise drew her eyes to the ceiling. Who—?

A chill prickled her skin. She listened, straining to hear another sound, but nothing came. *Too wound up*, she chided herself. With a mental shrug, she resumed her climb. Almost at the landing, a soft thud from the back bedroom snapped her head to the left. There *was* someone here. A burglar who'd read the obits? She'd heard of criminals who capitalized on death by burgling the homes of recently deceased people, sometimes during funerals. How dare someone violate her and Jason, steal his stuff! Rage spurred her.

"Get out!" She pounded down the hall and slammed open the bedroom door so it ricocheted off the wall. She took in the small room at a glance. No one. A flick of movement by the window. She dashed to it just in time to see a fluff of gray tail disappear off the balcony into Mrs. Colwell's yard.

Indigo. Damn cat. With trembling hands, Sydney pushed down the window sash and swiveled the stiff catch. Jason was always trying to get her to keep the windows closed, but she liked the soft breezes, found the air-conditioning sterile. But maybe Jason was right. She'd tell him … The truth of his absence hammered her and tears came so fast and thick she got the hiccups trying to gulp them back. She collapsed on the bed. Burying her face in his pillow, she breathed in his scent, knowing it would fade to nothing within days or weeks.

18

Paul
Friday, August 4

CONGRESSMAN MONTOYA WORKED FROM his expansive Maryland home on Friday mornings, Paul had discovered during his weeks of surveillance, then spent a couple of hours in his constituency office in the early afternoon. Only rarely did he go to his Capitol office on Fridays.

Usually father and son, who was somehow involved with the campaign, worked at the house together, with or without staffers from the office. Paul waited in his car down the road from the Montoya mansion, pleased that today there were no extra cars indicating staffers attending their boss at home. The wife had driven off earlier, so it was just father and son. There were neighbors in the area but not too close, not like in some communities where you could count the whiskers in your neighbor's sink by looking out your window into his bathroom. Like that contract he'd done in Wisconsin in February—

now that had been tricky, with the neighbors so close they could practically hear the target snoring.

He brought his thoughts back to the mission at hand. Separating father and son was the only trick, because he didn't want to take them both out. He prided himself on his precision and on limiting collateral damage. It shouldn't be a problem catching the target alone, because the congressman was in the habit of taking a five-mile jog along the quiet lanes that bordered the Pax River when he didn't go into DC.

The medications the doc had given him were wearing off and his shoulder pulsed with pain. The bandages itched, and even with the car pulled halfway off the road in the shade of a large tree, the rising heat and humidity were making him sweat. He wondered how his pop was doing today. He'd checked in with Moira earlier, but his father was still sleeping. He couldn't decide if he hoped his pop remembered shooting him or got the shooting mixed up with memories of his time on the force and whatever '70s detective shows he had watched recently.

Bullfrogs croaked from the river bank behind him and Paul tried to focus on the repetitive sound, let it help him find the zone. He scanned the road with his binoculars again, urging the congressman to appear. The weight of the Savage Arms Striker .22-250 he'd gotten from his safety deposit box was familiar and reassuring against the small of his back.

A flash of movement up the road caught his attention. Bingo. Clad in a white T-shirt and navy shorts, the man was jogging straight at Paul, his strides long and loose. Paul shrank down below dashboard level, cursing the pain in his shoulder as he bumped it. He counted slowly to one hundred, giving Montoya time to get past him, then eased himself up to peer over the dash. Montoya was a quarter mile down the left fork, oblivious to his surroundings. Good.

19

Fidel

FIDEL MONTOYA PICKED UP his pace. Damn but it felt good to stretch his legs, get away from paperwork and the goddamned phone. It never stopped ringing. He'd told his staff he didn't need them at the house today, mostly because he planned to take a long—a very long—lunch with Gillian March, a soccer mom and campaign volunteer. He'd see she was rewarded properly for her door-to-door campaigning on his behalf. A smile slipped onto his face. He'd seen the heat in her eyes when they rested on him, the way her tongue licked her lips. She was always touching him, on the shoulder, the hand, even the thigh once. She was ripe for the picking, married ten years to a husband who traveled a lot. Montoya preferred married conquests—that way they had as much to lose as he did, or almost.

Thinking about Gillian's long, muscled thighs under her short denim skirts made him half tumescent. Shit, he was acting like a horny fifteen-year-old. He shifted himself and lengthened his stride again. A woodpecker's rapid *rat-a-tat-tat-tat* sounded nearby, and a turkey gave his strangled gobble. As Montoya checked his watch, clocking his time, he heard the rumble of a car behind him and shifted onto the shoulder, soft from recent rains. His $140 running shoes sank into the mud and he cursed. Running through this muck would add several seconds to his time. No personal best today.

A gentle berm rose to his right, sloping down fifty feet through trees and underbrush to the Pax River. A bright red cardinal flitted from tree to tree and sunlight sparkled on the muddy river where it dodged away from the trees' shadows. The gurgle of the river and the pounding of his feet almost drowned out the sound of the approaching car. Step on it, buddy, Montoya thought, willing the car to move around him so he could edge back onto the solid macadam.

The car's engine growled and it suddenly sped past him, peppering him with mud. He jumped to the side, cursing. His right foot slipped in the mud just as the sound of a gunshot split the quiet morning air. Something whizzed past his shoulder. Instinctively, Montoya dove for the ground. He went over the berm, tumbling through the vines, ferns, and grasses that made up the undergrowth of a Maryland forest. Thorns and twigs clawed at the bare skin of his legs and arms as he folded them around his face to protect it. Jolting into a tree trunk knocked the breath out of him and he struggled to pull in air, listening for another shot or the car's engine. Had the shot come from the car?

Sydney Linn's—Ellison's—face popped into his head and he slid on his haunches toward the river, hearing again her story about a contract killer out to get him. Could this be … He thought he saw movement, a dark figure up at road level walking to the left, then to the right, starting down the hill at the point where he'd crashed into the woods. Stalking him. God, his imagination was working overtime. He almost called out, but stopped himself. There was something eerie in the quiet, something not right.

He tried to swallow, but his mouth was parched with fear and he only succeeded in creating a lump in his throat. The river beckoned. Montoya had survived a long time in the political jungle by trusting his instincts. With as little noise as possible, he scuffed off his shoes and slipped into the river. The cool of the water—he'd thought it would be warmer on such a hot day—caught him unaware and he stifled a gasp as his pores retracted and every cut and abrasion stung. Taking a deep breath, he dove beneath the murky surface, stroking for the middle as the current carried him downstream.

20

Sydney

WHEN SYDNEY WALKED INTO the Winning Ways offices on Friday morning, she knew immediately it had been a bad idea. Putting on a tan suit and navy shell as if it were a normal morning had felt like a positive step, but her staff were treading warily, slanting sympathetic looks her way, offering condolences, reminding her with every glance and breath and sentence that Jason was dead. Responding to "I'm so sorrys" wore her out before she even got to her office. She nodded and thanked everyone and told them she'd let them know when Jason's parents gave her details about the funeral. To solicitous inquiries of "How are you?" she said, "Coping," and left it at that. Her hand shook as she twisted the knob on her office door. She didn't even make it to the desk before her legs gave out. Sinking onto one of the green chairs, she wondered how long she had to stay before she could leave without looking like a total idiot.

The door flew open without ceremony, and D'won marched in. "What the hell are you doing here, Syd?" he asked, his frown a blend of annoyance and concern. His slim figure was clad in a navy suit with a lavender shirt and deeper purple tie speckled with parrots. Was she imagining it, or did his hair have purple highlights today? "You should be at your mama's house, letting her coddle you, not—"

"You've met Connie. Coddling is not her strong suit."

Her attempt at humor fell flat and D'won ignored it. "Go. Home."

She shook her head. "I can't. That's worse. I have to *do* something. I want to figure out who killed Jason, but I don't even know where to start. I thought that here, that I could..." She trailed off, not sure what she'd thought. She'd just known she couldn't mope in the town-house all day, sorting through Jason's things, seeing reminders of him everywhere. And she hadn't come up with a single idea for "summoning" Jason's killer, as Reese had put it. She felt useless at home. Here, she had a purpose.

D'won studied her for a moment, full lower lip thrust out, and then nodded sharply. "Okay then. If you're going to be here, you can teach the Interviewing Class. It starts in ten minutes. Trust Uncle D'won. You'll feel better if you get up off your butt and get into the classroom. We've got four new women—one of whom seems sharp—and a couple of retreads having another go at it. They'll take your mind off ... stuff."

"I don't know ..." She twiddled a paper clip.

"Just get your butt in the classroom. Muscle memory will take over from there."

She stood. D'won was right; teaching would help. She needed to get out of her head. "Have you considered a career as a radio psychologist?" She moved around him toward the door.

"And leave all this?" D'won said, gesturing to the office and shaping his face into an expression that suggested it was as luxurious as Versailles. "Although maybe I could moonlight. I could be Dr. Laura and Frasier Crane rolled into one, only handsomer and without the broomstick up my butt. The black hip radio psychologist to the disaffected millennials and Gen Yers. I can't call myself Dr. D'won, though—that sounds like a rap star. Dr. Do-good?"

Sydney gave a gurgle of laughter and he looked enormously pleased with himself. They left her office and started toward the classroom. Halfway there, Topaz Johnson, the receptionist, came scurrying down the hall, a gauzy skirt fluttering around her ankles, kohl-circled eyes wide. "Sydney, the police are here. They want—"

Before Sydney could process what Topaz was saying, a uniformed officer appeared, accompanied by Detective West. The hallway suddenly seemed crowded. Sydney searched West's face, unable to read his expression. His brown eyes seemed shuttered, his lips drawn into a thin line. "We have a warrant for your arrest," he said without preamble. "You have to come down to the station with us."

He was speaking Urdu as far as Sydney was concerned. "What?"

"That's the most ridiculous thing I've ever heard," D'won said, hands on his hips. Topaz nodded her agreement.

The uniformed officer—Salazar, his nametag said—reached for the cuffs on his belt, but West shook his head. "Look, is there a back way out of here? I'd just as soon dodge the media, and I assume you would, too. They're stacked up out front like vultures looking for fresh meat."

"This way." Sydney had recovered herself. She didn't know why West was arresting her, or why, given that he was hauling her off to the police station, he was helping her escape the media's scrutiny, but she was grateful for the consideration. She caught her breath between a laugh and a sob as she realized she was more upset at the prospect of facing reporters than being arrested.

West took her upper arm in a light grip and headed toward the stairway she'd indicated, Salazar trailing behind.

"Call Hilary Trent," she and West said in chorus to D'won.

Their eyes met and Sydney gave him a tiny smile, bewildered yet grateful for what seemed like his concern for her. West's fingers squeezed her upper arm tighter, not painfully, but almost as if he were trying to comfort her, and he gave D'won an address to pass on to Trent.

"I'll ring your mama, too," D'won called after them. "I guess this means I'm teaching the interviewing class." His voice said, *some people will do anything to duck their responsibilities.*

21

Paul

PAUL CURSED UNDER HIS breath. The sound of the rifle shot might have spurred a neighbor to summon the police; he couldn't risk it. His chance was gone for now. He returned to the car, where he'd left the door ajar so as not to alert the target with the sound of a car door slamming. As he eased it closed, he slapped on a baseball cap to change his profile. He'd memorized three routes out of the area and now stepped on the accelerator, his shoulder burning like a pack of wolverines was chewing on it. Keeping to the speed limit, he traversed the maze of secondary streets leading to the highway, alert for the sound of a cop's siren or unusual traffic.

Breathing easier once he reached the state highway, which would take him to the parking lot where he would dump the hot car, he jabbed the radio on.

An announcer was talking about Sydney Ellison: " ... arrested for the murder of Jason Nygaard. The detectives on the case are not revealing what evidence they may have, but we're expecting a news conference within the hour."

At least something was going right today. It seemed his client knew what he was talking about. With any luck, the police would discount anything Ellison had told them about a strange phone call now that they'd found the murder weapon in her possession. Still, with her connections, she'd be back on the street where he could get to her pronto. Maybe a suicide scenario would work . . . she'd lost her lover, been arrested and humiliated. He replayed a couple of successful contracts in his mind—hits written off as suicides by the local police. He could do Ellison like he had that radio guy in Syracuse. What was his name? Bekins. Yeah.

The radio station segued into a Jimi Hendrix number and Paul scanned the strip malls flashing past on either side, hoping to spot an acute care clinic. Maybe he could score some antibiotics with a tale about being exposed to his grandkid's strep throat. He'd feed 'em a story about being here on business, his wife calling to say little Paulie had strep throat, his fears of infecting the people he was here to deal with. He'd wave cash in their faces, hope the doc would fork over some samples. They always had plenty of samples on hand at these clinics, didn't they, from drug company reps pushing their products? He opened his mouth wide and examined his throat in the rear view mirror. It did look a bit red.

22

Fidel

FIDEL MONTOYA SCRAMBLED OUT of the river two miles downstream from where he'd gone in. Dark hair plastered to his skull, running shorts rendered almost transparent by the water, his first thought was to avoid being seen by a voter or, God forbid, a reporter until he could make himself more presentable. He patted the velcroed pocket of his shorts, knowing the only thing he'd find was his house key. No money, no wallet, no cell phone. Damn. He'd have to walk home, keeping to the woods, and hope no one spotted him. His fear of the assailant had diminished as the water chilled him, and now, as he trudged barefoot through the woods, he almost hoped he'd run into the bastard because he wanted to beat him to a pulp.

His route paralleled the road and he ducked deeper into the woods whenever the sound of a motor warned him of a car's approach. Twigs and thorns tore into his bare feet and his left leg throbbed from hip to ankle where he'd smacked it against the tree. His clothes steamed in the heat and sweat dripped from every pore, stinging the dozens of cuts and scrapes that scored his body. He judged he was about half a mile from his house when another car roared down the road, coming toward him. He jumped sideways into the underbrush, crouching, and knew from the instantaneous burning on his right foot and ankle that he'd landed in a patch of poison ivy. "Fuuck!" he bellowed as the car's wake kicked up leaves and dust.

From a copse of dogwood trees on the south end of his property, he surveyed the house, absently scratching his ankle. A man's silhouette moved in the downstairs office. Jimmy. Thank God. He limped to the kitchen door and pulled it open. They needed to be more careful about locking up. He made a mental note to remind Jimmy and Katya. Beelining for the freezer, he dragged a bottle of Grey Goose from the icy depths. He slugged back one shot, then another, before setting the bottle on the counter. Shower, anti-itch ointment, band-aids for his cuts, and food, in that order. Then he'd figure out what to do about the man who'd tried to kill him.

"Dad! What the hell?"

Jimmy's voice made him spin. His son's face was a study in astonishment, eyebrows raised, mouth agape. Montoya was conscious of a prickle of embarrassment at his appearance and covered it with outrage. "Someone just took a shot at me."

That statement made Jimmy's face go blank. Irritated with his son's slowness, Montoya took him through it all, starting with Sydney Ellison's visit to his office. While he was talking, Jimmy capped the vodka bottle and restored it to the freezer. The freezer belched cold air at them.

"It was probably some redneck getting a jump on hunting season," Jimmy said.

Montoya flared his nostrils. "Nothing's in season in August!"

"A poacher, then." Jimmy shrugged, obviously not impressed by Montoya's brush with death.

"Someone was stalking me. I saw him."

"You said you glimpsed someone. Coulda been a deer. There was a ten-point buck on the lawn this morning when I—"

"It wasn't a fucking deer!" Montoya stopped himself with an up-raised hand and sucked in a deep breath. "I need a shower." Leaving the kitchen, he headed down the hall.

Jimmy called after him, obviously anxious to make amends, "If you think there's something more to it, call Em's dad. Let him run it to ground."

Montoya grunted and kept going.

By the time he'd scoured away every molecule of river water, swallowed a Percocet left over from a root canal, and coated his shin, ankle, and foot with calamine, he knew what he *wouldn't* do about the situation. He was damn sure not going to publicize it in any way, leave an opening for his opponent in Tuesday's race. He could just see the head-lines. Either the press would ridicule him and call his story a cheap at-tempt to generate publicity or some wit like Howard Stern or Rush would start a lottery betting on his chances of surviving until the gen-eral election. He couldn't scare voters away faster if he said he had AIDS and fucked Rottweilers. The hell with that.

Jimmy's idea was, for once, the best one. He picked up the phone and dialed. When his chief of staff answered, he gave him few details. "I've got a situation that requires a cop, but I don't want to make it official. No publicity. Get here as soon as goddamn possible."

23

Sydney

HILARY TRENT HAD SYDNEY out of police custody in record time, before the interrogation even started, by producing an affidavit her investigator had just collected from a man who remembered seeing Sydney at the liquor store the afternoon Jason was killed. Making a face like she'd swallowed a beetle, the uptight Assistant DA looking to make her name with a high profile case slipped out of the interview room to call her boss. She returned and summoned West and Graves with a curt head jerk. Moments later, Hilary whisked Sydney out the station's back entrance and popped her into a taxi, commanding her to keep a low profile.

Sydney gave the driver her home address, but changed her mind a moment later and asked him to take her to the nearest mall, where she bought the least confining, brightest skirt and blouse she could find, abandoning the suit she'd been wearing in the fitting room.

Watching a noon newscast from home, Sydney looked on in awe as her lawyer handled the media on the steps of the courthouse. The woman was in her element. Striking in a butter-colored suit that set off her dark hair and eyes, she held up her right hand, a ten-carat sapphire glinting on one finger, to quiet the crowd of reporters hurling questions at her. Sydney shuddered at the thought of having to face the media after the humiliating experience of the arrest. Thank God Hilary had gotten her out so fast. She shivered, convinced an indefinable odor from the interrogation room still lingered even after the two showers she'd taken since arriving home. She turned the volume up.

"The police are harassing my client in a pathetic attempt to cover up the fact that they have absolutely no leads in the tragic slaying of Jason Nygaard. Yes, acting on a tip from an informant, who'd just happened to see my client on TV and immediately was overcome by the urge to do his civic duty and call the police to say he'd sold her a gun, they found a gun in my client's kitchen trash—because that's where anyone with an IQ over fifty would 'hide' a murder weapon, right?— and they have ascertained it was used to kill Jason. But"—she raised her hand higher to quell the excited babbling—"my client's fingerprints are not on this gun, she has never owned or even fired a gun of any kind, and she has an alibi for the time the murder was committed."

"We hear she visited Congressman Montoya the day of the murder," someone called from the back. "Do they have a relationship?" His inflection on "relationship" prompted sniggers from the crowd.

"Lamont, after the way your wife took you to the cleaners last year, I don't know if you want to be talking about relationships," Hilary shot back. The crowd broke into loud hoots at the mocking retort. "But to answer your question, Ms. Ellison visited Congressman Montoya's *office* on a business matter."

"Will your client be found innocent?" A woman packed into a baby-blue suit asked.

"Wilma, she *is* innocent. And there's no way this case will ever see the inside of a courtroom. The DA's office will never file charges. We urge the police to continue their investigation so the real killer can be apprehended and punished."

The doorbell's peal startled Sydney. Zapping off the television, she peered through the peephole, astonished and dismayed to see Marlon Hotchkiss on the doorstep, stiffly grave and clerical. For a moment, she considered tiptoeing away and letting him think she wasn't home. She should have gone to Connie's or a hotel, as Hilary Trent had suggested, but she was damned if she was going to let the media or anyone else chase her out of her home.

"Sydney." The board chairman's deep voice came through the closed door. Maybe he was here to offer pastoral comfort in her time of need. Yeah, right. Curiosity convinced her to open up.

She unlocked the door and pulled it open. Marlon was standing too close and she got a whiff of Brylcreem and body odor. Faint crescents of sweat showed under his arms. His white collar gleamed. Surely it was uncomfortable snugged up below his Adam's apple like that?

"It's been a rough day, as you can imagine, Marlon," Sydney started, not inviting him in. "And I'm—"

He gazed down at her from hooded eyes, his jaw working. "It would be more suitable to have this conversation inside," he said, with an assumption of authority that grated on her. He moved forward as if to enter.

She stretched out her arm to bar his way. "I've been packing Jason's things, the house is a mess," she lied. "You understand." She stepped onto the stoop, forcing him back a step, pulled the door shut, and stood looking at him with her arms crossed over her chest.

He halted, lower jaw shifting from side to side, and said, "I tried to call, but your phones went directly to voicemail."

"I didn't want to talk to reporters."

"Exactly," he said, as if she had admitted something. He had a trick of tucking his chin and gazing at people from under the shelf of his brow, and he looked at her that way now. "You were arrested."

What was she supposed to say? Sydney looked at him, keeping her face neutral, and chose not to respond. A breeze riffled the oak tree's leaves.

"I've talked to a few of the board members," he went on, steepling his fingers.

Sydney straightened, feeling an icy finger trace down her spine.

"And we've agreed to give you some time off."

"I don't want time off! I—"

"You've got more on your plate than anyone should be expected to handle. Your friend's death, your ... legal issues, the stress of running Winning Ways."

"It's not stressful. It's what keeps me—" She was going to say "sane" but stopped herself. "I'm perfectly capable—"

"It's not up for discussion, Sydney," he said. He squared his shoulders, and she flashed on a ridiculous image of him as an old-time priest in a Western, black cassock flapping around his legs, gun in one hand and crucifix in the other. She almost missed his next words.

"The board is concerned about how this looks for the organization. Having the executive director accused of murder is bad for our image. Distressing. I'd think you, of all people, could appreciate that. Of course, we know you'll be found innocent, and this time off will allow you to concentrate on proving it quickly."

His unctuous tone infuriated her. "It's supposed to be innocent until proven guilty."

"You can take some time off, or we can put you on administrative suspension."

He maintained an expression that suggested he was a good steward of the organization, forced to take action on behalf of Winning Ways, but she spotted the glint of self-righteous triumph in his eyes. She bent to pinch a wilted petunia off the plant flourishing in the ceramic pot by the door, not wanting him to read her reaction. She'd be damned if she'd give him the satisfaction of seeing what a blow this was. Composing herself, she turned. "Tell the board members I appreciate their thoughtfulness," she said, pleased at how calm her voice sounded.

Hotchkiss looked like he wanted to say more, but her expression backed him down the single step. He half stumbled but caught his balance, hesitated, and then turned and strode away. Sydney could almost hear the imaginary cassock snapping at his heels.

She held herself rigid until he was well and truly gone. Then her shoulders sagged and she pressed the heels of her hands to her eyes so tightly she saw stars, not sure she could bear the simultaneous losses of Jason and Winning Ways.

No, she hadn't lost Winning Ways, she reminded herself, stepping into the house; she was just taking a week or so of leave. Maybe less than that if Hilary was right about getting the charges dismissed for good. She wondered suddenly if her mother was one of the board members who'd recommended she take some time off. Pulling her cell phone out of her pocket to call Connie, she was surprised when it rang. She took a deep breath. "Hello?"

"Miss Ellison? Sydney? This is Fidel Montoya. I got your number from your mother. We need to talk."

The man sounded distraught. "What's wrong?"

"Not on a cell phone. Meet me at the National Arboretum. One hour."

24

Sydney

SYDNEY SPOTTED CONGRESSMAN MONTOYA as soon as she walked through the administrative building of the National Arboretum onto the patio shortly after noon. He was seated at an umbrella-topped table by the koi pond, dark sunglasses hiding his eyes and the *Post* screening his face, wearing navy slacks and a yellow golf shirt, his dark hair curling over the collar. The article facing her was headlined *Third Homeless Victim Burned*. The thought made her stomach heave.

On this sweltering August afternoon, no tourists crowded the koi pond's long rectangular edges, poking their fingers in the water to encourage the foot-long fish to nibble at them. The lilies, though, bloomed in pointed yellow, white, and pink abundance; it was a shame there was no one to admire them. Sidney had always thought the Arboretum was the DC area's most underrated attraction. As a teenager, she'd spent many an hour in the Asian Valley or the Herb Garden, scribbling in her diary and enjoying the tranquility woven by the trees, plants, and water features.

She crossed the flagstone patio to Montoya's table, sandals flapping against her soles. The new skirt swirled around her ankles, and the coordinating floral print blouse might have been the most colorful item she'd worn in the last fifteen years.

Montoya looked up and stood in one smooth movement. "Thank you for coming," he said, pulling out a chair for her and reseating himself. He took off his sunglasses, another courteous gesture she appreciated, and studied her. "You look—different," he said. Perhaps anxious that she not misinterpret that, he added, "Great. You look great." His deep-set eyes were red-tinged, and worry cut a line between his brows. "I think we can help each other," he said.

"With what?"

"With finding the man who's trying to kill us."

"Us? What happened?" Sydney leaned forward, her rib cage pressing against the table's edge. A hummingbird buzzed by, then zipped to a pot of orange trumpet flowers at the patio's edge.

"Your assassin took a shot at me while I was jogging this morning," Montoya said, his lips drawn into a grim line.

"He's not 'my' assassin!"

He continued as if she hadn't spoken. "Only I slipped in the mud and he missed." He rucked up his pants leg to show the deep purple bruises and poison ivy welts that discolored every inch of visible skin.

"How'd you get away?"

"I made it to the river and swam downstream. I guess he wasn't prepared for that."

"Would you recognize him?"

"No, I only caught a glimpse of him. It happened too fast."

Sydney sat silent for a moment, evaluating Montoya's story. He had no reason to lie, she decided. A bubble of relief swelled within her. His story would vindicate her. She clamped down on her rising excitement. "Why haven't I heard about this?" she asked, her eyes meeting his. "I'd think the attempted murder of a US Congressman would knock even the story of the former bimbette-turned-philanthropist being arrested for her fiancé's murder off of CNN."

Montoya frowned. "This can't make the news."

"Did you even tell the police?" Sydney asked.

He was quiet for a moment, his fingers fiddling with his sunglasses. "Not really."

"What the hell does that mean?"

"I've got a friend who used to be on the force. I told him in confidence. He's looking into it."

Sydney threw up her hands in disgust. "What kind of game are you playing here, Congressman?"

"Fidel. And it's not a game. The special election is Tuesday. I can't afford to have this splashed all over the media. My opponent would call it grandstanding, a publicity ploy. The voters... well, no one wants to vote for a Senatorial candidate who may be dead before the national election rolls around. This can't get out, at least not until after Tuesday."

"You realize your story would clear me, put the police on the track of the real killer, don't you? What happened to you proves I was telling the truth."

"I'm sorry," he said again.

The hell he was. "Then I don't think we have anything to talk about." Sydney scraped back her chair and rose, shaking with fury. How could he sit on this information, let her be pilloried in the press? Selfish bastard. *Politician.*

He stood, too, grabbing her wrist. "Sydney. Sit, please." The sincerity and worry in his face got to her and she sat. When he was sure she wouldn't bolt, he released her wrist and sat also, pulling his chair in closer so his knee banged hers. "Don't you want to clear your name, find out who killed your boyfriend?"

"Fiancé. Jason."

He nodded. "I can help. I've been thinking—ever since this morning, for God's sake—about why anyone would want to kill me. About what I could have done ... "

Despite herself, Sydney felt a twinge of sympathy for this man facing the knowledge that someone hated him enough to pay money to have him killed. "And?"

"And I'll share my thoughts with you, give you papers, phone numbers, whatever you need, if you'll follow up." He patted a bulky satchel in his lap. "John Favier, my chief of staff, pulled these together. They're the threats I've gotten from kooks in the last year. Some of them are pretty graphic. I can't go to an official investigator, not with the election on the line. You're the only one I can trust." He put his hand on hers where it lay on the table.

"I'm touched," Sydney said. Anything but. She pulled her hand away. "Why?"

A would-be-sheepish smile crept across his face at her tone. "Because you have everything to lose. If you go to the press and tell them my story, I'll deny everything, say you're lying to deflect suspicion from yourself. I'll tell them we were lovers and you've made up this whole charade to get back at me. I think both our histories make the story plausible."

Sydney eyed him with loathing. "You're despicable. I wouldn't vote for you if your opponent was Jack the Ripper."

Unfazed, he smiled. "Ah, but you don't vote in Maryland, do you? If you were one of my constituents, well, then I'd be a bit more circumspect."

"I hope you don't think your pseudo-honesty impresses me," she said. A fish broke the surface of the water with a plop and stole Sydney's attention. The water, dyed black to discourage algae, hid whatever lurked on the bottom. Kind of like the American political system, she thought cynically. On the surface it was glad-handing and high-minded public debate, kissing babies and standing up for veterans' benefits. Below it was backroom deals, backstabbing, and selling your immortal soul for re-election. The thought of working with Montoya made her gag, but did she have any choice?

"Okay," she said. "What have you got?"

———

When Montoya left twenty minutes later, Sydney remained at the table for a few minutes, one hand resting atop the box of threats the congressman had given her. The letters had been sorted by policy issue and included notes about follow-up actions and evaluation of the danger level. With the sun growing ever warmer and sweat dampening the hair at her temples, Sydney had taken a mere half page of notes during their conversation, getting Montoya's perspective on who might want to kill him. He kept referring her to the box, maintaining that the assassin must be connected to one of the letters. He didn't have any personal enemies, he insisted, and couldn't think of anyone in his personal life who would hire a contract killer to eliminate him.

Sydney had given him a skeptical look. "Everyone has enemies from adolescence on, especially politicians. You're telling me there's no pissed-off opponent or former political ally in your background, no volunteer you screwed who has it in for you, no wheeler-dealer who thinks you reneged on a deal? Not to mention that, statistically speaking, most murders are committed by spouses."

Without answering, Montoya had abruptly flattened his hands on the table and pushed to his feet. His shadow draped over her as he blocked the sun. "I've got a committee meeting. Keep me posted on your progress so I know—"

"I don't work for you."

"We're partners now, Sydney Linn Ellison, and don't you forget it. Your fate is tied to mine." He twined two fingers together. "Call me." Without waiting for her reply, he'd turned on the heel of one polished Italian shoe and strode away. A koi broke the surface of the pond with a plop as he passed.

Sydney now rose and exited the gardens, threading her way past a Japanese tour group gathered around a guide and two women pushing strollers and trying to herd five toddlers. She didn't want to be partners with Montoya, but she had to concede that in a random and unfair twist, fate had linked her with him. Why did it feel like she had an anaconda wrapped around her?

25

Sydney

TWO HOURS LATER, SYDNEY stood outside the emerald green door to Reese's Falls Church house, unable to make herself knock. She wiped sweaty palms down her skirted thighs. After spurning her sister's offer to help yesterday, she was now in the position of asking for assistance and she wasn't sure she could make her mouth form the words. She'd spent the better part of an hour tucked into the corner of a coffee shop, trying to think of a way around it, but had failed.

She focused on her surroundings. Reese's house was un-Reese-ish in her eyes, bright and welcoming. It was two stories, painted white with black trim. The green door made her think of Oz. The wraparound porch was made hospitable with a two-person swing, a small seating area, and masses of ferns and flowers in hanging baskets and ceramic pots. Bees buzzed. According to Connie, the profits from Reese's hugely successful true crime books had paid for this historic home, set apart from its neighbors by an acre of yard surrounded by a belt of trees.

Sydney dragged her thoughts back to why she was there. Asking Reese for help was the smart thing to do. No question. She had zero investigative experience and would waste too much time trying to figure out how to unearth the secrets in Montoya's life and locate an enemy—political or personal—willing to pay to have him killed. Reese, on the other hand, was a crack investigator. Even so, Sydney wasn't sure she could have brought herself to her sister's doorstep merely to help Montoya. She was here for Jason, to find the man who'd shot Jason in cold blood.

The question was: could she trust Reese to help and keep it quiet?

Reese wasn't a reporter anymore, she reminded herself, and she couldn't see any advantage Reese would gain by giving the story to someone at the *Post*. After the scandal, and then Dirk, Sydney had had trouble trusting her instincts about anyone, but years of working with the women at Winning Ways had gradually renewed her faith in her instincts. She could usually tell after half an hour which of the women were sincere about wanting to turn their lives around, which were going to fall back into the clutches of addiction or abusive relationships, and which were going to look for the easy way to make a buck or get ahead. She was afraid her instincts were off in her sister's case, scrambled by their history, but she didn't have a choice. *For Jason*, she told herself, stabbing the doorbell before she could change her mind. A *bong* worthy of a monastery bell resonated inside the house.

Barking and the tapping of doggie toenails on wood raised her brows. Since when did Reese have a dog? The door opened and Reese stood there, casual in shorts and a Hoyas T-shirt, smears of paint or caulk on her hands and one thigh. The dog, black and white with a pushed-in nose and bat ears, frisked around Sydney, sniffing her feet and then putting his paws on her knees. His stumpy tail wagged so hard his whole body shook.

"Off, Earl," Reese said.

The dog immediately sat. Trust Reese to have a well-trained dog.

Sydney bent to pat him, unable to resist his doggie grin. "Earl?"

"He was already Earl when I got him," Reese said, offering no further explanation. She gave Sydney a cool look. "To what do I owe the honor?"

Sydney straightened. Her sister wasn't going to make this easy. "I—" She cleared her throat. "I need your help."

"With?"

"Figuring out who put out a contract on Montoya." She rolled her neck to release the tension. "Look, can I come in and tell you about it?" She hefted the box she held in the crook of one elbow, hoping curiosity about its contents would break through her sister's reserve.

Reese hesitated a moment, long enough for Sydney to think she was going to turn her away, but then she pushed the screen door wider and said, "Why not?"

Sydney crossed the sanded, refinished oak planks of the entryway and followed Reese and Earl into the small living area on the left. The Boston terrier went to a dog bed by the open window and curled up on it. A cloth covered the floors, and stacks of tile stood neatly near the fireplace where two lines of square tiles had been affixed to the right of the opening. Reese had been refinishing the place since she'd bought it five years ago, according to Connie, who made a point of keeping Sydney updated on her sister's whereabouts and activities.

"Talk while I work," Reese commanded, sinking cross-legged in front of a bucket of mastic. "This'll dry out if I don't keep at it. I think better when my hands are busy anyway."

Sydney perched on the top of a step ladder. "It looks great," she said, delaying the need to talk about Montoya for a moment. "I love those tiles."

"They're vintage, made by the Trent Tile Company, and they match what was originally here. I got them at an auction and it was a bitch sanding them clean enough to install. I'm trying to be true to the period, but it's hard to find original fittings and tiles these days. I've had to use reproductions in a few places. I got lucky with the tiles."

Sydney got the feeling Reese was talking about tiles to ward off the silence and the awkwardness between them, which had expanded over the last decade and a half like foam insulation. Insulation was a good analogy, she decided. Conversation about unimportant things kept them insulated from feelings, from talking about the elephant in the room that they'd been studiously not talking about since one ugly, accusatory shout-fest fifteen years ago. Tiles were easy. While Reese troweled the thick glue onto the wall and pressed tiles onto it, Sydney finally told her about being summoned by Montoya and his "deal."

"Some deal," Reese said, looking up briefly. "Extortion, more like."

"Yeah, but he's right when he says we both benefit from ID-ing the man behind the killer. Montoya gets to live, and I get to find out who killed Jason."

"And not go to prison," Reese pointed out.

"That, too." Funnily enough, Sydney wasn't that worried about prison. Hilary said the case wouldn't go to trial, and she believed her. She was more worried that the damage to her reputation would be irreparable and that she'd permanently lose Winning Ways. The thought hollowed her stomach.

Reese worked in silence for a few minutes, and Sydney watched, thinking her sister had beautiful hands: slightly squarish, long-fingered and short-nailed, with strong bones. Not beautiful in the conventional sense of soft skin and manicures, but useful, competent, capable of creating beauty.

Using a level to check that her tiles weren't slanting, Reese said, "So, you want me to do what? Track down a hit man and ask him who hired him?"

Sydney flushed. "Help me figure out who might have. You have sources, research expertise." She shrugged. "I don't. I can analyze these"—she tapped the box of threatening letters—"but I don't know where to start with Montoya's personal life. He contends he has no enemies—"

Reese choked.

"I know, right?" Sydney said, smiling back. It felt surprisingly good. She couldn't remember the last time she and Reese had shared a laugh. "Anyway, I was thinking on the way over that the way to go at this might be to figure out who had both a grudge against Montoya—a worth-killing-for grudge—*and* access to a contract killer. I mean, there might be any number of cheated-on husbands out there, or spurned lovers or political rivals who would gladly run Montoya down if he stepped in front of their car, but how many of them have a hit man on speed dial? It's a Venn diagram." She made two circles with thumbs and forefingers and overlapped them slightly. "This one"—she pointed with her chin to her right hand—"represents everyone with a motive to kill Montoya. The left"—she touched that hand with her chin—"is people with the kind of connections to hire a contract killer. The space where they join is the pool of people we need to investigate."

Reese gave her a slightly surprised but approving look. "Good thinking."

"Don't look so surprised. I do have a brain, you know, and I didn't totally waste my time in college, even though I had to spend way too much of it guarding the graded term papers and exams people wanted to steal and post online to prove they knew the Manley Trap, or make fun of me, and ducking every time someone with a camera came within range. Forget about making friends. Sorry." Sydney stopped herself.

"I'm sorry. I wasn't going to drag all that up again." She was dismayed by how easily she'd fallen into a rant about Reese ruining her life.

Her sister swiveled on her butt to face her, eyes narrowed. "Get out right now if you're going to throw ancient history in my face every time you open your mouth."

Sydney reared back and the stepladder rocked. "I—"

"You think you were the only one who got mud splattered on you from that story?"

"You wrote it. It was your choice—"

Reese rose. Her nostrils flared. "In J-schools around the country, 'pulling a Linn' is synonymous with a reporter who goes to any lengths to get a story. I pretend to be proud of it, but it makes me squirm. You think I like having the whole world think I'm a Benedict Arnold?"

"Dad thought you were a rock star."

Reese nodded. She looked suddenly older. A gust of wind clattered the blinds behind her, but although she tensed, she didn't look around. "Everything I ever did—the grades, running track, Georgetown—I did for him, so he would be proud of me. I knew it disappointed him when I became a reporter instead of a lawyer, so I decided I'd be the best damn reporter there ever was. Well, there wasn't much scope for investigative reporting at the *Loudon Times-Mirror*. Two years of reporting on PTA meetings, city council elections, teen vandalism, and the occasional drug bust. Dad kept pressuring me to give it up, to go to law school—you remember."

Sydney did. Dinner conversations had been rancorous whenever Reese came home, which she did frequently since her reporter's salary barely paid for her studio apartment. Howard Linn haranguing Reese about following him into the law, Reese flaring that she had a right to live her own life, Connie blithely talking over both of them, relating the details of some social engagement that day, or a morsel of gossip she'd picked up at the tennis club.

"So, when I caught on to what you and Manley were up to, I wrote the story. You know what Dad said to me when it broke?"

Interested despite herself, Sydney shook her head.

"He said, 'You'd have made an outstanding lawyer. You've got the instincts of a shark.' He meant it as a compliment, but it didn't feel the way I'd always thought it would. I just felt ... empty."

For some reason, the word inflamed Sydney. She stood so fast the stepladder toppled with a clang. "'Empty'? Better that than 'betrayed,' 'abandoned,' 'abused.' You made me a pariah, and you didn't get the satisfaction out of it that you thought you would. Pardon me if I can't work up any tears for you." She tried to steady her voice. "You made the choice—"

"So. Did. You." Each word dropped with deadly precision. "No one made you sleep with George Manley. You might have been eighteen when the affair started, but you were twenty when it ended."

Old enough to know better, her tone said. The truth of it seared Sydney. It's not like she hadn't thought it a thousand times over the years. To drown out the guilt, she leaned forward, hands clenched at her sides, and almost yelled, "When *you* ended it!"

"Oh, please. The end was implicit from the beginning. Did you really think the Speaker of the House was going to ditch his career, his reputation, and his family to marry you? No twelve-year-old in this town is that naive." Reese cocked one brow. "Since 'choice' is your new favorite word, let me ask: did his wife have a choice?"

Sydney sucked in a breath, her mouth and throat dry. She felt like she'd inhaled talc. The air didn't reach her lungs and dizziness made her sway. Julie Manley. George's wife had come to see her after the story broke. Even now she couldn't make herself think about that meeting,

Julie's scorn, hurt, disgust. Sydney had vomited when Julie left. Her legs trembled so hard she reached for the wall to balance herself. This was a bad idea, a putrid one. She turned to go, gaining speed as she neared the door.

"That was low," Reese said. "I shouldn't have gone there."

She sounded sincere, but Sydney didn't even slow down. Reese's footsteps sounded behind her, and then she was in front of her, blocking the way. Sydney stopped, glaring at her. Earl barked and frisked around them like he thought they were playing a game.

"Hit me," Reese said.

Sydney's jaw sagged. "What?"

"Hit me. 'Sorry' isn't enough. It never will be. Giving money to Winning Ways isn't enough. You need to hit me."

"You never even said you were sorry, not and meant it!"

Reese's eyelids closed for a second. When she opened them, the futility in her eyes froze Sydney. "You never read my letters."

The letters. Sydney took a shuddering breath. The first one had arrived on the anniversary of the article's publication. Recognizing her sister's handwriting, Sydney, two days shy of her twenty-first birthday, had burned it unopened, taking savage satisfaction in watching the envelope start to smolder, the corner blacken and curl up, and then the burst of flames that resolved too quickly into ash. Letters postmarked on the anniversary had arrived for ten years, and then they had stopped. She had disposed of the first eight in various manners, but had kept the last two, unopened. They lay in a shoebox tucked onto her highest closet shelf. She hadn't thought about them for years. An unfamiliar twinge of guilt pulled at her. "I couldn't make myself—"

"No matter." Reese straightened her shoulders, abs tight and legs braced. Her arms hung loosely at her sides. She was still holding the trowel. When Sydney eyed it, she let it clatter to her refinished floor. "Do it." She squinched her eyes mostly closed, crow's feet fanning from the corners.

"That would be—"

"Hit me, damn it!"

Without thinking about it, Sydney pulled her fist back and launched it toward Reese's stomach, using the strength in her legs to power the punch. Her fist thudded into her sister's midsection. For that moment, she wanted to drive it through her abs and her internal organs, clear through to her spine. Reese folded forward and staggered back with a pained "Ungh."

Sydney rocked back on her heels and dropped her arms. Her right fist stung and her arm ached clear up to the shoulder socket. Hair fell over her eyes, and she *pffted* it back with a breath directed upward. She was breathing heavily, like she'd gone ten rounds with Mike Tyson. She felt no urge to hit Reese again. Earl's barks had changed to whimpers and he nosed Reese's ankle. Sydney actually felt worse about upsetting the dog than about slugging her sister.

Reese stayed hunched over, hands on her knees, but craned her neck to look at her sister. "Satisfied?"

Sydney took stock of her emotions. "Better," she admitted. She started to say "I'm sorry," but Reese stopped her with an upraised hand.

"Don't say it." She straightened slowly, probing her midsection with two fingers. "You pack a wicked punch."

They eyed each other. "Well," Sydney said.

"Well," Reese returned.

Sensing the changed atmosphere, Earl began barking again, in high, piercing yips.

"Shut up, Earl," they said in unison. Earl smacked his butt on the floor and panted happily. It brought tentative smiles to both their faces.

"Montoya?" Reese asked.

"Montoya," Sydney agreed.

26

Sydney

IN THE WARM HAVEN of the kitchen, surrounded by cream-colored walls, a farmhouse sink, and black-streaked bricks framing the six-burner stove and oven, Reese pulled leftover Chinese out of the fridge and Sydney got two forks from a drawer. She could feel how she and Reese were being careful with each other, choosing words with care, giving each other clearance so they didn't bump hips or tread—literally or figuratively—on toes, treating this fragile detente as if it were as brittle as a brandy snap. It felt almost like they needed to learn, or invent, a new language. They'd spoken Big Sister–Little Sister for the first twenty years, and since then they'd spoken only Surface Civil. Sydney tried to imagine what their new language might be called, assuming they created one. It was too early to know.

"Still haven't learned to cook, I see," she said, sniffing at a container labeled *Gen Tso's* before digging in. Then she worried that Reese would take that as a jab, and backtracked. "I didn't mean ... Chinese is my favorite ... "

"No point." Reese shrugged, unoffended. "No one's got time for celebrity chef TV shows or foo-foo ingredients like saffron threads or chanterelles in a war zone, and since I got into true crime, I live out of hotel rooms more often than not. Room service and delivery suit me fine."

Sydney secretly enjoyed cooking shows, but she didn't admit it. "Do you have a new project in mind yet?"

Reese shook her head. "No. I'm taking a break. A long break. This last one was hard."

Sydney saw something haunted in her eyes and wondered for the first time what kind of toll it must take, talking to serial killers or mass murderers, getting into their heads. It must be a different kind of carnage than Reese had seen on battlefields around the world, more personal. She sensed her sister didn't want to talk about the toll the Bingle investigation had taken, so she didn't ask. Another time. For the first time in forever, she thought that there might really be "another time," and a conversation that meant something.

"My publisher's got a two-week-long jaunt lined up when the book comes out in November. Until then ... " Reese gestured to their surroundings, and Sydney took it to mean she was going to occupy herself mainly with renovation projects.

Setting aside her *Gen Tso's*, Sydney pulled the lid off of Montoya's box of threats and slid her legal pad with notes across the butcher block countertop, which clearly was not original to the 1890s house but blended well.

"So," Reese asked, "is Montoya as sexy in real life as he is on the tube?"

Sydney jerked back. "What's that supposed to mean?"

A puzzled look crossed Reese's face, followed by an impatient one. "For God's sake, Sydney. It doesn't mean anything. Or maybe it means I haven't been laid for a while and I'm due."

Sydney calmed down. "He's a sleaze." She gave it more thought. "Which isn't to say he doesn't have a certain appeal, a combination of confidence and charm. But he's still a sleaze."

"Yeah, rumor has it that 'Fidel' is a real misnomer. I don't know why his wife puts up with it. She doesn't seem like the usual milquetoast, stand-by-your-man political wife, willing to suck up any amount of humiliation in order to call herself FLOTUS one day."

Like Julie Manley had been. Sydney let the thought go. "She's an architect, right?"

Reese nodded and tossed a bit of beef to a hopeful Earl. "Uh-huh."

"So, not much chance she knows any contract killers."

"Not so fast," Reese said. "Before she married Montoya at nineteen, her name was Katya Van Slyke, but her mother's maiden name was Utkin." At Sydney's blank stare, she added impatiently. "Do you live under a rock?"

"I certainly don't follow DC gossip, if that's what you mean. I know firsthand how vicious and wrong it is." Sydney slammed the counter in exasperation and her cardboard container jumped, rice fountaining from it. Earl eagerly licked up the pieces that hit the ground.

"It's not gossip—" Reese started. "Never mind." She grabbed a sponge and wiped up the rice. "Katya's uncle is a significant figure in the Russian Mafiya. He lives in New York. Her parents have always been careful to distance themselves from him, and of course there's no visible connection between him and Montoya—I don't even think Uncle Matvei was invited to the wedding—but I daresay he could pass a phone number to his niece if she asked. And then there's Jimmy."

"Montoya's son? I've seen him in the background when Montoya does events."

"Jimmy's got a gambling problem. Maybe addictive personalities run in the family—sex for Fidel, gambling for Jimmy. I don't know who he bets with, or if he owes money, but I can find out. If he's underwater with the wrong guys, Jimmy might be eager to come into his inheritance sooner rather than later. I've got a contact, a bookie friend—acquaintance, really—who owes me. He'll tell me who Jimmy's into."

"So much for Fidel's personal life," Sydney said, relieved that Reese knew how to find things out, just as she'd thought she would. "Now there's only this." She thumped the box of threats.

"Let's get to it."

An hour later, they'd both read all of the letters and taken notes. Sydney felt slimed by the hatred and vitriol pouring from the pages. The mail and email and social media drubbing she'd gotten after the scandal had been bad, but a lot of this was worse. No one had threatened to sodomize her and flay her alive before feeding her body to hogs. They were sitting on Reese's back deck, looking out over a rough-mown field so green it hurt her eyes, dotted with dandelions and wildflowers. Butterflies flitted. Birds twittered and chirruped from a line of woods edging the property. The people who'd written those letters couldn't live in the same world that she did.

Reese set down the last page and sat staring into space, drumming her fingers on the glass-topped table.

"Montoya seems pretty convinced the Imminent Revelation folks are the ones who hired the killer," Sydney said. "His second choice is his opponent in the election, with the national Democratic Party chair a distant runner-up because of what he calls 'intellectual differences.'" Sydney made air quotes.

"Yeah, he slept with the guy's wife," Reese said.

Sydney didn't ask her how she knew that. Reese knowing things was why she was here.

Her sister rose. "I need a drink. Get you anything?"

It was only three thirty. "A bit early for me. Water?"

Reese returned minutes later bearing what looked like a gin and tonic for herself, a half-full bottle of gin with a monkey on the label, and a bottle of chilled Perrier for Sydney. Reese drank a good third of the G&T, then set it down.

Sydney rolled the cold Perrier bottle across her forehead before opening it. It hissed. "You're—you *were*—the investigative reporter...how do we go about figuring out if any of these people or groups really hired a hit man?" She felt like she'd drifted into a spy novel, or *The Godfather*, using terms like "hit man" and "take out." Next thing she knew, she'd be saying "iced" or "sleeping with the fishes" or "collateral damage."

Reese shrugged one shoulder. "We talk to them, carefully. We talk to people who know them, even more carefully. We do our research before we talk to anybody." She knocked back most of the rest of her G&T with a rattle of ice.

"We've only got until Tuesday," Sydney reminded her. She sifted a page from the pile. "I think Montoya's right about the Imminent Revelationists. There's something angrier, more violent in their letters than in most of the others. They sound serious. They're calling out Montoya for 'polluting Adam's pure blood seedline by giving Jews, faggots, and the mud people access to America's land and treasure.' Repulsive. They threaten to blow him up, behead him, and give him a foretaste of the flames of hell, which must mean they want to burn him. I think we should look at them first."

"Agreed. You do that—it's a computer drill. I'll work my sources to find out more about Jimmy Montoya's situation and see if Katya's been lunching with Uncle Matvei." Reese poured another slug of gin into her glass and sipped.

Sydney worked hard to keep any hint of judgment or concern off her face, remembering Connie saying something in passing about Reese's drinking. She'd tuned it out at the time, as she'd tuned out any mention of Reese.

"Do you really donate to Winning Ways?" she asked, suddenly remembering Reese's remark before she'd hit her.

Reese swirled the liquid in her glass, letting the silver arc of it slice just to the rim, a hair's breadth from sloshing over. "People donate anonymously for a reason."

Sydney could have pushed it, but she let it go, a pea-sized bubble of happiness or hope rising within her from the knowledge that her sister had been donating to the cause closest to her heart. It might just have been guilt money, Judas's thirty pieces of silver, but it might also have been a bridge, a way to stay connected. She would think of it as the latter.

Setting the glass down, Reese pulled her laptop closer. "You know," she said, "we haven't paid any attention to that bit about 'Time for round two.' That may offer an alternate way to figure this out."

"How so?"

"If we take 'round two' to mean that they—the killer and his client—have already killed someone else, who was it? What's the connection with Montoya?"

"Another politician," Sydney said immediately. "Maybe they both supported a bill the mysterious client wants killed. Pun intended."

"À la *The Pelican Brief*?" Reese said skeptically. "How many politicians would you have to kill off to affect legislation? Still, we should check it out. What kind of timeline is reasonable? Six months?"

"Go back a year," Sydney said, watching Reese's fingers fly over the keyboard. A bee buzzed around her water bottle and she waved it away. "How many congressional members died in office in the past twelve months?"

It took only moments for the search engine to return an answer. "Three." Reese turned the screen so Sydney could see it.

While Sydney read, Reese recapped. "Congresswoman Beth Howser, from the Fifth District in Colorado, died of a heart attack last August, just a year ago. Rodney Portentos, Congressman from Alaska, was killed in a car wreck in February, and Armand Fewell, Maryland's senator, died in a hunting accident." She sipped her G&T and licked a drop off her lower lip.

"That's why there's the special election, to replace him," Sydney said slowly. "Was there any doubt about it being an accident? What happened?"

Reese scanned an article or two. "Doesn't seem to be," she said. "He was hunting turkey in South Dakota in May with a buddy, one Jermaine Washington, when he almost stepped on a rattlesnake, jumped and dropped his shotgun, and it went off. He was hit in the face and throat. Unlucky. They got him to a hospital and thought he was going to be okay, but he developed sepsis and died six weeks later. Not the way I want to go." She continued to scroll down the screen.

Sydney made a note to talk to Jermaine Washington or Fewell's wife. "If he was murdered, it seems like the killer almost screwed it up." She tapped her pen on the table, thinking. "Car wrecks can be arranged," she said, "and heart attacks can be faked." She felt faintly ridiculous even suggesting it.

"True," Reese said, "but unlikely. The *Colorado Springs Gazette* says Howser had a history of heart issues; it was her third heart attack that killed her."

"Probably not murder, then," Sydney agreed.

"And Portentos's crash was a single-car wreck on an icy road in Fairfax County."

"No cut brake lines or bullet hole in the tire?" Sydney asked, only half kidding.

"What kind of movies do you watch?" Reese asked, cocking a disdainful eyebrow.

Sydney didn't want to confess that she liked exactly the kind of action-packed thrillers that Reese's eyebrow was implicitly condemning. "The 'round two' bit could also refer to something personal to Montoya, couldn't it? Maybe someone has a grudge against his family, a personal thing, not a political thing."

"Possible. You'll have to ask him if any family members have died recently, though, because Montoya is too common a name, and it's not worth digging up his family tree to figure out his mom's maiden name and all that crap." Reese shut her laptop, downed the rest of her drink in one go, scraped back her chair, and stood, putting a hand on the table to steady herself. "Let's get going."

"Going? Where?"

"Your place. I'll get my gear. Ten minutes. I want to have a look around before dark."

"Wait." Sydney stood, too. "I told you, you don't need to move in with me."

Reese gave her a level look. "If you think I'm putting in the time and effort to track down Jason's killer and the guy who hired him, only to have him put a bullet in you, you're batshit crazy. He's already been back once to plant the gun. Until we get this figured out, I'm sticking to you like stink on shit." She headed for the stairs, no sign of the G&Ts in her steady walk.

"I don't need a bodyguard," Sydney called after her. The thought of having Reese around 24/7 made her itch with discomfort.

Reese spoke over her shoulder. "If you don't have any Monkey 47 on hand, put the bottle in your purse."

Sydney caved to the inevitable, stowed the gin bottle in her purse, and looked at Earl. "I suppose you think you're coming, too?"

He wagged his whole rear end and panted.

"Right. Then we'd better find you some food, because I don't think you'll like kiwi yogurt."

She located Earl's food, and she had the bag and a bowl tucked into the trunk of her Nissan Altima by the time Reese came back downstairs.

27

Sydney

LATER THAT EVENING, SYDNEY sat on her guest bed because Reese had said the balcony opening off the master bedroom made the room too vulnerable. When she'd testily asked what made Reese an expert on home security, her sister had said she'd picked up a few pointers while writing *Secret Silence*, her blockbuster about a Secret Service agent who was a serial killer. After poking about the house for twenty minutes, making notes, Reese had made Sydney drive them to the nearest hardware store, where they'd bought new locks and window latches. Reese installed the top-of-the-line deadbolts while Sydney put together a light dinner. The whirring of the drill intermittently drowned Earl's toenails clicking on the hardwood floor as he followed Sydney from stove to counter to fridge, hoping. The scents of tarragon and baked chicken still pervaded the house.

Reese was planning to sleep on the pull-out sofa downstairs. They hadn't talked much at dinner, and, when Sydney went upstairs, Reese was hunched forward studying her laptop screen, legs tucked under her, sipping a G&T and making notes on a legal pad. The living room was dark except for the computer's glow; it limned Reese's face, scooping hollows under her eyes, and made the chrome on Jason's bike glow. Earl had curled up on a blanket she'd unearthed from the linen closet and folded into a pad for him. Sydney felt certain he'd give warning of an assassin's entrance, since he'd already barked at Indigo, two youngsters rollerblading on the sidewalk, a squirrel traversing a branch, and numerous dog walkers, joggers, and commuters on their way home from the Metro. She thought about thanking Reese when she said good night, but didn't.

With a pillow scrunched at the small of her back and her laptop open beside her, Sydney let backed-up tears fall. She wore Jason's old plaid robe. It still smelled like him, which was mostly comforting. Shortly after she and Reese had gotten back from the hardware store, his parents, who lived in a tiny apartment in an assisted living facility, had called with details of the service, which was planned for the week after next in Saratoga Springs, New York, his home town. They'd also asked Sydney to clear out Jason's condo, keeping anything she wanted and disposing of the rest of his things as appropriate. If she came across anything small that she thought they would like, she should send it along, his mother said, her voice cracking with age and grief.

"You're not supposed to outlive your children," his father said through a barrage of throat clearing and nose honking, futile attempts to disguise his tears. That had cued the build-up of tears that Sydney had kept damned in her throat all evening, not wanting to break down in front of Reese.

Now, cried out, she blew her nose, collected the pyramid of sodden tissues to throw out, and opened her email.

One of the letters from Montoya's box—from Aaron Fisher, the Big Kahuna or Grand Wizard or whatever he called himself of the Imminent Revelation—lay beside her. Her Internet research earlier had revealed Fisher to be a product of Oral Roberts University and an ordained minister. The Imminent Revelation's slick website featured a photo of a fortyish man in a suit, who looked more like a businessman than the leader of a paramilitary organization devoted to influencing U. S. elections "by any means necessary." However, the Southern Poverty Law Center and Anti-Defamation League, who maintained thorough databases on hate groups, cited the IR and its founder as being among the most dangerous groups in the nation and the most likely to resort to "organized and scripted violence" to achieve their aims. True believers all had a two-inch-square entwined *A.S.*, for "Adam's Seed," branded on their chests. Sydney shuddered when she thought of it. She could not afford to underestimate Fisher, assuming she got to meet him.

She typed his email address into the "To" line on her computer. A plan for approaching him had come to her while she'd read up on his cult. She hadn't shared it with Reese, afraid her sister would put the kibosh on the idea. Fingers flying, she told Fisher they had a common goal: to keep Fidel Montoya from being elected.

I can make it happen, Sydney wrote. *Let's meet.* She sent the message and relaxed against the pillows. Die cast. She'd gotten in touch with a bunch of right-wing kooks. She hoped they'd respond in a conventional way, via email, rather than with a bomb or a bullet.

28

Paul
Saturday, August 5

EARLY SATURDAY MORNING, PAUL gingerly peeled back the bandage from his shoulder. In the sputtering fluorescent light of the DC motel room's tiny bathroom, the skin around the stitched bullet hole looked shiny and red. He poked at it, wincing. Infected. He didn't need this crap now. He hadn't been able to pry any antibiotics out of the doctor he'd visited, not when the rapid strep test came back negative. Who knew they had strep tests that gave almost immediate results these days? Last time he'd had a strep test, decades ago, it had taken over two days to get the results. His shoulder pulsed with pain and he pressed the heel of his hand against it, hoping to shut it up. Drenching a thin washcloth with the hottest water he could stand, he held it to his shoulder, letting the heat draw the poison to the surface. Repeating the process several times, he stared into the medicine cabinet mirror, seeing not the late-middle-aged man stripped to the waist whose skin was losing its grip on his musculature, sliding inexorably south, but his fifth-grade self reclining on the couch, his mother holding a hot cloth to his big toe with its infected ingrown toenail. Like she had, he pushed at the inflamed skin until the pus oozed out, dabbing it away with toilet tissue he pulled from a spare roll. He swabbed the area with the alcohol he'd picked up at a drug store and rubbed in antibiotic ointment before re-bandaging it. That would have to do.

Shrugging into a green polo shirt, he reviewed Plan B. There were contingency plans as well, but he didn't want to have to resort to them. The client's insistence on making the job look like an accident complicated things. Putting a bullet through a man's temple was so much simpler. Or tossing a grenade into his bedroom, like that mission in Hanoi—Ho Chi Minh City, as the gooks had taken to calling it—in '75. Simplicity and surprise were two of the principles of warfare that Clausewitz had espoused, and now Paul had neither on his side. He preferred Sun Tzu's war-fighting philosophies, but had to admit Clausewitz had a good thing going with his nine principles. Something about numbered lists was appealing, he thought, lacing his cross-trainers. *The Seven Habits of Highly Effective People*, Letterman's Top Ten lists.

The one good thing about this target, though, was that he could find out where Montoya was going to be at any hour of the day merely by checking the congressman's website for his appearance schedule. This close to the election, the candidate was stumping full-time, speaking at Kiwanis meetings over breakfast, visiting schools and factories in the mornings, lunching with union leaders, and so on, right up until his black-tie speaking engagement at an American Bar Association banquet that night. Folding up the print-out of Montoya's schedule, Paul put his gun in the gym bag and slung it over his good shoulder. Plan B called for interpreting "accident" in a somewhat liberal fashion.

29

Sydney

SYDNEY EXPECTED REESE TO be hungover and groggy Saturday morning, but she was up, dressed, and clear-eyed when Sydney came downstairs. Reese's short hair stuck out every which-way, and Sydney flashed back to how long it had been in high school and the way Reese had fussed with it every morning. Now she didn't look like a woman who even knew what a curling iron was, never mind one who'd once owned two hair dryers with detachable nozzles, three curling irons, hot rollers, and enough hair spray to supply the Dallas Cowboy cheerleaders for a month. Sydney wondered what she'd owned in high school that she would disdain now. Other than a collection of boy-band T-shirts and turquoise cream eyeshadow, she couldn't think of anything. Probably a bad sign, a sign that she hadn't moved on, grown, matured.

She told Reese, "I'm off to visit a rabid white supremacist today. What are you up to?"

Her flip tone didn't faze Reese. "Explain."

Sydney told her about contacting Aaron Fisher and read her the email he'd sent in reply to hers, which set up a time and place to meet in rural Maryland. He'd included a scan of a map that showed how to get to the meeting point, which she imagined to be at the Imminent Revelation compound.

"Shit," Reese muttered. "Let me think." Her thumb and forefinger pinched her brow above her nose, the way she'd worried at any problem since she was in grade school.

Earl barked imperatively, and Sydney opened the back door to let him out. As the door banged closed, Reese said, "Here's what we do."

———

Three hours later, Sydney slowed to twenty-five miles per hour; even so, the undercarriage of her car scraped the washboard ruts in the gravel road that led—she hoped—to the Imminent Revelation meeting site. Her teeth snapped together as the car jolted into a particularly deep pothole. She wrenched the steering wheel to the right and continued. Another third of a mile, if the directions were accurate. She scanned the verge on either side, seeing nothing but deciduous trees, brambly-looking undergrowth, an occasional bird. Spears of sunlight pierced the canopy and dappled the road, providing just enough brightness to keep her sight from adjusting to the shadows.

Blinking her eyes closed hard, Sydney opened them to see an area of trampled grass on her right. That must be the "parking area" indicated on her map. Backing into the lay-by, she cut the engine and took a deep breath—which whistled out in a muted scream as someone tapped on her window.

Her head jerked to the left, and a camo-clad figure motioned for her to get out. His pistol remained in the holster slung at his hip, but Sydney found that only minimally reassuring. Hesitantly, she unlocked the door and put a foot on the ground, slipping her key chain with the panic device into her front pocket.

"Miz Ellison?" The man, hardly more than a teen, had hair cut so short she couldn't tell if it was blond or brown. He stood about four inches taller than she did and was triathlete-lean in a tight T-shirt, his long legs ending in scuffed combat boots.

At her nod, he pulled a red and white bandanna from his pocket. "It's clean." Twirling a finger to get her to turn, he slipped the cloth over her eyes and tied it, catching a few hairs.

"Ow."

"Sorry, ma'am. OPSEC. We can't have anyone knowing our exact location for security reasons. You understand." Taking her upper arm in a firm grasp, he marched her along the roadside.

She could tell when they left the road and headed into the woods because the crunch and roll of gravel under her feet turned to the soft scrunch of grass and twigs. Her escort guided her by the pressure of his fingers on her arm. Feeling like a cross between a prisoner and someone playing that trust game that facilitators liked to force on participants at team-building events, she walked, trying to count her steps and keep track of turns. By the time they stopped, she figured they'd been walking fifteen minutes, plus or minus.

Her guide exchanged greetings with someone who called him Samuel. "This the one?" the new voice asked.

"Yes, sir. She's Mr. Fisher's guest."

"Take her on in, then."

They walked forward a short way on level ground before Samuel said, "Three stairs." She lifted her right foot, too high as it turned out, and stepped hard onto a wooden stair. Two more followed and then she was in a building. The cooler air was a relief after the muggy, hot walk. Fingers fumbled at the back of her head and the blindfold fell away. She checked her watch: eighteen minutes. Of course, Samuel could've led her in circles, so she might not be more than a few hundred yards away from her car.

She knew Reese was less than a mile away, due east of where she'd parked. They'd spoken for a moment before Sydney continued on to the rendezvous point.

"I'll move in closer if I can," Reese had said, pulling the bill of her baseball cap down. She tilted her head and Sydney imagined she was studying her from behind the sunglasses. "You sure you want to do this? Fisher and his fanatics aren't playing around. They're dangerous. I looked them up, you know. Nutjobs with branding irons. We can find some other way to suss out their involvement."

"Fisher and the Fanatics sounds like an alternative rock band," Sydney said, dodging the question.

Reese didn't smile at her joke; she just held Sydney's gaze seriously, silently asking her to consider her question. Hell no, she didn't want to do this, but it seemed like the fastest way to prove or disprove the Imminent Revelation's involvement in the plot to kill Montoya, so she was going to do it.

"I could go—" Reese started.

Sydney was shaking her head before her sister had finished. "They want to talk to me, and they said if I'm not alone, there'll be no meeting. Besides, you won't know if he's the one. I mean, I heard the man's voice on the cell phone. I want to hear Aaron Fisher's voice up close. Maybe I'll recognize it."

Reese had snorted but quit trying to argue her out of it. "Take this." She thrust a small gadget with a button at Sydney. "It's a panic button, like one of those 'I've fallen and I can't get up' devices. Hit it if it looks like things are going south. Don't wait too long, either. If you start to feel itchy, hit the damn button."

"What will you do?" Sydney had visions of her sister descending on the Imminent Revelationists, guns blazing, a cross between Rambo and Lara Croft.

Reese shoved her sunglasses up her nose. "Call the police."

Looking around the small room now, the kind of port-a-cabin used for construction site offices or overflow classrooms, she saw no phone. A map of the Eastern seaboard covered most of one wall and photos obscured the one opposite. A dorm-room-sized refrigerator and a two-burner stove huddled in one corner, a teakettle hissing atop the stove. A folding table sat at the far end of the room, ringed with five chairs. Two were occupied.

"Thank you, Samuel," the man seated closest to her said.

Aaron Fisher, she presumed. He held himself as erect as a king on a throne, despite the rickety metal chair he sat on. No more than medium height, he had short brown hair and wore a uniform that reminded her of photos of World War I–era German officers, complete with riding pants and glossy boots. He even held a crop in one hand.

"Did you search her?" His voice was nasal but deep, nothing like the voice she'd heard on the cell phone.

"N-no, sir," Samuel said, sounding unsure.

"Do you not understand the need for security?" In one motion, Fisher surged to his feet and slashed the crop across the young man's face. Sydney stifled a gasp and stepped back involuntarily. Samuel stood stoically, not even flinching, as a red weal wormed its way to the surface of his cheek.

"You're dismissed. Report to Daniel."

Did all the Imminent Revelation members have biblical names? Was it a condition for joining or were they assigned new names when they signed up?

"Yes, sir," Samuel said, swinging on his heel and clomping out of the building. Through the briefly open door, Sydney caught a glimpse of a small compound hedged with barbed wire and at least two other buildings. The door banged closed.

"Mo." Fisher jerked his head toward Sydney, and the other man stood.

Also clad in a uniform, more Army surplus store than movie set wardrobe, Mo was tall and lanky, with a neck that poked forward and hands covered with a thatch of black hair. He stopped in front of Sydney.

"I don't have a gun or anything," she said.

Fisher huffed a laugh as Mo's hands slid over her arms and down her sides. "I'm more concerned about a recorder than a weapon, Miss Ellison."

Mo patted her back and stomach, then slid his hands up her legs, lingering on her crotch. She was glad she'd worn jeans. He thrust a hand into her pocket, coming out with her keys. "What's this?" He pointed to the panic button.

"The remote for my car," she said. She held out her hand imperiously and, after a moment, he placed the key ring in it. Her fingers folded over it gratefully.

"She's clean," he told Fisher.

"Have a seat." Fisher pushed a chair forward with one foot.

Sydney was glad to sit and hide the trembling in her knees. The assault on Samuel and the thorough pat-down made her doubt her decision to approach Fisher. Clearly, these people relished violence. She'd let herself be misled by the professional website, the educated-sounding though repulsive rhetoric. Reese had tried to warn her.

Fisher tapped the crop on the table. "You intimated we could help each other, Miss Ellison," he said. "What did you have in mind?"

"You want to make sure Fidel Montoya doesn't get elected. I can help." She leaned forward, hoping to exude sincerity.

"You embrace our cause, then?" Fisher's eyes narrowed slightly.

"Let's just say I applaud your desire to keep Montoya out of office," Sydney replied, consciously adopting the more formal cadences of Fisher's speech. She'd read somewhere that it loosened up interview subjects if the reporter mimicked their speech patterns. Maybe Reese had told her that.

Fisher nodded. "How can you help us?"

"I have a ... relationship with Fidel. I have photos." A gleam in his eye told her she'd caught his interest. "For a fee, I could make those photos public and ruin his chances on Tuesday."

Shouts and the thud of marching feet drifted into the cabin. "Get in step, recruit!"

"If you have a 'relationship' with Congressman Montoya, why are you so eager to ruin him?" Fisher asked.

Was it her imagination, or had Mo inched closer? "I've come to realize that his policies would be damaging for America." That much was true.

"He dumped you, you mean, Miss Ellison? Your Latrino lover dumped you, just like that kike Manley, and you want revenge." At her startled look, Fisher continued. "Did you think we wouldn't research you before inviting you here?" The sweep of his arm took in the compound. "You're Sydney Linn, Jew-loving whore. Now you disgrace your race by trying to educate and raise up niggers. Your association with them is an abomination."

This was getting out of control fast. Sydney dropped a hand to her side and pushed the panic button. "I can see we have nothing to discuss," she said calmly, pushing back from the table. As she stood, Mo moved, quicker than she would've guessed he could, and grabbed her arm.

161

"What are you really after, Sidney Linn Ellison?" Fisher rose, too, and moved to stand a foot in front of her, his blue eyes probing hers. He breathed mouthwash into her face. "Are you a spy for Montoya?"

He slapped the crop lightly along the length of his leg and Sydney found her eyes drawn to it. "That's absurd. It's obvious you doubt my sincerity, so I'll just leave." She tried an affronted sniff and worked to still her racing mind so she could think. These men were not rational. Even though she'd suspected them of hiring a killer, she'd never entertained the idea that they might physically harm her. Now menace clouded the room, as real as Mo's stale coffee breath.

"Mo."

The single word from Fisher galvanized the larger man and he grabbed Sydney by the shoulders and forced her down into the chair. His fingers dug into the notch above her collarbones. Fisher strolled to the back of the room, stopping beside the small stove.

"I think you're lying to me, Miss Ellison," Fisher said. "And I take that as a sign of disrespect."

With jerky, agitated movements, he pulled on a single leather glove—was he going to beat her?—and picked up something propped against the stove. Sydney dug her nails into her palms as he stood upright with a metal shaft in his hand ... a branding iron topped with a backward *A.S.*

"You are still the seed of Adam, even if you've betrayed your blood," Fisher said, explaining the brand. "Maybe the purifying fire will set you on the straight and narrow, keep you from the eternal fires of damnation." As he spoke, he held the branding iron against the burner and it slowly turned from black to dull red. "An open flame works better, but we make do, Miss Ellison, we make do."

His voice was eerily calm, but the look in his eye when he turned to face Sydney made her feel like she'd been plunged into a bathtub of ice cubes. Her skin alternately tingled and burned, and she must have made an involuntary move because Mo's hands weighted her more heavily into her chair. Fisher stepped closer, stopping just on the far side of the table, the branding iron uplifted in one hand.

She'd gotten herself into this mess trying to trick Fisher. Maybe the truth would work. "This isn't necessary, Mr. Fisher. You're right. I lied to you and I'm sorry. My boyfriend was shot to death Wednesday and I'm … I'm searching for his killer."

The door burst open, ricocheting off the flimsy wall. "Fire!" A short man with grizzled hair huffed on the threshold. "Fire, sir," he told Fisher. "In the northeast bunkhouse."

"That's beside the ammo storage," Mo said, releasing Sydney's shoulders. "If it spreads—"

Fisher nodded, seemingly unperturbed. "Take care of it. And find out how it started."

As Mo and the other man trotted from the room, Fisher looking after them with his brows drawn into a line, Sydney seized her chance. She grabbed the edge of the table and exploded up with all the power in her thighs, driving it into Fisher's midsection.

"Oof!" He doubled over, the branding iron flying out of his hand and rolling to within three feet of her.

With a lunge, she grabbed it, then dropped it as the heated iron seared her palm. She kicked it away from Fisher and sped toward the door as he struggled to his feet. Yanking the door open, she paused. All the action was to her left, where billows of acrid smoke drifted skyward. She didn't see any flames, but shouts for buckets and hoses drifted toward her. She clattered down the stairs and veered right, desperate to disappear before Fisher emerged. She ducked behind the nearest building, a shed with sliding metal doors secured by a combination lock.

"Daniel!"

Fisher's voice made her hold her breath. Risking a peep around the side of the shed, she saw him standing at the foot of the stairs, talking to a man she hadn't seen before. The way he pointed made it clear he was ordering the man to search for her. She scanned the compound, tempted by a gate in the fence just twenty-five yards away. As she was contemplating making a run for it, a uniformed man with a rifle slung over his shoulder exited a gatehouse no bigger than a port-a-potty and gazed toward the fire. Clearly he had no intention of deserting his post, not even to help fight the fire. Damn. In a half crouch, Sydney darted from behind the shed toward a line of trees. With any luck … Yes! A chain-link fence topped with three strands of barbed wire lay just beyond the trees.

She wasted precious moments running alongside the fence, hoping for another gate, any kind of hole. Nothing. She stopped at an area hidden by trees and fastened her fingers into the chain link. Damage from barbed wire would be easier to bear than the pain Fisher and his cohorts would inflict if they caught her. She started to climb, then stopped, dropping to the ground. Her fingers fumbled with her blouse buttons and she ripped it off, wrapping it around her right hand. Sticking the toe of one shoe into a link, she pushed herself up with the other foot, quickly scaling the eight foot fence. Luckily the barbed wire canted outwards, intended to keep people from getting in, not to stop them escaping. Using her blouse wrapped hand, she held onto a strand while balancing on the thick metal pipe that topped the fence. It looked like a long way down. She swayed. Pulling the topmost strand down as far as she could, she closed her eyes and jumped, swinging her legs up and over the wire. A barb clutched at her jeans, ripping them and the flesh beneath.

She landed hard, winded, one arm trapped beneath her. Her leg burned and it hurt to breathe. Maybe she'd broken a rib. The musty scent of rotting leaves and moldy earth made her sneeze. Voices coming closer goosed her to her feet.

"This way," a man shouted.

Wincing as pain jolted up her leg, Sydney hobbled toward the trees and undergrowth twenty yards away. The Imminent Revelation took their security seriously; they'd burned and cleared the brush around the compound. Shades of the Berlin Wall.

Reaching the shelter of the woods, she stopped to gulp air. She wasn't safe yet. She had to put distance between herself and the compound, had to find her car. Which way was it? She turned in a full circle, but had no feel for the direction she needed to travel. Away. Just get away. She took off at a trot. Even if she didn't find her car, with any luck she'd come across a road, be able to flag someone down.

The forest grew denser. Trees pushed in on all sides and brambles scratched her exposed skin. She'd been jogging for ten minutes when it occurred to her to put on her shirt. She was too scared to laugh at the picture she must present, hair straggling down her back, topless except for a flesh-colored bra, ripped jeans. Thrusting one arm into her sleeve, she was struggling with the other one when an arm snaked around her waist and a hand clamped over her mouth. Sydney instinctively wriggled and stamped, trying to kick back at whoever held her.

"Ssh!" a voice hissed in her ear.

She recognized her sister's scent. If she'd been asked what Reese smelled like, she couldn't have answered, but her unconscious brain identified her.

"Okay?" Reese asked.

Sydney nodded, and the hand dropped from her mouth. Reese was stronger than she would have expected, even knowing she was a workout fiend. She leaned toward Reese and sniffed, picking up hints of gasoline and smoke. Her eyes widened.

"You started that fire!"

Even though she'd whispered, Reese held a finger to her lips. "Molotov cocktail. Gas, a bottle, some rags … break out the marshmallows. Let's go."

Reese took off through the woods and Sydney followed, saplings slapping at her face and thorny weeds dragging at her hems. After another ten minutes, Reese ran as easily as before, and Sydney's breath came in painful gulps but she couldn't hear sounds of pursuit.

"We're clear, I think," Reese said, pausing beside a gnarled oak. She raked her short bangs back. A leaf fluttered to the ground.

"Where's my car?"

Reese pointed back the way they'd come. "We're leaving it."

"What?"

"We can't risk walking into an ambush. My Highlander's five minutes this way."

"But my car—" Sydney cut herself off. If the Imminent Revelation had been planning to brand her for sleeping with a Jew, what would they do to a woman who'd burned down part of their complex? "Lead on."

Not more than three minutes later they burst out of the woods fifty yards south of Reese's SUV. Parked on a grassy verge, it looked untouched. Reese motioned for Sydney to stay back as she approached it. After a brief inspection, she beckoned. Was she looking for bombs? Another habit she'd picked up in Kabul or Darfur, Sydney guessed, scrambling into the front passenger seat. Reese *thunk*ed the locks closed.

"Let's get out of here," Sydney said, looking anxiously over her shoulder. No sign of Fisher's gang.

"I'm way ahead of you." Reese threw the car in gear, wrenched it onto the road, and floored the accelerator.

30

Fidel

FIDEL MONTOYA EXITED THE limo at the high school in Fredrick, Maryland, smiling and waving, his narrowed eyes scanning the crowd assembled for the state-wide track meet. Jimmy emerged from the car after him, straightening a tie that was too damn loud. It looked like a box of Crayolas had vomited on it. Montoya averted his gaze. Teachers and students, some with signs reading *Vote for Montoya* or *A Vote for Montoya is a Vote for America* crowded to the edges of the sidewalk at Lee High School, hemming him in. Ragged cheers flared up as his supporters caught sight of him. He ran a finger around his collar. Damn it. He wasn't going to be scared away from campaigning by his close encounter with an assassin's bullet. The vote was just days away and polls showed him neck-and-neck with his opponent. And this was a high school, for God's sake, not a meeting of the John Birch Society. Sure, high schoolers went postal now and then and shot each other or their teachers, but he'd never heard of one assassinating a political figure. The tension in his shoulders eased and he waved again, striding confidently forward to shake hands with the principal. Not a bad-looking woman, for someone his own age. Playmate-of-the-Month tits under a straw-colored suit jacket and a full lower lip he could suck on for days. And she found him attractive. Montoya held her hand a moment longer than necessary, looking deep into her eyes. Jimmy coughed behind him.

In his peripheral vision, Montoya glimpsed a student approaching on his left. At least he looked like a student, with lank hair brushing his shoulders and a pimply face. He wore a black T-shirt and cargo pants with a heavy chain threaded through the belt loops. Two silver hoops pierced his eyebrow, and an earring with a grinning skull dangled almost to his shoulder. A backpack hung from one hand. A tattoo of a black widow in a web crawled up his right forearm and disappeared under his sleeve. *Loser*, Montoya thought, then made himself think of the kid as a voter. He might be eighteen. He released Principal McDermott's hand to follow her into the auditorium, thanking God that Jimmy had never gone in for that Goth look. He'd dyed his hair green once, and he wore butt-ugly ties, but—

"Congress-dick Montoya!"

He turned involuntarily at the sound of his name. The loser was within feet of him, digging a hand into his backpack. Montoya froze. Jimmy, several steps in front, turned to cut off the teen, but it was too late. Even as Montoya broke free of his trance and moved toward the building, which was only steps away, the kid hurled something.

God, not a grenade! Montoya grabbed the principal's arm—was he going to use her as a shield or thrust her behind him?—and ducked.

Splat.

"Gross, dude" and "totally putrid" drifted from the assembled students and teachers as the rotten egg smacked into Montoya's back. A hideous stink fouled the air. The assailant was hightailing it off school grounds, backpack thumping against his leg as he ran. He bumped into a nondescript man watching from the sidewalk and then disappeared between two houses.

"Randall Eubanks, one of my problem children," Principal McDermott said into Montoya's ear. "Are you okay?"

"Sure," Montoya said, forcing himself to smile although a murderous rage was hammering in his skull. The kid had made him look like a coward, a clown. He took a deep breath and shrugged out of his Hugo Boss jacket, holding it at arm's length. Jimmy took it without being asked, his face paler than usual. "But I think I'll need a new jacket. Maybe you have an LHS letter jacket I could borrow? I lettered in basketball, back in the day."

Laughs and cheers greeted his attempt at humor and Montoya smiled through his anger. He didn't know who made him madder, the real assassin or the punk kid who'd made him look like a fool. He tried to figure out when he might have a five-minute hole in his schedule to call Sydney Ellison and find out what she'd learned.

31

Sydney

"IT'S NOT THE IMMINENT Revelation," Sydney told Fidel Montoya when he got hold of her ten minutes after she and Reese arrived home from the compound. She hadn't yet had time to change or think about her next move.

"How can you be sure?" Montoya asked in a whisper, and Sydney imagined he'd ducked into a hallway or restroom to make a quick call between campaign stops. "Those letters —"

"Take my word for it, Fidel. If these guys wanted to kill you, they'd do it themselves." She gave him a quick rundown of her encounter with Fisher.

"Jesus!" Montoya was silent for a moment. "What are you thinking, then? Who will you talk to next?"

"I'll be fine. Thanks for asking," she said drily. "And my car was two years old, after all. I might as well get a new one."

"Hey, get off my ass, Syd," Montoya snapped. "I'm sorry they roughed you up, but it's my life we're talking about here." His voice softened. "Look, fax the map to my aide and I'll have one of my guys pick up your car. Okay?"

"Thanks."

"So, what's your plan? Make it snappy … I've only got thirty seconds before my interview."

Maybe she'd tune in to the five o'clock news and see what he had to say, Sydney thought. She'd bet he wasn't this peremptory with the reporter. "Has anyone close to you died this year, in mysterious or unexplained circumstances?" She explained the logic behind the question.

"You think someone's got it in for the Montoya clan, that someone's killing us off one by one?" The congressman snorted with disbelief. When she didn't rise to the bait, he was silent a moment and then said, "My mother died in March, but since she was ninety-four and had been in a nursing home for a decade, I don't think we can call that a suspicious death."

"Anyone else?"

"No. My brother's got colon cancer, but he's not dead yet. No relative that I know of has tumbled off a convenient cliff, dropped dead of some unidentified poison, or drowned in the bathtub. You're thinking this is personal?"

Was that skepticism or worry in his voice? "It's certainly possible. I'd been thinking the hit must be a political thing, but now I'm wondering. I'm going to talk to Jimmy."

"Jimmy? My son?"

"Yeah. I understand he owes some people who might like to see him come into his inheritance sooner rather than later."

A ten-second pause followed her comment, and Sydney wondered if Montoya was trying to assimilate a new and unpalatable idea or if he was thinking of a way to head her off. "He'll be at the stables to-morrow morning early if you want to catch up with him," he sur-prised her by saying. "Sambrano's. Off 97."

"Thanks. Did you know Senator Fewell?"

She sensed his confusion. "Armand? Of course. Tragic, what hap-pened, a great loss for Amer—wait. You think his death is connected to this?"

She gave him points for catching on quickly. "Maybe. Were you close?"

"Not really. He batted for the other team, you know. Republicans. He was a leader in the Black Caucus, more honest than most, I hear. He died in a hunting accident. How could that be connected to some-one trying to shoot me?"

It really was all about him. Jason didn't count. "I don't know that it is, but I'm checking all the angles I can think of," she replied. "I want to talk to Fewell's wife and his hunting buddy."

"I can call Emma for you, pave the way. I'll try to set it up for to-morrow—the Fewells aren't far from the stable."

"Did you sleep with her?"

Sydney's suspicion seemed to amuse or flatter Montoya, although he expostulated, "For God's sake, Syd. I don't sleep with every attrac-tive woman who crosses my path. Besides, Emma Fewell's not my type."

"Too smart?" Sydney couldn't resist the barb.

"Too old. Too religious." A murmur of voices suggested someone had claimed his attention, and his tone was more curt when he spoke again. "Who else are you going to harass?"

"Your wife. Your uncle-in-law."

If she'd hoped to push him off-balance, she failed. "Matvei Utkin? Why? I hardly know the—ah, you're thinking he has a crew of contract killers. He might, at that." Montoya's tone was thoughtful. "Be careful with Utkin. He's the real deal. Katya sees him on occasion, but the guy makes me want to sit with my back to the wall. Don't go alone, and let someone know where you're going to be."

"This sudden concern for my welfare is touching," Sydney said acidly.

He laughed. "I like you, Syd, I do. I don't want to hear they've fished you out of the Anacostia with a bullet hole between your beautiful eyes. Besides, you're my best hope of finding out who's behind this. Don't get yourself killed." A ghost of a laugh echoed as he hung up.

Sydney lowered her cell phone, frowning. Fidel Montoya was something of an enigma. She couldn't afford to forget that he was, at heart, a politician, experienced at spinning six or seven different versions of a story depending on what he wanted from his audience. It looked like he wanted her to find the person or organization that had hired a hit man to kill him. But was that all he was after?

FIXED HABITS COULD BE fatal, as anyone who'd ever been through a counter-terrorism or counter-kidnapping course knew, but people fell into them as easily as rolling out of bed. Even if they'd been trained, they tumbled back into their ruts after a week or two of mixing things up. Habit was a force on par with gravity, in Paul's opinion. And he could tell that Montoya had never been encouraged to vary his routine. Tonight would be no different. After the congressman gave a speech at the American Bar Association's banquet, Montoya would walk back to his tiny apartment, a converted garage near the congressional offices where many congressmen, senators, and staffers rented apartments or rooms. Many of them shared. Thankfully, Montoya didn't have a roommate, although a cute blonde slept over from time to time. It was only six blocks from the hotel ballroom and the weather was good.

Paul waited in a stinking alley along Montoya's route, behind a restaurant and a dry cleaner. The smell of putrefying enchiladas wafted from the dumpster behind Tres Hombres. Just his luck the dumpsters hadn't been emptied in a week and the sun had baked their contents to a toxic sludge. He might never eat Mexican again. But he'd reconnoitered the terrain between the hotel and the apartment that afternoon and selected the alley as the best spot for an ambush. With any luck, Montoya'd be a bit drunk, easy to accost and shoot. The newspapers would write it up as another mugging and the cops would waste time bringing in the usual suspects. It might not be an "accident" in the sense the client intended, but it was close enough for government work. No one would think to call it an assassination. With small, precise twists, he fitted the silencer onto his weapon's muzzle.

A scuffle from his right caught Paul's attention and a scrawny tail slipped between two dumpsters. Rats. In Bangkok, they'd literally crawled over his head as he infiltrated the home of a rich VC sympathizer by wading through the khlong, breathing through a reed-like tube. Rotting fruit and God knows what else had bobbed around him on the dark water the locals used as both toilet and wash tub. The rats' claws had scraped his scalp as they'd leaped from his head to a pier littered with droppings from the morning's market. Paul shook his head sharply. He'd been thinking a lot about 'Nam lately, more than he had since his first couple years back, and it was distracting him. His pop's situation was distracting him. The gunshot wound—swollen and aching—was distracting him. Distractions landed you in prison. He needed to goddamn focus. He glanced at his watch. Any time now.

Footsteps approached. Paul tensed, holding his gun ready against his thigh. The steps stuttered to a halt and a shadow appeared at the mouth of the alley. Backlit by a streetlamp, the figure lifted a bottle to its mouth and guzzled. Not Montoya. Paul pressed himself back against the bricks, wincing as he jarred his injured shoulder. The clink of glass on concrete and a slurred curse told him the bum's bottle was empty.

Good, maybe he'd wander off in search of more oblivion. On the thought, the man slumped to the ground, half in and half out of the alley, and began to snore, one hand reaching toward the empty bottle.

Shit. Paul eased away from the wall and paced silently toward the man. Maybe he could roust him, get him to move along before Montoya showed up. Wet snores issued from the drunk's slack mouth, and he didn't stir.

As he studied the man, Paul felt his irritation drain away. Jug ears stuck out from beneath his navy watch cap, and a half inch of grizzled stubble roughened his jaw and concave cheeks. He looked about seventy but could have been as young as fifty, Paul figured. Life on the streets was no fountain of youth. The sour-sweet odor of cheap bourbon floated off him, reminding Paul of the one time he'd seen his pop drunk, the day after they buried Paul's mother. Let the old guy sleep it off, he told himself. He wasn't any threat as a witness. As quietly as he'd crept forward, Paul melted back into the shadows.

Taking slow, deep breaths, he slowed his heartbeat and respiration, sliding into the meditative state that enabled him to wait for hours, when necessary, to ambush a target. He wasn't sure how many minutes had passed when more footsteps sounded. His abdominal muscles clenched as he became fully alert instantaneously. Montoya? No. At least two people, maybe three, moving faster than Montoya was likely to walk. Paul relaxed but held himself still, secure in the alley's shadows. They'd pass by and—

"He's here."

The voice, young, taut with excitement, jarred Paul. Were they looking for him? How had they known—? His hand tightened around the gun.

"Fucking drunk." This voice was higher-pitched, also buzzing with anticipation.

They weren't looking for him; they were after the bum, for some reason. A meaty thunk was followed by a groan and a confused, "Wha—?"

The pallid slap of flesh on unresisting flesh told Paul that the teens—he could discern two figures dancing around the homeless man—were beating the man. Before he could decide whether or not to intervene, the first voice said, "You got the lighter fluid?"

"Oh, yeah." A sloshing of liquid and the scent of kerosene drifted to Paul. A giggle.

"No, no!" The terror-stricken denial came from the drunk, struggling to cover his head with his arms as the teenager directed a stream of fluid at him from a rectangular can.

Paul's mind flashed to the water buffalo his squad had set alight one morning at dawn. He'd only been in country two weeks and they'd lost three men overnight, including their lieutenant, when VC jumped them outside a small village. Daylight and a two-ship of A-10 Warthogs flying CAS had chased away the VC, and Paul had never been sure whether the buffalo was revenge or celebration. All he remembered was the sting of the gasoline in his nose as Dawson—he'd bought it only two days later, torn in half by a Bouncing Betty—doused the dumb animal with gasoline stores from their Jeep and Manny tossed a lighted match. The agonized bellows as the buffalo went up in a sheet of flame, stumbled to its knees, and then staggered, lowing, into a rice paddy with a hiss of steam still haunted him. As did the laughter.

The click of a lighter and the flicker of the small, blue flame pulled Paul forward the three strides necessary. His field of view collapsed to a narrow tunnel, with the old man's tormentors at the far end. As the boy closest to him half turned, alerted not by any sound Paul made but by instinct, he brought his arm up and fired. *Phut.* The alley's rough brick walls absorbed the sound of the silenced shot. The bullet ploughed through the boy's temple and he sagged to the ground.

The other teen, standing near the mouth of the alley, hesitated. In the sweeping light of a car's headlights, Paul read the evil intent on his face. The hand holding the lighter started to move. Without remorse, he raised the gun and fired twice, hitting the boy in the neck and face. Surprise and pain glazed the boy's eyes as the force of the bullets slammed him back, onto the sidewalk. He dropped the lighter as he fell, and his body smothered the flame.

Paul stared down at the bodies for a moment, alert for movement. A buttery leather bomber jacket on one, crocodile boots on the other, a gleam of platinum on an outflung wrist … rich kids out for kicks. *Rot in hell*. His unusually savage reaction startled him, and he turned away.

"They tried to … they wanted to …" the bum babbled. He fumbled with his grungy windbreaker, trying to shed the flammable garment. His hands were shaking so badly, from the liquor or fear, that he couldn't work the zipper. He wasn't looking at Paul, and Paul was certain he'd be unable to describe him, would have only a blurred memory of the evening's events by the time he dried out in some holding cell.

He leaned forward to help with the zipper, but the old guy's eyes widened in fear and he crab-walked backward. "Get away from me, mother fucker! Don't think I don't know. You're all in it." Spittle flecked at the corners of his mouth.

In what? Paul backed off a step.

"Get 'em off me!" The drunk began to scratch viciously at his arms and scalp. "They're all over me. Don't touch me!"

Understanding dawned. The DTs.

Hurrying footsteps approached and a woman screamed. A voice Paul recognized said, "Christ almighty! What's going on?"

Montoya. Shit. This mission was FUBAR. He was really losing it. With one last look at the bum, Paul loped down the alley to the door of the dry cleaning shop he'd jimmied earlier. Voices, sharp with excitement, floated from the front of the alley as he slipped inside the darkened shop that smelled of starch and chemical cleaners. He snapped off his latex gloves and shoved them in his pocket. Two deep breaths settled the last of his frustration. He eased himself out the front door onto the sidewalk, deserted at this hour except for a few people outside a bar two blocks down. He sucked in a deep breath, this time just to appreciate the clean air untainted by rotting food or chemicals, and then strode away from the late revelers and Montoya, headed for the Mall with its several Metro stops. It wouldn't do to use the one closest to the scene: if the cops were on top of things, they'd check the security videos.

At almost midnight, the air had cooled and the slight breeze felt good on his damp brow. Still, he was uncomfortably warm and the wound in his shoulder pulsed as if alive. Fever. He was sweating because he had a fever. He walked on, eyes searching the street for a likely sewer grate, saying a quiet "Good evening" to a young couple he passed. He wasn't much given to analyzing himself, but the irony of a killer shooting two killers and feeling righteous about it hit him as he walked. He didn't usually feel anything after a hit, not good, not bad, maybe just a twinge of satisfaction if it went well. What a lawyer felt when he won a case or a bricklayer felt when he finished a project. But tonight ... what he did for a living was surgical compared to what those psychos were planning to do, had already done, according to news reports. Setting people on fire ... Jesus!

He knew he should get rid of the gun and silencer, but when he spotted the gap in the curb he'd been searching for, he hesitated. He didn't have time to acquire yet another weapon. And the silencer was custom, hard to come by. There were no sounds of pursuit—he'd chance it. Cutting across the Mall, almost deserted at this hour, his steps slowed involuntarily as he neared the Vietnam Memorial. An uncompromising wall of black, the monument shimmered in the scant moonlight.

Something primeval rippled down Paul's spine. Despite frequent visits to DC, he'd never come to the Vietnam Memorial. Now it loomed in his peripheral vision. It dared him. He swung to face the wall and it glowered blackly. Slowly, slowly, he approached. Stopping a bare eighteen inches away, he could almost see his reflection. Almost, but not quite. He didn't see the men whose names scarred the polished granite either. Dawson's name would be there, and Manny's. Lieutenant Dixon, Jesus Gutierrez, and that boy from Kansas—Mathieson. Other names and faces churned in his head. Men Paul thought he'd forgotten. They were nothing but memories and names chiseled into stone. They weren't *here*. That print that was so popular, the one with the vet touching his hand to the memorial and the soldiers in the wall connecting to him—it wasn't like that. He was the only one here.

Warmth flushed through him, sending tingles to his fingertips. He'd survived it all, he thought, recognizing the savage emotion that rose in him as exultation. He was alive. Goddamned fucking alive. These men, they'd never left 'Nam. Coming home in a body bag didn't count. A capricious gust of wind knocked over a tribute of flowers in a metal vase. The clink roused Paul and he righted it, collecting the silk poppies and restoring them gently to the vase. He hesitated a moment, then turned his back on the wall and strode across the dark expanse of the Mall to the Metro station.

33

Sydney
Sunday, August 6

REESE WOKE SYDNEY AT seven o'clock the next morning. "Church starts at eight," she said. "Better get ready."

Half awake, Sydney blinked at her sister standing at her bedside, bony-slim in a cami and undies that doubled as sleepwear, freckles standing out on her chest. She had six-pack abs, Sydney noted ruefully, and some serious biceps. She wanted to complain about being wakened, but went with "You go to church?"

Reese nodded without a hint of self-consciousness. "I do. I make a point of trying different churches wherever I am. I've been to Baptist services and Catholic ones, to evangelical revivals, cowboy church, and Quaker meetings. Don't ask me why, because I don't know. It's something I do. I'm not leaving you here alone, so up and at 'em." Reese turned away, clearly considering the conversation finished.

More intrigued by a side of Reese she'd never guessed existed than annoyed by the early wake-up call, Sydney slid out of bed.

St. James Episcopal Church was only a half mile from the townhouse, and they walked to it. Lowering clouds like bursts of diesel exhaust locked in a mugginess that dampened Sydney's skin before they even reached the church. The interior was a cool relief. Reese selected a pew in the back, and they seated themselves just as the priest and his acolytes started up the aisle to the turgid strains of "A Mighty Fortress Is Our God." Sydney wished the organist would speed up so the hymn wasn't so dirge-like. At Nana Linn's funeral, it had sounded like a promise. She sang. Reese didn't.

Once seated for the lessons, Sydney looked around. Only a handful of elderly parishioners, mostly women, worshiped in twos and threes at this early service. She pegged a young couple half a dozen rows up as tourists, and briefly eyed the sixtyish man across the aisle studying the bulletin before deciding he had recently lost someone important to him, probably a wife since he was alone, and was searching for a way to make sense of his loss. She couldn't pinpoint why she thought that about him; he struck her as both hesitant and purposeful. Maybe it was something to do with the shaft of violet light from a stained glass depiction of the Last Supper that gave his jowly face a melancholy tinge.

Throughout the service, Sydney tried to worship, tried to ease herself into the familiar cadence of the liturgy Nana Linn had loved, but her mind kept returning to Jason and the events since his murder. She hoped the police would let her attend his funeral in New York. Not until the priest led the small congregation in saying "O Lamb of God, that takest away the sins of the world, grant us thy peace" did her heart and mind focus on the altar. *Grant me your peace, Father,* she prayed, going forward to take Communion. Reese stayed in the pew.

By the time they'd said the Prayer of Thanksgiving and sung the recessional hymn, she felt better, lighter.

When they left the church, the sun was rising and, with it, the humidity. Sydney felt the strands of hair along her face begin to curl. It was going to be a scorcher, the kind of day that made moving to northern Michigan seem like a good plan. She wanted to ask Reese what she'd gotten out of the service but didn't want to presume on their new relationship, with its foundation that felt no more stable than a bog. She didn't know where Reese's hot spots were, what she might consider prying or even criticism. Sydney did know that she wanted the chance to see if she and Reese could bridge the crevasse that had kept them apart for most of their adult lives. It was strange, she mused, keeping up with Reese's long-legged stride. If someone had asked her a week ago if she cared if she ever spoke to her sister again, she'd have said no. Now, though, she cared. A little bit.

They reached the townhouse and stood just outside the front gate. Mrs. Colwell peered at them from behind the lace curtain at her front window. The curtain dropped back into place when Sydney waved. A swell of irritation rolled through her, but she stifled it. Reese put her thoughts into words.

"Nosy old bat."

"She's probably lonely," Sydney said, trying to be charitable.

When Reese slanted a brow at her, she grinned. "No, you're right. She's a nosy old bat."

"You know how to find Jimmy's stables?" Reese asked.

Sydney nodded. "Yes. And I've got directions to Emma Fewell's place, too. Montoya texted that she's willing to see us this afternoon."

"Then let's change and saddle up," Reese said, "and go brace Junior. I'll bet he's just as full of shit as his daddy."

"No bet."

34

Sydney

"**THIS PLACE HAS TOO** much shit," Reese complained, scraping her sneaker in the grass to wipe off muck. "There are many reasons I hate horses, but horseshit is at the top of the list, closely followed by 'they bite' and 'they kick' and 'they stink.'"

Sydney gave her a sympathetic smile, in her element surrounded by green fields bounded by miles of white fencing with horses grazing. *Sambrano's Elite Training* read a small sign fronting the barn. *Tours daily*. The sun glossed the chestnut, bay, and palomino hides in the distance. Tails swished, flicking away the ubiquitous flies. One horse rolled in the grass, kicking her legs in the air, and Sydney smiled. Always nervous around horses, Reese had preferred softball and track, but Sydney had taken riding lessons from the time she was eight until she graduated from high school.

"It's a horse farm. Horse shit is part of the deal," she said.

"I'll wait," Reese said, propping herself against the hood of her Highlander and crossing her arms over her chest. "You can tackle this one on your own."

If Reese was willing to let her interview Jimmy Montoya alone, her fear of horses must be more intense than she'd let on, Sydney reflected. Reese's need to accompany her wouldn't be due to safety concerns this time—just to nosiness. Prying into others' lives was the equivalent of an addict shooting up for her, and she'd do a lot for that high. Sydney thought about her sister's adventures in war zones and the union exposé she'd written before turning to true crime. At least most of the murderers she talked to now were already behind bars.

Sydney crossed the barn's threshold and stepped into her past. The twilight gloom inside, with dust motes swirling in a shaft of sunlight; the smell of horse, hay, and liniment; and the soft whickers and thuds as the large animals moved about in their stalls transported her back to her days as a horse-crazy adolescent. Now, breathing in the familiar scent, she felt the old excitement rising, the love nurtured by reading *King of the Wind*, *Misty of Chincoteague*, and the Black Stallion series. Maybe she should take up riding again. She could even buy a horse, board it someplace like this ...

"Are you here for the tour? The next one is in twenty minutes." A friendly voice pulled Sydney out of her reverie.

She looked around to see a young woman with an open face, red hair in braids, and the bow-legged stance of a serious rider. Wearing jeans and work boots liberally spattered with Reese's favorite substance, she carried a shovel and a bucket.

"Actually, I'm looking for Jimmy Montoya. I was told he'd be here."

"Jimmy? He's watching Ed work Banger. That way." The girl pointed with the shovel handle to a door at the far end of the long corridor separating two rows of stalls.

"Who's Banger?"

The girl smiled, revealing a gap between her two front teeth. "Bang the Drum. Jimmy's Derby hopeful."

"Does he have a chance?"

The girl shrugged. "They all have a chance." She nodded goodbye to Sydney and nudged open an empty stall.

The scrape of the girl's shovel followed Sydney down the main corridor. An inquisitive gray accosted her by straining his neck to its full length and bumping her with his nose. "Whoa, you're a pushy one," she said.

He snorted and lowered his head to snuffle in the vicinity of her pockets. "Sorry, boy. No treats today." She wished she'd packed her pockets with carrots and apple bits.

He gazed at her reproachfully, his white forelock falling into his dark, liquid eyes. Giving his neck a final pat, she moved on. The far end of the barn opened on a paddock with a couple of leggy horses milling around. Beyond the fenced enclosure was a half-mile track, also ringed in gleaming white, where two men stood watching a pair of horses, jockeys high in the stirrups, canter toward the post. Sydney had never spent any time around racing—her interest had been in jumpers—and she watched with fascination as the jockeys reined in the horses and then let them go at a signal from one of the men. The horses flew around the track, hooves thudding up clods of dirt. Slowly but surely, the horse on the outside, a tall chestnut, pulled ahead of his rival, galloping past the men leaning on the rail. Judging from the way Jimmy Montoya was jumping and shouting, the winner was Banger.

Walking over, Sydney observed Jimmy as he high-fived the man beside him—Ed Sambrano, the trainer, maybe?—and stroked his colt's nose when the jockey brought him to the rail. He looked like a less dynamic copy of his father. He was a couple of inches shorter and thirty pounds lighter, with his father's dark hair but none of his air of command. He was dressed like a cross between the Marlboro man and a Ralph Lauren model in a four-hundred-dollar pair of jeans and a turquoise polo shirt. He sported hand-tooled ostrich-skin cowboy boots, and Sydney would have bet her entire trust fund that he'd never ridden a horse in his life.

"D'ja see that?" Jimmy startled her by asking. He'd turned to face her as Sambrano drifted off to give instructions to the jockey. "He was tearing up the track!" The young man struck her as callow and younger than his twenty-five years.

"He looked fast," Sydney said.

"Fast? He's greased lightning. Put your money on him for the Derby right now," Jimmy recommended, bringing a hand to his mouth and gnawing on the edge of his thumb. "You can't lose."

Unless he breaks a leg or gets colic or just feels "off" on the big day, or if there's a faster horse in the race, Sydney thought. Aloud, she said, "Thanks for the tip. I'm Sydney Ellison." She held out her hand and he shook it, his grip sweaty but firm.

"Jimmy Montoya. Nice to meet you." He looked her over without much interest and she doubted he could have described her outside of "white female between thirty and fifty." Clearly the horses, or gambling on horses, held his attention to the exclusion of everything else.

"Is he yours?" Sydney nodded toward the colt. The sun warmed her shoulders as she propped her forearms against the top rail, imitating Jimmy's posture.

"Yup. Bang the Drum. Out of Ophelia's Heaven by Dancing Admiral, a descendant of War Admiral, you know."

"Wow." That seemed like the response Jimmy was looking for. Sydney paused, expecting him to ask if she had a horse being trained by Sambrano, but Jimmy's absorption with himself was total. "I know your dad," she said finally.

That earned her a sideways look. "Yeah, well, lots of people know my dad," he said, fixing his eyes on a ladybug crawling along the fence rail.

"Do you think he'll win on Tuesday?"

"Sure. He always wins, whatever it takes." The words could've been bitter, but were delivered in a monotone that made it impossible for her to assess his feelings. Clearly Jimmy hadn't been bitten by the political bug, despite his position with his father's campaign. Sydney began to suspect that his job was nepotism, pure and simple. Either that or Montoya wanted to keep an eye on him. Jimmy put a finger in front of the ladybug and it crawled onto his nail. He watched it with the fascination of an eight-year-old.

"Politics is like horse-racing, don't you think?" Sydney asked, making a last ditch effort to snag his attention.

"How so?" He turned to face her squarely for the first time, waving his hand to dislodge the ladybug.

"Well, you have a field of contenders and everyone studies their records, trying to figure out who's likely to win. And you have gamblers betting on the outcome in each case. Folks put their money on a horse to win, hoping to cash in, and investors or PACs put money on a candidate, expecting a certain return if he or she ends up in office. And sometimes trainers or campaign managers resort to dirty tricks of one kind or another to ensure their 'horse' wins: giving a rival too much to drink right before a race to slow him down, drugs, negative campaigning, putting a hit out on an opponent." Sydney held her breath, afraid she'd been too explicit.

Jimmy's eyes blazed with interest. "Hey, I never thought about it before, but you're right. Wait'll I tell my dad. He's always trying to get me away from the horses, keep me from gambling. Makes me trek around with him to fundraisers and speeches and factory tours. Boring shit. Wait'll I tell him we're really in the same business." He laughed. "What'd you say your name was again?"

Before she could answer, a gruff voice with a slight accent sounded from behind her. "Hey, Jimmy, long time no see."

From the way Jimmy's face whitened, she assumed the newcomer wasn't a friend. Casually, she turned around as two men approached. The man in front was younger, about her age and height, with expertly barbered hair and beard, an expensive tweed coat over dark green slacks, and a pair of horn-rimmed glasses. He looked like the dean of a prep school. The older man trailing him looked more like Sydney's idea of a mob enforcer: burly, bull-necked, and with a suspicious bulge under his left arm.

"Mr. Avdonin," Jimmy stammered. "I've been meaning to—tell Uncle Mat that—"

The men had drawn level with them by this time and Avdonin studied Sydney with dark, detached eyes. "Does your fiancée know about this rendezvous, Jimbo? A stable. At first glance, not as convenient as a Motel 6, and yet there's something about a stable that makes a suitable setting for infidelity. Pheromones in the air. Stallions 'covering' mares. It's primal. There was a Tom Hanks movie some years back…never mind. I'm faithful to my wife, married nineteen years next Wednesday, but I can definitely see the attraction." He gave Sydney a considering look, like she was a Thoroughbred mare, she thought, and he a prospective bidder. "Definitely. But if she's going to rob the cradle, surely she can do better than a loser like you?"

"I'm not—" Sydney started, just as Jimmy said, "We just met—"

Avdonin acknowledged his mistake with an uplifted hand. "Ah. My apologies. Perhaps you'd excuse us then, miss? We have some business to conduct with Mr. Montoya." He scanned the fields behind Jimmy, apparently taking Sydney's departure for granted. "I saw your fiancée, the lovely Emily, in the newspaper this morning. At the American Bar Association ball last night. In the photo, she was dancing with her father. Nice. I assume you were there, too? My wife really liked that gown she was wearing, the white one with the ruffle. It looks like she's doing much better. The wedding's coming up, right? It would be a shame if she were to suffer another accident that would make it impossible to walk down the aisle. Or walk again ever." He shook his head in mock sorrow at the thought.

It was like listening to him discipline a student, Sydney thought, unable to get the image of him as a prep school headmaster out of her head.

"But we don't need to consider such an eventuality, do we, because I'm sure you're going to come up with the half mil you owe ... very, very soon." His eyes drilled into Jimmy's and beads of sweat pimpled the younger man's brow. A horse neighed loudly from the barn.

A half a million? That was serious money.

"Leave Em—I don't want—Banger's how I'm going to raise the money, Mr. Avdonin," Jimmy said, his voice a pathetic mix of enthusiasm and fear. "You can tell Uncle Mat he's a sure bet for the Derby. I'll be able to pay it all when he wins. And I'll keep up with the vig—"

"The Derby's not til next May, you moron," Avdonin snapped, the veneer of civility cracking like a thinly iced pond under a snowmobile. "Your uncle isn't going to wait nine months for his money. Your being his great-nephew isn't going to get in the way of business. Maybe your daddy can pull the half mil from one of his campaign coffers."

A touch on Sydney's shoulder made her turn. The burly man who'd accompanied Avdonin jerked his head toward the stable, suggesting she follow his boss's advice. A piece of blood-dotted tissue stuck to his stubbly jaw. Sydney's eyes fixed on it as she debated whether to do the smart thing—return to the stable and let Jimmy fend for himself—or the stupid thing and ask these men how badly Matvei Utkin wanted his money back. Bad enough to put a contract on Fidel Montoya, for instance? For all she knew, one of these men had killed Jason.

The thought brought a flush of anger to her skin. Her expression must have telegraphed something, because the man took her upper arm in a bruising grip and gave her a shove.

"Syd! You done *yet*?" Reese called from the barn, pointing at her watch. "You know we promised Ella and Shonda we wouldn't be late this time." Her manner and voice suggested she was an impatient friend or even lover. She held her cell phone up, as if to indicate a text from the fictional girlfriends, but Sydney saw it as a warning to Matvei Utkin's men. One touch and the police could be on their way. The bruiser dropped her arm, giving his boss a doubtful look.

All three men turned to stare at Reese. Avdonin's eyes narrowed at the sight of the cell phone. His sidekick unbuttoned his jacket but stopped there when Avdonin gave a slight headshake. Jimmy gawked, his mouth hanging open, and shot a look at Sydney.

"I got lots of horse photos," Reese yelled. "That one behind you is my fave. I just love gray horses." She steadied the phone, ostensibly to photograph a horse prancing past, but Sydney was sure she'd managed to get Avdonin and his sidekick in the frame. She felt an unwilling spark of admiration for her sister's tactics.

"Coming!" Sydney called in reply. "Nice meeting you gentlemen," she said, repressing the urge to rub the tender spot on her arm. "Jimmy, maybe we can talk more about your horse another time?"

He nodded, looking between her and Avdonin and Reese, completely out of his league. "Uh, sure."

She felt Avdonin's eyes stabbing her back as she made her way up the slight rise to Reese. He might look like an academic, but she had no doubt he'd order her death without blinking. She had to force herself not to break into a trot as she neared her sister.

"That'll teach me to let you go off on your own," Reese said, tossing Sydney the keys. "You drive. I leave you alone for ten seconds and turn around to find you hobnobbing with Misha Avdonin. He's Matvei Utkin's top man, you know."

"I gathered. How do you know him?" They buckled up and Sydney backed out and pointed the SUV down the mile-long drive.

"I don't personally know him, but his name's come up in conversation, especially when I was working on the union story. One of my sources got a bullet through the elbow. He told the police it was a hunting accident, but he quit talking to me after it happened. Avdonin's name was floated."

Rolling pastures, gnarled oaks, and two colts racing each other flashed past. Sidney filled Reese in on her conversation with Jimmy, adding, "So now we have proof that Jimmy Montoya has a relationship of sorts with Matvei Utkin, and that he probably knows a killer or two. We also know that Great-uncle Mat is impatient to get his money, so even if Jimmy didn't try to have his dad killed, Utkin might have. Probably did. There'd be no percentage in his killing Jimmy, but if he could arrange for Jimmy to get his inheritance soon ... "

"Possible," Reese said noncommittally.

Sydney took her eyes off the road long enough to look at her sister's unrevealing profile. Reese's lack of enthusiasm for her hypothesis stung. "Okay, what's your theory, then? If not Utkin or Jimmy, then who?"

Reese adjusted her sunglasses and said, "Don't get your panties in a wad. I didn't say it wasn't Utkin or Jimmy, although you said Jimmy didn't even blink when you mentioned people putting hits on politicians, so I'm thinking that's a point in his favor. He doesn't strike me as the deep, devious sort who could keep a straight face when confronted with something like that."

"Unlikely," Sydney reluctantly agreed. "Avdonin mentioned a fiancée, Emily Something. Know anything about her?"

Reese turned her head and gave Sydney a look over the top of her glasses. "You really do live under a rock, don't you?"

"Bite me."

Reese laughed. "Emily Favier, daughter of Montoya's best friend and chief of staff, John Favier. Longtime friends of the Montoya family. Emily and Jimmy grew up together and got engaged, oh, eighteen months ago. The wedding was supposed to be in May, but she cut herself on a rafting trip in Texas—some sort of freak thing, sheet metal in the river—and almost died. As if that wasn't enough tragedy, her mother was killed just a couple weeks later. Hit and run. Emily's been rehabbing somewhere in the area and I think the wedding's back on for Thanksgiving or Christmas time—the holidays, at any rate. It's going to be family only, not the extravaganza that was originally planned."

"Poor girl. I did read about that," Sydney said, negotiating past a moving van that rattled the SUV with its wake.

"Are you thinking she might figure in this somehow?" Reese asked, considering the idea.

"I don't see how, other than as a means for Avdonin and his thugs to keep Jimmy in line. Do you think they'd really hurt her?"

"In a heartbeat," Reese said. "Utkin's crew is famous for it. They don't damage the gambler—it might get in the way of his ability to pay them back. They hurt someone he loves. Surely even you heard about Donetta Hernandez, that boxer's wife, getting acid thrown in her face? That was Utkin. Her hubby didn't go down like he was supposed to, take a dive as was apparently prearranged. Donetta paid for his inconvenient attack of conscience or pride."

Sydney felt slightly sick, remembering the photos of the young Mrs. Hernandez after the attack. She'd been blinded in one eye and had most of her nose and her right cheek eaten away by the acid. She swallowed hard. "What exit do I take? We're due at Emma Fewell's in half an hour."

35

Paul

PAUL'S SUNDAY STARTED WITH following Sydney Ellison to church and went downhill from there. The remains of a dream refused to dissipate, leaving him unable to focus on the homily or his target. He'd dreamed about his pop, dreamed he was on fire, flailing about in a long nightshirt like the kind Scrooge wore in movie versions of *A Christmas Carol*. Nobody wore those anymore. But his pop had one on in the dream and it burned with a clean orange flame before he dove into a rice paddy. A flaming swan. *Hiss*. Paul put twenty dollars in the collection plate when it passed.

"We have sinned against you in thought, word, and deed," the congregation mumbled in unison.

It wasn't the thought of confessing his sins, so much, that had kept him away from church since his return from 'Nam. It was the realization that he and God didn't have much in common. No meeting place. He'd set out to serve his country four decades ago and become a killer. It was as simple as that. He didn't figure God had much to say to a killer, and an unrepentant one at that. And he sure as heck didn't have anything to say to God.

He blocked out most of the service by reading the announcements in the bulletin and thinking about his two uncompleted tasks. Rarely had an assignment carried with it this much frustration. He'd hoped to have a shot at Ellison that morning, but the woman with her complicated the scenario. The way she held herself, her fitness and alertness, suggested she might be a pro, a hired bodyguard. Studying the rangy woman seated beside his target, Paul recognized he might have to take her out, too. It might be impossible to get Ellison without eliminating her bodyguard. He was prepared to do that. The woman was a combatant. Fair game. Paul bent over, pretending to search the floor for something, as they passed him on the way out of the church.

He trailed them part of the way back to the townhouse, then broke off. Montoya was the primary target and time was running out. He wouldn't get paid if Montoya were still breathing come election day. He made his way back toward his target's Capitol Hill garage apartment, wanting to be in place before Montoya showed up at the café. Habits. Paul shook his head. The past two Sundays, Montoya had wandered down to the café at noon, bought a newspaper, and read it while eating his brunch at an outdoor table. Once he'd gone into the office for a couple of hours and once he'd met friends for dinner. Paul was prepared to follow up on any opportunity that presented itself today.

None did. Despite stationing himself on a bench in the small park across from Montoya's place, Paul never saw the man. He did the *New York Times* crossword, read for a bit, and watched a pair of sparrows fight over a hot dog bun. No Montoya. His shoulder began to throb; when he'd drained it that morning, he'd noted streaks of red shooting from the wound. It hurt like hell now and he swallowed four aspirins dry. He knew he would have to give in and see a doctor within a day or so.

By early afternoon, he was contemplating his options. Did he dare knock and force his way into the man's house in broad daylight? He'd made that approach work once before, in a suburban neighborhood with a man mowing his yard right next door. His vibrating cell phone cut into his planning.

"Paul, it's me. Pop. I think something's wrong with Moira." His father sounded lucid, but a cold chill ran down Paul's spine.

"What do you mean, Pop?" he asked, keeping his voice low so the two young skateboarders practicing tricks in front of him wouldn't hear. Their wheels rasped over the concrete, making it hard to make out his father's words.

"She's not moving."

"Where is she? What happened?"

His pop's voice became uncertain, perhaps in response to his sharper tone. "She's ... after I ... "

"After you what?" Paul tried to keep his voice calm, but he knew that his tension, his imaginings—had his pop found another gun, used a knife, hurt Moira?—oozed through the phone connection. "Let me talk to Moira."

A strange choking sound issued from the phone. Was his dad crying? "Pop? Pop?" Paul's voice rose to a shout, just as movement across the street caught his attention. Montoya, headed toward the café. Of all the shitty timing. With his cell phone pressed to his ear, Paul pushed to his feet, trailing Montoya, who eyed an attractive jogger as he ambled down the sidewalk. Across the street, Paul kept him in sight, saying, "Are you still there?" into the phone.

"Paulie ... I'm scared. I'd better—"

The line went dead.

Cursing, Paul punched in the number and got the buzzing of a busy signal. Shit! He hung up and redialed. Still busy. He glanced at Montoya from under his brows. The man had settled into a chair at the nearby café. He was sorting the newspaper into piles that looked like actual news on his right and the inserts and advertising fliers that doubled the size of the paper on his left. Pausing near a bus stop on the corner, Paul repeated the dialing and busy signal sequence fifteen or twenty more times before his battery died. He shook the phone.

Fuck. He didn't realize he'd said it aloud until a heavyset Hispanic woman waiting for the bus glared at him and ostentatiously shifted her bulk to the farthest end of the bench. What could be going on with Moira and Pop? Paul ground his teeth with frustration and indecision, his eyes glued to his target, who was now drinking a glass of grapefruit juice. The bus arrived with a whoosh of air brakes and a cloud of diesel fumes, cutting off Paul's view of Montoya. As if it had severed an invisible line, Paul broke into a jerky run, headed for a cab, his motel, and the phone charger.

Tossing T-shirts and socks into a gym bag an hour later, Paul tried to decide whether to just drive up to Pennsylvania or call Johanssen and have him send a car around to the house, check on things. But he was afraid of what they might find. If his father had done something ... no, he'd have to make the trip, he decided as the phone rang in its charging dock. He lunged for it. "Hello?"

Moira's voice came over the line and he sank onto the bed, his legs suddenly unable to bear his weight. "Paul." She sounded weak, out of breath.

"Moira, is everything all right? My pop called ... I've been worried sick." God, he sounded like a father whose daughter had stayed out past curfew.

"He saved my life."

"What? Who?"

"Your father. I must have miscalculated my insulin today. I got dizzy, passed out, couldn't get to the orange juice. He called 911 and saved my life."

"You're diabetic?" What else didn't he know about Moira King, the woman who lived in his house half the time and cared for his father? He'd thought he was the only one with secrets.

"Type one."

"Are you okay now?" he asked belatedly, his breathing returning to normal and a hint of anger making its way from his roiling gut to his voice. She should have told him. Guilt punched at him for the thoughts he'd had about his pop.

"Yes, thanks. The EMTs got me stabilized. They didn't even have to take me to hospital. Is something wrong?"

He debated telling her she was goddamn right something was wrong. She had a medical condition that could make it impossible for her to give his father the care he needed. She hadn't been honest with him. She'd probably scared Pop to death by falling into a diabetic coma. She—he stifled all the recriminations that jumped to his lips. They needed to talk in person. "No, nothing. I was just worried."

"Okay." He could tell she wasn't convinced. "Will you be home soon? Your dad misses you."

Did she? Where the hell did that thought come from? "Tuesday night." Come hell or high water.

As he ended the call, he thought again of another phone call, the automated voice from the dentist's office confirming Sydney Ellison's appointment... Tuesday morning. It hadn't been hard to find an address for Dr. Field's office. He wouldn't get a better shot at her.

And he was beginning to think she was a jinx. He'd had the Montoya assignment under control until she'd swiped his phone. He rubbed a hand across his forehead and it came away damp. He was burning up. Too much sun outside Montoya's apartment, he told himself. Heaving himself to his feet, he entered the bathroom and splashed cold water on his face. A little better. He chewed a few aspirins and winced at the sour taste. He stumbled to the bed. He'd rest just a short while before doing a recce at the dentist's building.

36

Sydney

ALTHOUGH HER EXPERIENCE WITH senators' homes was admittedly limited, Sydney was expecting something grander than the modest house they found at Emma Fewell's Carroll County address. Set back from a quiet residential street, it was a two-story Cape Cod–style home with weathered wood siding and gleaming white trim. Towering blue spruces blocked neighbors' sight lines. A door painted coral added a pop of color.

"You're sure you got the address right?" Reese asked, echoing Sydney thoughts.

The door opened and a woman, presumably Emma Fewell, beckoned them. "Yep," Sydney said, waving to Mrs. Fewell.

"I'll take the lead," Reese announced as they walked toward the waiting woman. "It's not exactly my first go-round with grieving widows."

Sydney let her silence be acquiescence. There was no harm in letting Reese steer the conversation; in fact, she was glad she didn't have to ask Fewell's widow if his death might really have been murder.

"You must be Sydney and Reese," the woman said when they were within earshot. "Now, which is which?"

Sydney and Reese identified themselves, and the woman said, "I'm Emma. I insist you call me that. I've been 'Mrs. Fewelled' to death ever since Armand got elected to the Senate thirty years ago." Her drawl revealed her Alabama origins.

Sydney instinctively liked Emma Fewell. Seventy-two, according to the bio Reese had given her, she wore her years lightly. She'd put on some weight, perhaps, and laugh lines made her face interesting, but her spine was straight and she moved with only a slight hitch in her step. Her face was makeup free, but strong brows brought the focus to her dark eyes. She wore a yellow cotton tunic and knit leggings with muddy knees, and no jewelry other than a modest diamond on her ring finger. Her graying hair spiraled in long dreadlocks, à la Maya Angelou, to mid-back.

"Come in, come in," she said, holding the door wide. "I've got a pitcher of tea on the back patio, if that's all right with y'all, and I thought we'd sit out there. I've been gardening. It's such a lovely day."

It was sweltering, but Sydney raised no objection. As they traversed a cool hall lined with family photos, and a kitchen that hadn't been updated since Jimmy Carter was president, she tried to figure out what made Emma Fewell so appealing. She was comfortable in her own skin, Sydney finally decided. Content with who she was and what she had. She reminded Sydney a little of Nana Linn.

"We're very sorry for your loss," Reese said when they reached the back patio, a brick semi-circle surrounded by lush gardens that testified to the love and hard work Emma Fewell poured into them. A pitcher sweated on a wrought-iron table with three acrylic glasses stacked beside it.

Sydney was afraid reference to her husband would make the recent widow tear up, but she replied calmly, "Thank you, dear. I haven't lost Armand, though; he's waiting for me on the other side, in the presence of our Lord Jesus Christ. He's at peace."

Something in her voice suggested he hadn't previously been at peace. Reese must have caught it, too, because she asked, "Was he worried about something before the hunting trip?"

"You don't mind if I work while we talk, do you?" Emma asked. She crossed to where two dozen small plastic pots, the disposable kind, held six-inch-high seedlings with toothy green leaves. A foot-wide dirt border that wound in front of a glorious display of ferns and hostas showed where the new plants would go. "If I don't get the Serbian bellflowers in, they're going to croak in this heat." Sinking heavily to her knees, she said, "Help yourselves to tea. Perhaps you wouldn't mind handing me the pots one at a time?" She smiled up at Sydney.

"Of course not." Awkwardly, Sydney lowered herself to the ground. She handed Emma one of the bellflower pots, thankful that they were in a corner shaded by a Japanese maple tree. She exchanged a look with Reese, who shrugged and went to pour three glasses of tea.

Crumbling the dirt around the seedling's roots, Emma said, "I was hoping that some time with Jermaine would do him good. He always enjoyed hunting, especially turkeys—he said they were awful wily for such a dumb bird—and he didn't get to do it as much as he liked, but ... " She shook her head. Using a trowel, she dug a hollow into the dirt and inserted the plant, tamping loam around it when it was positioned to her satisfaction.

"So Jermaine Washington was there when it happened? He saw the whole thing?" Reese asked. She was still standing, and her angular shadow draped over Sydney.

Emma apparently caught the edge in Reese's voice because she leveled a long look at her before saying, "Another one, please." Sydney handed over another bellflower, and then three more, feeling sweat trickle down her back. "Jermaine is a life-long friend and I have total faith in his integrity," Emma said, tucking the plants into place. "He's a man of good will. That's not a term you hear much anymore, is it? A man of good will. But that's what Jermaine is."

"So there's no chance at all that it wasn't an accident?" Reese prodded. "That Jermaine Washington might have been mistaken, that the bullet came from anywhere besides your husband's gun?"

Emma rocked back on her heels and looked from Reese to Sydney, a sad smile lurking in her eyes. "Well now, dear, that's two different questions, isn't it?"

Sydney's brow creased. What was the woman getting at? Reese apparently saw an opening because her voice sharpened. "So there *is* some doubt? The bullet might not have come from your husband's gun?"

"Why are you so interested in Armand's death? You know it's because of Armand's passing that Fidel is getting his shot at becoming a Senator—it's my husband's seat this election's meant to fill." Emma paused. "Fidel Montoya said it was important when he called, but he didn't say why." The easygoing timbre of her voice hadn't changed, but it was clear she wasn't continuing the conversation until she understood why they were there. "There's no crime involved here," she said, eyeing Reese in a way that made it clear she knew exactly what she did for a living. She thrust the trowel, blade down, into the dirt.

Jumping in before Reese could answer, Sydney said, "I—we—think it's possible your husband was murdered, and that the person who did it may be after another politician." She didn't name Montoya, knowing he'd deny any involvement if Emma asked him. She gave the woman a five-minute summary of the past week's events.

"My, my," Emma said slowly when she finished. "That's quite a tale." Sydney couldn't tell if she believed her or not.

"So," Reese put in, crouching slightly, "you can see why it's important that we know if there's any way, any way at all, that your husband's death wasn't an accident."

Emma blinked once, heavy eyelids shuttering her gaze. When she reopened her eyes, they brimmed with grief. "His death was definitely no accident," she said.

"What?" Reese peeled off her sunglasses to get a better look at the woman. Sydney could feel her sister's astonishment.

Emma stuck up a hand, her tunic sleeve sliding up to reveal a fleshy forearm. "Help me up, would you, there's a dear. The rest of these will have to wait."

Reese locked hands with her and helped haul her up. Sydney stood and brushed grass off her jeans.

"You don't believe your husband's death was an accident?" Sydney tried to rein in her excitement, her conviction that they were edging close to Jason's killer.

"I know it wasn't." Emma looked from Sydney to Reese and back to Sydney. "My Armand committed suicide. Jermaine, good friend that he is, made up that story about the rattlesnake so no one outside the family ever need know. I hope you won't feel the need to tell anyone; I wouldn't want Jermaine to get in any trouble with the police. He was only being the best friend he knew how to be, to Armand and to me."

Suicide! Sydney's hopes collapsed like a card house.

"Why would your husband kill himself?" Reese asked. Sydney hoped Emma didn't hear the thin edge of doubt that she did.

"He'd been heading toward suicide these twelve years and more," Emma said quietly. "Ever since we lost our son. A drunk driver took his life. Let's sit." She walked with weighted step to the iron table and lowered herself onto a chair. Reese passed her a glass of iced tea and she drank half of it before swiping the back of her wrist across her brow. Sydney and Reese sat on either side of her.

"I loved my Armand, Lord knows I did—do—and it about killed me that I couldn't help him. After Michael died, he was never the same. I'm sad about Michael every day, but I let joy back into my life after a year or so, mostly through my garden. I couldn't overlook the gift of a rose in bloom, or marigolds' bright happiness. And then there were the grandbabies, Michael's twins, and they were so full of life and energy, buzzing around, asking why and how, growing up so fast." She smiled, brown eyes sparkling, but then the liveliness drained out of her face. "But Armand … Armand, he kept himself closed off to joy. He still worked for his constituents, but it was out of duty, not passion, after Michael died.

"The first year, he focused on the trial, and after the conviction he campaigned for stiffer penalties for drunk drivers. He still went to church, but I could tell it wasn't the same for him. He loved Michael's kids and spent a lot of time with them, telling them stories about their dad, but he once said something to me about seeing Michael in them, especially little Colin, and it made me worry that he didn't love them for their own sakes as much as because he felt they were a link with Michael. From the start, he visited Michael's grave four or five times a week—got mad at me when I refused to go so often. It was one of the few times he was ever ugly to me." She looked pensive and was silent for a long moment. "He kept his grief alive, took it out and polished it every day." She mimed polishing as if she had a dust cloth folded over two fingers, rubbing them back and forth. "He had the shiniest, brightest grief you ever did see."

Her gaze drifted to the middle distance, and Sydney wondered what she was remembering. She shifted on her chair. She felt sad for Emma, but edgy, too, uncomfortable with the woman's expansive forgiveness, her seeming acceptance of death and her husband's depression. She compared Emma's grief to Connie's—their husbands had died not long apart—but it was apples and oranges. Or maybe not. Connie had lived with a husband physically disabled by a series of strokes, who'd needed nursing and care for almost two decades. Emma had lived with a husband crippled by grief. Were their cases so different? She put the thought aside to consider later.

"So, you see," Emma said in the voice of one reaching her conclusion, "there's no connection between Armand's death and what you're looking into."

"We're sorry for disturbing you," Reese said, gathering herself in as if she were ready to leave.

"I'm not disturbed." Emma smiled again. "I don't suppose I can talk you into helping with the rest of these bellflowers? I don't seem to have the stamina I used to."

Sydney and Reese left ninety minutes later, sweaty and coated with mulch dust after planting and mulching the bellflowers and moving a few heavy planters Emma wanted repositioned. As Reese backed out of the driveway, she muttered, "I know why she agreed to see us—she needed slave labor."

"I like her. Can I be like that when I'm seventy?"

"Black and fat? Probably not."

Sydney laughed long and hard and felt her muscles loosening and her stomach unknotting. It dispelled some of her disappointment that they hadn't made any progress toward ID-ing the killer by talking to

Emma Fewell. "Not that. At peace. Finding joy in little things. Not trying so hard anymore."

Reese favored her with a long, thoughtful look before turning her gaze back to the road. "Like I said: probably not."

Sydney punched her shoulder.

"Hey, not while I'm driving." But the corners of Reese's mouth turned in like she was holding back a smile.

37

Sydney

SYDNEY FELT RESTLESS WHEN they got back to the townhouse that evening, something in her stirred up by listening to Emma Fewell. When Earl yapped at them and ran toward his leash, she grabbed on to the idea of a walk with relief. She didn't want to sit, didn't want to think or contemplate. A walk would be just the ticket. She was half irritated when Reese insisted on coming along.

"What kind of bodyguard would I be if I let you wander around outside alone?" Reese asked, cocking a brow. She slung her purse over her shoulder. So she'd have the gun, Sydney realized. "Besides, he's my dog."

Resisting a sharp retort, Sydney leashed a happy Earl and the three of them turned right on the sidewalk with Earl taking the lead. One big happy, Sydney thought sourly. With twilight settling in and a breeze blowing, the temperature was more comfortable and Sydney gradually relaxed again. It was the heat making her snappy, she told herself. When they'd walked for fifteen minutes in a silence that Reese showed no inclination to break (not getting very far since Earl had to whiz on every tree, shrub, sign, lamppost, and hydrant they passed), Sydney said, "You researched Montoya's wife. Tell me about her so I know what we're walking into tomorrow."

Shifting the purse on her shoulder, Reese said, "Father a biochemist-turned-entrepreneur, mother a homemaker and sister of Matvei Utkin. A brother in Texas and a sister in North Carolina. Wellesley grad. Met Montoya at a fundraiser for a Democratic candidate and six months later they were married. He put her through grad school and she became an architect. After a few years, she branched out to become a builder—no one seems to know where the initial stake for that came from."

"Utkin?"

"Could be. Several profiles I scanned say her company is one of the most successful in eastern Maryland. Custom homes. She's rich in her own right, so why she sticks with Montoya, I don't know. He began screwing around on her about twenty minutes after they married, and she's put up with it all this time. I don't get the political wife ethos of 'stand by your man no matter what kind of pond scum he is.' What self-respecting woman would do that?"

Sydney almost felt Julie Manley's presence and tripped on an uneven slab of sidewalk. George's wife had told Sydney she was keeping their marriage together because she'd made a vow, that the church had joined them and no teenage slut with daddy issues was going to separate them. She'd said that George's political career was a calling that transcended his lapse—that's what she called the almost three-year affair, a 'lapse'—and that she wasn't going to let his sordid association with Sydney keep him from accomplishing everything she knew he could do for the American people. At the time, her words and disgust had devastated Sydney, but looking back, she wondered if Julie believed, really felt, what she was saying or if she'd scripted the speech and carefully chosen the dignified lavender suit for maximum impact. Shades of purple were mourning colors in Victorian times, Sydney knew, and she wondered if Julie was making a subtle statement about mourning her moribund marriage.

Reese's fingers snapping an inch from her nose brought her back. "Earth to Sydney. Where'd you go?"

"I'm right here," Sydney said, pulling Earl away from a fast-food bag he was investigating. He clamped it in his jaws and carried it with him. Her cell phone rang. She answered it, hoping it would be Montoya telling her one of his staff had located her car. Listening in disbelief to the voice squawking through the phone, she said, "Where?" and "Thank you" and hung up.

"That was the police," she told Reese. "They found my car."

"Superb. Let's go get it."

Sydney shook her head. "Nope. Someone hacked it up and set in on fire in the parking lot of an abandoned warehouse in Anacostia."

Reese whistled. "I guess those KKK guys were PO'd."

"Imminent Revelation."

"So they run around in camos instead of bed sheets." Prying the fast-food bag out of Earl's jaws and crinkling it into a ball, Reese shot it toward a rusted trash barrel. It swished in, startling a squirrel on the rim who fluffed his tail and chattered at them.

"Show-off."

"If you've got it, flaunt it." Reese grinned. "But I don't need to tell you that—you've done plenty of flaunting in your day. Even at seventeen, you had it going on, baby sister. The dress you wore to senior prom ..." She eyed Sydney's attire as if comparing it unfavorably with her former wardrobe. "You had it going on, but it looks like it got up and went."

Sydney's hand shook slightly and the leash rippled. The media and blogosphere had been brutal about her looks when the story broke, with paparazzi sneaking photos that emphasized her cleavage and editors digging up photos of her in that low-cut, tight-fitting green prom dress and running them over and over with her date cropped out. She didn't think Reese meant to be hurtful in this instance, and she wanted to preserve their soap-bubble-thin reconnection, but she couldn't keep all the irritation out of her response. "I don't need your fashion critiques, okay? My clothes suit me fine. They fit my job, who I am."

Reese let it go. "Who am I to judge?" She gestured to her camp shirt and khakis. "Whoever said 'clothes make the man'—or woman, in this case—was full of shit. Earl, it's time to go back."

38

Sydney
Monday, August 7

SHORTLY AFTER NOON ON Monday, Sydney and Reese pulled into the yard of a house under construction west of Annapolis. Sydney was driving Reese's Highlander while her sister worked on her tablet. A large sign in the yard proclaimed *Van Slyke Custom Builders*. A cement mixer trundled out of the rutted dirt driveway and workers crawled over the house like ants with hard hats.

"We're looking for Katya Van Slyke?" Sydney poked her head out the window to talk with an overalled man munching a sandwich.

"O'er dere," he mumbled around a mouthful. He jerked his head to the left of the house.

Sydney thanked him and steered the car carefully over the deep gouges in the roadway left by construction equipment.

"Shit," Reese exclaimed the third time they lurched into a pothole deep enough to double as a reservoir. "My ride's going to need an alignment when we get back."

"Quit whining. At least your car's not an arsonist's wet dream."

Reese's eyebrows soared and she chuckled. "I didn't know you had it in you, little sister. What would Connie say?"

"It's been a rough week," Sydney groused, putting the Highlander in park and unbuckling. "That's got to be her." She pointed toward a figure with a blond braid hanging from beneath its yellow hard hat.

They climbed out of the SUV and approached a tall woman studying a set of blueprints on the hood of a red F-250.

"Katya Van Slyke?" Sydney asked as they got closer. Fidel had warned her not to call his wife "Mrs. Montoya." "It makes her rabid," he'd said with a rueful note in his voice when he'd told Sydney where to find her. What did that say about their marriage?

The blonde looked up, showing ice blue eyes under pale brows, but she kept her finger on a spot on the documents. "Yes?" She looked from Sydney to Reese.

She came across like a middle-aged Viking warrior queen: six feet tall, big-boned, aloof. Sydney could easily imagine her wielding a hammer. "I'm Sydney Ellison and this is my sister, Reese Linn. Your husband said you might have a few minutes to talk to us about—"

"About this alleged assassin, yes?" Katya said, a thin smile stretching her lips.

"You don't think someone tried to kill your husband?"

She shrugged. "I think Fidel is a politician and he wants very much to win this election tomorrow. He subscribes to the 'any publicity is good publicity' theory."

"But he hasn't gone to the media with it, or even the police," Sydney said.

"Yet."

The single word hung between them. "Don't you want your husband to win?"

The woman's eyes crinkled at the corners and Sydney got the feeling she was laughing at her. "Of course I do. It's good for business. It would be better if he were a Republican, of course, from a commission standpoint—they're not as shamefaced about their conspicuous consumption as the Democrats, are they?—but being Congressman Montoya's wife nets me plenty of jobs." She extended a hand toward the house going up behind them. "Do you know what my profit on a fifteen-million-dollar home is?"

"Enough to buy Jimmy a racehorse?" Sydney didn't know where the idea came from; it jumped out of her mouth.

"Not even close." Katya's face shut down. "If I could, I'd buy Jimmy free of those monsters who have their hooks into him and lock him up in a recovery facility until he lost the urge to buy so much as a lottery ticket. There's one in Montana with a good reputation. But his father says he's got to live with the consequences of his decisions. Those men are going to hurt him. Matvei is … ruthless. Blood means nothing to him."

Although Katya spoke matter-of-factly, Sydney sensed a mother's fear for her son in the slight tightening of the cords in her neck. But Sydney found herself looking in vain for any resemblance between mother and son. Did it bother the woman to have left no physical stamp on her offspring?

"Do you think Utkin could be targeting your husband?" she asked. She stopped short of asking if Jimmy himself could be responsible.

"No one's 'targeting' Fidel," Katya said irritably. "So he heard a shot while he was jogging. A target shooter, a poacher, a homeowner scaring away a coyote. They are all more likely than an assassin, yes?"

"He says the bullet barely missed him."

She shrugged, seeming to imply that Montoya might have been exaggerating. "I've told him dozens of times he shouldn't run on the roads. That's what gyms and tracks are for."

The woman's lack of concern for her husband was unbelievable. Sydney told her about the cell phone switch and the call she'd received. Cold blue eyes locked onto hers.

"You have a history with politicians, do you not? And my husband has a weakness for attractive women." She said it the same way she might say, "My husband likes grape jelly."

The words stung Sydney like a cloud of mosquitoes. She slapped them away with a chop of her hand. "I am not sleeping with your husband! My fiancé was murdered by the man hired to kill your husband."

"So you say." The look in the blonde's eyes belied her cool tone.

"Maybe you're tired of Fidel's womanizing," Sydney suggested, pushed to her limit. "Maybe you hired the killer to get rid of him. If he was dead, you could spend his money to bail out your gambling-addict son before he gets himself beaten to a pulp by your uncle's goons."

"How dare you!" Katya banged her fist on the truck's hood with a loud clang. Several workers looked over and one took a step toward them, returning to his task when Reese stared him down.

"How dare *you* accuse me of sleeping with your sleazebag husband, just because I'm trying to keep him from getting killed and catch the bastard who shot my fiancé!"

The two women glared at each other over the truck's hood. Heat from the metal seeped into Sydney's hands and she realized she'd banged them down in her anger.

"Get the fuck off my job site," Katya said, her voice low and menacing. She leaned her torso across the truck and practically growled in Sydney's face. "And stay away from my family."

216

Sydney spun on her heel. Reese side-stepped with catlike agility before she could walk into her. In silence, they walked side-by-side back to the SUV.

"You were a big help back there," Sydney said, clambering into the driver's seat and jabbing the key into the ignition.

"Didn't look to me like you needed any help," Reese said, with a good humor that annoyed her more. "She has a longer reach, but I think you could've taken her. Interesting interview technique, by the way—pissing the subject off. I've used it myself. Of course, the object is to make the subject angry enough to say something he didn't mean to, but not so angry he takes a swing at you. It's a fine line." Her tone suggested she could give Sydney a few pointers on needling interview subjects.

"Do you think she hired someone to kill her husband?" Sydney craned her neck to look over her shoulder as she backed up the SUV.

"I don't know, but if I were Fidel Montoya, I'd hide the scissors before I went to sleep tonight," Reese said.

Sydney choked on a laugh despite her anger. "They're quite the dysfunctional family, aren't they?"

"Yeah, like the Menendezes were a dysfunctional family."

She shot her sister a look as she dodged a mason with trowel and hod. "You think Jimmy hired the hit man? The Menendezes were the sons who killed their parents, right?"

"Yeah." Reese pulled the visor down. "I didn't mean I necessarily think Jimmy's behind the assassination attempt. He seems pretty ineffectual, but sometimes the weakest-seeming men are the most vicious when they get the chance. They take years of abuse and put-downs and use them to fuel rage like you've never seen ... "

She trailed off, and Sydney said, "You're thinking about Ruben Panetta, aren't you?"

Reese swiveled her head toward her. "You've read my books?"

Sydney cursed herself inwardly. She didn't want Reese knowing she was interested enough to have followed her career. "I might have glanced at one or two."

Reese let it go. "Yeah, I was thinking about Panetta. He had some things in common with Jimmy Montoya. He was young—only twenty-three—when he started killing. He had a domineering father and was bullied in school. I'll bet Jimmy was bullied some. He just has that 'kick me' aura to him. But there are big differences, too. Panetta's father raped him repeatedly from the time he was five or six, and his mother let it happen. He had a history of bed-wetting and setting fires—all classic signs of a serial killer—and there's none of that in Jimmy Montoya's dossier."

"It's apples and oranges, right?" Sydney said, taking an exit ramp so fast that g-forces swayed Reese against the window. A detour forced them through a residential area of Annapolis streets. "Hiring a contract killer to take out your dad with filthy lucre as your motive is a far cry from being a serial killer."

"True." Reese was silent a moment, and then said, "When you talk to killers and victims all the time, you get to thinking that everyone is one or the other. Everyone around a killer is a victim, not just the people he actually kills. Parents, siblings, friends—they're all victims, too, to one degree or another. Panetta's sister ... I have to remind myself that it's not true that everyone is a killer or a victim. Some people lead perfectly ordinary lives, hurting each other in ordinary ways, kissing and making up, working, laughing, listening to music, losing their virginity to a high school sweetheart, celebrating quinceañeras." She gestured to a boisterous group of Latinos spilling out into the front yard they were passing, at their center a laughing teenage girl dressed in a tiered yellow gown and wearing a tiara.

"You know..." She spoke toward the window, and Sydney had to strain to hear her. "I spent ten years witnessing war in all of its ugliness, and the last six years chronicling the lives of the sickest, most depraved men—and one woman—in the country. It's gotten so I can't get it out of my head anymore."

A shaft of concern for her sister pierced Sydney. "Quit. Walk away."

Tilting her head back against the seat, Reese said, "And do what? This is what I'm good at."

"Take some time to figure it out. Go reno your house and just breathe."

"Is that what you did?" Reese asked the question facing straight ahead, not making eye contact.

Sydney knew what her sister meant. "Not soon enough," she said after a moment. She braked to let a gaggle of tourists and midshipmen from the Naval Academy cross the street. "Afterward, I hid in Europe. Then I married Dirk, thinking... hell, I couldn't have been thinking at all when I married Dirk." Lights from emergency vehicles strobed ahead of them and traffic was at a total standstill, so Sydney put the SUV in park and turned to face her sister's profile. "Nana Linn rescued me. She swooped down on me in Santa Monica—that's where we were living while Dirk pursued his 'acting' career—and took me home with her to Richmond. She made me get counseling and bullied me to finish my degree. Then, when I'd been with her almost a year, she gave me the keys to the cabin in West Virginia—"

"The one on Wood Lake, where we went on vacation a couple of times?" Reese looked interested.

Sydney nodded. "You told me we were swimming in fish pee and I wouldn't put my head underwater. Dad explained about dilution and threw me in off the dock."

"It was peaceful up there," Reese said, in a wistful voice that hinted she hadn't known peace in a while.

"It was," Sydney agreed. "Also lonely, cold—it was winter—and just what I needed. Nana Linn told me to hike, fish, chop wood, and not think at all. The result was a kind of healing; a strengthening, I guess you'd call it. I came back knowing I wanted to start Winning Ways. Well, not Winning Ways exactly, but something like it, a nonprofit that helped women. Nana Linn hooked me up with folks who knew the ins and outs of fundraising and could pinpoint an area where there was a need. I miss her." Her thoughts dwelled on the woman with the regal posture and the white hair always swept back in a chignon. She remembered the hands with their swollen knuckles and red nails, manicured weekly; the soft voice that somehow always made itself heard; the acerbic commentary on politics and the decline of Western culture; the surprising strength in the thin arms that would sweep her into a hug with no warning. She blinked back tears.

An ambulance maneuvered past, siren blaring, and the car in front of them chugged forward a few feet. Exhaust fumes choked the air. Sydney slipped the Highlander into gear and eased it forward.

"Solitude sounds blissful," Reese said. "She left you that place, didn't she?"

Sydney heard the unasked question. No, not quite a question, or even a hope; more like a dawning awareness of a previously unrecognized need. "I'll give you the keys when we get home, if we ever do," she said as the car in front of them slammed on its brakes to avoid hitting a motor scooter weaving through the halted cars. "You're welcome to stay as long as you want. I haven't been up there in a long time, so I can't vouch for the condition of the place. There's a caretaker, but—"

"Doesn't matter." After a pause, Reese added, "Thanks."

"You're welcome." The moment felt too heavy, almost meaning-ful, and it made her squirm. "I'll bet Earl will like swimming. Just don't tell him about the fish pee."

Reese chuckled. "He's afraid of water, the wussy, can't stand to get a bath. But he loves chasing squirrels."

"There are plenty of those."

In the mysterious way of traffic jams, the dam broke and suddenly they were moving.

39

Sydney

MAKING THE TURN ONTO G Street an hour later, Sydney was apprehensive at seeing a blue sedan drawn up in front of her house, a man's figure leaning against the passenger door.

"Who's that?" Reese asked, sitting up straight.

"The police," Sydney said hollowly. Was Detective West going to haul her off to jail? She slowed and found a parking spot halfway down the block.

"If you're going to hang with the handsome detective, I'm going to take care of a few things," Reese said, studying West in the rearview mirror. "You should be safe enough with him. Be back in a half hour."

Sydney nodded her agreement. She wasn't surprised that Reese didn't want to meet West, as she'd had some ugly run-ins with the police when she was a reporter. She stepped onto the sidewalk and West met her halfway between his car and the Highlander. Even though the sun was sliding toward the horizon, heat trapped by the asphalt and concrete of the city rose around them in almost visible waves. Despite the heat, someone was burning leaves, and the acrid odor made it feel hotter. Sydney tucked a lock of hair behind her ear, suddenly feeling the weight of the day's events descend on her shoulders.

"Who's your friend?" West's deep-set eyes studied Reese's lanky frame as she exited the passenger door and crossed in front of the SUV, out of their sight, to climb into the driver's side. Sydney thought she saw her hand upraised in a wave as she signaled and pulled away from the curb.

"Someone who takes my safety a bit more seriously than the MPD," Sydney said tartly. She passed West and opened the low gate to her yard. Indigo bounded over to greet her and she stroked him. He purred.

"A bodyguard?" West's brows climbed toward his hairline.

"My sister, actually. She's got a gun." She gave Indy a final pat and stood to unlock the front door. "Do I need to call my lawyer for this conversation?"

"Nope." West followed her into the foyer and shut the door, sending home the deadbolt. The cool relief of air conditioning settled on her skin as she headed for the kitchen and water. The heat and the dust from the construction site had parched her.

"Nice bike," West observed as they passed through the living room. "Yours?"

It was now. "Yes." She left it at that and beelined for the sink.

"I saw a report that your car was torched," he said. He leaned back against the counter as she filled a glass with water and glugged it. "Want to tell me about it?"

She filled the glass again before replying. "Want some?" When he shook his head, she took another long swallow, then gave him an appraising look. "I poked a hornet's nest and got stung."

"What hornets?"

After a moment's hesitation—what would Hilary say?—she told him about visiting the Imminent Revelation compound and her conversation with Aaron Fisher.

As she spoke, his brows contracted and the muscles in his jaw tensed. "You thought they might have hired a hit man to take out Montoya and you traipsed off to their hide-out alone?" Incredulity rang in his voice.

"Reese was nearby," she said defensively.

He was silent for a long moment, rubbing his eyebrow. When he spoke again, his tone said he'd come to a decision. "You're serious about this, about what you said. You're really trying to track down a hit man, aren't you?"

"Well, no one else is trying to find Jason's killer." She busied herself putting her glass in the sink to hide the tears that sprang to her eyes. "You all think I killed him."

"I'm willing to consider other possibilities."

Suddenly, he was beside her, a gentle hand turning her so he could study her face. He seemed taller close up; her nose was even with his jaw. She sniffed back her tears and met his gaze defiantly. "Really? Well, you fooled me with that whole arresting me thing."

"Sarcasm doesn't suit you."

"How would you know?" She held his gaze a moment longer, then turned away to push open the back door. She sank to the top step, wrapping her arms around her knees and hugging them to her chest. West joined her. He smelled like soap and limes and body heat as he sank down to the step, his thigh a whisper away from hers.

"Who else had a motive to kill Montoya?" he asked, pulling a small notebook and pen from his jacket pocket.

"You're finally taking me seriously?" Before he could change his mind, she poured out the results of the past two days' interviews and their research, watching the play of emotions across his face as she mentioned the Revelationists and their branding, Jimmy's gambling and Avdonin, Emma Fewell, Katya and her hostility.

"I originally thought it must be political, but after talking with Fisher, I realized that killing one congressman probably wouldn't clear the way for any big policy changes. So I started looking at his personal life. Plenty of people would benefit if Montoya died," she finished. The reds of her geraniums became muted and the glow of fireflies flitted at grass level as the sunlight faded. A sprinkler hissed nearby, scenting the air with warm water.

"So it would seem." He tucked the notebook back into his pocket.

How far should she trust West? Hilary's voice spoke in her right ear, telling her to shut up. She could just see D'won rolling his eyes at the idea of trusting a cop. Instinct made her say, "Someone shot at Montoya."

"What?!"

"But he won't confirm that," Sydney hastened to add. "He doesn't want to run the chance of losing the election." She told him what Montoya had said to her about the shooting incident, leaving out the bit where he'd blackmailed her into helping him.

West stood, brushing dirt from his slacks. "I'm going to look into this. You stop poking around. Stick close to your sister or, better yet, hire a real bodyguard. I could recommend someone."

He held out a hand to help her up, and after a moment she placed hers in it and let him tug her upright. She pulled her hand away as soon as she was standing. The stoop was so small that her back brushed against his chest as she pulled the storm door open. She scooted inside and turned to face him in the full glare of the kitchen's overhead fixture.

"Do you really believe me?" She gripped her lower lip between her teeth, waiting for his answer. Even though she didn't want it to, it mattered.

"I believe you're telling the truth as you know it."

She flapped an impatient hand at his ambiguity. "Do you think I killed Jason?"

He hesitated a beat, but when he spoke the words came out strong. "No. No, I don't."

She exhaled. "Are you supposed to tell me that?"

"Not really." He smiled ruefully, his mouth quirking up at one corner. "I'll dig myself in deeper and let you know the chief's ready to say you're no longer a suspect. There's nothing to tie you to the gun we found in here and we've got another witness who confirms your alibi. There should be an announcement in the morning. The chief's insisting the ADA be there to explain why we arrested someone without a case we're willing to take to trial. We're 'pursuing other leads,' mostly a kid who was in one of Nygaard's classes."

"It wasn't a student." Even though she knew they were looking in the wrong direction, at least they weren't looking at her anymore. A smile blossomed and she felt like someone had lifted a Volkswagen off her chest. She took a deep breath, feeling every rib expand.

"Well, we still need to find him, interview him. You keep your head down. No more visits to white supremacist encampments."

In another minute he'd be wagging his finger in her face. He didn't know her very well if he thought she was going to back off now. Rather than respond, she headed for the foyer. Floorboards creaked beneath their feet. Sydney flipped the deadbolt and pushed the door wide. "Thanks for coming by, Detective."

"Ben."

"I'll keep you posted."

West rolled his eyes but only said, "You do that."

40

Sydney
Tuesday, August 8

SYDNEY WOKE TUESDAY MORNING feeling dull and weighed down. Today was the special election. She'd failed to find the man behind the voice on the phone, failed to find the killer. Fidel Montoya might die today, and it would be partially her fault. If he survived, what would that mean? That she'd misunderstood the phone call in the first place? In which case, why was Jason dead? That she'd scared the killer away with her investigation? She gave that some thought as she splashed water on her face and dressed for the dental appointment. That could be counted as a partial win, she guessed, although the uncertainty made it a Pyrrhic victory at best. Flicking on some blush to give her pale cheeks a hint of color, she descended the stairs and stepped onto the front stoop to grab the newspaper. Earl peed on a shrub and challenged a squirrel that had the temerity to scamper up a tree in his territory.

Calling him back, Sydney returned to the house. Absently stripping the plastic sheath from the paper, she entered the kitchen and put water on to boil. Spreading the paper open on the kitchen table, she was setting aside the front page section, looking for the car sales pages, when the headline topping the local section plowed into her like a runaway horse: *Manley Trap Dukes It Out with Congressman's Wife*. Beneath it was a photo of her and Katya at the construction site, glaring at each other over the truck's hood. Hostility vibrated from them, even in the fuzzy newsprint.

A toxic cocktail of humiliation, fear that it was all starting again, and anger surged through her. Sydney collapsed into a chair and stilled her shaking hands by trapping them between her knees. How did the reporter—?

The answer was obvious. Grabbing the paper, Sydney scraped back her chair and stormed down the hall. She slammed open the powder room door, surprising Reese on the toilet.

"Don't you knock?" Reese started, but Sydney cut her off.

"How could you?" She slapped the paper down on the counter, knocking Reese's toothbrush and a compact to the floor. It splintered on the tile, sprinkling glass slivers and pressed powder across the tiny room. Sydney sneezed, which increased her fury. "I can't believe—"

"Give me a moment to see what you're going on about," Reese said, maddeningly calm. She leaned over and picked up the folded paper, saying, "That was my favorite compact, you know. I—oh." She raised her gaze from the page.

"Oh?" Heat flushed Sydney's face. "I thought I could trust you, that things were different between us. I'm an idiot."

"No argument there." Reese said, her voice as sharp as one of the glass splinters. "This"—she waved the paper before dropping it disdainfully in the sink—"was not me."

"You're a reporter—"

"*Was*. Even then, I didn't sneak around spying on politician's wives."

"No, you focused on their girlfriends."

Reese's face whitened, and she took a long moment before saying, "I have no way to make you believe me, but I had nothing to do with this. I don't know this"—she glanced at the byline—"Elaine Ng. I have absolutely no reason to let the press in on what we're doing."

Her use of "we're" gave Sydney pause. Drawing in a shaky breath, she fingered her hair off her forehead. She didn't know what to think. She'd been sure Reese was behind the story, but now ...

Reese interrupted her thoughts. "If you're going to hit me again, can I please get off the john first? Most fatal accidents in the home happen in the bathroom and I don't want to be that kind of statistic."

"I'm not going to hit you." Sydney stepped out of the bathroom and closed the door. The toilet flushed, a zipper whizzed, and water gurgled in the sink. Shoes crunching on glass heralded Reese's appearance. Sydney felt calmer but not quite ready to apologize. "Do you think the reporter was following me?"

"Maybe. Because of the arrest. I was keeping an eye out, but I might have missed a tail. Or she might have been following Katya, on spec as it were. Candidates' families, especially semi-estranged wives, can make good stories. Most likely someone at the site snapped a cell phone picture and called the *Post*."

"Could you find out?"

Reese cocked her head. "Maybe. Like I keep telling you, I don't have too many contacts at the *Post* anymore. I'm not sure it's worth it anyway."

Sydney inflated her whole torso with a deep breath. "I'm sorry."

"Forgiven."

Sydney gave a shaky laugh. "You're giving me a pass just to make me feel bad for hating you all these years."

"You hated me?" Reese's voice sounded tight.

Sydney hesitated. "Yes. At least, I think so. Especially early on."

"Well, that makes two of us. Hating me, I mean."

Not trusting herself to speak through the lump that rose in her throat, Sydney stood mute for a moment. Recovering, she said gruffly, "I don't hate you now. I'll get a dust pan."

"Then we can go buy a car."

"And a new compact, after my dentist appointment."

41

Paul

PAUL EASED HIMSELF THROUGH the roof access door of the building across from the Penn Professional Building where the dentist had his office. Sweat beaded his brow, and he drank thirstily from one of the bottled waters in his bag. Acid roiled his stomach, a result of the ibuprofen and acetaminophen he'd been taking for fever and pain. They were no longer doing the trick: his shoulder throbbed like a son of a bitch and the red streaks had grown longer. He had to gut it out today, finish the job, and then he'd find a doctor. His generic jumpsuit, with *Maintenance* stenciled on the back and *Lionel* in machine-embroidered script over his chest, had proved in the past to be the perfect disguise. A ball cap in a matching tan hid his face from cameras and ensured no one got a clear look at his features or hair. Nobody really looked at maintenance men, janitors, cable guys, or meter readers. A uniform and a clipboard or tool bag made you damned near invisible, Paul had discovered.

Clutching the duffel with his Savage Arms Striker .22-250 sniper pistol, he made his way around a shed-sized air-conditioning unit and dropped to one knee, leaning against the metal structure. It was still cool to the touch after a night in the sixties. Waves of dizziness and nausea struck him. Despite the over-the-counter painkillers touting their fever-reduction ingredients, he was burning up and the cool metal offered relief. The sun would heat it to egg-frying temperature by the time he completed his mission. Scanning the empty roof again, he drew the pistol with its long barrel from his bag. Even its relatively light weight sent jabs of pain radiating from his shoulder up his neck and down his arm. He cursed. There was a pharmacy two blocks from his motel. He could get antibiotics there. He'd looked it up on the Internet, knew what he needed. He could stick his gun in a white-coated jackass's face and they'd hand over the meds. It wasn't like he was after oxy.

He peered through the scope, cursing the faint tremble in his arm. The door of the Penn Professional Building loomed in vivid detail, seeming mere inches away instead of seventy-five yards.

He'd scouted the building Sunday night when everything was quiet. Two bums had huddled on the vent outside the place, and a handful of cars had traveled the famous avenue, but no one paid him any attention. The building looked like it might once have been a theater, with a broad lobby and high ceilings. Developers had modernized it and effaced most of its personality, converting it to a labyrinth of offices. By the elevators, Paul had studied the marquee listing the names and floors of a variety of professionals: doctors, dentists, CPAs, goddamned lawyers, shrinks—lots of shrinks. Paul was sure living in DC was enough to send everyone screaming for a therapist and medication. Dr. Field's office was on the third floor.

He'd trudged up the dimly lit stairs and studied the locked doors on the offices he passed. Light glowed from behind one frosted pane, but most were dark. Hmm. Too tight, too many people, no good way to make a fast exit. He'd have to do the job outside, maybe from the roof of the building across the way. A poster on a travel agency's door stopped him on his way out. Cruising through azure seas, a ship the size of a small city promised relaxation and adventure. Would Pop feel up to a cruise? Maybe when he'd completed this mission, he'd book a cruise, just a short one, to someplace warm. None of that Alaska stuff. Pop could lounge on a deck chair, benefiting from the sea air and sunshine, while he and Moira ...

A movement overhead drew Paul's attention and he whirled, bringing the pistol up. An angry hawk circled, then dive-bombed him. He flapped a gloved hand and the bird sheared away, veering toward the far corner of the roof. The rising sun burnished its glossy feathers, striking red from the spread tail. Using his hand as a visor, Paul made out the tips of sticks he assumed were a nest. The hawk's mate ruffled its feathers and glared at him as his attacker settled on a parapet nearby, keeping a fierce amber eye on Paul. He'd heard of raptors living in the city but had never seen any. What did they eat? Squirrels and pigeons, he decided after a moment's thought. Cats.

"You just have to share the roof with me for a couple of hours," he murmured, eliciting a threatening *shreee* from the bird. "Then I'll be out of your hair. Er, feathers."

42

Sydney

AT NINE O'CLOCK TUESDAY morning, Reese lounged in the dentist's waiting room, perusing a year-old *Good Housekeeping*, when Sydney came out of the treatment area swiping her tongue across smooth, clean teeth.

"You must be desperate," she observed, stepping to the receptionist's desk to take care of her co-pay.

"Don't knock it," Reese said. She put the magazine back on a listing tower of periodicals. "I found a great tip for cleaning grout that I'm going to try out. You rub a paste of baking soda and water on the grout, and then spray vinegar."

Sydney wrinkled her nose and handed the middle-aged receptionist her credit card. Without speaking, the sisters left the office and emerged onto Pennsylvania Avenue. Cars, trucks, SUVs, soccer-mom vans, and buses clogged the street, spewing fumes and heat as they idled for the traffic light. Bicycle messengers, pedestrian commuters, and vagrants dodged each other on the sidewalk as they hustled to their individual destinations or staked out their spots on benches and under awnings or eaves that promised shade. The sun had metamorphosed from the gentle warmth spilling through Sydney's window into a brutal glare that bounced off vehicles' chrome, shop windows, and even the patent leather heels of a businesswoman waiting for a bus. Sydney pulled her sunglasses from her purse and slid them onto her face with a sigh of relief.

"It's going to be a scorcher," she said as a blow caught her between the shoulder blades and knocked her to her knees on the concrete. As the pain of scraped knees and palms registered, she heard a gunshot, then another, and Reese toppled on top of her, mowing her flat.

"She's got a gun!" someone yelled.

Screams and pounding feet sounded as people scattered. Horns blared and tires squealed. "Call the cops," another voice yelled. A baby started crying.

43

Paul

EVEN THOUGH HIS STRIKER pistol could fire three shots, Paul only took one. When he saw the bodyguard fall, he cursed. She completely buried the target when she collapsed on top of her. Stuffing the gun into his duffel, Paul got to his feet, his knees crackling after such a long period of immobility. He swayed. He limped the first couple of steps, then regained his stride. He kept his mind from replaying the shot, intent on getting off the roof and away from the scene before the police arrived. He clattered down the stairs, fighting dizziness, and slowed as he reached the garage level. Easing the door open, he pretended to search for a tool in his bag to hide his face from the camera mounted overhead. His shoulder felt like the devil was gouging a red-hot poker into the wound, so he switched the duffel to his other hand. He stepped into the cool twilight of the garage and, still shielding his face, made his way toward the door that led to the street.

He was almost at his destination when a woman approached him on the narrow sidewalk that hugged the garage's inner wall. For a moment he saw two of her, but then she resolved into one plain, middle-aged woman. He mumbled "Good morning" and moved over to let her by.

The woman stopped, blocking his path. "Hey."

Push past her? He couldn't let her raise the alarm. With his heart-beat pounding in his ears, Paul hesitated.

The woman had springy brown hair and glasses with oval frames. She wore a blouse with a bow at the neck and a dirndl skirt even Paul knew was two decades out of style. Secretary, he decided.

"Lionel?" She sounded unsure.

Had she mistaken him for someone else? It took him a moment to place the name. His chest. She'd read the name off his uniform.

Not making eye contact, he said, "Yes'm?"

"The sink in our office kitchen—Suite 201—has been dripping for weeks and it's driving me absolutely batty. I put in a work order in early July but no one's been up to fix it. Do you think you could get to it today? My boss is on my back to get it fixed." She cocked her head, sparrow-like.

"Sure," he mumbled. "Be up after I take care of the clogged toilet in the men's room on four. Suite 201, right?"

"Thanks so much, Lionel," she said. "I'll be looking for you." She hesitated. "Are you okay?"

He must look as bad as he felt. "Yeah. Tummy troubles," he said vaguely.

"Oh. Sorry." She nodded and continued down the sidewalk toward the elevators.

Paul picked up his pace and cursed his bad luck. Ever since his father had shot him, nothing had gone right. He couldn't remember ever taking more than two attempts to eliminate a target. His shoulder pulsed with pain, he felt light-headed with fever, and now there was a witness who could describe him, at least partially, to the police. The hawks would recognize him, too. They knew who he was. A fellow predator. They hadn't taken their wild eyes off of him the whole morning. He'd felt the weight of their stares between his shoulder blades and expected their talons to tear into the flesh of his back. That was why he'd flinched when he'd pulled the trigger. The hawks ... He shook his head, trying to clear it. He needed to get away from here. Stooping behind a van near the door, he quickly shucked the jumpsuit and stuffed it and the cap in his bag. The suit he had underneath would get less notice on the sidewalk at this hour. He ran a hand over his head, smoothing his hair.

Sunlight stabbed his eyes as he stepped out of the garage, and he almost fell back into the comforting dimness. *Keep going.* Bowing his head, he shouldered through the crowd of commuters and looky-loos blocking the sidewalk. People lifted their cell phones over their heads and he tried to puzzle out what they were doing. He finally realized they were trying to film the body on the sidewalk. He took care to stay behind the amateur photographers, who were probably hoping to sell their filmmaking efforts to the nightly news.

"Must have been a crash," a man's voice said from behind him.

"No, I heard it was a jumper," a soprano voice said with ghoulish interest.

Paul kept going, keeping his pace at a fast walk—a man late for a meeting, not a hit man fleeing a botched assassination. Three blocks from the debacle, he could hear the sirens, or maybe it was the hunting call of the hawks, and imagined the commotion and confusion as traffic backed up and emergency vehicles tried to reach the scene. Pausing in the shade of a glorious chestnut tree, he held a hand to the stitch in his side. His breath came in short gasps. He felt hot, then cold, as if he was standing in front of an oven set to broil with the door open, then in front of a freezer gaping wide. He shook. Against his will, he sank to his haunches against the tree trunk, wrapping his arms around his shivering body. His bag fell to the ground with a muffled thud.

"You okay, mister?" A wino with a week's growth of stubble peered at him. A camo field jacket rank with mildew topped several layers of clothes that had seen their heyday in the Nixon years. His breath made Paul want to puke. A faded medal swung into Paul's view and he forced his eyes to focus. A Purple Heart.

"Should I call a medic?"

Paul's teeth were chattering too hard for him to answer the old vet, but he tried to shake his head.

"You don't look too good," the wino said, squatting so he was eye level with Paul. "I got a buddy wi' da malaria and he shakes like you when an attack gets him. You got malaria?"

"Don't let the hawks … " Paul felt himself listing to the left, and then everything went black.

44

Sydney

GRIT PRESSED INTO SYDNEY'S cheek as she breathed in a mix of dirt and exhaust. A flattened wad of chewing gum smudged the pavement inches from her nose. She tried to take a deep breath, but the weight on her back forced the air out of her lungs. She squirmed beneath Reese, short of breath from her sister pushing her into the sidewalk. Her breasts were squashed painfully to her chest and a throbbing ache told her she'd landed hard on her hip bone. A wet warmth pooled on her back. Had Reese peed on her? "Reese?"

"Hit ... roof." Her voice was a burbly whisper.

"Oh my God." It was Reese's blood soaking into her back. Sydney maneuvered her arms out from under both their bodies and managed to get her palms flat on the sidewalk. She tried to push up but couldn't budge her sister's dead weight without injuring her more. She couldn't be dead. "Reese?"

No reply.

Sydney stretched her arms out in front of her face and grasped the leg of a newspaper box bolted into the sidewalk. The metal cut into her palms as she pulled with all her strength and felt her body slide out from under Reese's. When her torso was free, she twisted around to sit and face Reese. Her hands supported her sister's shoulders, to keep her face from smashing into the sidewalk, as she edged her legs free.

She dragged in a deep breath. Reese lay prone, her face mashed against the rough concrete, her baseball cap in the gutter. The fall had knocked her sunglasses off and she looked younger, more vulnerable without them shielding her eyes. Sydney willed her to wake up, look at her, but Reese's eyes remained closed. Her hands extended to either side and the fingers of her right hand flopped inches from a gun. Had she fired one or both of the shots? It didn't matter. Sydney didn't see a wound or blood on her sister's back and allowed herself to feel hopeful. Maybe she wasn't hurt too badly. She reached for the wrist nearest her and put her fingers over the pulse. Reese's skin felt clammy, but her heart was beating: onetwothreefour. Too fast.

Sydney needed to call 911. She looked around frantically, but her purse, containing her cell phone, had disappeared.

"Someone help, please," she appealed to the milling crowd. "Call 911. Is anyone a doctor? I think she's been shot." The sound of approaching sirens told her someone had already phoned for help. Thank God.

No one stepped forward. Sydney reached up and grabbed the hand of a middle-aged man standing a step away. "Help me lift her."

The man gaped at her, then dropped reluctantly to his knees. Gently, they turned Reese over. Sydney gasped at the sight of the blood pooled beneath her—it looked like gallons—and still leaking from a wound in her abdomen. One hand flew to her mouth and she blinked back tears. "We need to stop the bleeding."

Without stopping to think, she ripped off her blouse, balled it up, and placed it over the wound. Blood soaked through it frighteningly fast and Sydney pressed down harder, barely feeling the warm trickle on her face.

"Maybe we should put her feet up?" her impromptu helper suggested. "Doesn't that help with shock?"

"Thanks," Sydney said.

He elevated Reese's feet and propped them on his briefcase.

"And we need a blanket. Does anyone have a coat, anything?" she appealed to the people still milling about. A woman handed over a cardigan sweater and a twenty-something man passed across a pinstriped suit jacket. Sydney kept her hand pressed tightly to the makeshift bandage as her helper draped the sweater over Reese's legs and folded the jacket to place under her head.

"Thanks," she whispered again. She pressed down harder, praying the EMTs would come, praying Reese would be okay. She'd lost so much blood. *Don't die, don't die, don't die…*

"Syd." The single word made her jump. Reese's eyes were open. They seemed glazed at first, but then her awareness seemed to sharpen as she focused on Sydney's face.

"Oh, thank God. You're going to be okay," she told her sister, putting a gentle hand on her cheek.

"…saying about victims and murderers?" Reese whispered. The corner of her mouth twitched as if she were trying to smile. "Guess I'm a victim after all. But not you." Her eyes fluttered closed and her head listed to the side.

"Reese! Reese!" Sydney stroked her sister's face repeatedly. "You're not a victim. You're going to be okay. Just talk to me, Reese. I'm right here. Right here. I'm not going anywhere, but you have to talk to me. Reese!"

After what seemed liked decades but was probably no more than another minute, the ambulance pulled up and EMTs jumped out, scattering the small knot of onlookers.

Sydney yielded her place to an efficient woman in a blue jumpsuit who opened a bag and got to work. Soon an IV line snaked into Reese's arm and the medics were loading her onto a gurney. Sydney glanced around and saw a skinny man reaching for Reese's gun where it lay forgotten on the sidewalk.

"Hey!" She lunged toward him and he scuttled back into the crowd. Gingerly, she picked up the gun and, spotting her purse under the newspaper box, put it in. Reese wouldn't want her gun in the hands of a junkie or a mugger.

A screech of tires and the whoop of a siren announced the arrival of the police. Two pairs of uniformed officers jumped from separate squad cars and the crowd immediately began to disperse, few people wanting to be tied up for hours giving witness statements. The two closest cops, a young white officer with jug ears and an older black man with grizzled hair wearing a sergeant's chevrons, assimilated the basic details in seconds from the EMTs and latched onto Sydney while the other cops rounded up witnesses.

"You were with the victim, ma'am?" the younger officer asked, pulling out a notebook. He had the earnest look of a young Ron Howard. Sydney named him "Opie" in her head. "Your name?"

"She's not a victim," Sydney said fiercely, then held up an apologetic hand. "Where are they taking her?" she asked as the ambulance pulled away from the curb, its lights and sirens clearing a path through the traffic like the prow of an icebreaker cleaving the polar seas.

"Howard University Hospital. But we need to get a statement from you." The black cop's nametag read *Morrison* and his voice held a Southern drawl. He shook off a homeless man trying to get his attention by tugging at his sleeve. "Later, bub."

"But someone's real sick. He needs a medic," the unkempt man said.

"Donnelly!" Sergeant Morrison beckoned to another cop and she hustled over and led the bum, carrying what was probably all his worldly goods on his back and in a gym bag, to the curb.

"I'm going to the hospital," Sydney said. She needed to be with Reese. She had a shivery feeling that the first shot she'd heard had been a bullet meant for her. And her sister had taken it. The least she could do was sit vigil at the hospital. She started for the curb, intending to flag a cab, but with a look at his partner, Opie said, "We'll drive you." He picked up the abandoned cardigan that had warmed Reese's legs. "Maybe you should put this on."

Suddenly conscious that she was standing on a busy street in her lacy bra, Sydney slipped her arms into the sweater and buttoned it with trembling fingers. The ride in the back seat of the police car passed in a blur of self-recrimination, chatter from the radio, and the smell of sweat and vomit from a previous occupant. When they pulled up at the Emergency entrance, Sydney tumbled out of the car and raced for the triage desk.

"My sister," she gasped. "Where is she? How is she?"

"Her name?" the nurse asked. She wore yellow scrubs dotted with flowers and had blond hair pulled back in a low ponytail. A stethoscope hung around her neck, along with a hospital badge.

"Reese Elizabeth Linn. The ambulance just brought her in. She was shot."

The nurse pursed her lips, clicked a few keys, and said, "She's going into surgery. You can go up to the waiting room on the third floor. It may be a few hours."

Sydney didn't move. She wanted more from the nurse, but she didn't know what. Reassurance? Direction?

A man's voice behind Sydney said, "Ma'am? My little boy's real sick."

She turned to see a thin, twenty-ish man holding a fever-flushed toddler against his shoulder. She blinked at him. Oh. He wanted her to move. The encounter reminded her of the crowded deli and the dad who needed to get his kids from daycare. With an apologetic noise, she stepped aside and looked blankly around a waiting room stuffed with runny-nosed children, coughing senior citizens, a man cradling his wrist in one hand, and several people staring blankly at the wall as if they'd lost all hope of ever setting eyes on a doctor. You should've gotten shot if you wanted fast attention, Sydney thought, threading her way through the room to the hallway to call Connie.

With a shaking hand, she dialed her mother's number. It went to voicemail. At the beep, she choked out, "Reese's been shot." The words hammered through her self-control and she started to sob. "Someone tried to shoot me and they hit Reese. You need to come. Howard University Hospital."

She swung away from the phone and found herself face to face with Opie and Sergeant Morrison.

"We need to get a statement from you, ma'am," Sergeant Morrison said.

"Okay." Sydney told them what she knew as they found the elevators and rode to the third floor. When the elevator doors slid open, she dashed down the hall toward a sign proclaiming *Surgical Waiting Area*, saying over her shoulder, "Call Detective West. He knows what this is about."

45

Sydney

NINETY MINUTES LATER, SYDNEY reclined on a padded gurney, watching blood flow from her vein into a collection pouch. Her left hand slowly squeezed and released a rubber ball as the technician bustled around checking the amount of blood in the pouch, making a note on a form, pulling a small can of apple juice from the refrigerator. Reese was still in surgery. When she'd asked what she could do, a nurse had suggested she donate blood. Turned out she and Reese were both O positive. It gave her some comfort to think that her blood might help save Reese's life as she'd saved hers.

"My God, what happened?" The worry in West's voice matched his expression as he charged into the room, flashing his badge at the nurse who moved to stop him.

"Someone tried to shoot me and my sister saved me," Sydney said, feeling again the thump between her shoulder blades that sent her to the ground.

"Tell me." West pulled up a metal-legged chair and straddled it.

Sydney filled him in on everything she remembered, mostly things she'd already told Sergeant Morrison and his partner. "Someone is trying to kill me," she finished, "and it's because of that phone call."

"Excuse me." The technician in his white lab coat wedged himself between West and Sydney. Withdrawing the needle from her arm, he put a cotton ball into the crook of her elbow and said, "Apply pressure and hold your arm straight up."

Sydney did as commanded, swinging her feet off the gurney so she faced West. She became conscious of how she must look, her bare legs scraped and dirty, her hair hanging in a tangled mass around her face, the cardigan and summer skirt splotched with Reese's blood. She tucked a hank of hair behind one ear and fought back tears.

"I'll find you something else to wear," West said.

He disappeared but returned while she was drinking her apple juice and munching the cookie the nurse forced on her. He bore a set of hospital scrubs, Dr. Seuss characters on a pink background. "Here. I'll be in the waiting room. We have to talk."

As soon as he left, Sydney stripped off the ruined clothes and shoved them into the container marked *Hazardous Waste*. She never wanted to see them again. Taking a quick sponge bath at the sink, using paper towels that left gritty brown bits where she scrubbed too hard, she slipped into the scrubs. They looked incongruous with her sandals, but she didn't have any other shoes and was reluctant to go barefoot in the hospital.

"Better?" West asked when she appeared in the waiting area.

"Much." She tried a smile. Anxious relatives of other patients who'd looked up when she entered went back to reading, handwringing, and quiet conversations. Armchairs upholstered in calming blues and deep greens were grouped around parquet-topped tables. Prince

William, with his arm around Kate Middleton and his face splotched by a coffee ring, grinned up at her from the cover of a magazine on the nearest table. The rich scent of brewed coffee drifted from a beverage bar tucked into a corner. Natural light streamed from a high window and nourished the peace lilies and ficuses in chunky ceramic planters. "Do you know how she is?"

West shook his head. "Still in surgery, I think. But she's young, fit … that's in her favor."

"Reese Linn? Next of kin for Reese?" A plump woman in surgical scrubs, hair scraped back from a high forehead, hovered in the doorway leading back to the operating rooms.

Sydney took a step forward. "Me. She's my sister."

The doctor motioned them into a private alcove and introduced herself as Dr. Tarkanian. She gave West a sharp look when he identified himself as a detective. Sydney's legs shook and West put an arm around her waist to steady her. She leaned against him as if he were a longtime friend, but straightened and pulled away when she remembered. He was a cop, here to investigate the shooting, nothing more.

"How is she? Is she going to be okay?"

The doctor tightened her full lips. "It's too early to tell. The bullet nicked her liver and tore a hole in her intestine. We had to resection it. And she's lost a lot of blood."

"Oh my God," Sydney said, squeezing her eyes shut for a moment of prayer. Reese had to live. She'd never forgive herself if she … She opened her eyes. "Can I see her?"

"Briefly. But she's still unconscious." The doctor took off at a brisk pace, ponytail bouncing against her neck, and halted at the nurse's station where she left them with the charge nurse, a fortyish Filipino man. He gave her a badge and escorted them to Reese's room, leaving them at the door. "Just five minutes, mind."

"I'll wait right here," West said, giving her a reassuring look.

Sydney edged into the room. Reese lay on her back with a sheet tucked under her armpits, and her arms, tan against the white sheets, resting atop them. The sheet rose and fell as she breathed. An IV line snaked to the vein in her left hand. Reese's long-fingered, competent hand seemed fragile in this setting, almost as if the needle were draining it of life rather than pumping in vital fluids. The skin seemed to have shrunken to fit the bones, outlining them clearly. Sydney put out a tentative hand and stroked her sister's middle finger. No response. A variety of machines blinked and chirped, monitoring blood pressure, pulse, and heaven knew what else. Tearing her gaze away from her sister's hand, Sydney studied the machine's green, blue, and yellow lines, but they revealed little. She turned her eyes to Reese's face.

Tears filled her eyes. "I'm so sorry, Ree-ree," she told her sister. "Sorry for getting you mixed up in this, for getting you shot. For hating you. I was so stupid! For everything. Just be okay, please? Earl needs you. And you need to finish renovating your house, and, and go to Nana Linn's cabin—we could go together—and ... " Sydney stopped her babbling by biting down hard on her lower lip.

Reese didn't stir. Only her chest rose and fell, rose and fell to the artificially slow beat of a machine. The movement was so slight, Sydney had to watch for it. She leaned down to kiss her sister on the cheek. "You are not a victim, Reese," she whispered in her ear. "Don't you dare be a victim."

Connie's voice spoke from the doorway. "Oh my God, oh my God. Reese. Baby. What has happened to you?" She surged forward, her tennis whites speaking to an interrupted game, her mussed hair telegraphing her distress.

Sydney stepped back so her mother could approach the bed, inhaling a whiff of Chanel No. 5 as she shouldered past. Connie stared down at her older daughter, and then stroked the hair back from her forehead.

Sydney felt her heart crack open at the expression of love and fear on Connie's face. Her mother was usually so ... *untouched* by life's harsher moments, preserving a facade of calm in the face of her daughter's disgrace, her husband's incapacitation and death, her own battle with breast cancer, that to see her laid bare like this made Sydney feel like she'd walked in on Connie naked. She shut her eyes.

"She's going to be all right," Connie said after a long minute. "The doctor said ... well, doctors are paid to be cautious, aren't they? My baby's strong. She's always been strong. And she's a fighter. Yes, you are, Reese Elizabeth, you're a fighter, so fight, damn it."

The nurse came to the doorway and motioned for them to leave the room. "Time's up," he said. "You can have another five minutes with her later."

Connie acted as if she hadn't heard him, continuing to encourage and chide Reese in a low voice. Sydney put a hand on her mother's shoulder. "Connie. Mom. She needs rest."

Squeezing Reese's hand, Connie let it slip slowly from hers and followed Sydney into the hall, where West was waiting. She blinked fast several times, then stood taller and looked from Sydney to West. "Someone tell me what the hell happened. Who shot my daughter? Why?"

Another nurse frowned at them and made shooing motions. West led the way back to the waiting area while Sydney summarized the morning's happenings for her mother in a low voice, concluding with, "The shooter was aiming for me, but he got Reese instead. She pushed me down. She saved my life."

"And you saved hers," West reminded them both. "If you hadn't stanched the blood, she'd have bled out before the EMTs got there."

"She wouldn't have needed saving except for me," Sydney said, her voice breaking. Guilt and fear for her sister threatened to overpower her, and she gripped her hands tightly together to keep them from shaking.

"Don't kid yourself," Connie surprised her by saying. "Reese has always had a mind of her own. From day one. Came out of the womb that way. She was the stubbornest…" She stopped and seemed to focus on two men praying together in the corner, hands entwined and eyes shut. She faced Sydney again, her eyes shining with tears that she refused to let fall. "She has a habit of putting herself in the line of fire, too. I blame Howard for that." She didn't explain why. "Don't think I don't blame you, too. If you'd gone to the police with that phone right away, or held onto your own phone in the first place, none of this would've happened. Certainly not Reese getting shot. But you chickened out. I don't know if I can forgive you or not." She said it flatly, and her lack of emotion was almost worse than tears or rage.

Sydney flinched and started to say, "I'm so sor—"

Connie cut her off. "The question is, why are you hanging around here when you should be out there"—she flung an arm out to indicate the world beyond the hospital—"catching the bastard who did this? Get going," Connie added forcefully, drawing the attention of the waiting room's other inhabitants, who cast furtive or disapproving looks their way.

For a startled moment, Sydney thought Connie was speaking to her, but then she saw that her minatory gaze was fixed on West. Even after she'd realized Connie was talking to the detective, Sydney felt the words vibrating inside her chest. She'd led a killer to Jason and now to Reese. She was going to track him down. She couldn't do anything for Reese here, but she could make sure that the man who shot her didn't get away with it.

West seemed amused rather than annoyed by Connie's command. He held up a placatory hand. "I'm on it."

"I'm coming with you," Sydney told West. "That is ... are you okay here by yourself, Connie? I can stay if you want ... "

Connie flapped a hand. "Hilary's coming. I'll be fine. I need to let some people know"—she held up her cell phone—"and then I can catch up on *People*. Apparently, Prince William is getting married." She cast a disparaging look at the waiting room's selection of outdated magazines. Sydney was sure she'd never read an issue of *People* in her life.

West guided Sydney from the room with a hand at her waist. She felt like a soldier must after a firefight—dazed, uncomprehending, shaky.

"Your sister'll be fine," he said. "She's tough. But she's clearly out of commission as your bodyguard, so I'm appointing a new one."

"No!" Sydney shook her head vehemently. "I can't let anyone else risk—" She dodged an empty wheelchair, grazing West.

He steadied her. "It's not up to you. You're a taxpayer—you get protection."

"Meaning?"

He smiled grimly. "You get me."

46

Paul

PAUL AWOKE, MOMENTARILY DISORIENTED by the smell of bleach and the feel of crisp sheets tucked under his armpits. *Where—?* Another second brought the realization that his injured shoulder hurt much less than earlier, and that his mind felt clearer, more focused. His eyes followed plastic tubing from his left hand to a stainless steel IV tree. The hospital. Of course. The almost-empty IV bag sagging from its hook must have contained antibiotics. A clean new bandage covered his wound, and the angry red streaks shooting down his arm had almost disappeared.

How long had he been here? Craning his head to see the watch on his wrist, he read the glowing numbers: 2:30. More than four hours since he'd missed his shot at the Ellison woman and escaped. He'd been talking to a wino … his bag! Where was his gym bag with the gun? Paul pushed to a half-sitting position, propped on his elbows, and scanned the counters and floor in the small exam room: a glass-fronted cabinet with gauze, bandages, gloves, and other medical supplies he couldn't identify; a red sharps disposal container; a sink with a soap dispenser; cupboards; monitoring machines on wheeled carts. No duffel. The police must have it. Maybe they'd already run ballistics—

Rings rattled around the metal rod as a nurse pushed back the curtain surrounding his bed. No one occupied the gurney on the other side of the curtain and a slice of hall was equally empty beyond the door. It wheezed shut.

"Ah, you're awake, good." Middle-aged, she moved with crisp efficiency to check the readings on the machine behind him. Something about the way she carried herself—maybe the sway of her ample hips—reminded him of Moira.

"Where—?"

"You're at Howard University Hospital. You had a nasty infection in your shoulder but the penicillin is doing its trick. Your temp's down and your blood pressure is much better than when they brought you in."

"My clothes? My duffel?" Paul held his breath, waiting for her answer.

"Your clothes, cell phone, and wallet are in that bag." She nodded to a plastic bag hanging from a drawer pull. "I don't think you had anything else with you. I can check."

"Thanks."

She squeezed the bag of fluids dripping into his IV. A laminated ID dangled from a chain around her neck. "Administration wants a chat with you when you're up to it—something about your insurance, and I understand the police have a few questions also." She smiled down at him. "I'll hold them all off for a while yet. You need more rest." She palpated the flesh around the bandage and gave a satisfied nod before bustling out of the exam room. A brisk tug slid the curtain around its rod again. A moment later, the door clunked shut.

Shit. The insurance card in his false name wouldn't hold up if the hospital ran it. And the police! Did they want to talk about the gun in his bag, the gunshot wound in his shoulder, or the killing on Pennsylvania Avenue? Whatever it was, he needed to get out of here. He shoved himself to a sitting position, wincing as the needle in the back of his hand shifted. With mordant humor he imagined himself sneaking out of the hospital and down the streets of Washington DC with the IV stand trailing behind him. The IV had to go. He peeled back the tape to expose the needle and a large bruise on the back of his hand. Steeling himself, he pressed the edge of the sheet against the point where the needle disappeared into his vein and pulled. The needle slid free and he applied pressure to the insertion site as he decided what to do next.

Easing himself off the gurney, he held onto it for a moment when his head swam. Soon, he felt steadier and headed naked for the cabinet with the bandages. He found one and stuck it on his hand. There. Clothes came next. Feeling stronger by the moment, better than he had in days, in fact, he quickly dressed and slipped his wallet and cell phone into his pocket. He paused for a moment, listening, but heard nothing but the usual clatter of an ER outside the room. Opening the door a crack, he peered out. No one in sight.

Feeling exposed, as if he were crossing a rice paddy, Paul stepped into the hall. Forcing himself to walk, he headed away from the sound of the noisy waiting room. A quick turn put him into another hall. A red exit sign beckoned from the far end. He sped up. Suddenly, a door opened in his path and a young woman backed into the hall, pulling a cart with what looked like a mobile x-ray machine. He ploughed into her.

She staggered, putting a hand to the red rectangular glasses he'd knocked askew. "What the he—" She bit back the word and glared at him.

"My daughter! They said she's having her baby. Do you know—" He didn't have to fake his panic and he knew it sounded in his voice.

The anger receded from the woman's face. "Labor and Delivery is on three," she said. "Just take those elevators and turn left." She pointed. "Your first grandbaby?"

"Yes. Thanks." He turned on his heel and walked in the direction she'd indicated. With her eyes on him, he pressed the call button and stepped on, flipping a brief wave at her. "Good luck, Grandpa," she called as the doors came together.

He stabbed the button "2" and got off at the next floor, merging with a group of visitors carrying flowers, balloons, and a large candle that leaked pungent bayberry from within its plastic wrapping. When they passed a stairwell, he peeled off and darted down the stairs, taking them two at a time. Any second now, if they hadn't already, they'd discover he was missing from the ER and raise the alarm—driven by the desire to get a valid insurance number from him, he thought cynically.

At the landing, he paused a moment outside the door stenciled "1" to catch his breath. The hallway was empty when he opened the door, and he heaved a sigh of relief. Only steps away was the exit door, this one marked *Emergency Exit Only. Alarm Will Sound.* A faint odor of stale cigarettes drifted to him. Maybe the unredeemed smokers snuck out this door to puff and had disabled the alarm. The hell with it. He banged the door open and ran. He thought he heard an alarm but then realized it was a siren from an approaching ambulance. A parking lot choked with cars, some illegally parked in the aisles and fire lanes, spread out ahead of him. He slowed to a walk, risking a glance over his shoulder as he reached the asphalt. No one behind him.

Threading his way through the densely packed cars, mothers with kids in strollers, and geriatrics hunched over walkers, he left the hospital grounds and looked for the Metro sign he knew must be nearby. Spotting the Shaw/Howard University Metro sign, he headed for the dark tunnel like a prairie dog for his burrow, sure of safety. As he put a foot on the escalator, his cell phone rang. He reached for it, stepping aside to let a paunchy businessman onto the escalator.

"What the hell are you doing?" The familiar voice bit at his ear. "You shot goddamned Reese Linn, the writer! It'll be a media feeding frenzy. Is this how you cover your tracks?"

"She jumped on top of Ellison," Paul said. Who the hell was Reese Linn? Obviously, the woman who took the bullet for Ellison, but why was it such a big deal? And why couldn't women have female names anymore? Susan and Pamela had been good enough for the girls in his generation. "Look—"

"No, you look. You concentrate on Montoya. Today's the election and I want him dead. D-E-A-D. I paid you a hefty sum up front and I want results. I don't want to have to spread the word that you're past it, Mr. Jones."

"You're the one who changed the assignment, tacked on Ellison," Paul said, his voice as cold as the client's. "You don't want to threaten me."

The client didn't back down. "You just fucking make it happen with Montoya. I'll take care of Ellison."

Paul found himself listening to silence when the client cut the connection. He slid the phone into his pocket slowly, misgiving and anger writhing in his gut. It might be time to implement his precautionary measures related to his mercurial client. Past time.

47

Sydney

"WHAT DID YOU MEAN, you're my bodyguard?" Sydney asked, taking long strides to keep up with West as he headed toward the hospital's front exit. He'd spoken to the officers who'd responded to the shooting, made a couple of calls to arrange for a forensics team to scour the roof of the building across from the dentist's office, and ordered a guard put on Reese, more to keep out the reporters than prevent the killer from making another attempt, he'd told Sydney.

Now he ignored her question. "I'm taking you to a safe house."

She stopped dead. "I am not going anywhere dressed like this. I look like I'm wearing my pajamas. I need to stop by my townhouse, get some clothes."

"Negative." He was shaking his head before she finished speaking. "Your townhouse is not on the agenda, not with a hit man out to kill you."

"So you believe me?" Her eyes widened and she hurried to catch up, almost knocking against a wizened man inching along the wall with a walker.

"Yep."

"Great. And all it took was my sister getting shot." Relief, bitterness, and guilt clashed within her.

"I'm sorry about that."

She waved his apology away, although the sincerity in his voice eased the tension clenching her stomach. "What do we do now?"

He slanted a look at her. His lashes really were absurdly long. "*We* don't do anything. You stay holed up in a safe place. I do the detecting and find this guy before he gets another chance at you or Montoya." Halfway across the lobby, he stopped. "Shit!"

"What?"

He pointed toward the tinted floor-to-ceiling wall of windows bracketing the revolving door at the hospital's entrance. "Reporters."

Sydney heard the din through the closed doors, a pack of hounds baying for the fox's blood. Or, in this case, the vixen's. She tamped down the anxiety rising within her, noting that the reporters' presence didn't panic her as much as usual. Their menace paled in comparison to the rest of the day's events.

"They're onto the shooting. Someone here leaked. C'mon," West said, spinning on his heel. "You don't want to deal with that right now."

No, she certainly didn't. She followed him as they retraced their steps.

"Detective West!"

The voice and heavy footsteps trotting their way stopped them just before they cleared the lobby. Sydney turned, wincing in anticipation of being pelted by a reporter's questions, to see one of the policemen who'd helped with Reese approaching them. West put out an arm to edge her slightly behind him.

"Glad I caught you, sir. Thought you'd want to know," Sergeant Morrison said. He had a stolid, capable presence Sydney felt would be comforting to find on your doorstep if you ever reported a prowler in the middle of the night. "Following the shooting incident, my partner and I were notified that another victim needed help, several blocks away. I sent Donnelly over and she said the man, white and in his sixties, was in a bad way."

"Yes?" West made a "get on with it" motion.

"Yes, sir. Well, the man had a GSW in his shoulder."

"What?"

"Yes, sir. The ER doc said the man had a bullet wound—two, three days old maybe—in his right shoulder. He was here, but he did a runner before we could talk to him about it. Doc said it looked like the wound had been professionally treated, but it was infected."

"They get a name?" West pulled out a notebook, prepared to write.

Sydney's gaze went from him to Sergeant Morrison, wondering what it meant. Gunshot wounds weren't all that unusual in downtown DC, after all.

"Yes, sir, but it was a fake. Anyway, what with the shooting and all, I thought you'd want to know about this guy. Especially since he matches the description of a strange man a witness saw in the garage of the building across the street from the Penn Professional Building just after the shooting. She said he was white, in his mid-to-late-sixties, and wore a ball cap and tan utility uniform that had the name 'Lionel' on the pocket. She thought he was a maintenance guy and seemed pissed he hadn't come to fix her sink."

Sydney paled. Was it possible that the man who'd killed Jason and shot Reese had been here, only a floor or two away from them if that? She shivered involuntarily. "Where—" she started, but West cut her off.

"You did good, Sergeant. I'll—"

"That's not all," the sergeant plowed on. "I called around to local motels to see if a Lionel Ross was registered—that's the name the guy used in the ER—and I got a hit at the Best Western over on Florida. I sent a patrol car over there—they don't think the guy'll be back. They say it feels like he's gone. Left his stuff, though, including a laptop, and they're taking it to the station."

"You did damn good! I'll mention it to your lieutenant. Put out an APB and let me know if you come up with anything interesting. And let's run any prints the team lifts, pronto."

"You got it, sir." Sergeant Morrison nodded twice, cast a curious look at Sydney, and turned away.

Sydney followed West down a smaller, quieter hall that smelled like hospital food—mushy peas, steamy metal from the lids that covered the dishes, and coffee.

"What was that all about?" she asked from half a step behind him.

"Could be the shooter, could be unconnected," he said.

"Doesn't sound unconnected," Sydney said, half jogging to draw even with him. The movement jarred her throbbing knee and made her aware of an aching shoulder and elbow.

"Agreed. Time—and evidence—will tell," he said. "For now, our best move is to put you somewhere the guy can't find you, and do the same for Montoya if he'll cooperate." West strode toward a small door with angry red signs warning *Emergency Exit Only. Alarm Will Sound.*

"Won't the alarm—?" she asked as he banged his palm against the bar. The door sprang open.

"Apparently not." Bright sunlight and a wall of heat clobbered them on the stoop as West got his bearings. Cigarette butts littered the ground around them and the smoky smell seemed to permeate the very brick of the walls. "C'mon." He grabbed Sydney's hand to pull her toward the parking lot.

"Hey, sleepyhead, we're here."

West's voice jolted Sydney. She must have fallen asleep on the ride to the safe house. How could she—? Her body's natural reaction to the aftermath of crisis, she realized. Out the car window, a block of condos, interchangeable with hundreds of similar buildings in the DC area, rose upward from a base of manicured grass. "Where are we?"

"My place."

She shot him a look.

"My intentions are pure," he said with a slight smile. "No one will think to look for you here. This takes less paperwork than getting you into an official safe house, and it's more secure. The fewer people who know where you are the better until I find this guy."

With a nod of acknowledgment, Sydney swung her legs out of the car and followed West into the building, noting an anonymous mélange of concrete, glass, tile, and potted plants. They got into an elevator along with a suited woman holding a six- or seven-year-old girl by the hand. The girl surveyed Sydney openly and finally asked, "Are you a doctor?"

Sydney laughed ruefully, looking down at her scrubs, and said, "No, honey. But I got these from a doctor."

The mother pulled her daughter closer, as if afraid of germs cascading off Sydney, and hustled the little girl off the elevator at the next floor.

Sydney crossed the threshold of West's condo like a scout moving into possibly hostile territory. The perfectly ordinary two-bedroom condo seemed alien. She felt strange staying at West's place with Jason dead less than a week. It wasn't that there was anything romantic or illicit to what she was doing; it just felt strange. It was the only word she could come up with. She dropped her purse on the narrow table in the entryway and folded her arms around her waist as West flipped through the mail littering the floor under the letter slot.

"The usual garbage," he said. "C'mon in."

She followed him into a small living room lined with books, photos, and traditional furniture in a dark wood upholstered in forest green and chocolate leather. Comfortable looking and typically masculine. She moved further into the room. West cut across to the kitchen and the clink of ice cubes drifted to Sydney as she studied a wall of photos all framed in silver metal.

"You ride?" she asked, looking at a picture of him on a horse, a huge grin plastered across his face. He looked young, tan, carefree, less guarded than he seemed now.

"I grew up on a ranch in Colorado," he said from the kitchen. "Riding was part of the deal. That and taking care of livestock, baling hay, the usual." He appeared in the doorway with two glasses of iced tea.

"Thanks," Sydney said, taking one. "So how come you're not Rancher Ben, riding the range?"

"My older brother, Brad, wanted to ranch and I didn't. I had a fling with rodeo, then decided I wanted to be able to walk when I was fifty, so I got out of that. I got a degree in criminal justice and joined the Air Force." He leaned against the door jamb, watching her as she peered at the photos.

"And now you're a cop."

"I was a cop in the Air Force, too. I enjoyed the military, even the deployments, but it was hard on my marriage. Claire got a better offer when I was in Iraq for a second tour. She and her new husband live in Maryland, so I got out of the Air Force to stay near Alexa. She'll be twelve in October."

"This her?" Sydney stopped in front of a photo of a girl with brown hair in ponytails and a braces-laden grin that mirrored the one from the other photo. "She's cute."

"As a baby wolverine," he said drily. Despite his tone, Sydney could feel the affection radiating from him.

Sydney laughed. The sound surprised her. She hadn't felt like laughing lately. "Just wait until she hits her teens. My mom says I was an unbearable combination of hormones and hostility from twelve to fifteen. Then I turned back into a human being, so there's hope."

"It seems like the list of things you have to worry about as a father just gets longer as your daughter gets older: driving, boys, grades, getting into college, skanky friends, online bullying, predators … you name it. I miss the days when my biggest worry was keeping her from sticking her finger in a socket or chewing on the toilet bowl brush."

"It must be wonderful," Sydney said softly, wondering if she'd ever have a child to raise. She'd hoped she and Jason … The colors in the room seemed muted all of a sudden.

"I've got to get back," West said with a look at his watch. "Make yourself at home. I'll give you a call in a couple of hours, let you know what's going on. Stick close, okay? Take a shower if you want." His brown eyes were serious as they met hers. "Don't do anything stupid, and don't tell anyone you're here."

She let the "stupid" comment slide. "I need to call the hospital and check on my sister."

"That should be okay. Just don't mention where you are, not even to your mother. She might let something slip without meaning to."

The seriousness with which he took the situation unnerved her a bit. She deadbolted the door behind him.

―――――

West had mentioned a shower, and Sydney suddenly couldn't wait to rinse the day's events off under pulsing water. Exploring a short hall, she found a bathroom that West's daughter used, if the lavender bathmat and plethora of fruit-scented body washes, gels, shampoos, and conditioners lining the tub were anything to go by. The collection spurred a small smile. She kicked off her sandals and wiggled her grateful toes. Every part of her body hurt. Her hand burned where the scab from the branding iron had been torn off by the asphalt when Reese pushed her down, and the barbed-wire gouge in her thigh stung. Bruises ached on her hips, legs, and shoulders as she stripped off the pink scrubs and her bloodstained bra. Her ankle was swollen to the size of a tennis ball.

Turning the water on as hot as she could stand it, she stepped into the tub and let the water sluice over her, carrying away the dried flakes of blood—Reese's blood—and some of her exhaustion. Lathering her hair with strawberry-scented shampoo, she massaged her scalp hard before squirting a dollop of kiwi-mango conditioner into her hand. She was going to smell like a fruit salad. The thought brought another smile. The smiles were coming easier. Reese was going to be okay. West was going to catch the killer. She switched the tap to cold for a few seconds before she jumped out and dried herself on a fluffy purple towel. She had to re-don the pink scrubs, and wrinkled her nose at them. Nothing could have made her wear the bloody bra, even though her breasts swinging free and heavy were disconcerting. As soon as she could, she'd duck back to the townhouse and get something more presentable. It was hard to feel confident, able to face down the media or a hit man, when braless and wearing pink scrubs.

She called Connie to check on Reese but got her voicemail. Of course; Connie wouldn't keep her phone on in the hospital. As she was about to dial the hospital's main number, the phone vibrated in her hand. Connie's number glowed at her.

With a sudden feeling of foreboding, Sydney answered. "Mom?"

"Your sister has gone back into surgery," Connie said, in a voice like a thread of glass likely to shatter at the slightest touch. "There was a blood clot. It … it broke free and caused a cerebrovascular incident."

A thousand thin metal flechettes buried themselves in Sydney's skin. Her every nerve ending felt seared. "A stroke?" she whispered. They were all familiar with the language of strokes after her father's strokes. "How is she—? Will she—? I'm on my way."

"No." Connie sounded stronger. "No, don't come to the hospital, Sydney. I can't—it's too much. Your father, Reese." She sounded as if she was going to say more, but then swallowed audibly. "Hilary's here, and a couple of friends from the neighborhood. I'll call you when I know anything. You might pray."

"But—"

Her mother hung up. Sydney slid down the wall to her haunches, putting a fist against her mouth. Her mother blamed her. For her father's death, and for Reese's condition. A single sob escaped before she bit down savagely on her inner cheek, determined to keep the tears back. If she gave in now, she would lose it, be no use to Reese or anyone. Pushing through her heels, she forced herself back up. Clothes. She had to have real clothes. Clutching her phone in her fist, willing it to ring with good news from Connie, she grabbed her purse and fumbled with the deadbolt. When it slid back, she hurried toward the elevator, not even thinking to lock West's door.

48

Paul

PAUL EMERGED FROM THE bank in Chevy Chase with his new identity safely stowed in his wallet and what he liked to think of as an insurance file tucked under his arm. His safety deposit boxes came in handy for securing more than cash, weapons, and the elements of clean identities.

With the Lionel Ross identity compromised by his visit to the ER, he couldn't risk returning to his room or retrieving his rental car. The cops might even now be sniffing around, lifting fingerprints. Inconvenient but not fatal. His prints would lead to the Army and the Army would pull up the bland file of a soldier killed at Ia Drang. The military bureaucracy had long ago erased any trace of his real identity when he became part of Operation Phoenix. There was nothing to tie him to Nygaard's murder since he'd ditched that gun at the Ellison woman's place, and nothing to tie him to today's fiasco. Except the sniper pistol in his gym bag, wherever the hell it was.

Crossing the street to a mall where he intended to replace his lost gym bag and purchase some clothes, toiletries, and a new laptop, he pondered the duffel's fate. With any luck the EMTs had overlooked it sitting on the sidewalk when they'd carted him off to the ER, and someone had stolen it. He regretted the loss of his laptop, though all his data was stored on the flash drive safely hooked to his key chain. He jiggled it in his pocket. A slight smile stretched his lips as he thought about the crackhead or petty thief getting arrested. The cops would find his gun, run ballistics, and tie the thief to Reese Linn's shooting if they recovered the bullet. Justice of a sort.

With the essentials packed in a new black backpack, Paul bought a sub sandwich in the mall's noisy food court and called home. No answer. He left a brief message for Moira and returned his cell phone to his pocket. A mother with twins in a stroller and a toddler lagging behind dumped her shopping bags on the table next to Paul's. One of the twins began squalling and the three-year-old demanded "fwen fwy." The harassed mother picked up the screaming baby, sat, and unbuttoned her blouse, draping a yellow blanket over her shoulder.

Time to go. Paul averted his eyes from the suckling baby and carried his tray to a nearby trash can where he dumped the remains of his meal. He felt tired and his shoulder ached, but the fever that had been clouding his head really was gone. Over dinner he had come up with a new plan for taking out Montoya, and it was time to set the plan in motion. Congressman Fidel Montoya wasn't going to care whether or not the voters thought he'd make a good senator.

49

Sydney

OUTSIDE WEST'S CONDOMINIUM COMPLEX, Sydney looked up, past the pitted brick walls of the building and its neighbors, surprised by the sky's blueness. On some unconscious level she'd expected darkness, even though it was only early evening and the light would linger till past nine.

She turned automatically toward the nearest Metro stop. The sun soaked into her pink top, trapping heat against her body. Feelings of overwhelming loss smothered her like cling wrap; she could see through the clear film, but nothing from outside permeated the barrier. People strode purposefully toward meetings or loitered outside shops; Sydney steered around them as if they were pylons, not hearing their conversations or their laughter, not smelling the warmth of too many bodies jammed together like logs floating toward a sawmill. Images of Jason sprawled on the floor, his blood pooled around his head, played in her mind, mixing with snapshots of Reese on the sidewalk. She felt Jason's terror as a stranger thrust a gun at him and fired, his pain as the bullet bored into his flesh, tearing skin and muscle, shattering bone. When the solid metal lump came to rest, had he felt it? Had Reese felt the bullet plowing into her intestines? Had it been cold and alien, lodged near her liver? Or had it been burning hot after its expulsion from the gun, searing her organs?

She descended into the darkness of the subway station, knowing she was responsible. The knowledge she'd been ducking since Jason's death clobbered her. If she hadn't been such a coward, if she'd taken the phone immediately to the police, Jason would be alive. She'd killed him, just like she'd killed her father. Like she'd maybe killed Reese by asking for her help. She boarded a train like an automaton, grabbing a strap to steady herself in the press of rush hour commuters. She rocked to the train's rhythm, bumping shoulders with a youth in a hoodie wearing pungent hair gel and a suited man who smelled vaguely like cat pee. Despite the wall of flesh around her, Sydney felt utterly alone. She became part of the flow surging toward the up escalator when the train stopped and threaded her way toward the exit. She couldn't stop herself from cycling through a litany of the injuries she'd done to people she loved.

The stroke her father suffered when the Manley scandal broke had killed him, even though he hadn't died for almost twenty more years. He'd been trapped in a body whose right side was locked up. He'd needed assistance with eating and bathing. He'd worn adult diapers. Worse, his spirit was imprisoned by a brain that could no longer access language except randomly. For a man celebrated for his oratory, his cogent arguments before the Supreme Court, it was a fate worse than being buried alive. Only Connie Linn seemed to know what he was trying to communicate, and then only occasionally. "For better or for worse" had turned into a twenty-year sentence for her mom. That was her fault, too. The thought that Reese might end up the same way...

She stepped off a curb and two cars and a bus squealed to a stop as she crossed against the light. Angry honking brought her head up. She stared at the driver of a green Saturn as he stuck his head out the window and raved at her. Not hearing a single word, she continued across the street, instinctively headed for home.

"You okay? Miss?" The tentative voice, words slurred through missing teeth, broke through Sydney's grief. She focused on the man and his dog standing in front of her. Eli, that was it. His bloodshot eyes held an anxious expression and the dog nosed her hand. She felt the wetness on her face and mopped the tears with the hem of her shirt.

"Yes. No." She floundered for words, undone by the real concern in the homeless man's voice. The dog sat and bit along the length of his tail. "Oh, I've got something for him." She fumbled with her purse and unearthed the flea collar she'd stuck in it days before. Before Jason died. She bent to buckle it around the dog's neck, grateful for the opportunity to hide her face. "What's his name?"

"Duke. After Ellington." The man shuffled his feet.

"Do you like jazz?"

"I played with Ellington once. Before the alcohol took away the music." He edged away, and Sydney understood he was regretting the impulse that led him to talk to her.

"I played clarinet in middle school," she offered. "I wasn't very good."

"Piano." He played a few notes in the air, his large, dusky hands unbearably graceful. Sydney didn't know much jazz, but she felt the music hovering in the air around them.

"You were good."

He nodded and let his hands drop to his side. "Still am." Summoning Duke with a slap on his thigh, he turned away.

"Thank you," Sydney called after them. She started homeward again, thinking about Eli and the other homeless people in DC. They were almost invisible, she thought, even though they lived out in the open, completely without physical privacy. Exposed, yet invisible at the same time. While she, able to afford fences and gates and a house with doors that locked, had not been able to escape total exposure in the newspapers and on TV. How utterly ironic. The knowledge that she wouldn't trade places with Eli for anything, not even anonymity, smote her.

Something about the encounter had freed her mind and she could think clearly again. The sadness still tugged at her, but she felt a new sense of resolve as she approached her townhouse, swept along by the sound of the Marine band practicing at the barracks. She'd found a purpose in life after the scandal, her dad's illness, and Dirk's betrayal by starting Winning Ways. Right now, her priority had to be finding the man who killed Jason and hurt Reese. Not just the man who'd pulled the trigger, but the one who put him up to it. West was on the case now, but she'd been investigating longer, and had the advantage of being the target.

Her mind assessing and discarding various plans for luring the killer into the open and getting him to implicate his employer, she swung open the gate to her tiny front yard. No sign of Indy. At least they'd dropped Earl at Connie's. Drooping feathers of salvia begging for water in their pots on either side of the door reminded her she'd neglected many home duties since Jason's death. She uncoiled the hose and turned on the faucet, rinsing the faint scent of flea collar chemicals off her hands before filling a watering can. As she was trickling the last of the water onto the grateful salvia, she noticed the corner of an envelope peeking from beneath her front door. Setting down the can, she bent to tug at the envelope. The corner tore off in her hand.

Damn. She fumbled for her keys and unlocked the door. Retrieving the envelope, she carried it upstairs and set it on the dresser while she stripped. She dug a clean bra out of her lingerie drawer and donned the first T-shirt that came to hand. With a crisp movement, she slid the closet door open to yank a pair of slacks off a hanger. A box on the top shelf caught her eye.

Oh, God. Reese's letters. She stretched on tiptoe to dislodge the box. It tilted and slid toward her in a poof of dust. She sneezed. Carrying the box to her bed, she sat. Even as she was thinking she didn't have time for this, she was lifting the lid off the shoe box. The two business-sized envelopes, one postmarked from Chicago and the other from Israel, lay atop a collection of Nana Linn's embroidered hankies, a box of seashells collected on a long-ago beach vacation, a well-read copy of *The Prophet*, and a dried corsage from prom. Treasures.

She ran two fingers the length of the smooth envelope. The gesture reminded her of Emma Fewell making a similar movement to demonstrate how her husband had shined his grief. She drew her hand back as if stung. Oh my God. She'd been doing the same thing, hanging onto her anger at Reese, keeping it alive by ignoring these apologies—she's always known the letters were apologies, of course she had—dwelling on her hurt, her sense of betrayal, the hardship. The stupidity and futility of it struck her with staggering force. Fifteen years wasted. Well, thirteen or fourteen, at least. Surely a year's anger was justified? Decisively, she fitted the lid back on the box. She didn't need to read the words to know Reese was sorry, to forgive her sister ... and maybe even herself? If—when—Reese recovered, maybe they'd talk about it. Or not.

Right now, she needed to figure out a way to smoke out the man who'd shot her sister. Her gaze fell on the other envelope, the one on the dresser. Her brows twitched together. It really didn't look like the junk flyer she'd assumed it was. Crossing to it, she inserted a finger into the torn corner and worked it open. She pulled out a folded photocopy of a newspaper photo. Flattening it against the dresser, she studied it. The picture was clearly taken at a funeral, and showed a solemn-faced Fidel Montoya headed away from an open grave, his arm around his wife. Three other mourners, two men and a woman, stood in the background, heads bent. There was no cutline or accompanying article.

Sydney knit her brows. Whose funeral was it? Who had shoved the photo under her door? Why? She couldn't tell if the photo was from last month or ten years ago. It was connected with Jason's death, though. It had to be.

The words from the phone call came back to her: "Time for round two." She was convinced, down to her bones certain, that the photo had something to do with "round one."

Without any clues to go by, any key words, finding the photo's provenance on the Internet was a lost cause. She wasn't going to waste her time on the computer when she knew someone who could tell at a glance where and when the photo had been taken. With any luck, he'd also know why someone had shoved it under her door.

Sydney punched a number into her cell phone and greeted Fidel Montoya when he answered.

"Your sister. Oh my God, Sydney, I heard about it on the news. What the hell happened?"

"It's a long story," she said, not wanting to go into it on the phone. "We need to talk. I've got something to show you."

"Really? Did you find something? Never mind. Tell me when you get here. I'm at the house." He gave her the address. "I never have an election night party. It's a superstition of mine. The night of my first election, for city council, I got bronchitis and couldn't speak at the supporters' dinner like I was supposed to. I spent the evening drinking cough syrup and watching a 007 movie marathon. I won. Ever since, I always spend election night watching James Bond. I've never lost."

"I'll bring the Robitussin," Sydney said.

He laughed. "Plan to stay for dinner," he added as he hung up.

The warmth in his voice gave her pause. Where was his wife? On the one hand, she didn't fancy another encounter with the hostile Ms. Katya Van Slyke. On the other, she didn't want to spend an evening alone with Montoya. Even if he didn't try anything, chances were some nosy reporter would make something of it. She hesitated a moment, then gave a fatalistic shrug. She'd ask him about the photograph and then leave. She'd be in and out in half an hour, tops.

She called Connie and learned that Reese was still in surgery, then hailed a taxi in the deepening twilight. Sliding onto the slick vinyl seat patched with duct tape in several places, she gave the cabbie the address, her eyes meeting his in the rearview mirror and daring him to complain about the semi-rural destination. With a grunt, he put the car in gear and pulled away from the curb, jerkily enough to bounce her against the door. She kept her mouth shut, figuring it would be worth it if she could finally get some answers. Almost to Montoya's, it occurred to her to call West, but she got his voicemail. She was cut off halfway through her explanation of finding the news clipping and where she was going with it. No matter—in all probability she'd be on her way back before he checked his messages.

50

Paul

HIS BODY HUMMING WITH energy as the antibiotics ran off the infection, Paul approached the target's place on foot, having left his stolen car a mile south. Clad in navy T-shirt and nylon pants and wearing a black fanny pack, he was just another aging jogger burning a few martini lunch calories as twilight slipped into night, trying to stay trim for a wife or, more likely, a mistress. Like Congressman Montoya, who got more than his share if the gossip columns got it right. Sneakered feet slapping the pavement, Paul imagined that he was a senator from a distant state, Idaho, maybe, who rented one of the apartments on this block while his family stayed home in Boise. Lots of Congress members, even those with homes in the Virginia or Maryland suburbs, rented apartments or small houses near the Capitol for those nights when sessions or fundraisers ran late. On second thought, a senator was too recognizable. A congressional staffer, then. Take off the fancy suits and there wasn't much to differentiate white, sixty-something men. The congressmen looked like plumbers, looked like math teachers. Or hit men, for that matter. Paul exhaled a laugh at the thought.

There were few people about: a man walking a rat dog with faux gems on its leash (the man and the dog should both be embarrassed), a couple of teens making a furtive exchange by a playground entrance. Idiots. He'd had the good sense to never do drugs, not even in 'Nam where a grunt could get marijuana or heroin with equal ease. He'd smoked, of course; they'd all smoked. The café down the street was closed, a security light giving off a dim glow inside the plate-glass window. No one paid him any attention.

Without hesitating, Paul cut down a narrow sidewalk between two houses, and came up on Montoya's place from behind. He grasped the lowest branch of a tree he'd climbed when surveilling the place over a week ago and hoisted himself up. Binoculars brought things into clear focus. He regretted the loss of the NVGs he'd had in his hotel room, but Montoya's apartment was so lit up he hardly needed night-vision goggles. A figure moved in the kitchen, and Paul watched as Montoya answered the phone then moved to the freezer and out of sight to the pantry. No girlfriend with him tonight. Good. Up against the client's deadline, he'd come prepared to take the woman out too, but he was relieved he wouldn't have to. It would be much easier to set up the "accident" he had in mind without another player.

A rustling in the grass below caught Paul's attention. He caught a glimpse of reddish fur and the gleam of inquisitive eyes before the critter vanished into a clump of holly. Sliding down the tree trunk, he listened for a moment but heard nothing more ominous than the drift of wind through the heavy branches, a woman a couple of houses away calling for a cat, and the shush of tires on the road. He crouched and made his way to the west side of the building, past two rubber trash cans.

The scent of grilling meat from someone's barbecue drifted toward him as he positioned himself beneath the bathroom window. Drawing on latex gloves, he tested the sash with a shove. Locked, damn it. Inconvenient but not unexpected. He withdrew a suction cup and a small ball peen hammer from his backpack. Licking the suction cup, he affixed it to the glass above the lock mechanism. One deft tap of the hammer on the rubber broke the glass. As he withdrew the larger piece with the suction cup, a fist-sized shard tinkled to the bathroom floor, landing on a red bathmat.

Fuck. He froze, listening for any sound from the front rooms. Had Montoya heard? The faint sounds of gunshots and squealing tires drifted to him. A TV show or movie. After two full minutes of immobility, during which he didn't hear approaching feet or doors opening, he took a deep breath. Clear. Reaching a gloved hand through the hole, he turned the lock and lifted the window an inch. Careful not to cut himself, he pulled his hand out and worked the fingers of both hands beneath the sash, heaving it up as far as it would go. He pulled paper booties from his pack and slipped them over his shoes, then swung his legs over the sill, lowered his backpack noiselessly to the floor, and slanted his body down until his toes touched the toilet seat. He was in.

First things first. He recovered the sliver of glass from the rug and tucked it into his backpack. After taking care of Montoya, he'd stash the glass in a bag at the bottom of one of the garbage bins. When found, as it would be if the homicide dick in charge was on the ball, it would suggest the window had been broken a couple of days before his entry. He could not leave any evidence that would cast doubt on a verdict of "accidental death." Closing the window—he didn't want a stray draft alerting the target—he surveyed the small room with its black and white tile, red rug and shower curtain, and magazine rack by the toilet. A jacuzzi tub dominated the space, big enough and deep enough to float the Titanic. Its tile surround gleamed, all 90 degree angles and sharp edges. Perfect. Edging behind the door, he slowed his breathing, prepared to wait.

51

Sydney

THE TAXI DROPPED SYDNEY in front of Fidel Montoya's house just before eight. The Pakistani driver took all her remaining cash and reversed at top speed, skidding into the road. The red of his brake lights faded to pinpricks and disappeared. Sydney stared in the direction of town, hoping Montoya would be chivalrous enough to drive her back. She walked toward the front door. The house was lit up like he was expecting two hundred guests for an election night victory party. Might as well get this over with.

A shadow moved at the tree line, where the glare of the security lights faded to umbra, and she halted. A fox skidded into view, something plump wriggling in its mouth. Piteous squeaks, growing weaker, betrayed the prey's plight. Spotting her, the fox stopped, sharp nose quivering.

Apparently deciding she was no threat, he trotted around a cement birdbath and merged into the shadows on the side of the house.

With a shiver, Sydney climbed the shallow steps leading to the double doors and rang the bell.

52

Paul

PAUL WAS PREPARED TO wait as long as necessary, but it was a mere half an hour before Montoya felt the need to empty his bladder. Creaking floorboards warned of his approach and Paul sucked in a deep breath, then let it out slowly. Whistling the theme from some movie Paul recognized but couldn't name, Montoya crossed directly to the john, unzipped, and began to urinate. Paul let the man have the satisfaction of a last long pee before making his move while Montoya was zipping up.

In a single motion, he burst from behind the bathroom door and secured Montoya's arms to his sides with both arms clamped around his chest. He kicked him off balance with a powerful sweep of his left leg and bore him downward, dragging him back as he fell. Montoya barely had time to let out a yelp of surprise and begin to twist away before Paul straddled his chest, knees planted on the floor, and pulled him up by the shoulders. He whammed the base of the man's skull against the tub's decorative tile surround.

Montoya's eyes widened and his breath came in a series of labored *huh-uh-huhs* for a long minute before stopping on one final hitch. Paul felt the man's muscles relax, and he slowly rose. Blood speckled the tile and oozed in a surprisingly small puddle beneath Montoya's head, matting his black hair. Paul was careful to avoid stepping in it or disturbing any of the spatter. Turning away from the dead, staring eyes, he pulled a thick sanitary pad from his pack and calmly went about stopping up the toilet. He added toilet paper and flushed, feeling the satisfaction of a job well done when the bowl filled and began to overflow. It soon wet Montoya's bare feet and soaked the hem of his pants.

Stepping back to survey the scene, Paul tried to see it through a cop's eyes. It played as an accident: Montoya comes into the bathroom, slips in the water from the overflowing toilet (stopped up by a careless woman friend), and cracks his head against the tub. Nothing argued against that scenario. A tragic accident. Very similar to the ones that killed a real estate baron in Phoenix, a city council member in Colorado Springs, and a dentist in Tupelo. Bathrooms were dangerous places.

Without being happy about the death, Paul was still conscious of the feeling of professional accomplishment that came over him at the successful conclusion of most contracts. He got a buzz from planning the mission, thinking through all the angles, executing it, and outwitting the police or insurance investigators. It was surprisingly like the feeling he used to get when the ball slapped into his glove, he tagged the runner, and then pivoted to pull off a double play. Pride, excitement, and a split second—gone before his palm quit stinging—of utter conviction of his invincibility.

He took a photo of the very dead, the *accidentally* dead, Jimmy Montoya. Clients liked proof before they paid.

Paul exited through the window he'd come in, stripping off boo-ties and gloves as soon as he hit the ground and tucking them into his pack. They'd go down a handy sewer grate. After hiding the window glass in a trash bag largely stuffed with reeking take-out containers, he eased back onto the sidewalk and began the slow jog to his car, hoping no one got close enough to smell him. As the adrenaline leached out of him, an ache in his calf began to bother him—had Montoya kicked him?—and jabbing pain from the bullet wound made him worry that he'd torn it open. He was tired. One more thing to take care of, and then he'd be on his way back to Pennsylvania, Pop, and Moira.

53

Sydney

MELODIOUS CHIMES RANG IN the depths of the house. Sydney waited for two full minutes. No one came. Where was Montoya? He knew she was coming. The bathroom, maybe. She frowned and rang again.

Finally, heavy footsteps approached. The door swung inward, loosing warm yellow light into the night. Fidel Montoya, dressed in casual black slacks and a garnet-red silk-blend T-shirt that made the most of his dark coloring, stood in the hallway holding a dish towel to the back of his head. "Sydney! Come in, come in." He leaned down to kiss her cheek.

She suffered the kiss but eluded a hug by stepping into the foyer. When she cast a curious look at the dish towel, he said, "Dropped a piece of ice and banged my head against the freezer door when I picked it up. Hurt like a son of a bitch. I've got a lump the size of a hubcap." He lowered the cloth and unwrapped it to show a few ice cubes.

"Ow," Sydney said, since he clearly wanted sympathy. She took in the polished walnut floors and contrasting cream walls, a perfect foil for the large canvases mounted at intervals designed to let each piece have its own space. A magnificent staircase soared to the upper story where four doors opened off a short hallway guarded by a wrought-iron banister. To her left, flickering lights from a television danced out of a den and to her right, a short hall led past a formal dining room to a kitchen. She studied the art as Montoya closed the door. Too abstract for her taste, the paintings rang with vibrant cobalts, scarlets, and golds. She peered at a powerful piece streaked with emerald along the lower edge.

"Let me get you a drink," Montoya said as she tried to decide if the painting was of a fish-filled sea or a pasture dotted with cows. Or sheep or horses. She gave it up and followed her host into the kitchen.

Shaking the ice cubes into the sink, he tossed the towel on the counter. "Vodka?" He lifted the Grey Goose bottle.

"I don't want a drink. I just want to ask—"

"Of course you want a drink. You probably prefer wine." He poured her a glass of red wine from a stoppered bottle on the counter, topped up his glass with the vodka, then peeked into a pot bubbling on the range. He stirred the contents with a spoon and a fragrant steam rose toward the ceiling. "Dinner," he said. "Linguine *alle vongole*. With clams. It's the only thing I know how to cook. When Katya's away I mostly make do with take-out. I hope you're not allergic?"

"I'm not staying."

When he started to protest, she talked over him. "Look, someone slipped this under my door." She pulled the page out of her purse and spread it on the counter. The bubbling pasta water spit on it and she moved it out of range.

"What's this?" His voice was brusque; he was annoyed that she wasn't staying. How had he envisioned the evening ending? She doubted he'd have been satisfied with watching James Bond movies and munching popcorn.

"I was hoping you could tell me," she said. "Do you know whose funeral this was?"

He found reading glasses on the counter and slipped them on, giving a half-embarrassed wince. "I never wear these in public." When Sydney didn't say anything, he picked up the photo. After a moment he raised his head slowly and looked at her over the top of the glasses. The slip of newsprint quivered in his hand. "What's this about? Where did you get this?"

"Someone put it under my door. I don't know when. I found it less than two hours ago."

"It's Carrie's funeral," he said.

She wasn't imagining it; his hand was shaking. "Carrie who?"

"Favier. John Favier's my chief of staff. Carrie is—was—his wife. She was killed by a hit-and-run driver earlier this summer. Tragic. She was … a special woman."

Sydney reclaimed the photo. "This"—she waved the paper— "Carrie's death, Jason's death, whoever's trying to kill you—it's all related. Did the police catch the driver?"

Slowly, Montoya shook his head. "No. Nothing to go on. No witnesses. Just the side mirror from an old Camry. There was a partial print on it, I remember the cops telling John. It sticks in my mind that they traced it to some private who died in Vietnam. A mistake, obviously." His tone said you couldn't count on the police to get things right.

Sydney stared him straight in the face and said, "Who would want to kill both Carrie Favier and you?"

He laughed uncomfortably and broke away from her gaze to lift the pasta pot from the stove and drain it into a colander. Steam billowed up, obscuring his features momentarily. "Sure you won't have some?" He filled a plate, topped it with sauce, and, with vodka glass in one hand and plate in the other, crossed the hall to a small den where

Daniel Craig as James Bond played on the large-screen television. Sydney followed him, incredulous that he could walk away from her and the conversation. She flung her purse onto an ottoman as he sank into a leather love seat and patted the place beside him. Yeah, when they took up bobsledding in hell. She remained standing.

"Sean Connery was the best Bond," he said, "but this guy's got a good take on the part." His comment and his attempt to entice her to join him felt awkward, strained, like he was going through the motions while his mind was elsewhere.

"Damn it!" Sydney shook with rage. He knew something, something about why Jason was killed and why Reese was lying in a hospital fighting for her life, and he was making small talk about a stupid movie. Hands on her hips, she stood in front of him, blocking his view of the television. "Tell me! You were screwing her, weren't you, this Carrie? Her husband found out and—"

"No." Montoya shook his head. "It wasn't like that. Yeah, Carrie and I had a thing, but it was damn near a quarter century ago. It didn't last twenty minutes. It's not like John's been a saint either. I covered for him more than once. He's got a thing for redheads." He eyed her auburn hair meaningfully. "He's my best friend. Take my word for it—he's not involved in this—whatever 'this' is."

Frustration bubbled up in Sydney. There had to be a connection between Carrie Favier's death and what was happening now. There had to be. Before she could puzzle through it, the doorbell rang.

54

Sydney

WANTING TO KEEP AN eye on Montoya and feeling foolish about it, Sydney followed him into the foyer. Without even checking the peep hole, he flipped the deadbolt and turned the doorknob.

"Don't—" Sydney started, remembering that an assassin was after him. After them.

Too late. Montoya had the door open and was regarding his chief of staff with bemusement. "John? What the hell—?" If he was discomfited by the appearance of the man he'd just admitted cuckolding, he didn't show it. The affair was woven so far back in the tapestry of their relationship, Sydney realized, that even though he knew the slub was there, he never focused on it.

The outside sconce shed a yellow light that draped Favier's square shoulders but left his face largely in shadow. His voice, though, was solemn. "I told the police—I needed to be the one to tell you. I didn't know you had a guest."

He leaned forward to stare at Sydney, and the porch light yellowed his eyes. She shrank away from his contempt, then straightened her back. Screw him. She was tired of people passing judgment on her. What was he doing here at this hour anyway, almost as if he'd been summoned by their talking about him? A chill seeped through her. "Don't let him—" She took a half step forward, but Montoya was already pulling the door wider.

"Tell me what?" Montoya made an impatient gesture. "Come in, damn it. What's this all about?"

Favier stepped across the threshold. In the chandelier's light he looked feverish, his face pale but with his cheeks flushed red. His eyes were glassy. "It's Jimmy," he said.

Montoya frowned, more irritated than worried, and started back toward the kitchen. "What's he done now? If it's more gambling losses, I don't want to hear about it. Want a drink? Some linguine? We just sat down to eat—"

"Jimmy's dead."

Sydney gasped. Montoya whirled so fast that he stumbled. He took two heavy steps back toward his friend. "That's not funny, John. What the hell are you playing at?"

"Oh, Fidel, I wish I didn't have to give you this news. Jimmy was like a son to me, too. You know that."

Sydney, her gaze glued to Favier, was convinced there was a distasteful avidity in the way he was watching Montoya's reaction to the news of Jimmy's death. He looked ... she searched for a word. Triumphant. She wished desperately that she had her phone on her, but it was in her purse in the den. Useless.

"There was an accident. He slipped in the bathroom and cracked his head open."

"Ay, *Dios mio*. My God!" Montoya cried, fingers writhing in his hair. It stood up in spiky clumps. His eyes widened by anguish, he stepped forward and shook Favier by the shoulders. "It's not true." His eyes searched his friend's face.

Favier disengaged himself by reaching into his pocket. Sydney tensed, but he brought out a phone. "I'm so sorry, my friend, but it's true. I have a photo." He held out his phone.

Sydney edged closer and glimpsed a bathroom with Jimmy Montoya's body sprawled on the floor. Montoya didn't make a sound, but tears rolled down his cheeks. Putting a sympathetic hand on his arm, moved by his silent grief, she fought back the tears that burned her eyes. If she started crying now—for Montoya, Jimmy, Reese, Jason, or out of sheer terror—Favier would win. Trying to keep her face from showing her thoughts, she forced herself to be analytical about the truth she'd instinctively recognized. There was no way John Favier should have a photo of Jimmy, no way the police would have told him about Jimmy's death before informing Fidel and Katya Montoya. He could only have one source for the photo: either he'd killed Jimmy himself, or the hit man had done it and provided him with the evidence that he'd completed his task. Sydney was betting on the latter.

"You need privacy to call your wife," she said. "I should go." Before either of them could stop her, she ducked into the den and grabbed her purse off the ottoman. A moment later, the phone was in her hand. "I'll just call a taxi," she said, pushing the redial button.

Before the call even went through, John Favier brought the butt of a gun down across her wrist. Sydney cried out and dropped the phone, which skipped once and disappeared under the entertainment center.

"My God, John—my friend—what are you playing at?" Montoya stepped toward Favier, only to be motioned back with a wave of the gun.

"Don't."

The word hummed with fury.

"What?" Montoya's confusion looked genuine.

"Don't come any closer and *don't* call yourself my friend."

Montoya stumbled back two steps, knocking against the cabinet and jarring the Grey Goose bottle, which shattered against the brick hearth. The three of them watched the clear liquid soak into the carpet and a hand-sized, curved shard of glass rocking back and forth.

Struggling to recover his sangfroid, Montoya spoke. "Come on, John. Whatever this is, we can talk it out. If I've done something to offend you..." He spread his arms wide and an earnest look filled his dark eyes.

He was good, Sydney had to admit. Her fingers crept into her purse as Favier rounded on the congressman.

"Something to offend me? Why, yes, I suppose you could call fucking my wife offensive! I may not be a hot-shot congressman, I may only be a simple country boy from Tennessee, but I have some decency. A friend's wife is off-limits. You bastard!"

Favier's voice shook with rage and the gun trembled in his large hand. Sydney didn't know much about guns, but she could see it was bigger than Reese's. Blue light from the flickering television screen danced along its silver length.

"And don't even try to deny it!" Favier almost shrieked as Montoya opened his mouth.

Montoya paused a moment, regrouping, then said simply, "I am so sorry, John. It was over between us decades ago, before you and I became friends, real friends. It only lasted a few months. I never meant... Why did you wait so long for..." He swirled one hand to encompass the week's events.

"I only found out recently," Favier replied.

Montoya's eyes widened with comprehension. "When Carrie died. Did she leave a diary, letters?"

"I found out *before* Carrie died," Favier said. His quiet emphasis on "before" hung in the room.

He'd killed his wife. Sydney knew it with chilling certainty. He'd arranged the hit-and-run "accident." That was definitely round one.

"Carrie. Oh my God." Montoya buried his face in his hands and his shoulders shook. After a moment he raised his head and glared at Favier. "You set that up. It wasn't an accident."

"Got it in one." Favier motioned with the gun for Montoya to join Sydney over near the loveseat. Heat and the stink of flop sweat radiated from him and she sidled away.

"Jimmy? Did you—tell me you didn't kill Jimmy?" Montoya's voice cracked.

"The same man who killed Carrie took care of Jimmy. The hit-and-run went flawlessly, or so it seemed at the time. No one ever suspected it wasn't an accident. Jimmy's didn't happen quite as planned, however. Mr. Jones must be losing his touch. First he let the Manley Trap here get hold of his phone, and then he fucked up and killed her boyfriend. To top it off, he shoots Reese Linn and leaves his goddamned fucking fingerprint in a hotel room where the police tracked him after the shooting today. Fingerprints that match a partial print they lifted from the car mirror that was knocked off in Carrie's accident."

Montoya stayed silent, and Favier stepped toward him threateningly. "A Detective West came by my office an hour ago to tell me he thought they were making progress on Carrie's case. What a clusterfuck. If Jones ever gets arrested, anywhere in the goddamned country, his fingerprints will tie him to both the murders. And he can tie me to them. Not that he's ever seen me, and our financial transactions have been anonymous, but how hard is it to figure out it's probably the husband that wants a woman killed? West has me in his sights, I can tell. I didn't like the tone of some his questions. Jones is the only link—without him they've got no way to prove anything. I have an alibi for both Carrie's death and Jimmy's. But that's for later," he said, making an obvious effort to calm himself. "The two of you are on tonight's agenda. It's serendipitous finding you here together."

"Katya will be home soon," Montoya said.

Favier snorted. "Weak, Fidel. You wouldn't have invited the Manley Trap over if that were the case. Maybe I'll do what I can to console Katya when you're gone." He leered at Montoya. "She does have the best rack I've ever seen on a fifty-year-old."

"*Maletón!*" Montoya lunged forward.

A percussive report filled the room, deafening Sydney. Montoya crumpled to the ground, keening and clutching at his knee. The scent of cordite and blood made her gag. Montoya's knee was nothing but pulped flesh and splinters of cartilage. A puddle of blood grew as she watched, bright red fading to maroon at the edges.

Favier grunted with dissatisfaction. "I didn't want to have to do that. It makes the murder-suicide scenario a little less tidy, but I think I can still make it work. It'll just look like Miss Ellison missed her first shot."

"I'll be crippled," Montoya moaned.

"That's the least of your worries."

Her ears still ringing from the shot, Sydney heard Favier's words as if from the end of a long tunnel. His head was turned as he focused on Montoya, and she slipped her hand into her purse to surreptitiously withdraw Reese's gun. It felt alien, cold and heavy against her palm. She had no idea how many bullets were in it, but she knew it was their only chance.

In one jerky motion, she raised her arm to shoulder height, her hand trembling from the weight of the pistol, and fired at Favier's torso. The bullet thudded into his chest, blasting him back until he slammed against the wall. His arms flew up and the silver gun slipped from his grasp, clunking to the floor. His eyes rolled back in his head as he slid down the wall.

Shuddering, Sydney dropped Reese's gun and ran to Montoya.

"911," he whispered.

"I've got to stop the bleeding first," she said, feeling a sense of déjà vu. Had it been only this morning that she'd been staunching Reese's blood? Unbuckling Montoya's belt and tugging it through the loops, she slipped it under his thigh, ignoring his cry of pain. Trying not to look at the mangled mess that had been his knee, she slid the free end through the buckle and cinched it tight above his knee. His skin felt clammy when she touched the back of her hand to his cheek and she knew he was in shock. She needed to find a blanket—

As she rose, something slammed into her temple, sending her to her knees. "You bitch!" Favier roared, standing over her, the gun in his hand smeared with her blood.

She put a hand to her temple, wiping away the blood dripping into her eye. Her head rang and she couldn't think straight. "How—?"

"Kevlar." Favier patted his tummy, making a dull, thwacking sound. "I never go into a tactical situation without it. Once a cop, always a cop. I think you cracked a rib though," he said, slapping her with his free hand. "Hurts like hell."

As her head whipped to her shoulder, Sydney felt the first cold fingers of despair working through her mind and numbing her body. It was a familiar feeling, but one she'd hoped was gone forever. After the scandal broke and she'd realized she was carrying George's baby, she'd stumbled through week after hopeless week with a cold black depression draining her energy and will to live. Only the baby's first kicks and her move to Europe had helped ease the darkness out of her heart and mind, so that she could see beyond the idea of death again— first in grays, then in color. Now that cold blackness was back, seeping into her marrow, urging her to give up. Tears mingled with the blood on her face.

Favier was moving around the small room, setting up his scene, as she pushed from her hands and knees to her haunches. "On the plus side," he said, "you've got GSR on your hands, so when the coroner tests it you'll come up positive. On the minus side, this has to go." He unbuckled the belt she'd bound around Montoya's thigh and the man moaned.

"How'd you find out, John?" he asked on an indraw of his breath. "After all this time..."

Favier's features froze into a mask of hatred. "It was Emily."

Montoya blinked several times, then forced his heavy lids open, trying to focus on Favier. "She didn't know. She wasn't even born."

"When she got hurt in Texas—when that damned piece of scrap metal opened up her leg—she needed blood, two pints. I offered mine. I'd have given anything to help her. But I'm type A and she's B so I couldn't donate to her. Worse, Carrie was type A like me." Favier ground his teeth. "It took me several minutes to figure out what that meant. I felt like I'd been kicked in the gut. When I asked Carrie, she admitted to your affair, said it was possible that you... that Emily..."

Sydney took her eyes off of Favier for a moment to see how his story was affecting Montoya. The congressman looked confused, and blinked slowly several times. Loss of blood, Sydney thought. Without treatment—

"You took my daughter away from me, and that's why I took your son," Favier bit out. Bleak satisfaction iced his words. "My sweet Emily, engaged to her half brother without knowing it. Sleeping with him. It was sick. Sick! I couldn't turn her away from him, not without telling her the truth. Believe me, I tried. Told her all about his gambling, but she just kept saying she loved him. It was all your fault. I wanted him dead before the election, so your win would be meaningless. I wanted everything to turn to ash for you, just as it has for me.

The whole world is gray now, ever since I found out. I was in New York on 911 and it's like that—the sky blotted out, ash raining down. Except nothing will clear this darkness away. Now you know what it's like." Favier scratched his chin with the gun's muzzle. "I wasn't going to kill you—I wanted you to suffer like I've suffered, but this will be better. Better for Emily. With both you and Jimmy dead, it'll be easier for her. She'll never have to know the truth."

Montoya struggled to push himself up on one elbow. "Jimmy. Jimmy can't be—I need... tell Katya. Is it true... Em's my daughter?" he asked, sounding woozy.

"Never!" Favier raised his gun and shot him point-blank in the forehead.

Sydney gasped and ducked involuntarily. She tried to crab-crawl away, but Favier was on her in an instant.

"You're what we call 'collateral damage,'" Favier told her, yanking her to her feet with a hand clamped around her upper arm. "And I'm sorry that it has to be this way, but I can't afford loose ends. Maybe I'll make a large donation to Winning Ways in your memory, suggest Em put in some volunteer hours down there. Yeah."

Sydney listened to him in shocked silence. The man was thinking at least three steps ahead. She tried to wrench her arm away as he dragged her to Montoya's side.

"A few bruises won't matter," he said, punching her cheek so hard she saw stars. He moved behind her, gripping her left shoulder and right wrist and pulling her back against his body. Her shoulder blades rubbed against the unyielding bulletproof vest. "It'll just look like Montoya roughed you up a bit before you shot him and killed yourself. I wonder how long your affair has been going on? Surely the journalists—they're so creative—will hint that you killed Nygaard so you could be with Fidel. Maybe he tossed you aside—being associated with you didn't do much for Manley's political career, after all—and you decided to kill him. In remorse, you shot yourself. Your body draped over his will be a nice touch."

Sydney found her voice. "No one will believe that. My mom—"

Favier laughed, his breath tickling her ear. "Oh, please. They'll lap it up. Now give me your hand." He pried open her fingers and laid the butt of his gun on her palm, wrapping her fingers around it. "There. That should do the trick for fingerprints."

Saying a quick prayer that her mother's grief wouldn't destroy her and that Reese would be okay, Sydney went limp, letting all her weight drop down so only Favier's hold on her left shoulder and right hand kept her from hitting the ground. Even if she couldn't save herself, she hoped to spoil the murder-suicide scene Favier was trying to create by making the bullet strike her at an angle that couldn't possibly be self-inflicted.

"Shit!"

Dangling in front of him, she had no leverage to wreak any damage with kicks, so she turned her head and sank her teeth into the fleshy part of his thumb where he gripped her hand that was holding the gun. With a yelp, he released her shoulder and smacked the back of her head with his left hand. She kept her teeth lodged in his flesh until a knee landed in her kidneys, the pain lightning bright, and jarred her loose. She sprawled across Montoya's body toward the hearth, screaming as a bone gave way in the wrist Favier still held in a grip of iron. The slick of light on glass caught her eye and before the thought was fully formed, she grabbed the neck of the broken Grey Goose bottle and twisted to slash the jagged edge back and up, burying it in the flesh of his upper arm. He released her hand and the gun fell to the floor between them.

"Hard to explain your … blood … at the scene," she taunted him.

His labored breaths came from behind her and she risked a glance backward as she scrabbled with her good hand for the gun. Blood welled from his triceps where the bottle had sliced it, but it was the look on his face that terrified her. His mouth snarled back from his teeth and his eyes burned like sunken coals in their sockets. He looked like the mask of a half-man, half-jaguar god she'd seen in a South American museum. Inhuman. He wrenched the gun from her hand and leveled it at her just as the room went dark.

55

Sydney

"**WHAT THE FUCK?**" **FAVIER'S** grip on Sydney's shoulder loosened and she twisted away from him as he fired. The bullet singed her cheek and ear, deafening her. Instinctively she went flat to the ground, rolling away. Two more shots rang out and a window shattered as she lodged against something. Her hand touched cooling flesh and viscous blood, and she recoiled. Montoya's body. She rolled again, toward the far side of the room and the window.

"Goddammit!" Favier's voice shook with fury and something else. Fear? "Who's there?"

Sydney felt it, too—another presence in the room. She couldn't hear the newcomer, who moved soundlessly as a hunting owl, but she felt a shift in the air and the flesh on her arms goose-pimpled in response. She bumped the far wall and pushed to her knees, careful not to jar her wrist any more than necessary.

"Who—?" Favier's voice, choked off mid-cry, asked the question in her mind.

Footsteps—surely more than one pair of feet?—and scuffling interspersed with grunts came to her ears as she felt her way along the wall in a half crouch until she came to a window. Her fingers fumbled with the latch and she shoved it open, letting in the scent of mown grass and a wisp of breeze.

She hooked one knee over the sill as a horrific gargling sound issued from behind her. Chancing a glance over her shoulder, she caught the dim outline of a mass swaying in the middle of the den. As she watched, her eyes now better adjusted to the darkness, the mass separated into two, part of it sliding to the ground like an iceberg calving. A stray moonbeam silvered a knife's blade and illuminated a man's pasty face, rigid with concentration. He looked up and caught her eye as she swung her other leg over the window ledge, rolled to her stomach, and slid out into the clutch of a forsythia bush.

Would he follow? Sydney tore free of the bush, stifling a cry as her broken wrist banged against a branch, and sprinted toward the front of the house and the road. The dark slowed her as she stumbled over a rock and clanged against metal trash cans, but it protected her, too. If the man in the den—was he the one who'd killed Jason?—had a gun, light would have made her exposed back an easy target. If she could just get to the road...

Footsteps pounded toward her from the road. "Sydney!"

She skidded to a halt and almost went down as the voice snagged her. Ben's voice. She caught her breath on a sob as he reached her and pulled her into his arms. She squeaked when pain jittered up her arm.

"Are you okay? Are you hurt?" His voice was urgent and she raised her eyes to his face, wondering at the anxiety she saw there.

"My wrist." She held it out, startled to see it distended like an anaconda's belly after a rodent snack.

"The paramedics are on their way," he said. "I radioed for back-up and medical fifteen minutes ago. When I got your call, I was already on my way here to tell Montoya about his son's death. I couldn't hear everything you were saying, but I heard the shots. I was afraid—"

"Montoya, Favier ... they're dead."

"Both of them?"

She nodded, impatiently swiping her hair off her face as it fell into her eyes. "Favier shot Montoya. He was going to shoot me, make it look like a murder-suicide, when the lights went out. Another man came in—"

"Who? Is he still there?" Ben's voice became clipped.

"I guess so."

"Wait here. Signal the cops or the ambulance when they arrive."

"No way." She grabbed his arm as he turned back to the house. "I am not staying here by myself."

After a single glance at her set face, he started forward again. "Stay behind me."

They jogged back to the house, Sydney moving awkwardly as she cradled her wrist against her chest, holding it with her good hand. They slowed as they approached the front door, which gaped wide. "Did you leave it like that?" West whispered.

Sydney shook her head. "I came out the window." She pointed.

"We need light. With an old house like this ... " West headed around the side of the house and apparently found the junction box to flip the master breaker to on. The night exploded with light.

Sydney blinked at the brightness but stayed with him as they returned to the front door. West went through it in one swift move, sweeping his weapon from one side to the other. "Clear. Where're Montoya and Favier?"

"In there." Sydney hung back as he eased open the door to the den, taking in the scene with one glance. Curiosity overcame her repulsion as he entered the room, and she followed him as far as the doorway.

"Don't come in." He stopped her with an uplifted hand. "We don't want to compromise the scene any more than necessary. I need to make sure they're beyond help."

The room was as she'd left it, except for a ghastly amount of blood spattered on the walls and soaked into the carpet. Favier's lifeless body stared up at her. A wide, red mouth gaped below his jaw.

"Oh my God." Her hand crept to her mouth, whether to stop herself from retching or block the coppery scent, she couldn't have said.

"Slit his throat," West said, walking around the blood-soaked patches as best he could, careful not to touch anything. He leaned down to touch his fingers to Montoya's wrist. A useless gesture, Sydney thought.

"He's dead. The forensics guys will have a field day with this." West spent one long moment staring at Montoya's corpse and returned to Sydney, who'd stayed in the doorway. He nudged her into the hall and looked around, then up the staircase, gun held at shoulder-height. Nothing moved. He motioned Sydney toward the door. "We'll wait outside for back-up before searching the house further. I'll bet this guy's fingerprints, if we find any, match up with a dead soldier's."

"Huh?"

"Can you describe him? Would you recognize him?"

Sydney screwed up her face. "White. Not young. It was dark. I don't think so." She wished she could describe the man, wished she could ID Jason's killer, but it had all happened so fast.

56

Paul

HEARING SYDNEY'S WORDS FROM his vantage point in the kitchen, Paul let go a sigh. He'd opened the front door, planning to follow her, unsure whether to take her out or not. He would never see any money for it, but if she could ID him ... When he heard the cop's voice mingling with hers, he'd retreated to the kitchen, jumping when the lights came on. Fucking cop must have found the junction box. He hovered, prepared for action, and listened as the cop and Ellison checked on the dead men. They left and he relaxed a notch. He had a few minutes. The kitchen smelled like musty pasta water and garlic and he took a quick moment to rinse his Ka-Bar in the sink. Favier's blood ran pinkly down the drain. Served him right.

Shortly after accepting the contract on Carrie Favier, Paul had deduced that John Favier was his client. It was always good insurance to know a little something about who he was working for, so whenever possible, he made some effort to ID the client. He always suspected spouses, and he'd followed Favier after accepting the job and called him while he was tailing him, knowing he'd guessed right as he watched the man answer the burner phone. Gotcha. He'd collected a little file on Favier, too, just in case. It was astonishing how many people thought they could cheat a contract killer they'd hired "anonymously" over the Internet and get away with it.

When Favier had threatened him that morning after his botched hit on Ellison, he'd extracted the newspaper clipping from the safe deposit box and planted it at Ellison's place, trusting she'd make a nuisance of herself with it like she'd been doing all week. He figured she might even take it to the police and give Favier some tense moments. A phone call to Favier would ensure his client knew where the photo had come from and encourage him to pay up and keep his mouth shut or face more dire consequences. He hadn't expected the woman to race out to Montoya's house with it, wasn't expecting to see her when he'd followed Favier there, but it had all turned out for the best. He'd shut Favier's mouth, discovered Ellison wasn't a threat, and gotten three-quarters of his fee—the half he'd been paid in advance and half of the remainder which Favier had wired him after he texted him the photo.

It was child's play to follow Favier. For a former cop, he took surprisingly few security precautions. The cushy political life had made him careless. Paul had positioned himself outside Favier's place before sending him the photo of a very dead Jimmy Montoya. Favier's flip response, a texted *Better late than never*, was followed almost immediately by a notification from the bank showing that Favier had deposited only half of the agreed-upon sum in his bank account. Bastard. Paul was prepared to encourage him to live up to his obligations. But before he could make a move, Favier's garage door went up and he backed out in his Mercedes sedan. Paul lost him on the dark Maryland lanes, but by then he knew exactly where he was heading. Letting the

Merc get ahead of him, Paul parked the stolen car in the same spot he'd left it on Friday when the poacher's shot had made him back away from killing Jimmy Montoya while his father was jogging, fearful that someone would call the police at the sound of the shot.

He'd entered the house through the kitchen door while Favier rang the doorbell and had been surprised to hear Ellison's voice. Two birds with one stone, maybe, he'd thought, grimly pleased that he'd taken the time to follow him to ensure Favier was going to honor their contract. Then, Favier had mentioned his name and Paul knew that he'd have to kill him. As Favier listed his screw-ups, Paul's anger grew, against Favier and against himself. Maybe he *was* losing it. Maybe it was time to retire.

He filed that thought away for another time. Sydney's words to the detective about not recognizing him stung him to action. He was glad he didn't have to kill her after all; he actually kind of admired her. Maybe he'd donate a little something to her charity, anonymously of course, as a kind of apology for causing her so much trouble. Enough. He needed to get out of the house, get back to his car before the cops arrived en masse. Gripping the knife in his right hand, he eased open the kitchen door with his left and slipped onto the stoop. He stuck to the shadows at the side of the house until he reached the point closest to the road. Staying low, he dashed across the open yard and the road, feeling a sense of calm as he dove into the bushes on the far side. His shoulder wound hurt—if he hadn't torn it killing Jimmy Montoya, he'd damn sure ripped it open wrestling with Favier—but he ignored it and jogged toward his car.

While he was still a quarter mile away, sirens split the quiet night and he jolted to a stop, listening. At least four cars, maybe five. Cops and an ambulance. Red and blue lights swirled. Fuck. He couldn't risk returning to his car with so many cops in the vicinity. They might already have spotted it, have someone posted near it. No, he wasn't going to chance it. He pushed deeper into the woods, away from the road.

The gurgling shush of the river sounded from up ahead. Not far. He'd take a leaf from his in-country playbook and use the river as an escape route. It should be cleaner than the Mekong. If he stayed in the water for eight or ten miles, he should emerge well outside any dragnet the cops had set up. Going with the current, it wouldn't be too hard.

At the river's edge, he hesitated, then walked into the chilly water fully clothed. His clothes would drag in the water, but he'd need clothes and shoes when he emerged. Naked men attracted a lot of unwelcome attention. He grinned, remembering a similar night in Laos and the two-sizes-too-small pants he'd ended up with off some gook's clothesline. When the water reached his neck, he started to swim downstream, a bullfrog's croak encouraging him.

57

Sydney

MONTOYA'S HOUSE AND YARD buzzed with cops. Sydney let a paramedic stabilize her wrist as she watched the cops in uniform prowl the perimeter of the yard and the forensic specialists in jumpsuits disappear into the house. Exclamations and speculation clouded the air as more and more people arrived: Maryland state troopers, the county sheriff, and FBI special agents drawn by Montoya's death. They all wanted to talk to her, but West and the EMTs kept them away. Sydney's head throbbed along with her wrist and she gratefully accepted painkillers from the paramedic, a burly woman with hair cut short as a man's and a tiny diamond stud piercing her nose. Sydney felt like she'd met more EMTs in the past week than in the past ten years combined.

A brief silence fell over the yard as the coroner's team appeared in the doorway with a dark bag zipped closed on a gurney. Sydney didn't know if the bag contained Montoya's body or Favier's, and she didn't know if the silence denoted respect, fear, or some other emotion. She was too tired to care. When Ben stopped beside her some minutes later, it took her a moment to recognize he was there. She raised her head to look into his face. His expression was set on "cop," but it softened as her eyes searched his.

"Go to the hospital," he ordered gently. "Let them fix your wrist. We'll take care of your statement in the morning. There's nothing more for you to worry about."

"I had it wrong from the get-go," she said wearily. "The killer wasn't after Fidel Montoya; he was after Jimmy. Poor Jimmy." Images of Montoya's son enthusiastically talking about his horse blurred with the photos of Jimmy dead on the bathroom floor. "Poor Jimmy," she whispered again.

"We all got it wrong," Ben said firmly. "This was an MPD case and we screwed it up royally, mostly by not taking you at your word. You aren't to blame for any of this. Not Nygaard, not your sister, not—"

"My sister—" Sydney couldn't believe she hadn't thought about Reese. "I need to know—"

"She's doing fine. I called the hospital looking for you when I couldn't get you on your cell; I wanted to tell you that we'd matched prints from the Favier hit-and-run scene with ones from the hotel room of the guy who shot your sister. I talked to your mother. They caught the stroke very early and there should be little to no long-term effects. She's going to be fine, Sydney. It's all going to be fine."

Sydney squeezed her eyes shut and swallowed around a lump in her throat. Her gratitude threatened to spill over as tears and she fought against them, saying with weak sarcasm, "There's still the journalists who will smear me for weeks, plus a broken wrist and nightmares."

"I'll do what I can to head off the reporters. Your wrist will heal and the nightmares will fade."

"Do you have an answer for everything?" She gave him a crooked smile.

"Not according to my daughter."

Sydney waved her good hand as the paramedic helped her climb into the ambulance. She thought Ben blew her a kiss as the EMT pulled the doors closed, but she might have been mistaken.

58

Paul
Wednesday, August 9

PAUL GOT OFF THE bus three blocks from his Barrytown house, grubby and weary. His clothes, though dry, smelled of river water, and he was pretty sure the pollutants in the river (or maybe it was fish piss) had re-infected his shoulder. No matter. Moira would know how to get him antibiotics. Emerging from the river some time after midnight, miles downstream of the Montoya place, he'd tromped through the woods, shoes squishing, until he came to a small town. Stealing a bicycle left unsecured on a front porch, he pedaled some twenty miles to a larger town and ditched the bike at a high school. Finding a public restroom, he'd cleaned up as best he could and, as dawn broke, he'd headed for the bus station.

The televisions in the bus station and a newspaper some passenger left on a chair overflowed with news and speculation about the incident at the Montoya house. Beyond confirming the deaths of Congressman Fidel Montoya (D/Maryland), 55, and John Favier, 58, Montoya's chief of staff, the cops were sticking with "No comment" and "We don't want to say anything that could disrupt an ongoing investigation." The paper reported that Sydney Ellison was "unavailable for comment."

Before approaching the ticket window, Paul scanned the columns for any mention of a suspect, any description of himself, and found nothing. *Home free*, he thought, knocking his knuckles on the faux wood of the chair's armrest. He stood in line behind a fat woman weighed down by three overstuffed shopping bags and told the clerk, "I need a ticket." Two transfers later, he was almost home.

His pace picked up as he rounded the corner and saw the small house, its white paint gleaming against the blue sky and the oranges and reds of the hollyhocks he'd planted in the spring. They brightened the place up, but did he need a taller shrub, maybe something with a dark green foliage, behind them? His pop sat in a folding chair on the lawn, face tilted toward the mid-day sun, his eyes closed. He must have heard the scrape of Paul's shoes against the sidewalk, though, because he sat up straighter, peered at Paul for a moment, then called over his shoulder, "Look, Angela, Eldon's home."

Angela was Paul's aunt, his father's youngest sister. Paul responded with "Hi, Pop" and kissed the old man's cheek, inhaling a menthol scent.

Moira appeared from the backyard, a trowel in her hand and a smudge of dirt on her forehead. "Hello." She smiled.

"Hello." He liked the way a strand of hair curled down onto her forehead, the way her eyes shifted between hazel and brown. Warm. He resisted the urge to hug her, saying, "I'm home."

"I see that." She set the trowel on the stoop and rubbed her hands along her thighs, suddenly uncertain. "I'll just clean up—"

"How do you feel about a cruise?"

Her astonished look pushed him to say, "I was thinking Pop might enjoy it, that the sea air would be good for him. And you've been alone with him so much lately, you deserve a vacation. I was thinking Puerto Vallarta, or maybe the Cayman Islands?"

"What about your work?" The note of hope and pleasure in her voice inflated a bubble inside him. He felt like a tulip bulb must when the sun and rains of spring tug at the flower inside, urging it to poke through the earth.

"It's a slow time."

He needed to let the dust from the Montoya job settle. A cruise—sunbathing, cocktails, a shore excursion or two—would give him some distance, let his shoulder heal properly. Moira might even want to try the one-day scuba diving course with him. Maybe he'd take on more commissions when they got back from the cruise and maybe he wouldn't. Retirement had its allure. His eyes dwelled on the hollyhocks. If he put a trellis on the wall behind them, he could train some morning glories up it, or even English ivy. He slipped his arm behind his father's back and helped him stand.

"It's good to see you, Eldon," his pop said, patting Paul's cheek with one horny-callused hand.

"Yeah, Pop. You, too." With Moira holding the door, he supported his father as the old man shuffled toward the house.

59

Sydney

HANDICAPPED BY A CAST that went from her hand to her elbow, Sydney struggled to get her arm through a sleeve and cursed the instinct that had led her to ask Connie to bring her a dress to wear home from the hospital. At her request, Connie had dug the classic Diane von Furstenberg number out of her closet at the townhouse and brought it to the hospital that morning. Sydney hadn't worn it in years but had seen similar wrap dresses in the fashion magazines lately and knew it was back in style. The soft jersey material draped her slim figure, even showing a hint of cleavage, and tied at the waist. The geometric shapes on an orange background seemed to infuse her with energy.

She'd barely smoothed it over her hips when a voice from the doorway said, "Whoa, boss, new look. Very nice. Powerful yet feminine. It suits you."

She turned, caught between laughter and tears, to see D'won on the threshold. "Old look, actually," she said. "I just haven't worn it since, well, since forever."

She smiled at her deputy and friend. He looked natty as ever, the purple gone from his hair, holding a vase of gerbera daisies in both hands. "Your favorites, right?" He lifted the vase with a gesture reminiscent of a priest raising a chalice.

"Oh, D'won."

"They're supposed to cheer you up, not make you cry," he observed, setting the flowers down and handing her a box of tissues.

She dabbed at her eyes. "Yeah, well, everything seems to make me cry right now."

He patted her back. "I read about some of what happened in the paper. They're calling you a heroine, boss."

Sydney frowned. "I don't know why. I screwed up by not going to the police right away with that phone, and four people died."

"Four people died because an evil man hired a conscienceless killer," D'won corrected her. "You exposed it all. You kept after it when the police were off the scent. Let them call you a heroine. Maybe you can make something of it, if not for yourself then for Winning Ways. It's a nice change of pace, right? The article I read didn't use the phrase 'Manley Trap' at all." He grinned, carving deep dimples in his dark cheeks.

Feeling shaky, Sydney perched on the edge of the bed. "How are things at the office?"

"Under control," D'won said. He shook an admonitory finger at her. "Don't you even think of showing your face there until you're feeling a lot stronger than you are now. You look downright peaky. I can cope with Reverend Hotchkiss until you're ready to come back. I got a commitment from Darkon Imaging to hire at least five of our graduates a year. Yes, I'm that good." He preened but then turned serious again. "I miss you, but I want you to get better." He surprised her by leaning down to kiss her cheek. "There. That's all I came to say. When are they springing you from this joint?"

"About noon. Connie's coming to pick me up. I have to give a statement to the police. After that, I don't know."

D'won drifted toward the door. "Just take it one day at a time, Syd. It'll all come right in the end. At least that's what my Aunt Hermione used to say, right up until Uncle Philemon got to thinking he could fix the hot water heater himself and blew the house and both of them to kingdom come."

A metallic clatter of something dropping in the hallway made Sydney jump. "D'won, that's awful! You're making that up."

He lifted a hand and gave an impish grin. "Ciao, boss."

After he left, she sat for a while thinking about what he'd said. Then she brushed her hair and put on makeup with the air of a knight donning armor before a battle. Lavish use of concealer and a swipe of blush made her look less peaky, she decided, peering at her reflection in the small bathroom mirror. Hooking her purse over her shoulder, and picking up the vase of daisies in her good hand, she straightened her back and marched down the corridor to Reese's room.

Reese had been moved out of the intensive care unit to a regular room where she would spend two or three more days, according to the doctor. Sydney observed her sister from the doorway. She appeared to be dozing, and Sydney hesitated on the threshold.

"Are you coming in or not?" Reese asked, eyes still closed. Her voice was strong, and when she opened her eyes they were clear and alert. Her blond hair spiked around her head like a corona. She seemed remarkably healthy for a woman who'd almost died the day before. A few stitches, a pint or two of blood, and presto.

Sydney crossed the room to stand by her sister's bedside. She set the vase down on a tray table that held a lidded tumbler with a built-in straw, a box of tissues, and a pocket-sized Bible. Reese's? She felt grateful and awkward and wished she'd prepared something to say. "Shall we compare scars?" she asked, wanting to recall the stupid question the moment she asked it.

"You don't stand a chance," Reese said.

"Probably not."

They both rushed to fill the awkward pause that ensued, with Reese saying, "Are you okay?" at the same time Sydney asked, "How are you?"

"I'll live," Reese said.

"Same here."

"I know you'll live," Reese said, "but are you really okay? You were shot at—"

"You were *shot!*"

"—you tried to save two injured people, one of whom died—not me, so thank you—and you watched two people die violent deaths. That's a lot to handle." Her voice said she'd been there, or somewhere very similar, and her arched brows and wrinkled forehead invited the truth.

Tears pricked the bridge of Sydney's nose at the unlooked-for perception. She pinched her nose hard and managed a half laugh. "I don't know how I am. I feel okay, relatively okay, but I suspect I can't be, not really. Not after all that. I've never watched someone die before, never had to fight for my life. It's given me a different perspective and I need time to think about it. I suspect I'll fall apart in a day or two when it catches up to me. Jason ... I miss him so much. I've still got my therapist on speed dial, though, so ..."

Reese nodded and Sydney was grateful she didn't offer platitudes such as "You'll get through it" or "This too shall pass." Connie had already trotted out both of those earlier that morning.

Silence once again threatened to overtake them, but Sydney powered through it. "I came to say thank you. You took a bullet for me."

"Must have internalized more than I realized when I was researching the Secret Service book." Reese reached for the tumbler of water on her bedside tray and winced.

Sydney picked up the tumbler, which chilled her palm, and handed it to Reese. "No, don't joke. You saved my life."

Reese took a long pull on the straw and then said in a low voice, "I owed you."

Sydney was shaking her head before Reese finished. "No, no you didn't. It's not like that."

"What's not like what?" Reese set the cup down.

Sydney cocked her head. "I know this isn't coming out right. You're the writer, not me. I've done a lot of thinking the last week, though, and I know that being sisters isn't about tit for tat, trading favors, or coming out even. Truth is, I've been a lousy sister to you." She forestalled Reese's attempt to say something. "I'm not saying you would have been my nominee for Sister of the Year, but I haven't been fair to you. I've been carrying a grudge for fifteen years, blaming you for everything that was wrong in my life. I wouldn't even read your letters because I wanted to stay mad at you, and I was afraid I couldn't stay mad if I read what you had to say. I knew they were apologies. Anyway, I'm really, truly sorry, and I'd like to do better in the future."

"Me, too," Reese said simply. "Want me to sign your cast?"

"Uh, sure." Sydney dug a marker out of her purse and handed it to her sister, balancing her forearm on the bedrail. Reese scribbled for long moments, the sharp, vaguely fruity odor of marker permeating the air. When she capped the marker and lay back, Sydney lifted her arm to read: *A little sisterly advice—stick to teaching interview techniques in future.* She'd signed it with her initials. No "love," no X's and O's, no mushy stuff.

Sydney snorted. "Let me get my hankie. You're making me tear up here."

"Not my style," Reese said with a smile.

Sydney scraped forward the straight-backed chair by the bed and sat. "Speaking of your style," she said in a leading way, "I was thinking we could write a book about all this." She rolled her hand to indicate their injuries and the events of the last week. "D'won stopped by to see me earlier and said the story's got some traction and that I—or Winning Ways, to be specific—might as well cash in on it. What do you think?"

Reese pushed up on one elbow, grimacing, and stared at Sydney in mock astonishment. "Let me get this straight—you *want* me to write about you? I must have a head injury the docs overlooked."

"Stop," Sydney said, but she smiled. "Yes, I'm tired of being defined by something I did when I was twenty. I made a stupid mistake—"

"Very stupid."

"—and it changed me, changed the course of my life. I hope for the better, even though it didn't feel like it at the time. Either way, it is what it is. If I can capitalize on my 'fame,' for want of a better word—"

"Infamy?" Reese suggested.

"Stop. If I can do that, and tell this story, and it can raise money for Winning Ways and let the world know what a wonderful person Jason was, then I want to do it. But only if you want to." She looked anxiously at Reese, trying to read her expression.

"My editor would jump at it. But we'd have to spend a lot of time together," Reese warned.

"Yeah, it'll be awful," Sydney said, "but I can put up with you if it means helping more women. Maybe we can go to Nana Linn's cabin when you feel up to it."

"Earl would like that."

"Connie's still got Earl, by the way," Sydney said, rising. "You may have trouble prying him away from her. He seems to have convinced her that you starve and deprive him, and she's made it her mission to make it all up to him."

Reese laughed, winced, and pressed down on her abdomen with the flat of her hand. "Don't make me laugh. It hurts too much. Where are you off to?"

"The police station. I've got to give a statement."

The thought sobered them both.

"See you later?" Reese finally asked.

"Yeah. Can I bring you anything?"

Reese slanted her a sly look. "Some Monkey 47?"

60

Sydney

A GAGGLE OF REPORTERS blocked access to police headquarters when Connie Linn dropped Sydney off to make her statement. Connie, who'd been playing "I've got a secret" since picking Sydney up at the hospital, slowed the car, eyeing the reporters narrowly. "I can come in with you," she offered, "or drive you around to a back entrance. There must be one. Maybe you should wait until Hil's available."

"It's okay," Sydney said. "I can handle it."

Connie studied her daughter's face for a moment, then nodded. "Okay. I'll be back in one hour, so you tell that detective that's all the time he has. You're injured and you need rest." Her fingers tapped restlessly on the steering wheel.

"What are you looking so smug about?" Sydney tried one last time to pry the surprise out of her mother. She'd probably arranged for some decadent spa treatments when Reese recovered, or scored tickets for the three of them to a hot show on Broadway.

Connie just looked mischievous and pulled an imaginary zipper closed across her lips."You'll know soon enough."

"Fine." Sydney stepped onto the curb and swung the door shut. She closed her eyes as her mother pulled into traffic without looking, making a bus driver stand on his brakes.

For once, the journalists crowding her like ants around a cake crumb didn't upset her. They wanted something from her, putting her in a power position she'd never appreciated before. Her orange dress gave her confidence. It would photograph well. Not for nothing had she spent over a decade helping women learn to present themselves effectively.

"Sydney, what happened at Montoya's house? Were you and he—?"

She held up a hand to silence the barrage of questions. "My personal life is off-limits. Surely your readers and viewers aren't shallow enough to be interested in the mundane details of an average working woman's life." That should slow them down. They could hardly say, "Yep, our readers are shallower than a mud puddle," even though they were.

"However," she continued, "I will be coauthoring a book with my sister, Reese Linn, that will discuss the events of the last week in the context of a dialogue on the nature of privacy and publicity in America. We'll be interviewing several well-known personalities—both those who chose to pursue fame and those who fell into it by accident. My share of the book's proceeds will be split between Winning Ways and a charity for the homeless people of the nation's capital."

The reporters bombarded her with questions, and she spent five minutes answering those related to the book and ignoring the others. D'won was certainly right, she reflected, turning her back on the journalists to ascend the steps. She could capitalize on her fame—her notoriety, call it what you will—and use it for her own purposes to raise money for causes she cared about.

"Just one thing more, Miss Ellison," a man's voice called. "About Winning Ways."

Sydney turned, raising her eyebrows.

"What's your reaction to Reverend Hotchkiss's resignation from the board and your reinstatement as director? Do you believe he really needs more time to tend to his parishioners as he told the board in emergency session this morning, or is something else going on?"

It took a moment for the words to sink in. So that was her mother's secret! How had Connie managed to strong-arm Hotchkiss into leaving? But Connie Linn had her ways. Sydney stifled a smile as she studied the young man with his steno pad ready to take down whatever she said. "Glory, hallelujah!" wouldn't do as a response. "I'm sure Reverend Hotchkiss's congregation will appreciate receiving his undivided attention."

Her feeling of satisfaction wilted in the somber atmosphere of the police station. Ben West met her in the lobby, an air of weariness undermining the effect of a close shave and crisp blue shirt. He scanned her face with concerned eyes. What he saw must have satisfied him because he put a hand to her elbow and escorted her to a conference room with padded chairs, windows, and Berber carpet in a blend of blues. "This is a bit nicer than before," she said, seating herself.

"Yeah. Sorry about last time. I'm going to record this, okay?"

She nodded assent and he punched a button on the recorder, reading in his name, hers, and the date. He questioned her for nearly an hour about the night's events before finally snapping off the recorder. He'd wrung details from her she didn't even know she remembered.

Finally, she felt free to ask the question that had been on her mind the whole time. "Do you think you'll ever catch him? The man who killed Jason?"

Ben rubbed his eyebrow and Sydney realized she'd come to expect this gesture when he was thinking. "It's hard to say, Syd. We have no leads right now. With Favier dead, there's no one to give us contact information or a name. The fingerprints are a dead end too, unless he gets arrested or applies for a job in a daycare center."

"Not very likely." Syd smiled sadly.

"I wouldn't think so. But we'll keep after it. This is one case that'll never end up in the 'cold case' files."

"Well, my mom will be waiting." Sydney pushed her chair back and rose. "I'd better go. If we're through?"

"Just one more thing." West rose, too, searching in his pocket for something. His hand emerged with a small manila envelope of the type salons used for tips. "This is for you."

"What is it?" Sydney held out her hand and he put the envelope in it, his warm fingers brushing hers.

"We gave Jason's effects to the Nygaards—the items he had on his body when he died. They thought you should have this. It was in his shirt pocket."

Her fingers trembling, Sydney pried up the flap and dumped the envelope over her left palm. Something gold and glittering tumbled out. A ring. A slender gold band with a one-carat diamond solitaire twinkled in her palm. Tears sprang to her eyes and she gasped. "Oh, Jason."

Ben curled her fingers over the ring. "I'm so sorry."

"No, I want to wear it." She slipped it onto her engagement finger, twisting her hand to see the play of light cutting through the diamond. "Thank you." She smiled mistily at Ben.

"Don't thank me—I'm just the delivery boy. Thank the Nygaards."

"I will." She surprised herself by leaning over and kissing Ben's warm cheek. "And I thank you, too, for everything you've done. For believing me. I'd probably be dead—"

He waved her thanks away and held the door open for her, walking her to the elevator. "Maybe in a few months, when you've had a little time, I could call you?" His brown eyes searched hers as he summoned the elevator. Those eyelashes...

A wisp of hope, of happiness, sparkled as brightly as the stone on her finger. She smiled. "You've got my number." An image of Jason's red bicycle popped in to her head. She could get the hang of it in a month or so. She pictured Jason shaking his head in mock disbelief and heard him saying, "Better late than never."

Her misty eyes made it hard to focus on Ben's face as she asked, "Do you like to bike?"

Epilogue

THE HEADLINE IN WEDNESDAY morning's paper read *Maryland Voters Elect Dead Man*. The right-wing pundits had a field day, suggesting that Fidel Montoya dead would make a better senator than any Democrat alive and distributing *Vote Montoya* buttons for November's general election. Reese gave one to Sydney and she chucked it in a kitchen drawer filled with scissors, tape, buttons, hair scrunchies, pencil stubs, paper clips, coupons, a pocket calendar from 2011, a bib left by a friend with a baby, a watch battery, and a few stray Cheerios.

The End

Note to Readers

Dear Readers,

Thank you for buying, borrowing, or stealing this book and taking the time to read it. I hope you enjoyed the journey. If you have five or ten minutes to spare, I would greatly appreciate it if you would post an honest review on Amazon, Goodreads, or similar sites. It doesn't have to be a lengthy summary or analysis—two sentences will do! You have no idea how helpful such reviews are to the author as well as to other readers.

Warm regards,

Laura

About the Author

National bestselling and award-winning author Laura DiSilverio served twenty years as an Air Force intelligence officer before becoming a full-time writer. Her Swift Investigations books were twice named Lefty Award finalists, and *The Reckoning Stones* won the Colorado Book Award for Mystery in 2016. She is a past president of Sisters in Crime and currently plots murder and parents teens—trying to keep the two tasks separate—in Colorado.